RICHARD
BROKEN ANGELS
MORGAN

The right of Richard Morgan to be identified as the author of
this work has been asserted by him in accordance with
the Copyright, Designs and Patents Act 1988.

First published in Great Britain in 2003 by

Gollancz
An imprint of the Orion Publishing Group
Orion House, 5 Upper St Martin's Lane,
London WC2H 9EA
An Hachette Livre UK Company

This edition published in Great Britain in 2008
by Gollancz

13

A CIP catalogue record for this book is
available from the British Library

ISBN 978 0 57508 1 253

Typeset by Deltatype Limited, Birkenhead, Merseyside

Printed and bound by CPI Group (UK) Ltd, Croydon, CRO 4YY

The Orion Publishing Group's policy is to use papers that
are natural, renewable and recyclable products and made
from wood grown in sustainable forests. The logging and
manufacturing processes are expected to conform to the
environmental regulations of the country of origin.

www.orionbooks.co.uk

'Morgan's depictions of road battles are truly stunning – I challenge you to fold the page and put the book down in the middle of one – you simply can't do it. Another "Certificate 18" killer read that you'd be a fool to miss!' *Infinity Plus*

'It's a bleak, violent portrait of a world which is only a few heartbeats and regime changes from our own. Imagine Michael Moore, George Orwell and Philip K Dick collaborating on a novel and you're halfway to realising what a mind-blowing book this is' *Ink Magazine*

BLACK MAN

'Since his ferocious debut novel *Altered Carbon* roared into town, Richard Morgan has been at the forefront of this breed of full-on, edgy science fiction, and his latest tech-noir thriller is also looking dangerously like his best yet. Smart, gripping, and downright indispensable – the search for the best sci-fi thriller of 2007 might just have come to an end' *SFX*

'Richard Morgan writes pumped-up steroid fuelled cyber punk. This is an unashamedly male, rip-roaring boy's own thriller for the 21st century. If Andy McNab ate a year's worth of issues of *New Scientist*, this is the kind of stuff he might write afterwards. *Black Man* is kick-ass SF from the hard end of the spectrum' *DeathRay Magazine*

This one's for Virginia Cottinelli –
compañera

afileres, camas, sacapuntas

PART ONE
Injured Parties

War is like any other bad relationship. Of course you want out, but at what price? And perhaps more importantly, once you get out, will you be any better off?

Quellcrist Falconer *Campaign Diaries*

CHAPTER ONE

I first met Jan Schneider in a Protectorate orbital hospital, three hundred kilometres above the ragged clouds of Sanction IV and in a lot of pain. Technically there wasn't supposed to be a Protectorate presence anywhere in the Sanction system – what was left of planetary government was insisting loudly from its bunkers that this was an internal matter, and local corporate interests had tacitly agreed to sign along that particular dotted line for the time being.

Accordingly, the Protectorate vessels that had been hanging around the system since Joshua Kemp raised his revolutionary standard in Indigo City had had their recognition codes altered, in effect being bought out on long-term lease by various of the corporations involved, and then reloaned to the embattled government as part of the – tax deductible – local development fund. Those that were not pulled out of the sky by Kemp's unexpectedly efficient second-hand marauder bombs would be sold back to the Protectorate, lease unexpired, and any net losses once again written off to tax. Clean hands all round. In the meantime, any senior personnel injured fighting against Kemp's forces got shuttled out of harm's way, and this had been my major consideration when choosing sides. It had the look of a messy war.

The shuttle offloaded us directly onto the hospital's hangar deck, using a device not unlike a massive ammunition feed belt to dump the dozens of capsule stretchers with what felt like unceremonious haste. I could hear the shrill whine of the ship's engines still dying away as we rattled and clanked our way out over the wing and down onto the deck, and when they cracked open my capsule the air in the hangar burnt my lungs with the chill of recently evacuated hard

3

space. An instant layer of ice crystals formed on everything, including my face.

'You!' It was a woman's voice, harsh with stress. 'Are you in pain?'

I blinked some of the ice out of my eyes and looked down at my blood-caked battledress.

'Take a wild guess,' I croaked.

'Medic! Endorphin boost and GP anti-viral here.' She bent over me again and I felt gloved fingers touch my head at the same time as the cold stab of the hypospray into my neck. The pain ebbed drastically. 'Are you from the Evenfall front?'

'No,' I managed weakly. 'Northern Rim assault. Why, what happened at Evenfall?'

'Some fucking terminal buttonhead just called in a tactical nuclear strike.' There was a cold rage chained in the doctor's voice. Her hands moved down my body, assessing damage. 'No radiation trauma, then. What about chemicals?'

I tilted my head fractionally at my lapel. 'Exposure meter. Should tell you. That.'

'It's gone,' she snapped. 'Along with most of that shoulder.'

'Oh.' I mustered words. 'Think I'm clean. Can't you do a cell scan?'

'Not here, no. The cellular level scanners are built into the ward decks. Maybe when we can clear some space for you all up there, we'll get round to it.' The hands left me. 'Where's your bar code?'

'Left temple.'

Someone wiped blood away from the designated area and I vaguely felt the sweep of the laser scan across my face. A machine chirped approval, and I was left alone. Processed.

For a while I just lay there, content to let the endorphin booster relieve me of both pain and consciousness, all with the suave alacrity of a butler taking a hat and coat. A small part of me was wondering whether the body I was wearing was going to be salvageable, or if I'd have to be re-sleeved. I knew that Carrera's Wedge maintained a handful of small clone banks for its so-called indispensable staff, and as one of only five ex-Envoys soldiering for Carrera, I definitely numbered among that particular elite. Unfortunately, indispensability is a double-edged sword. On the one hand it gets you elite medical treatment, up to and including total body replacement. On the downside, the only purpose of said treatment is to throw you back into the fray at the earliest possible opportunity. A plankton-standard grunt whose body was damaged beyond repair would just get his cortical stack excised from its snug little housing at the top of the spinal column then slung into a storage canister, where it would probably stay until the whole war was over. Not an ideal exit, and despite the Wedge's reputation for looking after their own there was no actual guarantee of re-sleeving, but at times in the screaming chaos of the last few months that step into stored oblivion had seemed almost infinitely desirable.

'Colonel. Hey, colonel.'

I wasn't sure if the Envoy conditioning was keeping me awake, or if the voice at my side had nagged me back to consciousness again. I rolled my head sluggishly to see who was speaking.

It seemed we were still in the hangar. Lying on the stretcher beside me was a muscular-looking young man with a shock of wiry black hair and a shrewd intelligence in his features that even the dazed expression of the endorphin hit could not mask. He was wearing a Wedge battledress like mine, but it didn't fit him very well and the holes in it didn't seem to correspond with the holes in him. At his left temple, where the bar code should have been, there was a convenient blaster burn.

'You talking to me?'

'Yes sir.' He propped himself up on one elbow. They must have dosed him with a lot less than me. 'Looks like we've really got Kemp on the run down there, doesn't it?'

'That's an interesting point of view.' Visions of 391 platoon being cut to shreds around me cascaded briefly through my head. 'Where do you think he's going to run *to*? Bearing in mind this is his planet, I mean.'

'Uh, I thought—'

'I wouldn't advise that, soldier. Didn't you read your terms of enlistment? Now shut up and save your breath. You're going to need it.'

'Uh, yes sir.' He was gaping a little, and from the sound of heads turned on nearby stretchers he wasn't the only one surprised to hear a Carrera's Wedge officer talking this way. Sanction IV, in common with most wars, had stirred up some heavy-duty feelings.

'And another thing.'

'Colonel?'

'This is a lieutenant's uniform. And Wedge command has no rank of colonel. Try to remember that.'

Then a freak wave of pain swept in from some mutilated part of my body, dodged through the grasp of the endorphin bouncers posted at the door of my brain and started hysterically shrilling its damage report to anyone who'd listen. The smile I had pinned to my face melted away the way the cityscape must have done at Evenfall, and I abruptly lost interest in anything except screaming.

Water was lapping gently somewhere just below me when I next woke up, and gentle sunlight warmed my face and arms. Someone must have removed the shrapnel-shredded remains of my combat jacket and left me with the sleeveless Wedge T-shirt. I moved one hand and my fingertips brushed age-smoothed wooden boards, also warm. The sunlight made dancing patterns on the insides of my eyelids.

There was no pain.

I sat up, feeling better than I had in months. I was stretched out on a small, simply-made jetty that extended a dozen metres or so out into what appeared to be a fjord or sea loch. Low, rounded mountains bounded the water on either side and fluffy white clouds scudded unconcernedly overhead. Further out in the loch a family of seals poked their heads above the water and regarded me gravely.

My body was the same Afro-Caribbean combat sleeve I'd been wearing on the Northern rim assault, undamaged and unscarred.

So.

Footsteps scraped on the boards behind me. I jerked my head sideways, hands lifting reflexively into an embryonic guard. Way behind the reflex came the confirming thought that in the real world no one could have got that close without my sleeve's proximity sense kicking in.

'Takeshi Kovacs,' said the uniformed woman standing over me, getting the soft slavic 'ch' at the end of the name correct. 'Welcome to the recuperation stack.'

'Very nice.' I climbed to my feet, ignoring the offered hand. 'Am I still aboard the hospital?'

The woman shook her head and pushed long, riotous copper-coloured hair back from her angular face. 'Your sleeve is still in intensive care, but your current consciousness has been digitally freighted to Wedge One Storage until you are ready to be physically revived.'

I looked around and turned my face upward to the sun again. It rains a lot on the Northern Rim. 'And where is Wedge One Storage? Or is that classified?'

'I'm afraid it is.'

'How did I guess?'

'Your dealings with the Protectorate have doubtless acquainted you with—'

'Skip it. I was being rhetorical.' I already had a pretty good idea where the virtual format was located. Standard practice in a planetary war situation is to fling a handful of low-albedo sneak stations into crazy elliptical orbits way out and hope none of the local military traffic stumbles on them. The odds are pretty good in favour of no one ever finding you. Space, as textbooks are given to saying, is big.

'What ratio are you running all this on?'

'Real time equivalence,' said the woman promptly. 'Though I can speed it up if you prefer.'

The thought of having my no doubt short-lived convalescence stretched out here by a factor of anything up to about three hundred was tempting, but if I was going to be dragged back to the fighting some time soon in real time, it was probably better not to lose the edge. Added to which, I wasn't sure that Wedge Command would let me do too much stretching. A couple of months pottering around, hermit-like, in this much natural beauty was bound to have a detrimental effect on one's enthusiasm for wholesale slaughter.

'There is accommodation,' said the woman, pointing, 'for your use. Please request modifications if you would like them.'

I followed the line of her arm to where a glass and wood two-storey structure stood beneath gull-winged eaves on the edge of the long shingle beach.

'Looks fine.' Vague tendrils of sexual interest squirmed around in me. 'Are you supposed to be my interpersonal ideal?'

The woman shook her head again. 'I am an intra-format service construct for Wedge One Systems Overview, based physically on Lieutenant Colonel Lucia Mataran of Protectorate High Command.'

'With that hair? You're kidding me.'

'I have latitudes of discretion. Do you wish me to generate an interpersonal ideal for you?'

Like the offer of a high-ratio format, it was tempting. But after six weeks in the company of the Wedge's boisterous do-or-die commandos, what I wanted more than anything was to be alone for a while.

'I'll think about it. Is there anything else?'

'You have a recorded briefing from Isaac Carrera. Do you wish it stored at the house?'

'No. Play it here. I'll call you if I need anything else.'

'As you wish.' The construct inclined her head, and snapped out of existence. In her place, a male figure in the Wedge's black dress uniform shaded in. Close-cropped black hair seasoned with grey, a lined patrician face whose dark eyes and weathered features were somehow both hard and understanding, and beneath the uniform the body of an officer whose seniority had not removed him from the battlefield. Isaac Carrera, decorated ex-Vacuum Command captain and subsequently founder of the most feared mercenary force in the Protectorate. An exemplary soldier, commander, and tactician. Occasionally, when he had no other choice, a competent politician.

'Hello, Lieutenant Kovacs. Sorry this is only a recording, but Evenfall has left us in a bad situation and there wasn't time to set up a link. The medical report says your sleeve can be repaired in about ten days, so we're not going to go for a clone-bank option here. I want you back on the Northern Rim as soon as possible, but the truth is, we've been fought to a standstill there for the moment and

8

they can live without you for a couple of weeks. There's a status update appended to this recording, including the losses sustained in the last assault. I'd like you to look it over while you're in virtual, set that famous Envoy intuition of yours to work. God knows, we need some fresh ideas up there. In a general context, acquisition of the Rim territories will provide one of the nine major objectives necessary to bring this conflict . . .'

I was already in motion, walking the length of the jetty and then up the sloping shore towards the nearest hills. The sky beyond was tumbled cloud but not dark enough for there to be a storm in the offing. It looked as if there would be a great view of the whole loch if I climbed high enough.

Behind me, Carrera's voice faded on the wind as I left the projection on the jetty, mouthing its words to the empty air and maybe the seals, always assuming they had nothing better to do than listen to it.

CHAPTER TWO

I n the end, they kept me under for a week.

I didn't miss much. Below me, the clouds roiled and tore across the face of Sanction IV's northern hemisphere, pouring rain on the men and women killing each other beneath. The construct visited the house regularly and kept me abreast of the more interesting details. Kemp's offworld allies tried and failed to break the Protectorate blockade, at the cost of a brace of IP transports. A flight of smarter-than-average marauder bombs got through from somewhere unspecified and vaporised a Protectorate dreadnought. Government forces in the tropics held their positions while in the northeast the Wedge and other mercenary units lost ground to Kemp's elite presidential guard. Evenfall continued to smoulder.

Like I said, I didn't miss much.

When I awoke in the re-sleeving chamber, I was suffused in a head-to-foot glow of well-being. Mostly, that was chemical; military hospitals shoot their convalescent sleeves full of feelgood stuff just before download. It's their equivalent of a welcome-home party, and it makes you feel like you could win this motherfucking war *singlehanded* if they'd only let you up and at the bad guys. Useful effect, obviously. But what I also had, swimming alongside this patriot's cocktail, was the simple pleasure of being intact and installed with a full set of functioning limbs and organs.

Until I talked to the doctor, that is.

'We pulled you out early,' she told me, the rage she'd exhibited on the shuttle deck tamped a little further down in her voice now. 'On orders from Wedge command. It seems there isn't time for you to recover from your wounds fully.'

'I feel fine.'

'Of course you do. You're dosed to the eyes with endorphins. When you come down, you're going to find that your left shoulder only has about two-thirds functionality. Oh, and your lungs are still damaged. Scarring from the Guerlain Twenty.'

I blinked. 'I didn't know they were spraying that stuff.'

'No. Apparently nobody did. A triumph of covert assault, they tell me.' She gave up, the attempted grimace half formed. Too, too tired. 'We cleaned most of it out, ran regrowth bioware through the most obvious areas, and killed the secondary infections. Given a few months of rest, you'd probably make a full recovery. As it is . . .' She shrugged. 'Try not to smoke. Get some light exercise. Oh, for fuck's sake.'

I tried the light exercise. I walked the hospital's axial deck. Forced air into my scorched lungs. Flexed my shoulder. The whole deck was packed five abreast with injured men and women doing similar things. Some of them, I knew.

'Hey, lieutenant!'

Tony Loemanako, face mostly a mask of shredded flesh pocked with the green tags where the rapid regrowth bios were embedded. Still grinning, but far too much of far too many teeth visible on the left side.

'You made it out, lieutenant! Way to go!'

He turned about in the crowd.

'Hey, Eddie. Kwok. The lieutenant made it.'

Kwok Yuen Yee, both eye sockets packed tight with bright orange tissue incubator jelly. An externally-mounted microcam welded to her skull provided videoscan for the interim. Her hands were being regrown on skeletal black carbon fibre. The new tissue looked wet and raw.

'Lieutenant. We thought—'

'Lieutenant Kovacs!'

Eddie Munharto, propped up in a mobility suit while the bios regrew his right arm and both legs from the ragged shreds that the smart shrapnel had left.

'Good to see you, lieutenant! See, we're all on the mend. The 391 platoon be back up to kick some Kempist ass in a couple of months, no worries.'

Carrera's Wedge combat sleeves are currently supplied by Khumalo Biosystems. State-of-the-art Khumalo combat biotech runs some charming custom extras, notable among them a serotonin shutout system that improves your capacity for mindless violence and minute scrapings of wolf gene that give you added speed and savagery together with an enhanced tendency to pack loyalty that hurts like upwelling tears. Looking at the mangled survivors of the platoon around me, I felt my throat start to ache.

'Man, we tanked them, didn't we?' said Munharto, gesturing flipper-like with his one remaining limb. 'Seen the milflash yesterday.'

Kwok's microcam swivelled, making minute hydraulic sounds.

'You taking the new 391, sir?'

'I don't—'

'Hey, Naki. Where are you, man? It's the lieutenant.'

I stayed off the axial deck after that.

Schneider found me the next day, sitting in the officers' convalescent ward, smoking a cigarette and staring out of the viewport. Stupid, but like the doctor said *for fuck's sake*. Not much point in looking after yourself, if that same self is liable at any moment to have the flesh ripped off its bones by flying steel or corroded beyond repair by chemical fallout.

'Ah, Lieutenant Kovacs.'

It took me a moment to place him. People's faces look a lot different under the strain of injury, and besides we'd both been covered in blood. I looked at him over my cigarette, wondering bleakly if this was someone else I'd got shot up wanting to commend me on a battle well fought. Then something in his manner tripped a switch and I remembered the loading bay. Slightly surprised he was still aboard, even more surprised he'd been able to bluff his way in here, I gestured him to sit down.

'Thank you. I'm, ah, Jan Schneider.' He offered a hand that I nodded at, then helped himself to my cigarettes from the table. 'I really appreciate you not ah, not—'

'Forget it. I had.'

'Injury, ah, injury can do things to your mind, to your memory.' – I stirred impatiently – 'Made me mix up the ranks and all, ah—'

'Look, Schneider, I don't really care.' I drew an ill-advisedly deep lungful of smoke and coughed. 'All I care about is surviving this war long enough to find a way out of it. Now if you repeat that, I'll have you shot, but otherwise you can do what the fuck you like. Got it?'

He nodded, but his poise had undergone a subtle change. His nervousness had damped down to a subdued gnawing at his thumbnail and he was watching me, vulture-like. When I stopped speaking, he took his thumb out of his mouth, grinned, then replaced it with the cigarette. Almost airily, he blew smoke at the viewport and the planet it showed.

'Exactly,' he said.

'Exactly what?'

Schneider glanced around conspiratorially, but the few other occupants of the ward were all congregated at the other end of the chamber, watching Latimer holoporn. He grinned again and leaned closer.

'Exactly what I've been looking for. Someone with some common sense. Lieutenant Kovacs, I'd like to make you a proposition. Something that will involve you getting out of this war, not only alive but rich, richer than you can possibly imagine.'

'I can imagine quite a lot, Schneider.'

He shrugged. 'Whatever. A lot of money, then. Are you interested?'

I thought about it, trying to see the angle behind. 'Not if it involves changing sides, no. I have nothing against Joshua Kemp personally, but I think he's going to lose and—'

'Politics.' Schneider waved a hand dismissively. 'This has nothing to do with politics. Nothing to do with the war, either, except as a circumstance. I'm talking about something solid. A product. Something any of the corporates would pay a single figure percentage of their annual profits to own.'

I doubted very much whether there was any such thing on a backwater world like Sanction IV, and I doubted even more that someone like Schneider would have ready access to it. But then, he'd scammed his way aboard what was in effect a Protectorate warship and got medical attention that – at a pro-government estimate – half a million men on the surface were screaming for in vain. He might have *something*, and right now *anything* that might get me off this mudball before it ripped itself apart was worth listening to.

I nodded and stubbed out my cigarette.

'Alright.'

'You're in?'

'I'm listening,' I said mildly. 'Whether or not I'm in depends on what I hear.'

Schneider sucked in his cheeks. 'I'm not sure we can proceed on that basis, lieutenant. I need—'

'You need me. That's obvious, or we wouldn't be having this conversation. Now shall we proceed on that basis, or shall I call Wedge security and let them kick it out of you?'

There was a taut silence, into which Schneider's grin leaked like blood.

'Well,' he said at last. 'I see I've misjudged you. The records don't cover this, ah, aspect of your character.'

'Any records you've been able to access about me won't give you the half of it. For your information, Schneider, my last official military posting was the Envoy Corps.'

I watched it sink in, wondering if he'd scare. The Envoys have almost mythological status throughout the Protectorate, and they're not famous for their charitable natures. What I'd been wasn't a secret on Sanction IV, but I tended not to mention it unless pressed. It was the sort of reputation that led to at best a nervous silence every time I walked into a mess room and at worst to insane challenges from young first-sleevers with more neurachem and muscle grafting than sense. Carrera had carpeted me after the third (stack retrievable) death. Commanding officers generally take a dim view of murder within the ranks. You're supposed to reserve that kind of enthusiasm for the enemy. It was agreed that all references to my Envoy past would be buried deep in the Wedge datacore, and superficial records would label me a career mercenary via the Protectorate marines. It was a common enough pattern.

But if my Envoy past was scaring Schneider, it didn't show. He hunched forward again, shrewd face intense with thought.

'The Es, huh? When did you serve?'

'A while ago. Why?'

'You at Innenin?'

His cigarette end glowed at me. For a single moment it was as if I was falling into it. The red light smeared into traceries of laser fire, etching ruined walls and the mud underfoot as Jimmy de Soto wrestled against my grip and died screaming from his wounds, and the Innenin beachhead fell apart around us.

I closed my eyes briefly.

'Yeah, I was at Innenin. You want to tell me about this corporate wealth deal or not?'

Schneider was almost falling over himself to tell someone. He helped himself to another of my cigarettes and sat back in his chair.

'Did you know that the Northern Rim coastline, up beyond Sauberville, has some of the oldest Martian settlement sites known to human archaeology?'

Oh well. I sighed and slid my gaze past his face and back out to the view of Sanction IV. I should have expected something like this, but somehow I was disappointed in Jan Schneider. In the short minutes of our acquaintance, I thought I'd picked up on a gritty core that seemed too tightly wired for this kind of lost civilisation and buried techno-treasure bullshit.

It's the best part of five hundred years since we stumbled on the mausoleum of Martian civilisation, and people still haven't worked out that the artefacts our extinct planetary neighbours left lying around are largely either way out of our reach or wrecked. (Or very likely both, but how would we know?) About the only truly useful things we've been able to salvage are the astrogation charts whose vaguely understood notation enabled us to send our own colony ships to guaranteed terrestroid destinations.

This success, plus the scattered ruins and artefacts we've found on the worlds the maps gave us, have given rise to a widely varied crop of theories, ideas and cult beliefs. In the time I've spent shuttling back and forth across the Protectorate, I've heard most of them. In some places you've got the gibbering paranoia that says the whole thing is a cover-up, designed by the UN to hide the fact that the astrogation maps were really provided by time travellers from our own future. Then there's a carefully articulated religious faith that believes we're the lost descendants of the Martians, waiting to be reunited with the spirits of our ancestors when we've attained sufficient karmic enlightenment. A few scientists entertain vaguely hopeful theories that say Mars was in fact only a remote outpost, a colony cut off from the mother culture, and that the hub of the civilisation is still out there somewhere. My own personal favourite is that the Martians moved to Earth and became dolphins in order to shrug off the strictures of technological civilisation.

In the end it comes down to the same thing. They're gone, and we're just picking up the pieces.

Schneider grinned. 'You think I'm nuts, don't you? Living something out of a kid's holo?'

'Something like that.'

'Yeah, well just hear me out.' He was smoking in short, fast drags that let the smoke dribble out of his mouth as he talked. 'See, what everyone assumes is that the Martians were like us, not like us physically, I mean we assume their civilisation had the same cultural bases as ours.'

Cultural bases? This didn't sound like Schneider talking. This was something he'd been told. My interest sharpened fractionally.

'That means, we map out a world like this one, everyone creams themselves when we find centres of habitation. Cities, they figure. We're nearly two light years out from the main Latimer system, that's two habitable biospheres and three that need a bit of work, all of them with at least a handful of ruins, but as soon as the probes get here and register what look like cities, everyone drops what they're doing and comes rushing across.'

'I'd say rushing was an exaggeration.'

At sub-light speeds, it would have taken even the most souped-up colony barge the best part of three years to cross the gap from Latimer's binary suns to this unimaginatively named baby brother of a star. Nothing happens fast in interstellar space.

'Yeah? You know how long it took? From receiving the probe data via hypercast to inaugurating the Sanction government?'

I nodded. As a local military adviser it was my duty to know such facts. The interested corporates had pushed the Protectorate Charter paperwork through in a matter of weeks. But that was nearly a century ago, and didn't appear to have much bearing on what Schneider had to tell me now. I gestured at him to get on with it.

'So then,' he said, leaning forward and holding up his hands as if to conduct music, 'you get the archaeologues. Same deal as anywhere else; claims staked on a first come, first served basis with the government acting as broker between the finders and the corporate buyers.'

'For a percentage.'

'Yeah, for a percentage. Plus the right to expropriate quote under suitable compensation any findings judged to be of vital importance to Protectorate interests etcetera etcetera, unquote. The point is, any decent archaeologue who wants to make a killing is going to head for the centres of habitation, and that's what they all did.'

'How do you know all this, Schneider? You're not an archaeologist.'

He held out his left hand and pulled back his sleeve to let me see the coils of a winged serpent, tattooed in illuminum paint under the skin. The snake's scales glinted and shone with a light of their own and the wings moved fractionally up and down so that you almost seemed to hear the dry flapping and scraping that they would make. Entwined in the serpent's teeth was the inscription *Sanction IP Pilot's Guild* and the whole design was wreathed with the words *The Ground is for Dead People*. It looked almost new.

I shrugged. 'Nice work. And?'

'I ran haulage for a group of archaeologues working the Dangrek coast north-west of Sauberville. They were mostly Scratchers, but—'

'Scratchers?'

Schneider blinked. 'Yeah. What about it?'

'This isn't my planet,' I said patiently, 'I'm just fighting a war here. What are Scratchers?'

'Oh. You know, kids.' He gestured, perplexed. 'Fresh out of the Academy, first dig. Scratchers.'

'Scratchers. Got it. So who wasn't?'

'What?' he blinked again.

'Who wasn't a Scratcher? You said *they were mostly Scratchers, but*. But who?'

Schneider looked resentful. He didn't like me breaking up his flow.

'They got a few old hands, too. Scratchers have to take what they can find in any dig, but you always get some vets who don't buy the conventional wisdom.'

'Or turn up too late to get a better stake.'

'Yeah.' For some reason he didn't like that crack either. 'Sometimes. Point is we, they, found something.'

'Found what?'

'A Martian starship.' Schneider stubbed out his cigarette. 'Intact.'

'Crap.'

'Yes, we did.'

I sighed again. 'You're asking me to believe you dug up an entire spaceship, no sorry, *star*ship, and the news about this somehow hasn't got round? No one saw it. No one noticed it lying there. What did you do, blow a bubblefab over it?'

Schneider licked his lips and grinned. Suddenly he was enjoying himself again.

'I didn't say we dug it up, I said we *found* it. Kovacs, it's the size of a fucking asteroid and it's out there on the edges of the Sanction system in parking orbit. What we dug up was a gate that leads to it. A mooring system.'

'A gate?' Very faintly, I felt a chill coast down my spine as I asked the question. 'You talking about a hypercaster? You sure they read the technoglyphs right?'

'Kovacs, it's a *gate*.' Schneider spoke as if to a small child. 'We opened it. You can see right through to the other side. It's like a cheap experia special effect. Starscape that positively identifies as local. All we had to do was walk through.'

'Into the ship?' Against my will, I was fascinated. The Envoy Corps teaches you about lying, lying under polygraph, lying under extreme stress, lying in whatever circumstances demand it and with total conviction. Envoys lie better than any other human being in the Protectorate, natural or augmented, and looking at Schneider now I knew he was not lying. Whatever had happened to him, he believed absolutely in what he was saying.

'No.' He shook his head. 'Not into the ship, no. The gate's focused on a point about two kilometres out from the hull. It rotates every four and a half hours, near enough. You need a spacesuit.'

'Or a shuttle.' I nodded at the tattoo on his arm. 'What were you flying?'

He grimaced. 'Piece of shit Mowai suborbital. Size of a fucking house. It wouldn't fit through the portal space.'

'What?' I coughed up an unexpected laugh that hurt my chest. 'Wouldn't fit?'

'Yeah, you go ahead and laugh,' said Schneider morosely. 'Wasn't for that particular little logistic, I wouldn't be in this fucking war now. I'd be wearing out a custom-built sleeve in Latimer City. Clones on ice, remote storage, fucking immortal, man. The whole programme.'

'No one had a spacesuit?'

'What for?' Schneider spread his hands. 'It was a suborbital. No one was expecting to go offworld. Fact, no one was *allowed* offworld 'cept via the IP ports at Landfall. Everything you found on site had to be checked through Export Quarantine. And that was something else no one was real keen to do. Remember that expropriation clause?'

'Yeah. Any findings judged to be of vital importance to Protectorate interests. You didn't fancy the suitable compensation? Or you didn't figure it'd be suitable?'

'Come on, Kovacs. What's suitable compensation for finding something like this?'

I shrugged. 'Depends. In the private sector it depends very much on who you talk to. A bullet through the stack, maybe.'

Schneider skinned me a tight grin. 'You don't think we could have handled selling to the corporates?'

'I think you would have handled it very badly. Whether you lived or not would have depended on who you were dealing with.'

'So who would you have gone to?'

I shook out a fresh cigarette, letting the question hang a little before I said anything. 'That's not under discussion here, Schneider. My rates as a consultant are a little out of your reach. As a partner, on the other hand, well.' I offered him a small smile of my own. 'I'm still listening. What happened next?'

Schneider's laugh was a bitter explosion, loud enough to hook even the holoporn audience momentarily away from the lurid airbrushed bodies that twisted in full-scale 3-D reproduction at the other end of the ward.

'What happened?' He brought his voice down again, and waited until the flesh fans' gazes were snagged back to the performance. 'What happened? This war is what fucking happened.'

CHAPTER THREE

Somewhere, a baby was crying.

For a long moment I hung by my hands from the hatch coaming and let the equatorial climate come aboard. I'd been discharged from the hospital as fit for duty, but my lungs still weren't functioning as well as I would have liked, and the soggy air made for hard breathing.

'Hot here.'

Schneider had shut down the shuttle's drive and was crowding my shoulder. I dropped from the hatch to let him out and shaded my eyes against the glare of the sun. From the air, the internment camp had looked as innocuous as most scheme-built housing, but close up the uniform tidiness went down under assault from reality. The hastily-blown bubblefabs were cracking in the heat and liquid refuse ran in the alleys between them. A stench of burning polymer wafted to me on the scant breeze; the shuttle's landing field had blown sheets of waste paper and plastic up against the nearest stretch of perimeter fence, and now the power was frying them to fragments. Beyond the fence, robot sentry systems grew from the baked earth like iron weeds. The drowsy hum of capacitors formed a constant backdrop to the human noises of the internees.

A small squad of local militia slouched up behind a sergeant who reminded me vaguely of my father on one of his better days. They saw the Wedge uniforms and pulled up short. The sergeant gave me a grudging salute.

'Lieutenant Takeshi Kovacs, Carrera's Wedge,' I said briskly. 'This is Corporal Schneider. We're here to appropriate Tanya Wardani, one of your internees, for interrogation.'

The sergeant frowned. 'I wasn't informed of this.'

'I'm informing you now, sergeant.'

In situations like this, the uniform was usually enough. It was widely known on Sanction IV that the Wedge were the Protectorate's unofficial hard men, and generally they got what they wanted. Even the other mercenary units tended to back down when it came to tussles over requisitioning. But something seemed to be sticking in this sergeant's throat. Some dimly remembered worship of regulations, instilled on parade grounds back when it all meant something, back before the war cut loose. That, or maybe just the sight of his own countrymen and women starving in their bubble-fabs.

'I'll have to see some authorisation.'

I snapped my fingers at Schneider and held out a hand for the hardcopy. It hadn't been difficult to obtain. In a planet-wide conflict like this, Carrera gave his junior officers latitudes of initiative that a Protectorate divisional commander would kill for. No one had even asked me what I wanted Wardani for. No one cared. So far the toughest thing had been the shuttle; they had a use for that and IP transport was in short supply. In the end I'd had to take it at gunpoint from the regular-forces colonel in charge of a field hospital someone had told us about south-east of Suchinda. There was going to be some trouble about that eventually, but then, as Carrera himself was fond of saying, this was a war, not a popularity contest.

'Will that be sufficient, sergeant?'

He pored over the printout, as if he was hoping the authorisation flashes would prove to be peel-off fakes. I shifted with an impatience which was not entirely feigned. The atmosphere of the camp was oppressive, and the baby's crying ran on incessantly somewhere out of view. I wanted to be out of here.

The sergeant looked up and handed me the hardcopy. 'You'll have to see the commandant,' he said woodenly. 'These people are all under government supervision.'

I shot glances past him left and right, then looked back into his face.

'Right.' I let the sneer hang for a moment, and his eyes dropped away from mine. 'Let's go talk to the commandant then. Corporal Schneider, stay here. This won't take long.'

The commandant's office was in a double-storey 'fab cordoned off from the rest of the camp by more power fencing. Smaller sentry units squatted on top of the capacitor posts like early millennium gargoyles and uniformed recruits not yet out of their teens stood at the gate clutching oversize plasma rifles. Their young faces looked scraped and raw beneath the gadgetry-studded combat helmets. Why they were there at all was beyond me. Either the robot units were fake, or the camp was suffering from severe overmanning. We passed through without a word, went up a light alloy staircase that someone had epoxied carelessly to the side of the 'fab and the sergeant buzzed the door. A securicam set over the lintel dilated briefly and the door cracked open. I stepped inside, breathing the conditioning-chilled air with relief.

Most of the light in the office came from a bank of security monitors on the far wall. Adjacent to them was a moulded plastic desk dominated on one side by a cheap datastack holo and a keyboard. The rest of the surface was scattered with curling sheets of hardcopy, marker pens and other administrative debris. Abandoned coffee cups rose out of the mess like cooling towers in an industrial wasteland, and in one place light-duty cabling snaked across the desktop and down to the arm of the sideways slumped figure behind the desk.

'Commandant?'

The view on a couple of the security monitors shifted, and in the flickering light I saw the gleam of steel along the arm.

'What is it, sergeant?'

The voice was slurred and dull, disinterested. I advanced into the cool gloom and the man behind the desk lifted his head slightly. I made out one blue photoreceptor eye and the patchwork of prosthetic alloy running down one side of the face and neck to a bulky left shoulder that looked like spacesuit armour but wasn't. Most of the left side was gone, replaced with articulated servo units from hip to armpit. The arm was made of lean steel hydraulic systems that ended in a black claw. The wrist and forearm section was set with a half dozen shiny silver sockets, into one of which the cabling from the table was jacked. Next to the jacked socket, a small red light pulsed languorously on and off. Current flowing.

I stood in front of the desk and saluted.

'Lieutenant Takeshi Kovacs, Carrera's Wedge,' I said softly.

'Well.' The commandant struggled upright in his chair. 'Perhaps you'd like more light in here, lieutenant. I like the dark, but then,' he chuckled behind closed lips. 'I have an eye for it. You, perhaps, have not.'

He groped across the keyboard and after a couple of attempts the main lights came up in the corners of the room. The photoreceptor seemed to dim, while beside it a bleary human eye focused on me. What remained of the face was fine featured and would have been handsome, but long exposure to the wire had robbed the small muscles of coherent electrical input and rendered the expression slack and stupid.

'Is that better?' The face attempted something that was more leer than smile. 'I imagine it is; you come after all from the Outside World.' The capitals echoed ironically. He gestured across the room at the monitor screens. 'A world beyond these tiny eyes and anything their mean little minds can dream of. Tell me, lieutenant, are we still at war for the raped, I mean raked, archaeologically rich and raked soil of our beloved planet?'

My eyes fell to the jack and the pulsing ruby light, then went back to his face.

'I'd like to have your full attention, commandant.'

For a long moment, he stared at me, then his head twisted down like something wholly mechanical, to look at the jacked-in cable.

'Oh,' he whispered. 'This.'

Abruptly, he lurched round to face the sergeant, who was hovering just inside the door with two of the militia.

'Get out.'

The sergeant did so with an alacrity that suggested he hadn't much wanted to be there in the first place. The uniformed extras followed, one of them gently pulling the door shut behind him. As the door latched, the commandant slumped back in his chair and his right hand went to the cable interface. A sound escaped his lips that might have been either sigh or cough, or maybe laughter. I waited until he looked up.

'Down to a trickle, I assure you,' he said, gesturing at the still winking light. 'Probably couldn't survive an outright disconnection at this stage in the proceedings. If I lay down, I'd probably never get up again, so I stay in this. Chair. The discomfort wakes me. Periodically.' He made an obvious effort. 'So what, may I ask, do Carrera's Wedge want with me? We've nothing here of value, you know. Medical supplies were all exhausted months ago and even the food they send us barely makes full rations. For my men, of course; I'm referring to the fine corps of soldiers I command here. Our residents receive even less.' Another gesture, this time turned outwards to the bank of monitors. 'The machines, of course, do not need to eat. They are self-contained, undemanding, and have no inconvenient empathy for what they are guarding. Fine soldiers, every one. As you see, I've tried to turn myself into one, but the process isn't very far along yet—'

'I haven't come for your supplies, commandant.'

'Ah, then it's a reckoning, is it? Have I overstepped some recently drawn mark in the Cartel's scheme of things? Proved an embarrassment to the war effort, perhaps?' The idea seemed to amuse him. 'Are you an assassin? A Wedge enforcer?'

I shook my head.

'I'm here for one of your internees. Tanya Wardani.'

'Ah yes, the archaeologue.'

A slight sharpening stole through me. I said nothing, only put the hardcopy authorisation on the table in front of the commandant and waited. He picked it up clumsily and tipped his head to one side at an exaggerated angle, holding the paper aloft as if it were some kind of holotoy that needed to be viewed from below. He seemed to be muttering something under his breath.

'Some problem, commandant?' I asked quietly.

He lowered the arm and leant on his elbow, wagging the authorisation to and fro at me. Over the movements of the paper, his human eye looked suddenly clearer.

'What do you want her for?' he asked, equally softly. 'Little Tanya the Scratcher. What's she to the Wedge?'

I wondered, with a sudden iciness, if I was going to have to kill this man. It wouldn't be difficult to do, I'd probably only be cheating the wire by a few months, but there was the sergeant outside the door and the militia. Bare-handed, those were long odds, and I still didn't know what the programming parameters of the robot sentries were. I poured the ice into my voice.

'That, commandant, has even less to do with you than it does with me. I have my orders to carry out, and now you have yours. Do you have Wardani in custody, or not?'

But he didn't look away the way the sergeant had. Maybe it was something from the depths of the addiction that was pushing him, some clenched bitterness he had discovered whilst wired into decaying orbit around the core of himself. Or maybe it was a surviving fragment of granite from who he had been before. He wasn't going to give.

Behind my back, preparatory, my right hand flexed and loosened.

Abruptly, his upright forearm collapsed across the desk like a dynamited tower and the hardcopy gusted free of his fingers. My hand whiplashed out and pinned the paper on the edge of the desk before it could fall. The commandant made a small dry noise in his throat.

For a moment we both looked at the hand holding the paper in silence, then the commandant sagged back in his seat.

'Sergeant,' he bellowed hoarsely.

The door opened.

'Sergeant, get Wardani out of 'fab eighteen and take her to the lieutenant's shuttle.'

The sergeant saluted and left, relief at the decision being taken out of his hands washing over his face like the effect of a drug.

'Thank you, commandant.' I added my own salute, collected the authorisation hardcopy from the desk and turned to leave. I was almost at the door when he spoke again.

'Popular woman,' he said.

I looked back. 'What?'

'Wardani.' He was watching me with a glitter in his eye. 'You're not the first.'

'Not the first what?'

'Less than three months ago.' As he spoke, he was turning up the current in his left arm and his face twitched spasmodically. 'We had a little raid. Kempists. They beat the perimeter machines and got inside, very high tech considering the state they're in, in these parts.' His head tipped languidly back over the top of the seat and a long sigh eased out of him. 'Very high tech. Considering. They came for. Her.'

I waited for him to continue, but his head only rolled sideways slightly. I hesitated. Down below in the compound, two of the militia looked curiously up at me. I crossed back to the commandant's desk and cradled his face in both hands. The human eye showed white, pupil floating up against the upper lid like a balloon bumping the roof of a room where the party has long since burnt itself out.

'Lieutenant?'

The call came from the stairway outside. I stared down at the drowned face a moment longer. He was breathing slackly through half-open lips, and there seemed to be the crease of a smile in the corner of his mouth. On the periphery of my vision, the ruby light winked on and off.

'Lieutenant?'

'Coming.' I let the head roll free and walked out into the heat, closing the door gently behind me.

Schneider was seated on one of the forward landing pods when I got back, amusing a crowd of ragged children with conjuring tricks. A couple of uniforms watched him at a distance from the shade of the nearest bubblefab. He glanced up as I approached.

'Problem?'

'No. Get rid of these kids.'

Schneider raised an eyebrow at me, and finished his trick with no great hurry. As a finale, he plucked small plastic memory form toys from behind each child's ear. They looked on in disbelieving silence while Schneider demonstrated how the little figures worked. Crush them flat and then whistle sharply and watch them work their way, amoeba-like, back to their original shape. Some corporate gene lab ought to come up with soldiers like that. The children watched open-mouthed. It was another trick in itself. Personally, something that indestructible would have given me nightmares as a child, but then, grim though my own childhood had been, it was a three-day arcade outing compared with this place.

'You're not doing them any favours, making them think men in uniform aren't all bad,' I said quietly.

Schneider cut me a curious glance and clapped his hands loudly. 'That's it, guys. Get out of here. Come on, show's over.'

The children sloped off, reluctant to leave their little oasis of fun and free gifts. Schneider folded his arms and watched them go, face unreadable.

'Where'd you get those things?'

'Found them in the hold. Couple of aid packages for refugees. I guess the hospital we lifted this boat from didn't have much use for them.'

'No, they've already shot all the refugees down there.' I nodded at the departing children, now chattering excitedly over their new acquisitions. 'The camp militia'll probably confiscate the lot once we're gone.'

Schneider shrugged. 'I know. But I'd already given out the chocolate and painkillers. What are you going to do?'

It was a reasonable question, with a whole host of unreasonable answers. Staring out the nearest of the camp militia, I brooded on some of the bloodier options.

'Here she comes,' said Schneider, pointing. I followed the gesture and saw the sergeant, two more uniforms and between them a slim figure with hands locked together before her. I narrowed my eyes against the sun and racked up the magnification on my neurachem-aided vision.

Tanya Wardani must have looked a lot better in her days as an archaeologue. The long-limbed frame would have carried more flesh, and she would have done something with her dark hair, maybe just washed it and worn it up. It was unlikely she would have had the fading bruises under her eyes either, and she might even have smiled faintly when she saw us, just a twist of the long, crooked mouth in acknowledgement.

She swayed, stumbled and had to be held up by one of her

escorts. At my side, Schneider twitched forward, then stopped himself.

'Tanya Wardani,' said the sergeant stiffly, producing a length of white plastic tape printed end to end with bar code strips and a scanner. 'I'll need your ID for the release.'

I cocked a finger at the coding on my temple and waited impassively while the red light scan swept down over my face. The sergeant found the particular strip on the plastic tape that represented Wardani and turned the scanner on it. Schneider came forward and took the woman by the arm, pulling her aboard the shuttle with every appearance of brusque detachment. Wardani herself played it without a flicker of expression on her pallid face. As I was turning to follow the two of them, the sergeant called after me in a voice whose stiffness had turned suddenly brittle.

'Lieutenant.'

'Yes, what is it?' Injecting a rising impatience into my tone.

'Will she be coming back?'

I turned back in the hatchway, raising my eyebrow in the same elaborate arch that Schneider had used on me a few minutes earlier. He was way out of line, and he knew it.

'No, sergeant,' I said, as if to a small child. 'She won't be coming back. She's being taken for interrogation. Just forget about her.'

I closed the hatch.

But as Schneider spun the shuttle upward, I peered out of the viewport and saw him still standing there, buffeted by the storm of our departure.

He didn't even bother to shield his face from the dust.

CHAPTER FOUR

We flew west from the camp on grav effect, over a mixture of desert scrub and blots of darker vegetation where the planet's flora had managed to get a lock on shallow-running aquifers. About twenty minutes later we picked up the coast and headed out to sea over waters that Wedge military intelligence said were infested with Kempist smart mines. Schneider kept our speed down, subsonic the whole time. Easy to track.

I spent the early part of the flight in the main cabin, ostensibly going through a current affairs datastack that the shuttle was pulling down from one of Carrera's command satellites, but in reality watching Tanya Wardani with an Envoy-tuned eye. She sat slumped in the seat furthest from the hatch and hence closest to the right side viewports, forehead resting against the glass. Her eyes were open, but whether she was focusing on the ground below was hard to tell. I didn't try to speak to her – I'd seen the same mask on a thousand other faces this year, and I knew she wasn't coming out from behind it until she was ready, which might be never. Wardani had donned the emotional equivalent of a vacuum suit, the only response left in the human armoury when the moral parameters of the outside environment have grown so outrageously variable that an exposed mind can no longer survive unshielded. Lately, they've been calling it War Shock Syndrome, an all-encompassing term which bleakly but rather neatly puts the writing on the wall for those who would like to treat it. There may be a plethora of more and less effective psychological techniques for repair, but the ultimate aim of any medical philosophy, that of prevention rather than cure, is in this case clearly beyond the wit of humanity to implement.

To me it comes as no surprise that we're still flailing around with Neanderthal spanners in the elegant wreckage of Martian civilisation without really having a clue how all that ancient culture used to operate. After all, you wouldn't expect a butcher of farm livestock to understand or be able to take over from a team of neurosurgeons. There's no telling how much irreparable damage we may have already caused to the body of knowledge and technology the Martians have unwisely left lying around for us to discover. In the end, we're not much more than a pack of jackals, nosing through the broken bodies and wreckage of a plane crash.

'Coming up on the coast,' Schneider's voice said over the intercom. 'You want to get up here?'

I lifted my face away from the holographic data display, flattened the data motes to the base and looked across at Wardani. She had shifted her head slightly at the sound of Schneider's voice, but the eyes that found the speaker set in the roof were still dulled with emotional shielding. It hadn't taken me very long to extract from Schneider the previous circumstances of his relationship with this woman, but I still wasn't sure how that would affect things now. On his own admission it had been a limited thing, abruptly terminated by the outbreak of war almost two years ago and there was no reason to suppose it could cause problems. My own worst-case scenario was that the whole starship story was an elaborate con on Schneider's part for no other purpose than to secure the archaeologue's release and get the two of them offworld. There had been a previous attempt to liberate Wardani, if the camp commandant was to be believed, and part of me wondered if those mysteriously well equipped commandos hadn't been Schneider's last set of dupes in the bid to reunite him with his partner. If that turned out to be the case, I was going to be angry.

Inside me, at the level where it really mattered, I didn't give the idea much credence; too many details had checked out in the time since we'd left the hospital. Dates and names were correct – there had been an archaeological dig on the coast north-west of Sauberville, and Tanya Wardani was registered as site regulator. The haulage liaison was listed as Guild Pilot Ian Mendel, but it was Schneider's face, and the hardware manifest began with the serial number and flight records of a cumbersome Mowai Ten Series suborbital. Even if Schneider had tried to get Wardani out before, it was for far more material reasons than simple affection.

And if he hadn't, then somewhere along the line someone else had been dealt into this game.

Whatever happened, Schneider would bear watching.

I closed down the data display and got up, just as the shuttle banked seaward. Steadying myself with a hand on the overhead lockers, I looked down at the archaeologue.

'I'd fasten your seatbelt if I were you. The next few minutes are likely to be a little rough.'

She made no response, but her hands moved in her lap. I made my way forward to the cockpit.

Schneider looked up as I entered, hands easy on the arms of the manual flight chair. He nodded at a digital display which he'd maximised near the top of the instrument projection space.

'Depth counter's still at less than five metres. Bottom shelves out for kilometres before we hit deep water. You sure those fuckers don't come in this close?'

'If they were in this close, you'd see them sticking out of the water,' I said, taking the co-pilot's seat. 'Smart mine's not much smaller than a marauder bomb. Basically an automated mini-sub. You got the set online?'

'Sure. Just mask up. Weapon systems on the right arm.'

I slid the elasticated gunner's eyemask down over my face and touched the activate pads at the temples. A seascape in bright primaries wrapped around my field of vision, pale blue shaded deeper grey with the landscape of the seabed beneath. Hardware came through in shades of red, depending on how much it corresponded to the parameters I'd programmed in earlier. Most of it was light pink in colour, inanimate alloy wreckage devoid of electronic activity. I let myself slide forward into the virtual representation of what the shuttle's sensors were seeing, forced myself to stop actively looking for anything and relaxed the last mental millimetres into the Zen state.

Minesweeping was not something the Envoy Corps taught as such, but the total poise that only comes, paradoxically, with an utter lack of expectation was vital to the core training. A Protectorate Envoy, deployed as digital human freight via hyperspatial needle-cast, can expect to wake up to literally anything. At the very least, you habitually find yourself in unfamiliar bodies on unfamiliar worlds where people are shooting at you. Even on a good day, no amount of briefing can prepare you for a total change of environment like that, and in the invariably unstable to lethally dangerous sets of circumstances the Envoys have been created to deal with, there just isn't any point.

Virginia Vidaura, Corps trainer, hands in the pockets of her coveralls, looking us over with calm speculation. Day one induction.

Since it is logistically impossible to expect everything, she told us evenly, *we will teach you not to expect anything. That way, you will be ready for it.*

I didn't even consciously see the first smart mine. There was a red flare in the corner of one eye, and my hands had already matched coordinates and loosed the shuttle's hunter-killer micros. The little missiles ran green traces across the virtual seascape, plunged beneath the surface like sharp knives in flesh and pricked the squatting mine before it could either move or respond. Flash blast of detonation and the surface of the sea heaved upward like a body on an interrogation table.

Once upon a time men had to run their weapons systems all by themselves. They went up in the air in flyers not much bigger or better equipped than bathtubs with wings, and fired off whatever clumsy hardware they could squeeze into the cockpit with them. Later, they designed machines that could do the job faster and more accurately than humanly possible and for a while it was a machine's world up there. Then the emerging biosciences began to catch up and suddenly the same speed and precision capacity was available as a human option again. Since then it's been a race of sorts between technologies to see which can be upgraded faster, the external machines or the human factor. In that particular race, Envoy psychodynamics were a sharp surprise sprint up the inside lane.

There are war machines that are faster than me, but we weren't lucky enough to have one aboard. The shuttle was a hospital auxiliary, and its strictly defensive weaponry ran to the micro turret in the nose and a decoy-and-evade package that I wouldn't have trusted to fly a kite. We were going to have to do this ourselves.

'One down. The rest of the pack won't be far away. Kill your speed. Get us down on the deck and arm the tinsel.'

They came from the west, scuttling across the seabed like fat-bodied cylindrical spiders, drawn to the violent death of their brother. I felt the shuttle tip forward as Schneider brought us down to barely ten metres altitude and the solid thump as the tinsel bomb racks deployed. My eyes flickered across the mines. Seven of them, converging. They usually ran five to a pack so this had to be the remnants of two groups, though who'd thinned their numbers out so much was a mystery to me. From what I'd read in the reports, there'd been nothing in these waters but fishing boats since the war began. The seabed was littered with them.

I acquired the lead mine and killed it almost casually. As I watched, the first torpedoes erupted from the other six and rose through the water towards us.

'They're on us.'

'Seen them,' said Schneider laconically, and the shuttle flinched into an evasive curve. I peppered the sea with micros on autoseek.

Smart mine is a misnomer. They're actually pretty stupid. It stands to reason, they're built for such a narrow range of activity it isn't advisable to programme in much intellect. They attach themselves to the seabed with a claw for launch stability, and they wait for something to pass overhead. Some can dig themselves deep enough to hide from spectroscanners, some camouflage themselves as seabed wreckage. Essentially, they're a static weapon. On the move, they can still fight but their accuracy suffers.

Better yet, their minds have a dogmatic either/or target acquisition system that tags everything surface or airborne before it fires on it. Against air traffic it uses surface-to-air micros, against shipping the torpedoes. The torpedoes can convert to missile mode at a pinch, shedding their propulsion systems at surface level and using crude thrusters to get aloft, but they're *slow*.

At nearly surface level and throttled back almost to hovering, we'd been made as a ship. The torpedoes came up for air in our shadow, found nothing and the autoseek micros destroyed them while they were still trying to shrug off their underwater drives. Meanwhile, the spread of micros I'd launched sought and destroyed two, no, wait, three of the mines. At this rate—

Malfunction.

Malfunction.

Malfunction.

The fail light pulsed in the upper left field of my vision, detail scrolling down. I had no time to read it. The fire controls were dead in my hands, jammed solid, the next two micros unarmed in their launch cradles. *Fucking mothballed UN surplus* flashing through my mind like a falling meteor. I slammed the emergency autorepair option. The shuttle's rudimentary troubleshooter brain leapt down into the jammed circuits. No time. It could take whole minutes to fix. The remaining three mines launched surface to air at us.

'Sch—'

Schneider, whatever his other failings, was a good flyer. He flung the shuttle on its tail before the syllable was out of my mouth. My head snapped back against the seat as we leapt into the sky, trailing a swarm of surface-to-air missiles.

'I'm jammed.'

'I know,' he said tautly.

'Tinsel them,' I yelled, competing with the proximity alerts that screamed in my ears. The altitude numerals flashed over the kilometre mark.

'On it.'

The shuttle boomed with the tinsel bombs' launch. They detonated two seconds in our wake, sowing the sky with tiny electronic appetisers. The surface-to-air fire spent itself amongst the decoys. On the weapons board at the side of my vision, a cleared light flashed green, and as if to prove the point the launcher executed its last jammed command and launched the two waiting micros into the targetless space ahead of us. Beside me, Schneider whooped and spun the shuttle about. With the high-manoeuvre fields belatedly compensating, I felt the turn slop through my guts like choppy water and had time to hope that Tanya Wardani hadn't eaten recently.

We hung for an instant on the wings of the shuttle's AG fields, then Schneider killed the lift and we plunged a steep line back towards the surface of the sea. From the water, a second wave of missiles rose to meet us.

'*Tinsel!!!*'

The bomb racks banged open again. Sighting on the three undamaged mines below, I emptied the shuttle's magazines and hoped, breath held back. The micros launched clean. At the same moment, Schneider threw on the grav fields again and the little vessel shuddered from end to end. The tinsel bombs, now falling faster than the crash-reversed shuttle that had launched them, exploded fractionally ahead and below us. My virtual vision flooded with crimson sleet from the storm of decoy broadcast, and then the explosions of the surface-to-air missiles as they destroyed themselves amidst it. My own micros were away, fired through the tiny window of opportunity before the tinsel blew and locked onto the mines somewhere below.

The shuttle spiralled down behind the debris of tinsel and misled missiles. Scant moments before we hit the surface of the sea, Schneider fired one more, carefully doctored pair of tinsel bombs. They detonated just as we slipped below the waves.

'We're under,' said Schneider.

On my screen, the pale blue of the sea deepened as we sank, nose down. I twisted around, searching for the mines and found only a satisfying array of wreckage. I let out the last breath I'd drawn somewhere up in the missile-strewn sky and rolled my head back in the seat.

'That,' I said to no one in particular, 'was a mess.'

We touched bottom, stuck for a moment and then drifted fractionally upward again. Around us, the shrapnel from the doctored tinsel bombs settled slowly to the seabed. I studied the pink fragments with care and smiled. I'd packed the last two bombs myself – less than an hour's work the night before we came to get Wardani, but it had taken three days reconnoitring deserted battlezones and bombed-out landing fields to gather the necessary pieces of hull casing and circuitry to fill them.

I peeled off the gunner's mask and rubbed at my eyes.

'How far off are we?'

Schneider did something to the instrument display. 'About six hours, maintaining this buoyancy. If I help the current along with the gravs we could do it in half that.'

'Yeah, and we could get blown out of the water too. I didn't go through the last two minutes for target practice. You keep the fields banked all the way, and use the time to figure out some way to wipe the face off this bucket.'

Schneider gave me a mutinous look.

'And what are you going to be doing all that time?'

'Repairs,' I said shortly, heading back for Tanya Wardani.

CHAPTER FIVE

The fire threw leaping shadows, making her face into a camouflage mask of light and dark. It was a face that might have been
handsome before the camp swallowed her, but the rigours of
political internment had left it a gaunt catalogue of bones and
hollows. The eyes were hooded, the cheeks sunken. Deep inside the
wells of her gaze, firelight glittered on fixed pupils. Stray hair fell
across her forehead like straw. One of my cigarettes slanted between
her lips, unlit.

'You don't want to smoke that?' I asked after a while.

It was like talking on a bad satellite link – a two-second delay
before the glitter in her eyes shifted upward to focus on my face.
Her voice ghosted out, rusty with disuse.

'What?'

'The cigarette. Site Sevens, best I could get outside Landfall.' I
handed the packet across to her and she fumbled it, turning it over a
couple of times before she found the ignition patch and touched it to
the end of the cigarette in her mouth. Most of the smoke escaped
and was carried away on the soft breeze, but she took some down
and grimaced as it bit.

'Thanks,' she said quietly, and held the packet in cupped hands,
looking down at it as if it were a small animal she had rescued from
drowning. I smoked the rest of my own cigarette in silence, gaze
flickering along the treeline above the beach. It was a programmed
wariness, not based on any real perception of danger, the Envoy
analogue of a relaxed man beating time to music with his fingers. In
the Envoys you're aware of potential hazards in the surroundings,
the way most people are aware that things will fall out of their hands

if they let them go. The programming goes in at the same instinctual level. You don't let down your guard ever, any more than a normal human being would absent-mindedly let go of a filled glass in mid-air.

'You've done something to me.'

It was the same low voice she had used to thank me for the cigarette, but when I dropped my gaze from the trees to look at her, something had kindled in her eyes. She was not asking me a question. 'I can feel it,' she said, touching the side of her head with splayed fingers. 'Here. It's like. Opening.'

I nodded, feeling cautiously for the right words. On most worlds I've visited, going into someone's head uninvited is a serious moral offence, and only government agencies get away with it on a regular basis. There was no reason to assume the Latimer sector, Sanction IV or Tanya Wardani would be any different. Envoy co-option techniques make rather brutal use of the deep wells of psychosexual energy that drive humans at a genetic level. Properly mined, the matrix of animal strength on tap in those places will speed up psychic healing by whole orders of magnitude. You start with light hypnosis, move into quick-fix personality engagement and thence to close bodily contact that only misses definition as sexual foreplay on a technicality. A gentle, hypnotically induced orgasm usually secures the bonding process, but at the final stage with Wardani, something had made me pull back. The whole process was uncomfortably close to a sexual assault as it was.

On the other hand, I needed Wardani in one psychic piece, and under normal circumstances that would have taken months, maybe years, to achieve. We didn't have that kind of time.

'It's a technique,' I offered tentatively 'A healing system. I used to be an Envoy.'

She drew on her cigarette. 'I thought the Envoys were supposed to be killing machines.'

'That's what the Protectorate wants you to think. Keeps the colonies scared at a gut level. The truth is a lot more complex, and ultimately it's a lot more scary, when you think it through.' I shrugged. 'Most people don't like to think things through. Too much effort. They'd rather have the edited visceral highlights.'

'Really? And what are those?'

I felt the conversation gathering itself for flight, and leaned forward to the heat of the fire.

'Sharya. Adoracion. The big bad high-tech Envoys, riding in on hypercast beams and decanting into state-of-the-art biotech sleeves to crush all resistance. We used to do that too, of course, but what most people don't realise is that our five most successful deployments ever were all covert diplomatic postings, with barely any bloodshed at all. Regime engineering. We came and went, and no one even realised we'd been there.'

'You sound proud of it.'

'I'm not.'

She looked at me steadily. 'Hence the "used to"?'

'Something like that.'

'So how does one stop being an Envoy?' I was wrong. This wasn't conversation. Tanya Wardani was sounding me out. 'Did you resign? Or did they throw you out?'

I smiled faintly. 'I'd really rather not talk about it, if it's all the same to you.'

'You'd rather not talk about it?' Her voice never rose, but it splintered into sibilant shards of rage. 'Goddamn you, Kovacs. Who do you think you are? You come to this planet with your fucking weapons of mass destruction and your profession-of-violence airs, and you think you're going to play the injured-child-inside with me. Fuck you and your pain. I nearly died in that camp. I watched other women and children die. I don't fucking care what you went through. You answer me. Why aren't you with the Envoys any more?'

The fire crackled to itself. I sought out an ember in its depths and watched it for a while. I saw the laser light again, playing against the mud and Jimmy de Soto's ruined face. I'd been to this place in my mind countless times before, but it never got any better. Some idiot once said that time heals all wounds, but they didn't have Envoys back when that was written down. Envoy conditioning carries with it total recall, and when they discharge you, you don't get to give it back.

'Have you heard of Innenin?' I asked her.

'Of course.' It was unlikely she hadn't – the Protectorate doesn't get its nose bloodied very often, and when it happens the news travels, even across interstellar distances. 'You were there?'

I nodded.

'I heard everybody died in the viral strike.'

'Not quite. Everybody in the second wave died. They deployed the virus too late to get the initial beachhead, but some of it leaked over through the communications net and that fried most of the rest of us. I was lucky. My comlink was down.'

'You lost friends?'

'Yes.'

'And you resigned?'

I shook my head. 'I was invalided out. Psych-profiled unfit for Envoy duties.'

'I thought you said your comlink—'

'The virus didn't get me; the aftermath did.' I spoke slowly, trying to keep a lock on the remembered bitterness. 'There was a Court of Enquiry – you must have heard about that too.'

'They indicted the High Command, didn't they?'

'Yeah, for about ten minutes. Indictment quashed. That's roughly when I became unfit for Envoy duties. You might say I had a crisis of faith.'

'Very touching.' She sounded abruptly tired, the previous anger too much for her to sustain. 'Pity it didn't last, eh?'

'I don't work for the Protectorate any more, Tanya.'

Wardani gestured. 'That uniform you're wearing says otherwise.'

'This uniform,' I fingered the black material with distaste, 'is strictly a temporary thing.'

'I don't think so, Kovacs.'

'Schneider's wearing it too,' I pointed out.

'Schneider . . .' The word gusted out of her doubtfully. She obviously still knew him as Mendel. 'Schneider is an asshole.'

I glanced down the beach to where Schneider was banging about in the shuttle with what seemed like an inordinate degree of noise. The techniques I'd used to bring Wardani's psyche back to the surface hadn't gone down well with him, and he'd liked it even less when I'd told him to give us some time alone by the fire.

'Really? I thought you and he . . .'

'Well.' She considered the fire for a while. 'He's an attractive asshole.'

'Did you know him before the dig?'

She shook her head. 'Nobody knew anybody before the dig. You just get assigned, and hope for the best.'

'You got assigned to the Dangrek coast?' I asked casually.

'No.' She drew in her shoulders as if against cold. 'I'm a Guild Master. I could have got work on the Plains digs if I'd wanted to. I chose Dangrek. The rest of the team were assigned Scratchers. They didn't buy my reasons, but they were all young and enthusiastic. I guess even a dig with an eccentric's better than no dig at all.'

'And what were your reasons?'

There was a long pause, which I spent cursing myself silently for the slip. The question had been genuine – most of my knowledge of the Archaeologue Guild was gleaned from popular digests of their history and occasional successes. I had never met a Guild Master before, and what Schneider had to say about the dig was obviously a filtered version of Wardani's pillow talk, stepped on by his own lack of deeper knowledge. I wanted the full story. But if there was one thing that Tanya Wardani had seen a surplus of during her internment, it was probably interrogation. The tiny increment of incisiveness in my voice must have hit her like a marauder bomb.

I was marshalling something to fill the silence, when she broke it for me, in a voice that only missed being steady by a micron.

'You're after the ship? Mende—' She started again. 'Schneider told you about it?'

'Yeah, but he was kind of vague. Did you know it was going to be there?'

'Not specifically. But it made sense; it had to happen sooner or later. Have you ever read Wycinski?'

'Heard of him. Hub theory, right?'

She allowed herself a thin smile. 'Hub theory isn't Wycinski's; it just owes him everything. What Wycinski said, among others at the time, is that everything we've discovered about the Martians so far points to a much more atomistic society than our own. You know – winged and carnivorous, originally from airborne predator stock, almost no cultural traces of pack behaviour.' The words started to flow – conversational patterns fading out as the lecturer in her tuned in unconsciously. 'That suggests the need for a much broader personal domain than humans require and a general lack of sociability. Think of them as birds of prey if you like. Solitary and aggressive. That they built cities at all is evidence that they managed at least in part to overcome the genetic legacy, maybe in the same way humans have got a halfway lock on the xenophobic tendencies that pack behaviour has given us. Where Wycinski differs from most of the experts is in his belief that this tendency would only be repressed to the extent that it was sufficiently desirable to group together, and that with the rise of technology it would be reversible. You still with me?'

'Just don't speed up.'

In fact, I wasn't having a problem, and some of this more basic stuff I'd heard before in one form or another. But Wardani was relaxing visibly as she talked, and the longer that went on the better chance there was of her recovery remaining stable. Even during the brief moments it had taken her to launch into the lecture, she had grown more animated, hands gesturing, face intent rather than distant. A fraction at a time, Tanya Wardani was reclaiming herself.

'You mentioned hub theory, that's a bullshit spin-off; fucking Carter and Bogdanovich whoring off the back of Wycinski's work on Martian cartography. See, one of the things about Martian maps is, there are no common centres. No matter where the archaeologue teams went on Mars, they always found themselves at the centre of the maps they dug up. Every settlement put itself slap in the middle of its own maps, always the biggest blob, regardless of actual size or apparent function. Wycinski argued that this shouldn't surprise anybody, since it tied in with what we'd already surmised about the way Martian minds worked. To any Martian drawing a map, the most important point on that map was bound to be where the map maker was located at the time of drawing. All Carter and Bogdanovich did was to apply that rationale to the astrogation charts. If every Martian city considered itself the centre of a planetary map, then every colonised world would in turn consider itself the centre of the Martian hegemony. Therefore, the fact that

Mars was marked big and dead centre on all these charts meant nothing in objective terms. Mars might easily be a recently colonised backwater, and the real hub of Martian culture could be literally any other speck on the chart.' She pulled a disdainful face. 'That's hub theory.'

'You don't sound too convinced.'

Wardani plumed smoke into the night. 'I'm not. Like Wycinski said at the time, so fucking what? Carter and Bogdanovich completely missed the point. By accepting the validity of what Wycinski said about Martian spatial perceptions, they should have also seen that the whole concept of hegemony was probably outside Martian terms of reference.'

'Uh-oh.'

'Yeah.' The thin smile again, more forced this time. 'That's where it started to get political. Wycinski went on record with that, saying that wherever the Martian race had originated, there was no reason to suppose that the mother world would be accorded any more importance in the scheme of things than quote absolutely essential in matters of basic factual education unquote.'

'Mummy, where do we come from? That sort of thing.'

'That sort of thing exactly. You might point it out on the map, *that's where we all came from once*, but since *where we are now* is far more important in real, day-to-day terms, that's about as far as the mother world homage would ever get.'

'I don't suppose Wycinski ever thought to disown this view of things as intrinsically and irreconcilably unhuman, did he?'

Wardani gave me a sharp look. 'How much do you really know about the Guild, Kovacs?'

I held up finger and thumb a modest span apart. 'Sorry, I just like to show off. I'm from Harlan's World. Minoru and Gretzky went to trial about the time I got into my teens. I was in a gang. Standard proof of how antisocial you were was to carve air graffiti about the trial in a public place. We all had the transcripts by heart. *Intrinsically and irreconcilably unhuman* came up a lot in Gretzky's recantation. Seemed like it was the standard Guild statement for keeping your research grants intact.'

She lowered her gaze. 'It was, for a while. And no, Wycinski wouldn't play that tune. He loved the Martians, he admired them, and he said so in public. That's why you only hear about him in connection with fucking hub theory. They pulled his funding, suppressed most of his findings and gave it all to Carter and Bogdanovich to run with. And what a blowjob those two whores gave in return. The UN commission voted a seven per cent increase in the Protectorate strategic budget the same year, all based on paranoid fantasies of a Martian overculture somewhere out there waiting to jump us.'

'Neat.'

'Yeah, and totally impossible to disprove. All the astrogation charts we've recovered on other worlds bear out Wycinski's finding – each world centres itself on the map the way Mars did, and that single fact is used to scare the UN into keeping a high strategic budget and a tight military presence across the whole Protectorate. No one wants to hear about what Wycinski's research really means, and anybody who talks too loud about it, or tries to apply the findings in research of their own is either defunded overnight or ridiculed, which in the end comes to the same thing.'

She flicked her cigarette into the fire and watched it flare up.

'That what happened to you?' I asked.

'Not quite.'

There was a palpable click to the last syllable, like a lock turning. Behind me, I could hear Schneider coming up the beach, his checklist for the shuttle or maybe just his patience exhausted. I shrugged.

'Talk about it later, you want to.'

'Maybe. How about you tell me what all that macho high-G manoeuvre bullshit was today?'

I glanced up at Schneider as he joined us beside the fire. 'Hear that? Complaint about the in-flight entertainment.'

'Fucking passengers,' Schneider grunted, picking up the clowning cue flawlessly as he lowered himself to the sand. 'Nothing ever changes.'

'You going to tell her, or shall I?'

'Was your idea. Got a Seven?'

Wardani held up the packet, then tossed them into Schneider's grasp. She turned back to me. 'Well?'

'The Dangrek coast,' I said slowly, 'whatever its archaeological merits may have been, is part of the Northern Rim territories and the Northern Rim has been designated by Carrera's Wedge as one of nine primary objectives in winning the war. And judging from the amount of organic damage going on up there at the moment, the Kempists have come to the same conclusion.'

'So?'

'So, mounting an archaeological expedition while Kemp and the Wedge are up there fighting for territorial dominance isn't my idea of smart. We have to get the fighting diverted.'

'*Diverted?*' The disbelief in her voice was gratifying to hear. I played to it, shrugging again.

'Diverted, or postponed. Whatever works. The point is, we need help. And the only place we're going to get help of that order is from the corporates. We're going to Landfall, and since I'm supposed to be on active service, Schneider's a Kempist deserter, you're a prisoner-of-war and this is a stolen shuttle, we need to shed a little heat before we do that. Satellite coverage of our little run-in with the smart mines back there will read like they took us down. A search of the seabed will show up pieces of wreckage compatible with that. Allowing that no one looks at the evidence too closely, we'll be filed as missing presumed vaporised, which suits me fine.'

'You think they'll let it go at that?'

'Well, it's a war. People getting killed shouldn't raise too many eyebrows.' I picked a stray length of wood out of the fire and started tracing a rough continental map in the sand. 'Oh, they may wonder what I was doing down here when I'm supposed to be taking up a command on the Rim, but that's the kind of detail that gets sifted in the aftermath of a conflict. Right now, Carrera's Wedge are spread pretty thin in the north and Kemp's forces are still pushing them towards the mountains. They've got the Presidential Guard coming in on this flank,' I prodded at the sand with my makeshift pointer, 'And sea-launched air strikes from Kemp's iceberg fleet over here. Carrera's got a few more important things to worry about than the exact manner of my demise.'

46

'And you really think the Cartel are going to put all that on hold just for you?' Tanya Wardani swung her burning gaze from my face to Schneider's. 'You didn't really buy into this, did you, Jan?'

Schneider made a small gesture with one hand. 'Just listen to the man, Tanya. He's jacked into the machine, he knows what he's talking about.'

'Yeah, *right*.' The intense, hectic eyes snapped back to me. 'Don't think I'm not grateful to you for getting me out of the camp, because I am. I don't think you can imagine quite how grateful I am. But now I'm out, I'd quite like to live. This, this *plan*, is all bullshit. You're just going to get us all killed, either in Landfall by corporate samurai or caught in the crossfire at Dangrek. They aren't going to—'

'You're right,' I said patiently, and she shut up, surprised. 'To a point, you're right. The major corporates, the ones in the Cartel, they wouldn't give this scheme a second glance. They can murder us, stick you into virtual interrogation until you tell them what they want to know and then just keep the whole thing under wraps until the war is over and they've won.'

'If they win.'

'They will,' I told her. 'They always do, one way or the other. But we aren't going to the majors. We've got to be smarter than that.'

I paused and poked at the fire, waiting. Out of the corner of my eye, I saw how Schneider craned forward with tension. Without Tanya Wardani aboard, the whole thing was dead in the water and we all knew it.

The sea whispered itself up on the beach and back. Something popped and crackled in the depths of the fire.

'Alright.' She moved slightly, like someone bedridden shifting to a less aching posture. 'Go on. I'm listening.'

Relief gusted out of Schneider audibly. I nodded.

'This is what we do. We target one corporate operator in particular, one of the smaller, hungrier ones. Might take a while to sound out, but it shouldn't be difficult. And once we've got the target, we make them an offer they can't refuse. A one-time only, limited period, bargain basement, satisfaction guaranteed purchase.'

I saw the way she exchanged glances with Schneider. Maybe it was all the monetary imagery that made her look to him.

'Small and hungry as you like, Kovacs, you're still talking about a corporate player.' Her eyes locked onto mine. 'Planetary wealth. And murder and virtual interrogation are hardly expensive. How do you propose to undercut that option?'

'Simple. We scare them.'

'You *scare* them.' She looked at me for a moment, and then coughed out a small, unwilling laugh. 'Kovacs, they should have you on disc. You're perfect post-trauma entertainment. So, tell me. You're going to *scare* a corporate block. What with, slasher puppets?'

I felt a genuine smile twitch at my own lips. 'Something like that.'

CHAPTER SIX

It took Schneider the better part of the next morning to wipe the shuttle's datacore, while Tanya Wardani walked aimless scuffing circles in the sand or sat beside the open hatch and talked to him. I left them alone and walked up to the far end of the beach where there was a black rock headland. The rock proved simple to scale and the view from the top was worth the few scrapes I picked up on the way. I leaned my back against a convenient outcrop and looked out to the horizon, recalling fragments of a dream from the previous night.

Harlan's World is small for a habitable planet and its seas slop about unpredictably under the influence of three moons. Sanction IV is much larger, larger even than Latimer or Earth, and it has no natural satellites, all of which makes for wide, placid oceans. Set against the memories of my early life on Harlan's World, this calm always seemed slightly suspicious, as if the sea were holding its watery breath, waiting for something cataclysmic to happen. It was a creepy sensation and the Envoy conditioning kept it locked down most of the time by the simple expedient of not allowing the comparison to cross my mind. In dreamsleep, the conditioning is less effective, and evidently something in my head was worrying at the cracks.

In the dream, I was standing on a shingle beach somewhere on Sanction IV, looking out at the tranquil swells, when the surface began to heave and swell. I watched, rooted to the spot, as mounds of water shifted and broke and flowed past each other like sinuous black muscles. What waves there were at the water's edge were gone, sucked back out to where the sea was flexing. A certainty made in equal parts of cold dread and aching sadness rose in me to match the disturbances offshore. I knew beyond doubt. Something monstrous was coming up.

But I woke up before it surfaced.

A muscle twitched in my leg and I sat up irritably. The dregs of the dream rinsed around the base of my mind, seeking connection with something more substantial.

Maybe it was fallout from the duel with the smart mines. I'd watched the sea heave upward as our missiles detonated beneath the surface.

Yeah, right. Very traumatic.

My mind skittered through a few other recent combat memories, looking for a match. I stopped it, rapidly. Pointless exercise. A year and a half of hands-on nastiness for Carrera's Wedge had laid up enough trauma in my head to give work to a whole platoon of psychosurgeons. I was entitled to a few nightmares. Without the Envoy conditioning, I'd probably have suffered a screaming mental collapse months ago. And combat memories weren't what I wanted to look at right now.

I made myself lie back again and relax into the day. The morning sun was already beginning to build towards semi-tropical midday heat, and the rock was warm to the touch. Between my half-closed eyelids, light moved the way it had in the lochside convalescent virtuality. I let myself drift.

Time passed unused.

My phone hummed quietly to itself. I reached down without opening my eyes and squeezed it active. Noted the increased weight of heat on my body, the light drenching of sweat on my legs.

'Ready to roll,' said Schneider's voice. 'You still up on that rock?'

I sat up unwillingly. 'Yeah. You make the call yet?'

'All cleared. That scrambler uplink you stole? Beautiful. Crystal clear. They're waiting on us.'

'Be right down.'

Inside my head, the same residue. The dream had not gone.

Something coming up.

I stowed the thought with the phone, and started downward.

*

Archaeology is a messy science.

You'd think, with all the high-tech advances of the past few centuries, that we'd have the practice of robbing graves down to a fine art by now. After all, we can pick up the telltale traces of Martian civilisation across interplanetary distances these days. Satellite surveys and remote sensing let us map their buried cities through metres of solid rock or hundreds of metres of sea, and we've even built machines that can make educated guesses about the more inscrutable remnants of what they left behind. With nearly half a millennium of practice, we really ought to be getting good at this stuff.

But the fact is, no matter how subtle your detection science is, once you've found something, you've still got to dig it up. And with the vast capital investment the corporates have made in the race to understand the Martians, the digging is usually done with about as much subtlety as a crew night out in Madame Mi's Wharfwhore Warehouse. There are finds to be made and dividends to be paid, and the fact that there are – apparently – no Martians around to object to the environmental damage doesn't help. The corporates swing in, rip the locks off the vacated worlds, and stand back while the Archaeologue Guild swarm all over the fixtures. And when the primary sites have been exhausted, no one usually bothers to tidy up.

You get places like Dig 27.

Hardly the most imaginative name for a town, but there was a certain amount of accuracy in the choice. Dig 27 had sprung up around the excavation of the same name, served for fifty years as dormitory, refectory and leisure complex for the archaeologue workforce, and was now in steep decline as the seams of xenoculture ore panned out to the dregs. The original dighead was a gaunt centipedal skeleton, straddling the skyline on stilled retrieval belts and awkwardly bent support struts as we flew in from the east. The town started beneath the drooping tail of the structure and spread from it in sporadic and uncertain clumps like an unenthusiastic concrete fungus. Buildings rarely heaved themselves above five storeys, and many of those that had were rather obviously derelict, as if the effort of upward growth had exhausted them beyond the ability to sustain internal life.

Schneider banked around the skull end of the stalled dighead, flattened out and floated down towards a piece of wasteground between three listing pylons which presumably delineated Dig 27's landing field. Dust boiled up from the badly kept ferrocrete as we hovered and I saw jagged cracks blown naked by our landing brakes. Over the comset, a senile navigation beacon husked a request for identification. Schneider ignored it, knocked over the primaries and climbed from his seat with a yawn.

'End of the line, folks. Everybody out.'

We followed him back to the main cabin and watched while he strapped on one of the unsubtle sawn-off particle throwers we'd liberated with the shuttle. He looked up, caught me watching and winked.

'I thought these were your friends.' Tanya Wardani was watching as well, alarmed if the expression on her face was anything to go by.

Schneider shrugged. 'They were,' he said. 'But you can't be too careful.'

'Oh great.' She turned to me. 'Have you got anything a bit less bulky than that cannon that I could maybe borrow. Something I can lift.'

I lifted the edges of my jacket aside to show the two Wedge-customised Kalashnikov interface guns where they rested in the chest harness.

'I'd lend you one of these, but they're personally coded.'

'Take a blaster, Tanya,' said Schneider without looking up from his own preparations. 'More chance you'll hit something with it anyway. Slug throwers are for fashion victims.'

The archaeologue raised her eyebrows. I smiled a little. 'He's probably right. Here, you don't have to wear it around your waist. The straps web out like this. Sling it over your shoulder.'

I moved to help her fit the weapon and as she turned towards me something indefinable happened in the small space between our bodies. As I settled the holstered weapon at the downward slope of her left breast, her eyes slanted upward to mine. They were, I saw, the colour of jade under swift-flowing water.

'That comfortable?'

'Not especially.'

I went to move the holster and she raised a hand to stop me. Against the dusty ebony of my arm, her fingers looked like naked bones, skeletal and frail.

'Leave it, it'll do.'

'OK. Look, you just pull down and the holster lets it go. Push back up and it grips again. Like that.'

'Got it.'

The exchange had not been lost on Schneider. He cleared his throat loudly and went to crack the hatch. As it hinged outward, he held onto a handgrip at the leading edge and swung down with practised flyer nonchalance. The effect was spoiled slightly as he landed and began coughing in the still settling dust our landing brake had raised. I suppressed a grin.

Wardani went after him, letting herself down awkwardly with the heels of her palms on the floor of the open hatchway. Mindful of the dust clouds outside, I stayed in the hatchway, eyes narrowed against the airborne grit in an attempt to see if we had a reception committee.

And we did.

They emerged from the dust like figures on a frieze gradually sandblasted clean by someone like Tanya Wardani. I counted seven in all, bulky silhouettes swathed in desert gear and spiky with weapons. The central figure looked deformed, taller than the others by half a metre but swollen and misshapen from the chest up. They advanced in silence.

I folded my arms across my chest so my fingertips touched the butts of the Kalashnikovs.

'Djoko?' Schneider coughed again. 'That you, Djoko?'

More silence. The dust had settled enough for me to make out the dull glint of metal on gun barrels and the enhanced vision masks they all wore. There was room for body armour beneath the loose desert gear.

'Djoko, quit fucking about.'

A high-pitched, impossible laugh from the towering, misshapen figure in the centre. I blinked.

'Jan, Jan, my good friend.' It was the voice of a child. 'Do I make you so nervous?'

'What do you think, fuckwit?' Schneider stepped forward and as I watched the huge figure spasmed and seemed to break apart. Startled, I cranked up the neurachem vision and made out a small boy of about eight scrambling down from the arms of the man who held him to his chest. As the boy reached the ground and ran to meet Schneider, I saw the man who had carried him straighten up into a peculiar immobility. Something quickened along the tendons in my arms. I screwed up my eyes some more and scanned the now unremarkable figure head to foot. This one was not wearing the EV mask and his face was . . .

I felt my mouth tighten as I realised what I was looking at.

Schneider and the boy were trading complicated handshakes and spouting gibberish at each other. Midway through this ritual, the boy broke off and took Tanya Wardani's hand with a formal bow and some ornate flattery that I didn't catch. He seemed insistent on clowning his way through the meeting. He was spouting harmlessness like a tinsel fountain on Harlan's Day. And with the worst of the dust down where it belonged, the rest of the reception committee had lost the vague menace their silhouettes had given them. The clearing air revealed them as an assortment of nervous-looking and mostly young irregulars. I saw one wispy-bearded Caucasian on the left chewing his lip below the blank calm of the EV mask. Another was shifting from foot to foot. All of them had their weapons slung or stowed and as I jumped down from the hatch, they all flinched backward.

I raised my hands soothingly shoulder height, palms outward.

'Sorry.'

'Don't apologise to this idiot.' Schneider was now trying to cuff the boy around the back of the head, with limited success. 'Djoko, come here and say hello to a real live Envoy. This is Takeshi Kovacs. He was at Innenin.'

'Indeed?' The boy came and offered his hand. Dark-skinned and fine-boned, it was already a handsome sleeve – in later life it would be androgynously beautiful. It was dressed immaculately in a tailored mauve sarong and matching quilted jacket. 'Djoko Roespinoedji, at your service. I apologise for the drama, but one cannot be too careful in these uncertain times. Your call came in on satellite frequencies that no one outside Carrera's Wedge has access to and Jan, while I love him like a brother, is not known for his connections in high places. It could have been a trap.'

'Mothballed scrambler uplink,' said Schneider importantly. 'We stole it from the Wedge. This time, Djoko, when I say I'm jacked in, I mean it.'

'Who might be trying to trap you?' I asked.

'Ah.' The boy sighed with a world-weariness several decades out of place in his voice. 'There is no telling. Government agencies, the Cartel, corporate leverage analysts, Kempist spies. None of them have any reason to love Djoko Roespinoedji. Remaining neutral in a war does not save you from making enemies as it should. Rather, it loses you any friends you might have and earns you suspicion and contempt from all sides.'

'The war isn't this far south yet,' Wardani pointed out.

Djoko Roespinoedji placed a hand gravely on his chest. 'For which we are all extremely grateful. But these days, not being on the front line merely means you are under occupation of one form or another. Landfall is barely eight hundred kilometres to our west. We are close enough to be considered a perimeter post, which means a state militia garrison and periodic visits from the Cartel's political assessors.' He sighed again. 'It is all *very* costly.'

I looked at him suspiciously. 'You're garrisoned? Where are they?'

'Over there.' The boy jerked a thumb at the ragged group of irregulars. 'Oh, there are a few more back at the uplink bunker, as per regulations, but essentially what you see here is the garrison.'

'*That's* the state militia?' asked Tanya Wardani.

'It is.' Roespinoedji looked sadly at them for a moment, then turned back to us. 'Of course, when I said it was costly, I was referring mostly to the cost of making the political assessor's visits congenial. For us and for him, that is. The assessor is not a very sophisticated man, but he does have substantial, um, appetites. And of course ensuring that he remains *our* political assessor displaces a certain amount of expenditure too. Generally they are rotated every few months.'

'Is he here now?'

'I would hardly have invited you here if he were. He left only last week.' The boy leered, unnerving to watch on a face that young. 'Satisfied, you might say, with what he found here.'

I found myself smiling. I couldn't help it.

'I think we've come to the right place.'

'Well that will depend on what you came for,' said Roespinoedji, glancing at Schneider. 'Jan was far from explicit. But come. Even in Dig 27 there are more congenial places than this to discuss business.'

He led us back to the little group of waiting militiamen and made a sharp clucking sound with his tongue. The figure who had been carrying him before stooped awkwardly and picked him up. Behind me, I heard Tanya Wardani's breath catch slightly as she saw what had been done to the man.

It was by no means the worst thing I'd ever seen happen to a human being, wasn't in fact even the worst I'd seen recently; still there was something eerie about the ruined head and the silvery alloy cement that had been used to patch it together. If I'd had to guess, I would have said this sleeve had been struck by flying shrapnel. Any kind of deliberate, directional weapon just wouldn't have left anything to work with. But someone somewhere had taken the trouble to repair the dead man's skull, seal up the remaining gaps with resin and replace the eyeballs with photoreceptors that sat in the gutted sockets like cyclopic silver spiders waiting for prey. Then, presumably, they'd coaxed enough life back into the brain-stem to operate the body's vegetative systems and basic motor functions, and maybe respond to a few programmed commands.

Back before I got shot up on the Rim, I'd had a Wedge noncom working with me whose Afro-Caribbean sleeve was actually his own. One night, waiting out a satellite bombardment in the ruins of some kind of temple, he'd told me one of the myths his people, in chains, had taken across an ocean on Earth, and later, in hope of a new beginning, across the gulfs of the Martian astrogation charts to the world that would later become known as Latimer. It was a story of magicians and the slaves they made of bodies raised from the dead. I forget what name he gave to these creatures in the story, but I know he would have seen one in the thing that held Djoko Roespinoedji in its arms.

'Do you like it?' The boy, cuddled up obscenely close to the ravaged head, had been watching me.

'Not much, no.'

'Well, aesthetically, of course . . .' The boy let his voice trail off delicately. 'But with judicious use of bandaging, and some suitably ragged clothing for me, we should make a truly pitiful ensemble. The wounded and the innocent, fleeing from the ruins of their shattered lives – ideal camouflage, really, should things become extreme.'

'Same old Djoko.' Schneider came up and nudged me. 'Like I told you. Always one step ahead of the action.'

I shrugged. 'I've known refugee columns get gunned down just for target practice.'

'Oh, I'm aware of that. Our friend here was a tactical marine before he met his unfortunate end. Still quite a lot of ingrained reflex left in the cortex, or wherever it is they store that kind of thing.' The boy winked at me. 'I'm a businessman, not a technician. I had a software firm in Landfall knock what was left into usable shape. Look.'

The child's hand disappeared into his jacket and the dead man snatched a long-barrelled blaster from the scabbard across his back. It was very fast. The photoreceptors whirred audibly in their sockets, scanning left to right. Roespinoedji grinned broadly and his hand emerged clutching the remote. A thumb shifted and the blaster was returned smoothly to its sheath. The arm supporting the boy had not shifted an inch.

'So you see,' the boy piped cheerfully, 'where pity cannot be mined, less subtle options are always available. But really, I'm optimistic. You'd be surprised how many soldiers still find it difficult to shoot small children, even in these troubled times. Now. Enough chatter, shall we eat?'

Roespinoedji had the top floor and penthouse of a raddled warehouse block not far off touching distance from the tail of the dighead. We left all but two of the militia escort outside in the street and picked our way through cool gloom to where an industrial elevator stood in one corner. The animated dead man dragged the cage door aside with one hand. Metallic echoes chased around the empty space over our heads

'I can remember,' said the boy as we rose towards the roof, 'when all this was stacked with grade-one artefacts, crated and tagged for airlift to Landfall. The inventory crews used to work shifts round the clock. The dighead never stopped, you could hear it running day and night under all the other sounds. Like a heartbeat.'

'Is that what you used to do?' asked Wardani. 'Stack artefacts?'

I saw Schneider smile to himself in the gloom.

'When I was younger,' said Roespinoedji, self-mocking. 'But I was involved in a more. Organisational capacity, shall we say?'

The elevator passed through the roof of the storage area and clanged to a halt in suddenly bright light. Sunlight strained through fabric-curtained windows into a reception lounge screened from the rest of the floor by amber-painted internal walls. Through the elevator cage I saw kaleidoscopic designs on carpets, dark wood flooring and long, low sofas arranged around what I took to be a small, internally-lit swimming pool. Then, as we stepped out, I saw that the floor recess held not water but a wide horizontal video screen on which a woman appeared to be singing. In two corners of the lounge, the image was duplicated in a more viewable format on two vertical stacks of more reasonably sized screens. The far wall held a long table on which someone had laid out enough food and drink for a platoon.

'Make yourselves comfortable,' said Roespinoedji, as his corpse guardian bore him away through an arched doorway. 'I'll only be a moment. Food and drink over there. Oh, and volume, if you want.'

The music on the screen was suddenly audible, instantly recognisable as a Lapinee number, though not her debut cover of the junk salsa hit *Open Ground* that had caused so much trouble the previous year. This one was slower, merged in with sporadic sub-orgasmic moaning. On screen, Lapinee hung upside down with her thighs wrapped around the barrel of a spider tank gun and crooned into the camera. Probably a recruiting anthem.

Schneider strode to the table and began piling a plate with every type of food the buffet had to offer. I watched the two militiamen take up station near the elevator, shrugged and joined him. Tanya Wardani seemed about to follow suit, but then she changed course abruptly and walked to one of the curtained windows instead. One narrow-boned hand went to the patterns woven into the fabric there.

'Told you,' said Schneider to me. 'If anyone can jack us in on this side of the planet, Djoko can. He's interfaced with every player in Landfall.'

'You mean he was before the war.'

Schneider shook his head. 'Before and during. You heard what he said about the assessor. No way he could pull that kind of gig if he wasn't still jacked into the machine.'

'If he's jacked into the machine,' I asked patiently, eyes still on Wardani, 'how come he's living in this shithole town?'

'Maybe he likes it here. This is where he grew up. Anyway, you ever been to Landfall? Now *that's* a shithole.'

Lapinee disappeared from the screen, to be replaced by some kind of documentary footage on archaeology. We carried our plates to one of the sofas where Schneider was about to start eating when he saw that I wasn't.

'Let's wait,' I said softly. 'It's only polite.'

He snorted. 'What do you think; he's going to poison us? What for? There's no angle in it.'

But he left the food alone.

The screen shifted again, war footage this time. Merry little flashes of laser fire across a darkened plain somewhere and the carnival flare of missile impacts. The soundtrack was sanitised, a few explosions muffled by distance and overlaid with dry-voiced commentary giving innocuous-sounding data. Collateral damage, rebel operations neutralised.

Djoko Roespinoedji emerged from the archway opposite, minus his jacket and accompanied by two women who looked as if they'd stepped straight out of the software for a virtual brothel. Their muslin-wrapped forms exhibited the same airbrushed lack of blemishes and gravity-defying curves, and their faces held the same absence of expression. Sandwiched between these two confections, the eight-year-old Roespinoedji looked ludicrous.

'Ivanna and Kas,' he said, gesturing in turn to each woman. 'My constant companions. Every boy needs a mother, wouldn't you say? Or two. Now,' he snapped his fingers, surprisingly loudly, and the two women drifted across to the buffet. He seated himself in an adjacent sofa. 'To business. What exactly can I do for you and your friends, Jan?'

'You're not eating?' I asked him.

'Oh.' He smiled and gestured at his two companions. 'Well, they are, and I'm really very fond of both of them.'

Schneider looked embarrassed.

'No?' Roespinoedji sighed and reached across to take a pastry from my plate at random. He bit into it. 'There, then. Can we get down to business now? Jan? Please?'

'We want to sell you the shuttle, Djoko.' Schneider took a huge bite out of a chicken drumstick and talked through it. 'Knockdown price.'

'Indeed?'

'Yeah – call it military surplus. Wu Morrison ISN-70, very little wear and no previous owner of record.'

Roespinoedji smiled. 'I find that hard to believe.'

'Check it if you like.' Schneider swallowed his mouthful. 'The datacore's wiped cleaner than your tax records. Six hundred thousand klick range. Universal config, hard space, suborbital, submarine. Handles like a whorehouse harpy.'

'Yes, I seem to remember the seventies were impressive. Or was it you that told me that, Jan?' The boy stroked his beardless chin in a gesture that clearly belonged to a previous sleeve. 'Never mind. This knockdown bargain comes armed, I assume.'

Schneider nodded, chewing. 'Micromissile turret, nose-mounted. Plus evasion systems. Full autodefensive software, very nice package.'

I coughed on a pastry.

The two women drifted over to the sofa where Roespinoedji sat and arranged themselves in decorative symmetry on either side of him. Neither of them had said a word or made a sound that I could detect since they walked in. The woman on Roespinoedji's left began to feed him from her plate. He leaned back against her and eyed me speculatively while he chewed what she gave him.

'Alright,' he said finally. 'Six million.'

'UN?' asked Schneider, and Roespinoedji laughed out loud.

'Saft. Six million saft.'

The Standard Archaeological Find Token, created back when the Sanction government was still little more than a global claims administrator, and now an unpopular global currency whose performance against the Latimer franc it had replaced was reminiscent of a swamp panther trying to climb a fricfree-treated dock ramp. There were currently about two hundred and thirty saft to the Protectorate (UN) dollar.

Schneider was aghast, his haggler's soul outraged. 'You cannot be serious, Djoko. Even six million UN's only about half what it's worth. It's a Wu Morrison, man.'

'Does it have cryocaps?'

'Uhhh . . . No.'

'So what the fuck use is it to me, Jan?' Roespinoedji asked without heat. He glanced sideways at the woman on his right, and she passed him a wineglass without a word. 'Look, at this precise moment the only use anyone outside the military has for a space rig is as a means of lifting out of here, beating the blockade and getting back to Latimer. That six-hundred-thousand-kilometre range can be modified by someone who knows what they're doing, and the Wu Morrisons have goodish guidance systems, I know, but at the speed you'll get out of an ISN-70, especially backyard customised, it's still the best part of three decades back to Latimer. You need cryocapsules for that.' He held up a hand to forestall Schneider's protest. 'And I don't know anyone, *anyone*, who can get cryocaps. Not for cunt nor credit. The Landfall Cartel know what they're about, Jan, and they've got it all welded shut. No one gets out of here alive – not until the war's over. That's the deal.'

'You can always sell to the Kempists,' I said. 'They're pretty desperate for the hardware, they'll pay.'

Roespinoedji nodded. 'Yes, Mr Kovacs, they will pay, and they'll pay in saft. Because it's all they've got. Your friends in the Wedge have seen to that.'

'Not my friends. I'm just wearing this.'

'Rather well, though.'

I shrugged.

'What about ten,' said Schneider hopefully. 'Kemp's paying five times that for reconditioned suborbitals.'

Roespinoedji sighed. 'Yes, and in the meantime I have to hide it somewhere, and pay off anyone who sees it. It's not a dune scooter, you know. Then I have to make contact with the Kempists, which as you may be aware carries a mandatory erasure penalty these days. I have to arrange a covert meeting, oh and with armed back-up in case these toy revolutionaries decide to requisition my merchandise instead of paying up. Which they often do if you don't come heavy. Look at the logistics, Jan. I'm doing you a favour, just taking it off your hands. Who else were you going to go to?'

'Eight—'

'Six is fine,' I cut in swiftly. 'And we appreciate the favour. But how about you sweeten our end with a ride into Landfall and a little free information? Just to show we're all friends.'

The boy's gaze sharpened and he glanced towards Tanya Wardani.

'Free information, eh?' He raised his eyebrows, twice in quick succession, clownishly. 'Of course there's really no such thing, you know. But just to show we're all friends. What do you want to know?'

'Landfall.' I said. 'Outside of the Cartel, who are the razorfish? I'm talking about second-rank corporates, maybe even third rank. Who's tomorrow's shiny new dream at the moment?'

Roespinoedji sipped meditatively at his wine. 'Hmm. Razorfish. I don't believe we have any of those on Sanction IV. Or Latimer, come to that.'

'I'm from Harlan's World.'

'Oh, really. Not a Quellist, I assume.' He gestured at the Wedge uniform. 'Given your current political alignment, I mean.'

'You don't want to oversimplify Quellism. Kemp keeps quoting her, but like most people he's selective.'

'Well, I really wouldn't know.' Roespinoedji put up one hand to block the next piece of food his concubine was readying for him.

'But your razorfish. I'd say you've got a half dozen at most. Late arrivals, most of them Latimer-based. The interstellars blocked out most of the local competition until about twenty years ago. And now of course they've got the Cartel and the government in their pocket. There's not much more than scraps for everybody else. Most of the third rank are getting ready to go home; they can't really afford the war.' He stroked at his imagined beard. 'Second rank, well . . . Sathakarn Yu Associates maybe, PKN, the Mandrake Corporation. They're all pretty carnivorous. Might be a couple more I can dig out for you. Are you planning to approach these people with something?'

I nodded. 'Indirectly.'

'Yes, well, some free advice to go with your free information, then. Feed it to them on a long stick.' Roespinoedji raised his glass towards me and then drained it. He smiled affably. 'Because if you don't, they'll take your hand off at the shoulder.'

CHAPTER SEVEN

L ike a lot of cities that owe their existence to a spaceport, Landfall had no real centre. Instead it sprawled haphazardly across a broad semi-desert plain in the southern hemisphere where the original colony barges had touched down a century ago. Each corporation holding stock in the venture had simply built its own landing field somewhere on the plain and surrounded it with a ring of ancillary structures. In time those rings had spread outwards, met each other and eventually merged into a warren of acentric conurbation with only the vaguest of overall planning to link it all together. Secondary investors moved in, renting or buying space from the primaries and carving themselves niches in both the market and the rapidly burgeoning metropolis. Meanwhile, other cities arose elsewhere on the globe, but the Export Quarantine clause in the Charter ensured that all the wealth generated by Sanction IV's archaeological industries had at some point to pass through Landfall. Gorged on an unrestricted diet of artefact export, land allocation and dig licensing, the former spaceport had swelled to monstrous proportions. It now covered two-thirds of the plain and, with twelve million inhabitants, was home to almost thirty per cent of what was left of Sanction IV's total population.

It was a pit.

I walked with Schneider through badly-kept streets full of urban detritus and reddish desert sand. The air was hot and dry and the shade cast by the blocks on either side provided little respite from the high-angled rays of the sun. I could feel sweat beading on my face and soaking the hair at the back of my neck. In windows and mirror-shielded frontages along the way, our black-uniformed reflections kept pace. I was almost glad of the company. There was no one else out in the midday heat and the shimmering stillness of it was uncanny. The sand crunched audibly underfoot.

The place we were looking for wasn't hard to find. It stuck up at the edge of the district like a burnished bronze conning tower, double the height of the surrounding blocks and utterly featureless from the outside. Like much of the architecture in Landfall, it was mirror-surfaced and the reflected sun made its edges difficult to look at directly. It wasn't the tallest tower in Landfall, but the structure had a raw power to it that throbbed across the surrounding urban sprawl and spoke volumes about its designers.

Testing the human frame to destruction

The phrase flopped out of my memory like a corpse from a closet.

'How close you want to get?' asked Schneider nervously.

'A bit closer.'

The Khumalo sleeve, like all Carrera's Wedge custom, had a satdata locational display wired in as standard and reckoned to be quite user-friendly when not fucked up by the webs of jamming and counter-jamming that currently swathed most of Sanction IV. Blinked up to focus now, it gave me a mesh of streets and city blocks covering my whole left field of vision. Two tagged dots pulsed minutely on a thoroughfare.

Testing the—

I overcued the tightlock fractionally and the view dizzied up until I was looking at the top of my own head from block-top height.

'Shit.'

'What?' Beside me, Schneider had tensed up in what he obviously imagined was a stance of ninja combat readiness. Behind his sunlenses, he looked comically worried.

Testing—

'Forget it.' I scaled back up until the tower re-emerged on the edge of the display. A shortest-possible route lit up obligingly in yellow, threading us to the building through a pair of intersections. 'This way.'

Testing the human frame to destruction is only one of the cutting-edge lines

A couple of minutes down the yellow line, one of the streets gave onto a narrow suspension bridge over a dry canal. The bridge sloped upward slightly along its twenty-metre length to meet a raised concrete flange on the far side. Two other bridges paralleled the crossing a hundred metres down on either side, also sloping upward. The floor of the canal bore a scattering of the debris any urban area will breed – discarded domestic devices spilling circuitry from cracked casings, emptied food packages and sun-bleached knots of cloth that reminded me of machine-gunned bodies. Over it all and on the other side of this dumping ground, the tower waited.

Testing the human

Schneider hovered on the threshold of the bridge.

'You going across?'

'Yeah, and so are you. We're partners, remember.' I shoved him lightly in the small of the back and followed up so close he'd have to go on. There was a slightly hysterical good humour brewing in me as the Envoy conditioning strove to fend off the unsubtle doses of combat prep hormones my sleeve sensed were required.

'I just don't think this is—'

'If anything goes wrong, you can blame me.' I nudged him again. 'Now come on.'

'If anything goes wrong, we'll be dead,' he muttered morosely.

'Yeah, at least.'

We crossed, Schneider holding onto the rails as if the bridge were swaying in a high wind.

The flange on the other side turned out to be the edge of a featureless fifty-metre access plaza. We stood two metres in, looking up at the impassive face of the tower. Whether intentionally or not, whoever had built the concrete apron around the building's base had created a perfect killing field. There was no cover in any direction and the only retreat was back along the slim, exposed bridge or a bone-shattering jump into the empty canal.

'*Open ground*, all around,' sang Schneider under his breath, picking up on the cadence and lyrics of the Kempist revolutionary hymn of the same name. I couldn't blame him. I'd caught myself humming the fucking thing a couple of times since we got into the unjammed airspace around the city – the Lapinee version was everywhere, close enough to the Kempist original to activate recall from last year. Back then, you could hear the original playing on the Rebels' propaganda channels whenever and wherever the government jamming went down. Telling the – apparently edifying – story of a doomed platoon of volunteers holding a position against overwhelming odds for love of Joshua Kemp and his revolution, the anthem was sung against a catchy junk salsa backdrop that tended to stick in your head. Most of my men in the Northern Rim assault force could sing it by heart, and often did, to the fury of Cartel political officers, who were mostly too scared of the Wedge uniforms to make something of it.

In fact, the melody had proven so virulently memetic that even the most solidly pro-corporate citizens were unable to resist absent-mindedly humming it. This, plus a network of Cartel informers working on a commission-only basis, was enough to ensure that penal facilities all over Sanction IV were soon overflowing with musically-inclined political offenders. In view of the strain this put on policing, an expensive consulting team was called in and rapidly came up with a new set of sanitised lyrics to fit the original melody. Lapinee, a construct vocalist, was designed and launched to front the replacement song, which told the story of a young boy, orphaned in a Kempist sneak raid but then adopted by a kindly corporate bloc and brought up to realise his full potential as a top-level planetary executive.

As a ballad, it lacked the romantic blood and glory elements of the original, but since certain of the Kempist lyrics had been mirrored with malice aforethought, people generally lost track of which song was which and just sang a mangled hybrid of both, sewn together with much salsa-based humming. Any revolutionary senti-ments got thoroughly scrambled in the process. The consulting team got a bonus, plus spin-off royalties from Lapinee, who was currently being plugged on all state channels. An album was in the offing.

Schneider stopped his humming. 'Think they've got it covered?'

'Reckon so.' I nodded towards the base of the tower, where burnished doors fully five metres high apparently gave access. The massive portal was flanked by two plinths on which stood examples of abstract art each worthy of the title *Eggs Collide in Symmetry* or – I racked up the neurachem to be sure – *Overkill Hardware Semi-deployed.*

Schneider followed my gaze. 'Sentries?'

I nodded. 'Two slug autocannon nests and at least four separate beam weapons that I can see from here. Very tastefully done, too. You'd barely notice them in amongst all that sculpture.'

In a way, it was a good sign.

In the two weeks we'd spent in Landfall so far, I hadn't seen much sign of the war beyond a slightly higher uniform count on the streets in the evenings and the occasional cyst of a rapid response turret on some of the taller buildings. Most of the time, you could have been forgiven for thinking it was all happening on another planet. But if Joshua Kemp did finally manage to fight his way through to the capital, the Mandrake Corporation at least looked to be ready for him.

Testing the human frame to destruction is only one of the cutting-edge lines central to the Mandrake Corporation's current research programme. Maximum utility for ALL resources is our ultimate goal.

Mandrake had only acquired the site a decade ago. That they had built with armed insurrection in mind showed strategic thinking way in advance of any of the other corporate players at this particular table. Their corporate logo was a chopped strand of DNA afloat on a background of circuitry, their publicity material was just the right side of shrill in its aggressive, more-for-your-investment-dollar new-kid-on-the-block pitch, and their fortunes had risen sharply with the war.

Good enough.

'Think they're looking at us now?'

I shrugged. 'Always someone looking at you. Fact of life. Question is whether they noticed us.'

Schneider pulled an exasperated face. 'Think they *noticed* us, then?'

'I doubt it. The automated systems won't be tuned for it. War's too far off for emergency default settings. These are friendly uniforms, and curfew isn't till ten. We're nothing out of the ordinary.'

'Yet.'

'Yet,' I agreed, turning away. 'So let's go and get noticed.'

We headed back across the bridge.

'You don't look like artists,' said the promoter as he punched in the last of our encoding sequence. Out of uniform and into nondescript civilian clothing bought that morning, we'd been calibrated the moment we walked in the door and, by the look of it, found lacking.

'We're security,' I told him pleasantly. 'She's the artist.'

His gaze flipped across the table to where Tanya Wardani sat behind winged black sunlenses and a clamp-mouthed grimace. She had started to fill out a little in the last couple of weeks, but beneath the long black coat, it didn't show, and her face was still mostly bone. The promoter grunted, apparently satisfied with what he saw.

'Well.' He maximised a traffic display and studied it for a moment. 'I have to tell you, whatever it is you're selling, you're up against a lot of state-sponsored competition.'

'What, like Lapinee?'

The derision in Schneider's voice would have been apparent across interstellar distances. The promoter smoothed back his imitation military goatee, sat back in his chair and stuck one fake combat-booted foot on the desk edge. At the base of his shaven skull, three or four battlefield quickplant software tags stuck out from their sockets, too shiny to be anything but designer copies.

'Don't laugh at the majors, friend,' he said easily. 'I had even a two per cent share in the Lapinee deal, I'd be living in Latimer City by now. I'm telling you, the best way to defuse wartime art is buy it up. Corporates know that. They've got the machinery to sell it at volume and the clout to censor the competition out of existence. Now,' he tapped the display where our upload sat like a tiny purple torpedo waiting to be fired. 'Whatever it is you've got there, better be pretty fucking hot if you expect it to swim against that current.'

'Are you this positive with all your clients?' I asked him.

He smiled bleakly. 'I'm a realist. You pay me, I'll shunt it. Got the best anti-screening intrusion software in Landfall to get it there in one piece. Just like the sign says. We Get You Noticed. But don't expect me to massage your ego too, because that isn't part of the service. Where you want this squirted, there's too much going on to be optimistic about your chances.'

At our backs, a pair of windows were open onto the noise of the street three floors below. The air outside had cooled with the onset of evening, but the atmosphere in the promoter's office still tasted stale. Tanya Wardani shifted impatiently.

'It's a niche thing,' she rasped. 'Can we get on with this.'

'Sure.' The promoter glanced once more at the credit screen and the payment that floated there in hard green digits. 'Better fasten your launch belts. This is going to cost you at speed.'

He hit the switch. There was a brief ripple across the display and the purple torpedo vanished. I caught a glimpse of it represented on a series of helix-based transmission visuals, and then it faded, swallowed behind the wall of corporate data security systems and presumably beyond the tracking capacity of the promoter's much-vaunted software. The green digit counters whirled into frantic, blurred eights.

'Told you,' said the promoter, shaking his head judiciously. 'High-line screening systems like that, would have cost them a year's profits just for the installation. And cutting the high line costs, my friends.'

'Evidently.' I watched our credit decay like an unprotected antimatter core and quelled a sudden desire to remove the promoter's throat with my bare hands. It wasn't really the money; we had plenty of that. Six million saft might have been a poor price for a Wu Morrison shuttle, but it was going to be enough for us to live like kings for the duration of our stay in Landfall.

It wasn't the money.

It was the designer fashion war gear and the drawled theories on what to do with wartime art, the fake seen-it/been-it worldweariness, while on the other side of the equator men and women blew each other apart in the name of minor adjustments to the system that kept Landfall fed.

'That's it.' The promoter played a brisk drumroll across his console with both hands. 'Gone home, near as I can tell. Time for you boys and girls to do the same.'

'Near as you can tell,' said Schneider. 'What the fuck is that?'

He got the bleak smile again. 'Hey. Read your contract. To the best of our ability, we deliver. And that's to the best of anyone else's ability on Sanction IV. You bought state of the art, you didn't buy any guarantees.'

He ejected our eviscerated credit chip from the machine and tossed it onto the table in front of Tanya Wardani, who pocketed it, deadpan.

'So how long do we wait?' she asked through a yawn.

'What am I, clairvoyant?' The promoter sighed. 'Could be quick, like a couple of days, could be a month or more. All depends on the demo, and I didn't see that. I'm just the mailman. Could be never. Go home, I'll mail you.'

We left, seen out with the same studied disinterest with which we'd been received and processed. Outside, we went left in the evening gloom, crossed the street and found a terrace café about twenty metres up from the promoter's garish third-floor display holo. This close to curfew, it was almost deserted. We dumped our bags under a table and ordered short coffees.

'How long?' Wardani asked again.

'Thirty minutes.' I shrugged. 'Depends on their AI. Forty-five, the outside.'

I still hadn't finished my coffee when they came.

The cruiser was an unobtrusive brown utility vehicle, ostensibly bulky and underpowered but to a tutored eye very obviously armoured. It slunk round a corner a hundred metres up the street at ground level and crawled down towards the promoter's building.

'Here we go,' I murmured, wisps of Khumalo neurachem flickering into life up and down my body. 'Stay here, both of you.'

I stood up unhurriedly and drifted across the street, hands in pockets, head cocked at a rubbernecker's angle. Ahead of me the cruiser floated to a curb hugging halt outside the promoter's door and a side hatch hinged up. I watched as five coverall-clad figures climbed out and then vanished into the building with a telltale economy of motion. The hatch folded back down.

I picked up speed fractionally as I made my way among the hurrying last-minute shoppers on the pavement, and my left hand closed around the thing in my pocket.

The cruiser's windscreen was solid-looking and almost opaque. Behind it, my neurachem-aided vision could just distinguish two figures in the seats and the hint of another body bulking behind them, braced upright to peer out. I glanced sideways at a shop frontage, closing the last of the gap up to the front of the cruiser.

And time.

Less than half a metre, and my left hand came out of its pocket. I slammed the flat disc of the termite grenade hard against the windscreen and stepped immediately aside and past.

Crack!

With termite grenades you've got to get out of the way quickly. The new ones are designed to deliver all their shrapnel and better than ninety-five per cent of their force to the contact face, but the five per cent that comes out on the opposite side will still make a mess of you if you stand in the way.

The cruiser shuddered from end to end. Contained within the armoured body, the sound of the explosion was reduced to a muffled crump. I ducked in through the door to the promoter's building and went up the stairs at a run.

(At the first floor landing I reached for the interface guns, the bioalloy plates sewn beneath the palms of my hands already flexing, yearning.)

They'd posted a single sentry on the third-floor landing, but they weren't expecting trouble from behind. I shot him through the back of the head as I came up the last flight of stairs – *splash of blood and paler tissue in clots across the wall in front of him* – made the landing before he'd hit the ground and then erupted around the corner of the promoter's office door.

The echo of the first shot, like the first sip of whisky, burning . . .

Splinters of vision . . .

The promoter tries to rise from his seat where two of them have him pinned and tilted back. One arm thrashes free and points in my direction.

'That's hi—'

The goon nearest the door, turning . . .

Cut him down. Three-shot burst, left-handed.

Blood splatters the air – I twist, neurachem hyperswift, to avoid it.

The squad leader – recognisable, somehow. Taller, more presence, something, yelling, 'What the fu—'

Body shots. Chest and weapon arm, get that firing hand *wrecked*.

The right-hand Kalashnikov spurts flame and softcore anti-personnel slugs.

Two left, trying to shrug themselves free of the half-pinioned, flailing promoter, to clear weapons that . . .

Both hands now – head, body, anywhere.

The Kalashnikovs bark like excited dogs.

Bodies jerking, tumbling . . .

And done.

Silence slammed down in the tiny office. The promoter cowered under the body of one of his slain captors. Somewhere, something sparked and shorted out in the console – damage from one of my slugs that had gone wide or through. I could hear voices out on the landing.

I knelt beside the wreckage of the lead goon's corpse and set down the smart guns. Beneath my jacket, I tugged the vibroknife from its sheath in the small of my back and activated the motor. With my free hand I pressed down hard on the dead man's spine and started cutting.

'Ah, *fuck*, man.' The promoter gagged and threw up across his console. 'Fuck, *fuck*.'

I looked up at him.

'Shut up, this isn't easy.'

He ducked down again.

After a couple of false starts, the vibroknife took and sliced down through the spinal column a few vertebrae below the point where it met the base of the skull. I steadied the skull against the floor with one knee, then pressed down again and started a new incision. The knife slipped and slithered again on the curve of the bone.

'Shit.'

The voices out on the landing were growing in number and, it seemed, creeping closer. I stopped what I was doing, picked up one of the Kalashnikovs left-handed and fired a brace of shots out of the doorway into the wall opposite. The voices departed in a stampede of feet on stairs.

Back to the knife. I managed to get the point lodged, cut through the bone, and then used the blade to lever the severed section of spine up out of the surrounding flesh and muscle. Messy, but there wasn't a lot of time. I stuffed the severed bone into a pocket, wiped my hands on a clean portion of the dead man's tunic and sheathed the knife. Then I picked up the smart guns and went cautiously to the door.

Quiet.

As I was leaving, I glanced back at the promoter. He was staring at me as if I'd just sprouted a reef demon's fangs.

'Go home,' I told him. 'They'll be back. Near as I can tell.'

I made it down the three flights of stairs without meeting anyone, though I could feel eyes peering from other doors on the landings I passed. Outside, I scanned the street in both directions, stowed the Kalashnikovs and slipped away, past the hot, smouldering carapace of the bombed-out cruiser. The pavement was empty for fifty metres in both directions and the frontages on either side of the wreck had all cranked down their security blinds. A crowd was gathering on the other side of the street, but no one seemed to know what exactly to do. The few passers-by who noticed me looked hurriedly away as I passed.

Immaculate.

CHAPTER EIGHT

Nobody said much on the way to the hotel.

We did most of it on foot, doubling back through covered ways and malls to blind any satellite eyes the Mandrake Corporation might have access to. Breathless work, weighed down with the carryall bags. Twenty minutes of this found us under the broad eaves of a refrigerated storage facility, where I waved a transport pager at the sky and eventually succeeded in flagging down a cab. We climbed in without leaving the cover of the eaves and sank back into the seats without a word.

'It is my duty to inform you,' the machine told us prissily, 'that in seventeen minutes you will be in breach of curfew.'

'Better get us home quick then,' I said and gave it the address.

'Estimated trajectory time nine minutes. Please insert payment.'

I nodded at Schneider, who produced an unused credit chip and fed it to the slot. The cab chittered and we lifted smoothly into a night sky almost devoid of traffic before sliding off westward. I rolled my head sideways on the back of the seat and watched the lights of the city pass beneath us for a while, mentally backtracking to see how well we'd covered ourselves.

When I rolled my head back again, I caught Tanya Wardani staring straight at me. She didn't look away.

I went back to watching the lights until we started to fall back towards them.

The hotel was well chosen, the cheapest of a row built under a commercial freight overpass and used almost exclusively by prostitutes and wireheads. The desk clerk was sleeved in a cheap Syntheta body whose silicoflesh was showing signs of wear around the knuckles and had a very obvious re-upholstering graft halfway up the right arm. The desk was heavily stained in a number of places and nubbed every ten centimetres along its outer edge with shield generators. In the corners of the dimly-lit lobby, empty-faced women and boys flickered about wanly, like flames almost out.

The desk clerk's logo-scribbled eyes passed over us like a damp cloth.

'Ten saft an hour, fifty deposit up front. Shower and screen access is another fifty.'

'We want it for the night,' Schneider told him. 'Curfew just came down, case you hadn't noticed.'

The clerk stayed expressionless, but then maybe that was the sleeve. Syntheta have been known to skimp on the smaller facial nerve/muscle interfaces.

'Then that'll be eighty saft, plus fifty deposit. Shower and screen fifty extra.'

'No discount for long-stay guests?'

His eyes switched to me, and one hand disappeared below the counter. I felt the neurachem surge, still jumpy after the firefight.

'You want the room or not?'

'We want it,' said Schneider with a warning glance at me. 'You got a chip reader?'

'That's ten per cent extra.' He seemed to search his memory for something. 'Handling surcharge.'

'Fine.'

The clerk propped himself to his feet, disappointed, and went to fetch the reader from a room in back.

'Cash,' murmured Wardani. 'We should have thought of that.'

Schneider shrugged. 'Can't think of everything. When was the last time you paid for something without a chip?'

She shook her head. I thought back briefly to a time three decades gone and a place light years distant where for a while I'd used tactile currency instead of credit. I'd even got used to the quaint plastified notes with their ornate designs and holographic panels. But that was on Earth, and Earth is a place straight out of a pre-colonial period experia flick. For a while there I'd even thought I was in love and, motivated by love and hate in about equal proportions, I'd done some stupid things. A part of me had died on Earth.

Another planet, another sleeve.

I shook an unfairly well-remembered face from my mind and looked around, seeking to embed myself back in the present. Garishly painted faces looked back from the shadows, then away.

Thoughts for a brothel lobby. Ye Gods.

The desk clerk came back, read one of Schneider's chips and banged a scarred plastic key card on the counter.

'Through the back and down the stairs. Fourth level. I've activated the shower and screen till curfew break. You want any of it longer, you'll need to come up and pay again.' The silicoflesh face flexed in what was probably supposed to be a grin. He shouldn't have bothered. 'Rooms are all soundproofed. Do what you like.'

The corridor and steel frame stairwell were, if anything, worse lit than the lobby. In places the illuminum tiles were peeling off the walls and ceiling. Elsewhere they had just gone out. The stair rail was painted luminous but that too was fading, coming off microns at a time with every hand that gripped and slid along the metal.

We passed a scattering of whores on the stairs, most with customers in tow. Little bubbles of fake hilarity floated around them, tinkling. Business seemed to be brisk. I spotted a couple of uniforms among the clientele, and what looked like a Cartel political officer leant on the second level landing rail, smoking pensively. No one gave us a second glance.

The room was long and low-ceilinged with a quickmould resin cornice-and-pillar effect epoxied onto the raw concrete walls, the whole then painted in violent primary red. About halfway down, two bedshelves jutted out from opposing walls with a half metre of space between their adjacent sides. The second bed had plastic chains moulded into the four corners of the shelf. At the far end of the room stood a self-contained shower stall wide enough to take three bodies at a time, should the occasion so require. Opposite each bed was a wide screen with a menu display glowing on a pale pink background.

I looked around, puffed a single breath out into blood-warm air and then stooped to the carryall at my feet.

'Make sure that door's secured.'

I pulled the sweeper unit out of the bag and waved it around the room. Three bugs showed up in the ceiling, one above each bed and one in the shower. Very imaginative. Schneider snapped a Wedge standard limpet neutraliser onto the ceiling next to each one. They'd get into the bugs' memories, pull out whatever had been stored there over the last couple of hours and then recycle it endlessly. The better models will even scan the content and then generate plausible improvised scenes from stock, but I didn't think that was going to be necessary here. The desk clerk had not given the impression that he was fronting a high-security operation.

'Where do you want this stuff?' Schneider asked Wardani, unpacking one of the other carryalls onto the first bed shelf.

'Right there is fine,' she said. 'Here, I'll do it. It's, uhm, complicated.'

Schneider raised an eyebrow. 'Right. Fine. I'll just watch.'

Complicated or not, it only took the archaeologue about ten minutes to assemble her equipment. When she was done, she took a pair of modified EV goggles from the flaccid skin of the empty carryall and settled them over her head. She turned to me.

'You want to give me that?'

I reached into my jacket and produced the segment of spine. There were still fresh streaks of gore clinging to the tiny bumps and crannies of the bone, but she took it without apparent revulsion and dumped it into the top of the artefact scrubber she'd just finished snapping together. A pale violet light sprang up under the glass hood. Schneider and I watched fascinated as she jacked the goggles into one side of the machine, picked up the connected handset and settled cross-legged to work. From within the machine came tiny crackling sounds.

'Working alright?' I asked.

She grunted.

'How long is this going to take?'

'Longer, if you keep asking me stupid questions,' she said without looking away from what she was doing. 'Don't you have anything else to do?'

Out of the corner of my eye, I caught Schneider grinning.

By the time we'd put together the other machine, Wardani was almost done. I peered over her shoulder into the purple glow and saw what remained of the spinal segment. Most of it was gone, and the final pieces of vertebrae were being eaten away from the tiny metal cylinder of the cortical stack. I watched, fascinated. It wasn't the first time I'd seen a cortical stack removed from a dead spine, but it had to be amongst the most elegant versions of the operation I'd ever witnessed. The bone retreated, vanishing one minute increment at a time as Tanya Wardani cut it away with her tools, and the stack casing emerged scrubbed clean of surrounding tissue and shiny as new tin.

'I do know what I'm doing, Kovacs,' Wardani said, voice slow and absent with concentration. 'Compared to scrubbing the accretion off Martian circuitboards, this is like sandblasting.'

'I don't doubt it. I was just admiring your handiwork.'

She did look up then, sharply, pushing the goggles up on her forehead to see if I was laughing at her. When she saw I wasn't, she lowered the goggles again, made a couple of adjustments to something on the handset then sat back. The violet light went out.

'It's done.' She reached into the machine and removed the stack, holding it between thumb and forefinger. 'Incidentally, this isn't great equipment. In fact it's the sort of thing Scratchers buy for their thesis work. The sensors are pretty crude. I'm going to need a lot better than this up on the Rim.'

'Don't worry.' I took the cortical stack from her and turned to the machine on the other bed. 'If this works out, they'll build your gear to custom order. Now, listen carefully, both of you. There may well be a virtual environment tracer built into this stack. A lot of corporate samurai are wired that way. This one may not be, but we're going to assume he is. That means we've got about a minute of safe access before the trace powers up and kicks in. So when that counter hits fifty seconds, you shut everything down. This is just a casualty ID&A, but cranked up we'll still get a ratio of about thirty-five to one, real time. Little over half an hour, but that ought to be enough.'

'What are you going to do to him?' This was Wardani, looking unhappy.

I reached for the skullcap. 'Nothing. There isn't time. I'm just going to talk to him.'

'Talk?' There was a strange light in her eyes.

'Sometimes,' I told her. 'That's all it takes.'

It was a rough ride in.

Casualty Identification and Assessment is a relatively new tool in military accounting. We didn't have it at Innenin; the prototype systems didn't appear until after I'd bailed out of the Corps, and even then it was decades before anyone outside Protectorate elite forces could afford it. The cheaper models came out about fifteen years ago, much to the delight of military auditors everywhere, though of course they weren't ever the ones who had to ride the system. ID&A is a job usually done by battlefield medics trying to pull the dead and wounded out, often under fire. Under those circumstances, smooth-format transition tends to be seen as a bit of a luxury, and the set we'd liberated from the hospital shuttle was definitely a no-frills model.

I closed my eyes in the concrete-walled room and the induction kicked me in the back of the head like a tetrameth rush. For a couple of seconds I sank dizzyingly through an ocean of static, and then that snapped out, replaced by a boundless field of wheat that stood unnaturally still under a late afternoon sun. Something hit me hard in the soles of the feet, jolting upward, and I was standing on a long wooden porch looking out over the field. Behind me was the house the porch belonged to, a single-storey wood-frame place, apparently old but too perfectly finished for anything that had genuinely aged. The boards all met with geometric precision and there were no flaws or cracks anywhere that I could see. It looked like something an AI with no humanity interface protocols would dream up from image stock, and that's probably exactly what it was.

Thirty minutes, I reminded myself.

Time to Identify and Assess.

It's in the nature of modern warfare that there often isn't very much left of dead soldiers, and that can make life difficult for the auditors. Certain soldiers will always be worth re-sleeving; experienced officers are a valuable resource and a grunt at any level may have vital specialist skills or knowledge. The problem lies in identifying these soldiers rapidly and separating them out from the grunts who aren't worth the cost of a new sleeve. How, in the screaming chaos of a war zone, are you going to do this? Barcoding burns off with the skin, dog tags melt or get inconveniently shredded by shrapnel. DNA scanning is sometimes an option, but it's chemically complicated, hard to administer on a battlefield and some of the nastier chemical weapons will fuck up the results completely.

Worse still, none of this will tell you if the slain soldier is still a psychologically viable unit for re-sleeving. How you die – fast, slow, alone, with friends, in agony or numb – is bound to affect the level of trauma you suffer. The level of trauma affects your combat viability. So too does your re-sleeving history. Too many new sleeves too fast leads to Repeat Re-sleeve Syndrome, which I'd seen the year before in a once-too-often retrieved Wedge demolitions sergeant. They'd downloaded him, for the ninth time since the war began, into a clone-fresh twenty-year-old sleeve, and he sat in it like an infant in its own shit, screaming and weeping incoherently in between bouts of introspection in which he examined his own fingers as if they were toys he didn't want any more.

Oops.

The point is there's no way to learn these facts with any degree of certainty from the broken and charred remnants the medics are often faced with. Fortunately for the accountants, though, cortical stack technology makes it possible not only to identify and tag individual casualties, but also to find out if they have gone irretrievably screaming insane. Snugged inside the spinal column, just below the skull, the mind's black box is about as safe as it's possible to make it. The surrounding bone in itself is remarkably resistant to damage, and just in case good old evolutionary engineering isn't up to the job, the materials used to make cortical stacks are among the hardest artificial substances known to man. You can sandblast a stack clean without worrying about damaging it, jack it into a virtual environment generator by hand and then just dive in after your subject. The equipment to do all this will fit into a large carryall.

I went to the perfect wooden door. Chiselled into a copper plate on the boards beside it was an eight-digit serial number and a name: *Deng Zhao Jun*. I turned the handle. The door swung inward noiselessly and I walked through into a clinically tidy space dominated by a long wooden table. A pair of mustard-cushioned armchairs stood off to one side, facing a grate in which a small fire crackled. At the back of the room, doors appeared to lead off to a kitchen and a bedroom.

He was seated at the table, head in his hands. Apparently he hadn't heard the door open. The set would have brought him online a few seconds before it let me in, so he'd probably had a couple of minutes to get over the initial shock of arrival and realise where he was. Now he just had to deal with it.

I coughed gently.

'Good evening, Deng.'

He looked up and dropped his hands back to the table when he saw me. The words came out of him in a rush.

'We were set up man, it was a fucking set-up. Someone was waiting for us, you can tell Hand his security's fucked. They must—'

His voice dried up and his eyes widened as he recognised me.

'Yes.'

He jerked to his feet. *'Who the fuck are you?'*

'That's not really important. Look—'

But it was too late, he was up and coming for me round the table, eyes slitted with fury. I stepped back.

'Look, there's no point—'

He closed the gap and lashed out, knee-height kick and mid-level punch. I blocked the kick, locked up the punching arm and dumped him on the floor. He tried another kick as he landed and I had to dodge back out of reach to avoid getting hit in the face. Then he slithered to his feet, and came at me again.

This time I stepped in to meet him, deflecting his attacks with wing blocks and butterfly kicks and using knee and elbows to take him down. He grunted gut-deep with the blows and hit the floor for the second time, one arm folded beneath his body. I went down after him, landed on his back and dragged the available wrist up, locking out the arm until it creaked.

'Right, that's enough. You are in a fucking *virtuality*.' I got my breath back and lowered my voice. 'Plus, any more shit out of you and I'll break this arm. Got it?'

He nodded as best he could with his face pressed into the floorboards.

'Alright.' I lessened the pressure on the arm a fraction. 'Now I'm going to let you up and we're going to do this in a civilised fashion. I want to ask you some questions, Deng. You don't have to answer them if you don't want to, but it'll be in your best interests, so just hear me out.'

I got up and stepped away from him. After a moment he climbed to his feet and limped back to his chair, massaging his arm. I sat down at the other end of the table.

'You wired for virtual trace?'

He shook his head.

'Yeah, well, you'd probably say that even if you were. It isn't going to help. We're running a mirror-code scrambler. Now, I want to know who your controller is.'

He stared at me. 'Why should I tell you a fucking thing?'

'Because if you do, I'll turn your cortical stack back over to Mandrake and they'll probably re-sleeve you.' I leaned forward in the chair. 'That's a one-time special offer, Deng. Grab it while it lasts.'

'If you kill me, Mandrake'll—'

'No.' I shook my head. 'Get a sense of reality about this. You're what, a security operations manager? Tactical deployment exec? Mandrake can get a dozen like you from stock. There are platoon noncoms on the government reserve who'd give blowjobs for the chance to duck out of the fighting. Any one of them could do your job. And besides, the men and women you work for would sell their own children into a brothel if it meant getting their hands on what I showed them tonight. And alongside that, my friend, you. Don't. Matter.'

Silence. He sat looking at me, hating.

I deployed one from the manual.

'They might like to do a retribution number on general principles, of course. Make it known that their operatives are not to be touched without dire consequences. Most hardline outfits like to whistle that tune, and I don't suppose Mandrake is any different.' I gestured with one open hand. 'But we're not operating in a context of general principles here, are we, Deng? I mean, you know that. Have you ever worked a response that rapid before? Ever had a set of instructions so total? How did it read? Find the originators of this signal and bring them back stack intact, all other costs and considerations subordinate? Something like that?'

I let the question hang out in the air between us, a rope casually thrown out but aching to be grabbed.

Go on. Grab. Only takes a monosyllable.

But the silence held. The invitation to agree, to speak, to let go and answer, creaking under its own weight where I'd built it out into the air between us. He compressed his lips.

Try it again.

'Something like that, Deng?'

'You'd better go ahead and kill me,' he said tautly.

I let the smile come out slow –

'I'm not going to kill you, Deng.'

– and waited.

As if we had the mirror-code scrambler. As if we couldn't be tracked. As if we *had* the time. *Believe* it.

All the time in the universe.

'You're—?' he said, finally.

'I'm not going to kill you, Deng. That's what I said. I'm. Not. Going to kill you.' I shrugged. 'Far too easy. Be just like switching you off. You don't get to be a corporate hero that easy.'

I saw the puzzlement sliding into tension.

'Oh, and don't get any ideas about torture either. I don't have the stomach for that. I mean, who knows what kind of resistance software they've downloaded into you. Too messy, too inconclusive, too long. And I can get my answers somewhere else if I have to. Like I said, this is a one-time special offer. Answer the questions now, while you've still got the chance.'

'Or *what?*' *Almost* solid bravado, but the new uncertainty made it slippery at base. Twice he'd prepped himself for what he thought

84

was coming, and twice he'd had his assumptions cut out from under him. The fear in him was fume thin, but rising.

I shrugged.

'Or I'll leave you here.'

'*What?*'

'I'll leave you here. I mean, we're out in the middle of the Chariset Waste, Deng. Some abandoned dig town, I don't think it even has a name. An even thousand kilometres of desert in every direction. I'm just going to leave you plugged in.'

He blinked, trying to assimilate the angle. I leaned in again.

'You're in a Casualty ID&A system. Runs off a battlefield powerpack. It's probably good for decades on these settings. Hundreds of years, virtual time. Which is going to seem pretty fucking real to you, sitting in here watching the wheat grow. *If* it grows in a format this basic. You won't get hungry here, you won't get thirsty, but I'm willing to bet you'll go insane before the first century's out.'

I sat back again. Let it sink into him.

'Or you can answer my questions. One-time offer. What's it going to be?'

The silence built, but it was a different kind this time. I let him stare me out for a minute, then shrugged and got to my feet.

'You had your chance.'

I got almost to the door before he cracked.

'Alright!' There was a sound like piano wire snapping in his voice. 'Alright, you got it. You got it.'

I paused, then reached for the door handle. His voice scaled up.

'I said you *got it*, man. Hand, man. *Hand*. Matthias Hand. He's the man, he sent us, fucking stop man. I'll tell you.'

Hand. The name he'd blurted earlier. Safe to bet he'd cracked for real. I turned slowly back from the door.

'Hand?'

He nodded jerkily.

'Matthias Hand?'

He looked up, something broken in his face. 'I got your word?'

'For what it's worth, yeah. Your stack goes back to Mandrake intact. Now. Hand.'

'Matthias Hand. Acquisitions Division.'

'He's your controller?' I frowned. 'A divisional exec?'

'He's not really my controller. All the tactical squads report to the Chief of Secure Operations, but since the war they've had seventy-five tac operatives seconded directly to Hand at Acquisitions.'

'Why?'

'How the fuck would I know?'

'Speculate a little. Was it Hand's initiative? Or general policy?'

He hesitated. 'They say it was Hand.'

'How long's he been with Mandrake?'

'I don't know.' He saw the expression on my face. 'I don't fucking know. Longer than me.'

'What's his rep?'

'Tough. You don't cross him.'

'Yeah, him and every other corporate exec above departmental head. They're all such tough motherfuckers. Tell me something I can't already guess.'

'It isn't just talk. Two years ago some project manager in R&D had Hand up in front of the policy board for breach of company ethics—'

'Company *what?*'

'Yeah, you can laugh. At Mandrake that's an erasure penalty if it sticks.'

'But it didn't.'

Deng shook his head. 'Hand squared it with the board, no one knows how. And two weeks later this guy turns up dead in the back of a taxi, looking like something exploded inside him. They say Hand used to be a hougan in the Carrefour Brotherhood on Latimer. All that voodoo shit.'

'All that voodoo shit,' I repeated, not quite as unimpressed as I was playing it. Religion is religion, however you wrap it, and like Quell says, a preoccupation with the next world pretty clearly signals an inability to cope credibly with this one. Still, the Carrefour Brotherhood were as nasty a bunch of extortionists as I'd ever run across in a tour of human misery that took in, among other highlights, the Harlan's World yakuza, the Sharyan religious police and, of course, the Envoy Corps itself. If Matthias Hand were ex-

Carrefour, he'd be stained a deeper darker shade than the average corporate enforcer. 'So apart from *all that voodoo shit*, what else do they say about him?'

Deng shrugged. 'That he's smart. Acquisitions muscled in on a lot of government contracts just before the war. Stuff the majors weren't even looking at. The word is Hand's telling the policy board it'll have a seat on the Cartel by this time next year. And no one I know's laughing at that.'

'Yeah. Too much danger of a career change, decorating the inside of taxis with your guts. I think we'll—'

Falling.

Leaving the ID&A format turned out to be about as much fun as coming in. It felt as if a trapdoor had opened in the floor under my chair and dropped me down a hole drilled right through the planet. The sea of static slithered in from all sides, eating up the darkness with a hungry crackling and bursting against my combined senses like an instant empathin hangover. Then it was gone, leached out and sucking away just as unpleasantly, and I was reality-aware again, head down and a tiny string of saliva drooling from one corner of my mouth.

'You OK, Kovacs?'

Schneider.

I blinked. The air around me seemed unreasonably twilit after the static rush, as if I'd been staring into the sun for too long.

'Kovacs?' This time it was Tanya Wardani's voice. I wiped my mouth and looked around. Beside me the ID&A set was humming quietly, the glowing green counter numerals frozen at 49. Wardani and Schneider stood on either side of the set, peering at me with almost comical concern. Behind them, the resin-moulded tawdriness of the whoring chamber lent the whole thing an air of badly staged farce. I could feel myself starting to smirk as I reached up and removed the skullcap.

'Well?' Wardani drew back a little. 'Don't just sit there grinning. What did you get?'

'Enough,' I said. 'I think we're ready to deal now.'

PART TWO
Commercial Considerations

In any agenda, political or otherwise, there is a cost to be borne. Always ask what it is, and who will be paying. If you don't, then the agenda-makers will pick up the perfume of your silence like swamp panthers on the scent of blood, and the next thing you know, the person expected to bear the cost will be you. And you may not have what it takes to pay.

Quellcrist Falconer *Things I Should Have Learnt By Now Vol II*

CHAPTER NINE

'Ladies and gentlemen, your attention please.'

The auctioneer tapped a finger delicately onto the bulb of her no-hands mike and the sound frub-frubbed through the vaulted space over our heads like muffled thunder. In keeping with tradition, she was attired, minus helmet and gloves, in a vacuum suit of sorts, but it was moulded in lines that reminded me more of the fashion houses on New Beijing than a Mars exploratory dig. Her voice was sweet, warm coffee laced with overproof rum. 'Lot seventy-seven. From the Lower Danang Field, recent excavation. Three-metre pylon with laser-engraved technoglyph base. Opening offers at two hundred thousand saft.'

'Somehow I don't think so.' Matthias Hand sipped at his tea and glanced idly up to where the artefact turned in holographic magnification just beyond the edge of the clearing balcony. 'Not today, and not with that bloody great fissure running through the second glyph.'

'Well you never know,' I said easily. 'No telling what kind of idiots are wandering around with too much money in a place like this.'

'Oh, quite.' He twisted slightly in his seat, as if scanning the loosely knotted crowd of potential buyers scattered around the balcony. 'But I really think you'll see this piece go for rather less than a hundred and twenty.'

'If you say so.'

'I do.' An urbane smile faded in and then out across the chiselled Caucasian planes of his face. He was, like most corporate execs, tall and forgettably good-looking. 'Of course, I have been wrong in the past. Occasionally. Ah, good, this looks like ours.'

The food arrived, dispensed by a waiter on whom had been inflicted a cheaper and less well-cut version of the auctioneer's suit. He unloaded our order with remarkable grace, considering. We both waited in silence while he did it and then watched him out of sight with symmetrical caution.

'Not one of yours?' I asked.

'Hardly.' Hand prodded doubtfully at the contents of the bento tray with his chopsticks. 'You know, you might have picked another cuisine. I mean, there's a war on and we are over a thousand kilometres from the nearest ocean. Do you really think sushi was such a good idea?'

'I'm from Harlan's World. It's what we eat there.'

Both of us were ignoring the fact that the sushi bar was slap in the middle of the clearing balcony, exposed to sniper view from positions all over the auction house's airy interior. In one such position, Jan Schneider was at that moment huddled up with a snub-barrelled hooded-discharge laser carbine, looking down a sniper-scope at Matthias Hand's face. I didn't know how many other men and women might be in the house doing the same thing to me.

Up on the holodisplay over our heads, the opening price slithered in warm orange numerals, down past a hundred and fifty and unchecked by the imploring tones of the auctioneer. Hand nodded towards the figure.

'There you are. The corrosion begins.' He started to eat. 'Shall we get down to business then?'

'Fair enough.' I tossed something across the table to him. 'That's yours, I think.'

It rolled on the surface until he stopped it with his free hand. He picked it up between a well-manicured finger and thumb and looked at it quizzically.

'Deng?'

I nodded.

'What did you get out of him?'

'Not much. No time with a virtual trace set to blow on activation, you know that.' I shrugged. 'He dropped your name before he realised I wasn't a Mandrake psychosurgeon, but after that he pretty much clammed up. Tough little motherfucker.'

Hand's expression turned sceptical, but he dropped the cortical stack into the breast pocket of his suit without further comment. He chewed slowly through another mouthful of sashimi.

'Did you really have to shoot them all?' he asked finally.

I shrugged. 'That's the way we do things up north these days. Maybe you haven't heard. There's a war on.'

'Ah, yes.' He seemed to notice my uniform for the first time. 'So you're in the Wedge. I wonder, how would Isaac Carrera react to news of your incursions into Landfall, do you suppose?'

I shrugged again. 'Wedge officers get a lot of latitude. It might be a little tricky to explain, but I can always tell him I was undercover, following up a strategic initiative.'

'And are you?'

'No. This is strictly personal.'

'And what if I've recorded this and I play it back to him?'

'Well, if I'm undercover, I have to tell you something to maintain that cover, don't I. That would make this conversation a double bluff. Wouldn't it.'

There was a pause while we looked impassively at each other across the table, and then another smile spread slowly onto the Mandrake executive's face. This one stayed longer and was unmanufactured, I thought.

'Yes,' he murmured. 'That is so very elegant. Congratulations, lieutenant. It's so watertight I don't know what to believe, myself. You *could* be working for the Wedge, for all I know.'

'Yes, I could.' I smiled back. 'But you know what? You don't have time to worry about that. Because the same data you received yesterday is in locked-down launch configuration at fifty places in the Landfall dataflow, preprogrammed for high-impact delivery into every corporate stack in the Cartel. And the clock is running. You've got about a month to put this together. After that, well, all your heavyweight competitors will know what you know, and a certain stretch of coastline is going to look like Touchdown Boulevard on New Year's Eve.'

'Be quiet.' Hand's voice stayed gentle, but there was a sudden spike of steel under the suave tones. 'We're in the open here. If you want to do business with Mandrake, you're going to have to learn a little discretion. No more specifics, please.'

'Fine. Just as long as we understand each other.'

'I think we do.'

'I hope so.' I let my own tone harden a little. 'You underestimated me when you sent the goon squad out last night. Don't do it again.'

'I wouldn't dream—'

'That's good. Don't even dream about it, Hand. Because what happened to Deng and his pals last night doesn't come close to some of the unpleasantries I've been party to in the last eighteen months up north. You may think the war's a long way off right now, but if Mandrake tries to shaft me or my associates again, you'll have a Wedge wake-up call rammed so far up your arse you'll be able to taste your own shit in the back of your throat. Now, do we understand each other?'

Hand made a pained face. 'Yes. You've made your point very graphically. I assure you, there will be no more attempts to cut you out of the loop. That's provided your demands are reasonable, of course. What kind of finder's fee were you looking for?'

'Twenty million UN dollars. And don't look at me like that, Hand. It's not even a tenth per cent of what Mandrake stands to make from this, if we're successful.'

Up on the holo, the asking price seemed to have braked at a hundred and nine and the auctioneer was now coaxing it upward a fraction at a time.

'Hmm.' Hand chewed and swallowed while he thought about it. 'Cash on delivery?'

'No. Up front, on deposit in a Latimer City bank. One-way transfer, standard seven-hour reversibility limit. I'll give you the account codes later.'

'That's presumptuous, lieutenant.'

'Call it insurance. Not that I don't trust you, Hand, but I'll feel happier knowing you've already made the payment. That way, there's no percentage in Mandrake fucking me over after the event. You don't stand to gain anything from it.'

The Mandrake exec grinned wolfishly. 'Trust works both ways, lieutenant. Why should we pay you before the project matures?'

'Other than because if you don't I'll walk away from this table and you'll lose the biggest R&D coup the Protectorate has ever seen, you mean?' I let that sink in for a moment before I hit him with the relaxant. 'Well, look at it this way. I can't access the money from here as long as the war's on; the Emergency Powers Directive ensures that. So your money's gone, but I don't have it either. To get paid, I have to be on Latimer. That's your guarantee.'

'You want to go to Latimer *as well*?' Hand raised an eyebrow. 'Twenty million UN *and* passage offworld?'

'Don't be obtuse, Hand. What did you expect? You think I want to wait around until Kemp and the Cartel finally decide it's time to negotiate instead of fight? I don't have that kind of patience.'

'So.' The Mandrake exec set down his chopsticks and steepled his hands on the table. 'Let me see if I've got this straight. We pay you twenty million UN dollars, now. That's non-negotiable.'

I looked back at him, waiting.

'Is that right?'

'Don't worry, I'll stop you if you get off track.'

The faint there-and-gone smile again. 'Thank you. Then, upon successful completion of this project, we undertake to freight you, and presumably your associates, by needlecast to Latimer. Are those all of your demands?'

'Plus decanting.'

Hand looked at me strangely. I guessed he wasn't used to his negotiations taking this path.

'Plus decanting. Any specifics I should know about there?'

I shrugged. 'Selected sleeves, obviously, but we can discuss the specifics later. Doesn't have to be custom. Something top of the range, obviously, but off the rack will do fine.'

'Oh, good.'

I felt a grin floating up, tickling the inner surfaces of my belly. I let it surface. 'Come on Hand. You're getting a fucking bargain, and you know it.'

'So you say. But it isn't that simple, lieutenant. We've checked the Landfall artefact registry for the past five years, and there's no trace of anything like the item you describe.' He spread his hands. 'No evidence. You can see my position.'

'Yeah, I can. In about two minutes you're about to lose the biggest archaeological coup of the past five hundred years, and you're going to do it because there's nothing in your *files* about it. If that's your position, Hand, I'm dealing with the wrong people.'

'Are you saying this find went unregistered? In direct breach of the Charter?'

'I'm saying it doesn't matter. I'm saying what we sent you looked real enough for either you or your pet AI to authorise a full urban commando strike inside half an hour. Maybe the files got wiped, maybe they were corrupted or stolen. Why am I even discussing this? *Are you going to pay us, or are you going to walk?*'

Silence. He was pretty good – I still couldn't tell which way he was going to jump. He hadn't shown me a single genuine emotion since we sat down. I waited. He sat back and brushed something invisible from his lap.

'I'm afraid this will require some consultation with my colleagues. I'm not authorised to sign off on deals of this magnitude, with this little up front. Authorisation for the DHF needlecasting alone will need—'

'Crap.' I kept it friendly. 'But go ahead. Consult. I can give you half an hour.'

'Half an hour?'

Fear – the tiniest flicker of it at the narrowed corners of his eyes, but it was there and I felt the satisfaction come surging up from my stomach in the wake of the grin, savage with nearly two years of suppressed rage.

Got you, motherfucker.

'Sure. Thirty minutes. I'll be right here. I hear the green tea sorbet's pretty good in this place.'

'You're not serious.'

I let the savagery corrode the edge of my voice. 'Sure, I'm serious. I warned you about that. Don't underestimate me again, Hand. You get me a decision inside thirty minutes or I walk out of here and go talk to someone else. I might even stiff you with the bill.'

He jerked his head irritably.

'And who would you go to?'

'Sathakarn Yu? PKN?' I gestured with my chopsticks. 'Who knows? But I wouldn't worry about it. I'll work something out. You'll be busy enough trying to explain to the policy board how you let this slip through your fingers. Won't you?'

Matthias Hand compressed a breath and got up. He sorted out a thin smile and flashed it at me.

'Very well. I'll be back shortly. But you have a little to learn about the art of negotiation, Lieutenant Kovacs.'

'Probably. Like I said, I've spent a lot of time up north.'

I watched him walk away between the potential buyers on the balcony, and could not repress a faint shiver. If I was going to get my face lasered off, there was a good chance it would happen now.

I was banking hard on an intuition that Hand had licence from the policy board to do pretty much what he wanted. Mandrake was the commercial world's equivalent of Carrera's Wedge, and you had to assume a corresponding approach to latitudes of initiative at executive levels. There was really no other way for a cutting-edge organism to work.

Don't expect anything, and you will be ready for it. In Corps-approved fashion, I stayed in surface neutral, defocused, but underneath it all I could feel my mind worrying at the details like a rat.

Twenty million wasn't much in corporate terms, not for a guaranteed outcome like the one I was sketching for Mandrake. And hopefully I'd committed enough mayhem the night before to make them wary of risking another grab at the goods without paying. I was pushing hard, but it was all stacked up to fall in the desired direction. It made sense for them to pay us out.

Right, Takeshi?

My face twitched.

If my much-vaunted Envoy intuition was wrong, if Mandrake execs were leashed tighter than I thought, and if Hand couldn't get a green light for cooperation, he might just decide to try smash and grab after all. Starting with my death and subsequent re-sleeving in an interrogation construct. And if Mandrake's assumed snipers took me down now, there wasn't much Schneider and Wardani could do but fall back and hide.

Don't expect anything and—

And they wouldn't be able to hide for long. Not from someone like Hand.

Don't—

Envoy serenity was getting hard to come by on Sanction IV.

This fucking war.

And then Matthias Hand was there, threading his way back through the crowd, with a faint smile on his lips and decision written into the lines of his stride as if he were marketing the stuff. Above his head, the Martian pylon turned in holo, orange numerals flaring to a halt and then to the red of arterial spray. Shutdown colours. One hundred and twenty-three thousand seven hundred saft.

Sold.

CHAPTER TEN

Dangrek.

The coast huddled inward from a chilly grey sea, weathered granite hills thinly clothed with low growing vegetation and a few patches of forest. It was clothing that the landscape started shrugging off in favour of lichen and bare rock as soon as height permitted. Less than ten kilometres inland the bones of the land showed clean in the tumbled peaks and gullies of the ancient mountain range that was Dangrek's spine. Late-afternoon sunlight speared in through shreds of cloud caught on the few remaining teeth the landscape owned and turned the sea to dirty mercury.

A thin breeze swept in off the ocean and buffeted good-naturedly across our faces. Schneider glanced down at his ungoosefleshed arms and frowned. He was wearing the Lapinee T-shirt he'd got up in that morning, and no jacket.

'Should be colder than this,' he said.

'Should be covered in little bits of dead Wedge commandos as well, Jan.' I wandered past him to where Matthias Hand stood with his hands in the pockets of his board-meeting suit, looking up at the sky as if he expected rain. 'This is from stock, right? Stored construct, no real time update?'

'Not as yet.' Hand dropped his gaze to meet my eye. 'Actually, it's something we've worked up from military AI projections. The climate protocols aren't in yet. It's still quite crude, but for locational purposes . . .'

He turned expectantly to Tanya Wardani, who was staring off across the rough grass hillscape in the opposite direction. She nodded without looking round at us.

'It'll do,' she said distantly. 'I guess an MAI won't have missed much.'

'Then you'll be able to show us what we're looking for, presumably.' A long, tuned-out pause, and I wondered if the fastload therapy I'd done on Wardani might be coming apart at the seams. Then the archaeologue turned about.

'Yes.' Another pause. 'Of course. This way.'

She set out across the side of the hill with what seemed like overlong strides, coat flapping in the breeze. I exchanged a glance with Hand, who shrugged his immaculately tailored shoulders and made an elegant *after you* gesture with one hand. Schneider had already started out after the archaeologue, so we fell in behind. I let Hand take the lead and stayed back, watching amused as he slipped on the gradient in his unsuitable boardroom shoes.

A hundred metres ahead, Wardani had found a narrow path worn by some grazing animal and was following it down towards the shore. The breeze kept pace across the hillside, stirring the long grass and making the stiff petalled heads of spider-rose nod in dreamy acquiescence. Overhead, the cloud cover seemed to be breaking up on a backdrop of quiet grey.

I was having a hard time reconciling it all with the last time I'd been up on the Northern Rim. It was the same landscape for a thousand kilometres in either direction along the coast, but I remembered it slick with blood and fluids from the hydraulic systems of murdered war machines. I remembered raw granite wounds torn in the hills, shrapnel and scorched grass and the scything blast of charged particle guns from the sky. I remembered screaming.

We crested the last row of hills before the shore and stood looking down on a coastline of jutting rock promontories tilted into the sea like sinking aircraft carriers. Between these wrenched fingers of land, gleaming turquoise sand caught the light in a succession of small, shallow bays. Further out, small islets and reefs broke the surface in places, and the coast swept out and round to the east where—

I stopped and narrowed my eyes. On the eastern edge of the long coastal sweep, the virtuality's fabric seemed to be wearing through, revealing a patch of grey unfocus that looked like old steel wool. At irregular intervals, a dim red glow lit the grey from within.

'Hand. What's that?'

'That?' He saw where I was pointing. 'Oh, that. Grey area.'

'I can see that.' Now Wardani and Schneider had both stopped to peer along the line of my raised arm. 'What's it doing there?'

But some part of me recently steeped in the dark and spiderweb green of Carrera's holomaps and geolocational models was already waking up to the answer. I could feel the pre-knowledge trickling down the gullies of my mind like the detritus ahead of a major rock fall.

Tanya Wardani got there just ahead of me.

'It's Sauberville,' she said flatly. 'Isn't it?'

Hand had the good grace to look embarrassed. 'That is correct, Mistress Wardani. The MAI posits a fifty per cent likelihood that Sauberville will be tactically reduced within the next two weeks.'

A small, peculiar chill fell into the air, and the look that passed from Schneider to Wardani and back to me felt like current. Sauberville had a population of a hundred and twenty thousand.

'Reduced how?' I asked.

Hand shrugged. 'It depends who does it. If it's the Cartel, they'll probably use one of their CP orbital guns. Relatively clean, so it doesn't inconvenience your friends in the Wedge if they fight their way through this far. If Kemp does it, he won't be so subtle, or so clean.'

'Tactical nuke,' said Schneider tonelessly. 'Riding a marauder delivery system.'

'Well, it's what he's got.' Hand shrugged again. 'And to be honest, if he has to do it, he won't want a clean blast anyway. He'll be falling back, trying to leave the whole peninsula too contaminated for the Cartel to occupy.'

I nodded. 'Yeah, that makes sense. He did the same thing at Evenfall.'

'Motherfucking psycho,' said Schneider, apparently to the sky.

Tanya Wardani said nothing, but she looked as if she was trying to loosen a piece of meat trapped between her teeth with her tongue.

'So.' Hand's tone shifted up into a forced briskness. 'Mistress Wardani, you were going to show us something, I believe.'

Wardani turned away. 'It's down on the beach,' she said.

The path we were following wound its way around one of the bays and ended at a small overhang that had collapsed into a cone of shattered rock spilling down to the pale blue shaded sand. Wardani jumped down with a practised flex in her legs and trudged across the beach to where the rocks were larger and the overhangs towered at five times head height. I went after her, scanning the rise of land behind us with professional unease. The rock faces triangled back to form a long, shallow Pythagorean alcove about the size of the hospital shuttle deck I'd met Schneider on. Most of the space was filled with a fall of huge boulders and jagged fragments of rock.

We assembled around Tanya Wardani's motionless figure. She was faced off against the tumbled rock like a platoon scout on point.

'That's it.' She nodded ahead. 'That's where we buried it.'

'Buried it?' Matthias Hand looked around at the three of us with an expression that under other circumstances might have been comical. 'How exactly did you bury it?'

Schneider gestured at the fall of debris, and the raw rock face behind it. 'Use your eyes, man. How do you think?'

'You blew it up?'

'Bored charges.' Schneider was obviously enjoying himself. 'Two metres in, all the way up. You should have seen it go.'

'You.' Hand's mouth sculpted the words as if they were unfamiliar. 'Blew up. An artefact?'

'Oh, for God's sake, Hand.' Wardani was looking at him in open irritation. 'Where do you think we found the fucking thing in the first place? This whole cliff wall came down on it fifty thousand years ago, and when we dug it up it was still in working order. It's not a piece of pottery – this is hypertechnology we're talking about. Built to last.'

'I hope you're right.' Hand walked about the skirts of the rockfall, peering in between the larger cracks. 'Because Mandrake isn't going to pay you twenty million UN dollars for damaged goods.'

'What brought the rock down?' I asked suddenly.

Schneider turned, grinning. 'I told you, man. Bored—'

'No.' I was looking at Tanya Wardani. 'I mean originally. These are some of the oldest rocks on the planet. There hasn't been any serious geological activity up on the Rim for a lot longer than fifty thousand years. And the sea sure as hell didn't do it, because that would mean this beach was created by the fall. Which puts the original construction under water, and why would the Martians do that. So, what happened here fifty thousand years ago?'

'Yeah, Tanya,' Schneider nodded vigorously. 'You never did nail that one, did you? I mean we talked about it, but . . .'

'It's a good point.' Matthias Hand had paused in his explorations and was back with us. 'What kind of explanation do you have for this, Mistress Wardani?'

The archaeologue looked around at the three men surrounding her, and coughed up a laugh.

'Well, *I* didn't do it, I assure you.'

I picked up on the configuration we'd unconsciously taken around her, and broke it by moving to seat myself on a flat slab of rock. 'Yeah, it was a bit before your time, I'd agree. But you were digging for months here. You must have some ideas.'

'Yeah, tell them about the leakage thing, Tanya.'

'Leakage?' asked Hand dubiously.

Wardani shot Schneider an exasperated glance. She found a rock of her own to sit on and produced cigarettes from her coat that looked suspiciously like the ones I'd bought that morning. Landfall Lights, about the best smoking that money could buy now Indigo City cigars were outlawed. Tapping one free of the packet, she rolled it in her fingers and frowned.

'Look,' she said finally. 'This gate is as far ahead of any technology we have as a submarine is ahead of a canoe. We know what it does, at least, we know *one* thing that it does. Unfortunately we don't have the faintest idea *how* it does it. I'm just guessing.'

When no one said anything to contradict this, she looked up from the cigarette and sighed.

'Alright. How long does a heavy load hypercast usually last? I'm talking about a multiple DHF needlecast transmission. Thirty seconds, something like that? A minute absolute maximum? And to open and hold that needlecast hyperlink takes the full capacity of our best conversion reactors.' She put the cigarette in her mouth and applied the end to the ignition patch on the side of the packet. Smoke ribboned off into the wind. 'Now. When we opened the gate last time, we could see through to the other side. You're talking about a stable image, metres wide, infinitely maintained. In hypercast terms, that's *infinite* stable transmission of the data contained in that image, the photon value of each star in the starfield and the coordinates it occupied, updated second by second in real time, for as long as you care to keep the gate up and running. In our case that was a couple of days. About forty hours, that's two thousand, four hundred minutes. Two and a half thousand times the duration of the longest needlecast hyperlink event we can generate. And no sign that the gate was ever running at anything other than standby. Begin to get the idea?'

'A lot of energy,' said Hand impatiently. 'So what's this about leakage?'

'Well, I'm trying to imagine what a glitch in a system like that would look like. Run any kind of transmission for long enough, and you'll get interference. That's an unavoidable fact of life in a chaotic cosmos. We know it happens with radio transmission, but so far we haven't seen it happen to a hypercast.'

'Maybe that's because there's no interference in hyperspace, Mistress Wardani. Just like it says in the textbooks.'

'Yeah, maybe.' Wardani blew smoke disinterestedly in Hand's direction. 'And maybe it's because we've been lucky so far. Statistically, it wouldn't be all that surprising. We've been doing this for less than five centuries and with an average 'cast duration of a few seconds, well, it doesn't add up to much air time. But if the Martians were running gates like these on a regular basis, their exposure time would be way up on ours, and given a civilisation with millennial hypertechnology, you'd have to expect an occasional blip. The problem is that with the energy levels we're talking about, a blip coming through this gate would probably be enough to crack the planet's crust wide open.'

'Oops.'

The archaeologue flicked me a glance not much less dismissive than the exhaled smoke she'd pushed at Hand's Protectorate-sanctioned schoolroom physics.

'Quite,' she said acidly. 'Oops. Now the Martians weren't stupid. If their technology was susceptible to this sort of thing, they'd build in a fail-safe. Something like a circuit breaker.'

I nodded. 'So the gate shuts down automatically at the surge—'

'And buries itself under five hundred thousand tonnes of cliff face? As a safety measure, that seems a little counterproductive, if you don't mind me saying so, Mistress Wardani.'

The archaeologue made an irritable gesture. 'I'm not saying it was intended to happen that way. But if the power surge was extreme, the circuit breaker might not have operated fast enough to damp down the whole thing.'

'Or,' said Schneider brightly, 'it could just have been a microme-teorite that crashed the gate. That was my theory. This thing was looking out into deep space, after all. No telling what might come zipping through, given enough time, is there?'

'We already talked about this, Jan.' Wardani's irritation was still there, but tinged this time with the exasperation of long dispute. 'It's not—'

'It's *possible*, alright.'

'Yes. It's just not very *likely*.' She turned away from Schneider and faced me. 'It's hard to be sure – a lot of the glyphs were like nothing I'd ever seen before, and they're hard to read, but I'm pretty certain there's a power brake built in. Above certain velocities, nothing gets through.'

'You don't know that for certain.' Schneider was sulking. 'You said yourself you couldn't—'

'Yes, but it makes *sense*, Jan. You don't build a door into hard space without some kind of safeguard against the junk you're likely to find out there.'

'Oh, come *on* Tanya, what about—'

'Lieutenant Kovacs,' said Hand loudly. 'Perhaps you could come with me down to the shoreline. I'd like a military perspective on the outlying area, if you wouldn't mind.'

'Sure.'

We left Wardani and Schneider bickering among the rocks, and set out across the expanse of blued sand at a pace dictated largely by Hand's shoes. To begin with, neither of us had anything to say, and the only sounds were the quiet compression of our steps in the yielding surface underfoot and the idle lapping of the sea. Then, out of nowhere, Hand spoke.

'Remarkable woman.'

I grunted.

'I mean, to survive a government internment camp with so little apparent scarring. That alone must have taken a tremendous effort of will. And now, to be facing the rigours of technoglyph operational sequencing so soon . . .'

'She'll be fine,' I said shortly.

'Yes, I'm sure she will.' A delicate pause. 'I can see why Schneider is so burned on her.'

'That's over, I think.'

'Oh, really?'

There was a fractional amusement buried in his tone. I shot him a narrow sideways glance, but his expression was blank and he was looking carefully ahead at the sea.

'About this military perspective, Hand.'

'Oh, yes.' The Mandrake exec stopped a few metres short of the placid ripples that passed for waves on Sanction IV and turned about. He gestured at the folds of land rising behind us. 'I'm not a soldier, but I would hazard a guess that this isn't ideal fighting ground.'

'Got it in one.' I scanned the beach end to end, looking vainly for something that might cheer me up. 'Once we get down here, we're a floating target for anyone on the high ground with anything more substantial than a sharp stick. It's an open field of fire right back to the foothills.'

'And then there's the sea.'

'And then there's the sea,' I echoed gloomily. 'We're open to fire from anyone who can muster a fast assault launch. Whatever we have to do here, we'll need a small army to keep us covered while we do it. That's unless we can do this with a straight recon. Fly in, take pictures, fly out.'

'Hmm.' Matthias Hand squatted and stared out over the water pensively. 'I've talked to the lawyers.'

'Did you disinfect afterwards?'

'Under incorporation charter law, ownership of any artefact in non-orbital space is only considered valid if a fully operational claim buoy is placed within one kilometre of said artefact. No loopholes, we've looked. If there's a starship on the other side of this gate, we're going to have to go through and tag it. And from what Mistress Wardani says, that's going to take some time.'

I shrugged. 'A small army, then.'

'A small army is going to attract a lot of attention. It'll show up on satellite tracking like a holowhore's chest. And we can't really afford that, can we?'

'A holowhore's chest? I don't know, the surgery can't be that expensive.'

Hand cocked his head up to stare at me for a moment, then emitted an unwilling chuckle. 'Very droll. Thank you. We can't really afford to be satellite-tagged, can we?'

'Not if you want an exclusive.'

'I think that goes without saying, lieutenant.' Hand reached down and idly traced a pattern on the sand with his fingers. 'So then. We have to go in small and tight and not make too much noise. Which in turn means this area has to be cleared of operational personnel for the duration of our visit.'

'If we want to come out alive, yes.'

'Yes.' Unexpectedly, Hand rocked back on his heels and dumped himself into a sitting position in the sand. He rested his forearms on his knees and seemed lost in searching the horizon for something. In the dark executive suit and white winged collar, he looked like a sketch by one of the Millsport absurdist school.

'Tell me, lieutenant,' he said finally. 'Assuming we can get the peninsula cleared, in your professional opinion, what's the lower limit on a support team for this venture? How few can we get away with?'

I thought about it. 'If they're good. Spec ops, not just plankton-standard grunts. Say six. Five, if you use Schneider as flyer.'

'Well, he doesn't strike me as the sort to be left behind while we look after his investment for him.'

'No.'

'You said spec ops. Do you have any specific skills in mind?'

'Not really. Demolitions, maybe. That rock fall looks pretty solid. And it wouldn't hurt if a couple of them could fly a shuttle, just in case something happens to Schneider.'

Hand twisted his head round to look up at me. 'Is that likely?'

'Who knows?' I shrugged. 'Dangerous world out there.'

'Indeed.' Hand went back to watching the place where the sea met the grey of Sauberville's undecided fate. 'I take it you'll want to do the recruiting yourself.'

'No, you can run it. But I want to sit in, and I want veto on anyone you select. You got any idea where you're going to get half a dozen spec ops volunteers? Without ringing any alarm bells, I mean.'

For a moment I thought he hadn't heard me. The horizon seemed to have him body and soul. Then he shifted slightly and a smile touched the corners of his mouth.

'In these troubled times,' he murmured, almost to himself, 'it shouldn't be a problem finding soldiers who won't be missed.'

'Glad to hear it.'

He glanced up again and there were still traces of the smile clinging to his mouth.

'Does that offend you, Kovacs?'

'You think I'd be a lieutenant in Carrera's Wedge if I offended that easily?'

'I don't know.' Hand looked back out to the horizon again. 'You've been full of surprises so far. And I understand that Envoys are generally pretty good at adaptive camouflage.'

So.

Less than two full days since the meeting in the auction hall, and Hand had already penetrated the Wedge datacore and unpicked whatever shielding Carrera had applied to my Envoy past. He was just letting me know.

I lowered myself to the blued sand beside him and picked my own point on the horizon to stare at.

'I'm not an Envoy any more.'

'No. So I understand.' He didn't look at me. 'No longer an Envoy, no longer in Carrera's Wedge. This rejection of groupings is verging on pathological, lieutenant.'

'There's no verging about it.'

'Ah. I see some evidence of your Harlan's World origins emerging. *The essential evil of massed humanity*, wasn't that what Quell called it?'

'I'm not a Quellist, Hand.'

'Of course not.' The Mandrake exec appeared to be enjoying himself. 'That would necessitate being part of a group. Tell me, Kovacs, do you hate me?'

'Not yet.'

'Really? You surprise me.'

'Well, I'm full of surprises.'

'You honestly have no feelings of rancour towards me after your little run-in with Deng and his squad.'

I shrugged again. 'They're the ones with the added ventilation.'

'But I sent them.'

'All that shows is a lack of imagination.' I sighed. 'Look, Hand. I knew *someone* in Mandrake would send a squad, because that's the way organisations like yours work. That proposal we sent you was practically a dare to come and get us. We could have been more careful, tried a less direct approach, but we didn't have the time. So I flashed my fishcakes under the local bully's nose, and got into a fight as a result. Hating you for that would be like hating the bully's wrist bones for a punch that I ducked. It served its purpose, and here we are. I don't hate you personally, because you haven't given me any reason to yet.'

'But you hate Mandrake.'

I shook my head. 'I don't have the energy to hate the corporates, Hand. Where would I start? And like Quell says, *rip open the diseased heart of a corporation and what spills out?*'

'People.'

'That's right. People. It's all people. People and their stupid fucking groups. Show me an individual decision-maker whose decisions have harmed me, and I'll melt his stack to slag. Show me a group with the united purpose of harming me and I'll take them all down if I can. But don't expect me to waste time and effort on abstract hate.'

'How very balanced of you.'

'Your government would call it antisocial derangement, and put me in a camp for it.'

Hand's lip curled. 'Not my government. We're just wet-nursing these clowns till Kemp calms down.'

'Why bother? Can't you deal direct with Kemp?'

I wasn't looking, but I got the sense that his gaze had jerked sideways as I said it. It took him a while to formulate a response he was happy with.

'Kemp is a crusader,' he said finally. 'He has surrounded himself with others like him. And crusaders do not generally see sense until they are nailed to it. The Kempists will have to be defeated, bloodily and resoundingly, before they can be brought to the negotiating table.'

I grinned. 'So you've tried.'

'I didn't say that.'

'No. You didn't.' I found a violet pebble in the sand and tossed it into the placid ripples in front of us. Time to change the subject. 'You didn't say where you were going to get our spec ops escort, either.'

'Can't you guess?'

'The soul markets?'

'Do you have a problem with that?'

I shook my head, but inside me something smoked off the detachment like stubborn embers.

'By the way.' Hand twisted around to look back at the rock fall. 'I have an alternative explanation for that collapsed cliff.'

'You didn't buy the micrometeorite, then?'

'I am inclined to believe in Mistress Wardani's velocity brake. It makes sense. As does her circuit-breaker theory, to a point.'

'That point being?'

'That if a race as advanced as the Martians appear to have been built a circuit breaker, it would work properly. It would not leak.'

'No.'

'So we are left with the question. Why, fifty thousand years ago, did this cliff collapse. Or perhaps, why *was* it collapsed?'

I groped around for another pebble. 'Yeah, I wondered about that.'

'An open door to any given set of coordinates across interplanetary, possibly even interstellar distances. That's dangerous, conceptually and in fact. There's no telling what might come through a door like that. Ghosts, aliens, monsters with half-metre fangs.' He glanced sideways at me. 'Quellists, even.'

I found a second, larger stone somewhere back behind me.

'Now that *would* be bad,' I agreed, heaving my find far out into the sea. 'The end of civilisation as we know it.'

'Precisely. Something which the Martians, no doubt, also thought of and built for. Along with the power brake and the circuit breaker, they would presumably have a monster-with-half-metre-fangs contingency system.'

From somewhere Hand produced a pebble of his own and spun it out over the water. It was a good throw from a seated position, but it still fell a little short of the ripples I had created with my last stone. Wedge-customised neurachem – hard to beat. Hand clucked in disappointment.

'That's some contingency system,' I said. 'Bury your gate under half a million tonnes of cliff face.'

'Yes.' He was still frowning at the impact site of his throw, watching as his ripples merged with mine. 'It makes you wonder what they were trying to shut out, doesn't it.'

CHAPTER ELEVEN

'You like him, don't you?'

It was an accusation, dealt face up in the low gleam from the muffled illuminum bar top. Music twanged, irritatingly sweet, from speakers not nearly high enough above our heads. Crouched at my elbow like a large comatose beetle, the personal space resonance scrambler that Mandrake had insisted we carry at all times showed a clear green functioning light, but apparently wasn't up to screening out external noise. Pity.

'Like who?' I asked, turning to face Wardani.

'Don't be obtuse, Kovacs. That slick streak of used coolant in a suit. You're fucking bonding with him.'

I felt the corner of my mouth quirk. If Tanya Wardani's archaeologue lectures had seeped into some of Schneider's speech patterns during their previous association, it looked as if the pilot had given as good as he'd got.

'He's our sponsor, Wardani. What do you want me to do? Spit at him every ten minutes to remind us all how morally superior we are?' I tugged significantly at the shoulder flash of the Wedge uniform I was wearing. 'I'm a paid killer, Schneider here is a deserter and you, whatever your sins may or may not be, are encoded all the way with us in trading the greatest archaeological find of the millennium for a ticket offworld and a lifetime pass to all the ruling-elite fun-park venues in Latimer City.'

She flinched.

'He tried to have us killed.'

'Well, given the outcome, I'm inclined to forgive him that one. Deng's goon squad are the ones who ought to be feeling aggrieved.'

Schneider laughed, then shut up as Wardani cut him a freezing stare.

'Yes, that's right. He sent those men to their deaths, and now he's cutting a deal with the man who killed them. He's a piece of shit.'

'If the worst Hand ever scores is eight men sent to their deaths,' I said, more roughly than I'd intended, 'then he's a lot cleaner than me. Or anyone else with a rank that I've met recently.'

'You see. You're defending him. You use your own self-hatred to let him slide off the scope and save yourself a moral judgment.'

I looked hard at her, then drained my shot glass and set it aside with exaggerated care.

'I appreciate,' I said evenly, 'that you've been through a lot recently, Wardani. That's why I'm cutting you some slack. But you're not an expert on the inside of my head, so I'd prefer it if you'd keep your fucking amateur psychosurgeon bullshit to yourself. OK?'

Wardani's mouth compressed to a thin line. 'The fact remains—'

'Guys,' Schneider leaned across Wardani with the rum bottle and filled my glass. 'Guys, this is supposed to be a celebration. If you want to fight, go north, where it's popular. Right here, right now, I'm celebrating the fact I won't ever have to get in a fight again, and you two are spoiling my run-up. Tanya, why don't you—'

He tried to top up Wardani's glass, but she pushed the neck of the bottle aside with the edge of one hand. She was looking at him with a contempt that made me wince.

'That's all that matters to you, Jan, isn't it?' she said in a low voice. 'Sliding out from under with heavy credit. The quick-fix, short-cut, easy-solution route to some swimming-pool existence at the top of the pile. What happened to you, Jan? I mean, you were always shallow, but . . .'

She gestured helplessly.

'Thanks, Tanya.' Schneider knocked back his shot, and when I could see his face again, he was grinning fiercely. 'You're right, I shouldn't be so selfish. I ought to have stuck with Kemp for a while longer. After all, what's the worst that can happen?'

'Don't be childish.'

'No, really. I see it all so much more clearly now. Takeshi, let's go tell Hand we've changed our minds. Let's all go down fighting, it's so much more *significant*.' He stabbed a finger at Wardani. 'And you. You can go back to the camp we pulled you out of because I wouldn't want you to miss out on any of this noble suffering.'

'You pulled me out of the camp because you needed me, Jan, so don't pretend any different.'

Schneider's open hand was well into the swing before I realised he intended to hit her. My neurachem-aided responses got me there in time to lock down the slap, but I had to lunge across Wardani to do it and my shoulder must have knocked her off the stool. I heard her yelp as she hit the floor. Her drink went over and spilled across the bar.

'That's enough,' I told Schneider quietly. I had his forearm flattened to the bar under mine, and my other hand floating in a loose fist back at my left ear. My face was close enough to his to see the faint tear sheen on his eyes. 'I thought you didn't want to fight any more.'

'Yeah.' It came out strangled. He cleared his throat. 'Yeah, that's right.'

I felt him relax, and unlocked on his arm. Turning, I saw Wardani picking her stool and herself up from the floor. Behind her, a few of the bar's table occupants had come to their feet and were watching uncertainly. I met their eyes, and they seated themselves hurriedly. A graft-heavy tactical marine in one corner lasted longer than the rest, but in the end even she sat down, unwilling to tussle with the Wedge uniform. Behind me, I felt more than saw the bartender clearing up the spilled drink. I leaned back on the newly dried surface.

'I think we'd better all calm down, agreed?'

'Suits me.' The archaeologue set her stool back on its feet. 'You're the one that knocked me over. You and your wrestling partner.'

Schneider had hooked the bottle and was pouring himself another shot. He downed it and pointed at Wardani with the empty glass.

'You want to know what happened to me, Tanya? You—'

'I have a feeling you're going to tell me.'

'—really want to know? I got to watch a six-year-old-girl.

Fucking die of shrapnel. Fucking shrapnel wounds that I fucking inflicted because she was hiding in an automated bunker I rolled fucking grenades into.' He blinked and trickled more rum into his glass. 'And I'm not going to fucking watch anything like that ever again. I'm out, whatever it takes. However *shallow* that makes me. For your fucking information.'

He looked back and forth between us for a couple of seconds, as if he couldn't honestly remember who either of us were. Then he got off his stool and walked an almost straight line to the door and out. His last drink stood untouched on the muted glow of the bar top.

'Oh shit,' said Wardani, into the small silence left beside the drink. She was peering into her own empty glass as if there might be an escape hatch at the bottom.

'Yeah.' I wasn't about to help her get off the hook with this one.

'You think I should go after him?'

'Not really, no.'

She put down the glass and fumbled for cigarettes. The Landfall Lights pack I'd noticed in the virtuality came out and she fed herself one mechanically. 'I didn't mean . . .'

'No, I thought you probably didn't. So will he, once he sobers up. Don't worry about it. He's most likely been carrying that memory around in sealwrap since it happened. You just fed him enough catalyst to vomit it up. Probably better that way.'

She breathed the cigarette into life and glanced sideways at me through the smoke. 'Does none of this touch you any more?' she asked. 'How long does it take to get like that?'

'Thank the Envoys. It's their speciality. How long is a meaning-less question. It's a system. Psychodynamic engineering.'

This time she turned on her stool and stayed facing me. 'Doesn't that ever make you angry? That you've been tampered with like that?'

I reached across for the bottle, and topped up both our drinks. She made no move to stop me. 'When I was younger, I didn't care. In fact, I thought it was great. A testosterone wet dream. See, before the Envoys, I served in the regular forces and I'd already used a lot of quickplant jack-in software. This just seemed like a super-ramped version of the same thing. Body armour for the soul. And by the time I got old enough to think any differently, the conditioning was in to stay.'

'You can't beat it? The conditioning?'

I shrugged. 'Most of the time, I don't want to. That's the nature of good conditioning. And this is a very superior product. I work better when I go with it. Fighting it is hard work, and it slows me down. Where did you get those cigarettes?'

'These?' She looked down at the packet absently. 'Oh, Jan, I think. Yeah, he gave them to me.'

'That was nice of him.'

If she noticed the sarcasm in my voice, she didn't react. 'You want one?'

'Why not? By the look of it, I'm not going to be needing this sleeve much longer.'

'You really think we're going to get as far as Latimer City.' She watched me shake out a cigarette and draw it to life. 'You trust Hand to keep his side of this bargain?'

'There's really very little point in him double crossing us.' I exhaled and stared at the smoke as it drifted away across the bar. A massive sense of departure from something was coursing unlooked-for through my mind, a sense of unnamed loss. I groped after the words to sew everything back together again. 'The money's already gone, Mandrake can't get it back. So if it cuts us out, all Hand saves himself is the cost of the hypercast and three off-the-rack sleeves. In return for which he gets to worry forever about automated reprisals.'

Wardani's gaze dropped to the resonance scrambler on the bar. 'Are you sure this thing is clean?'

'Nope. I got it from an indie dealer, but she came Mandrake-recommended, so it could be tagged for all I know. It doesn't really matter. I'm the only person who knows how the reprisals are set up, and I'm not about to tell you about it.'

'Thanks.' There was no appreciable irony in her tone. An internment camp teaches you things about the value of not knowing.

'Don't mention it.'

'And what about silencing us after the event?'

I spread my hands. 'What for? Mandrake isn't interested in silence. This'll be the biggest coup a single corporate entity have ever pulled off. It'll want it known. Those time-locked data launches we set are going to be the oldest news on the block when they finally decay. Once Mandrake has got your starship hidden away some-where safe, it'll be dropping the fact through every major corporate dataport on Sanction IV. Hand's going to use this to swing instant membership of the Cartel, and probably a seat on the Protectorate Commercial Council into the bargain. Mandrake'll be a major player overnight. Our significance in that particular scheme of things will be nil.'

'Got it all worked out, huh?'

I shrugged again. 'This isn't anything we haven't already discussed.'

'No.' She made a small, oddly helpless gesture. 'I just didn't think you'd be so, fucking, congenial with that piece of corporate shit.'

I sighed.

'Look. My opinion of Matthias Hand is irrelevant. He'll do the job we want him to do. That's what counts. We've been paid, we're on board and Hand has marginally more personality than the average corporate exec, which as far as I'm concerned is a blessing. I like him well enough to get on with. If he tries to cross us, I'll have no problem putting a bolt through his stack. Now, is that suitably detached for you?'

Wardani tapped the carapace of the scrambler. 'You'd better hope this isn't tagged. If Hand's listening to you . . .'

'Well,' I reached across her and picked up Schneider's untouched drink. 'If he is, he's probably having similar thoughts about me. So cheers, Hand, if you can hear me. Here's to mistrust and mutual deterrence.'

I knocked back the rum and upended the glass on the scrambler. Wardani rolled her eyes.

'Great. The politics of despair. Just what I need.'

'What you need,' I said, yawning, 'is some fresh air. Want to walk back to the tower? If we leave now, we should make it before curfew.'

'I thought, in that uniform, the curfew wasn't an issue.'

I looked down at the black jacket and fingered the cloth. 'Yeah, well. Probably isn't, but we're supposed to be profiling low right now. And besides, if you get an automated patrol, machines can be bloody-minded about these things. Better not to risk it. So what do you think, want to walk?'

'Going to hold my hand?' It was meant to be a joke, but it came out wrong. We both stood up and were abruptly, awkwardly inside each other's personal space.

The moment stumbled between us like an uninvited drunk.

I turned to crush out my cigarette.

'Sure,' I said, trying for lightness. 'It's dark out there.'

I pocketed the scrambler, and stole back my cigarettes in the same movement, but my words had not dispersed the tension. Instead, they hung there like the afterimage of laser fire.

It's dark out there.

Outside, we both walked with hands crammed securely into pockets.

CHAPTER TWELVE

The top three floors of the Mandrake Tower were executive residential, access barred from below and topped off with a multilevel roof complex of gardens and cafés. A variable permeate power screen strung from parapet pylons kept the sun finetuned for luminous warmth throughout the day, and in three of the cafés, you could get breakfast at any hour. We got it at midday and were still working our way through the last of the spread when an immaculately-attired Hand came looking for us. If he'd been listening in to last night's character assassination, it didn't seem to have upset him much.

'Good morning Mistress Wardani. Gentlemen. I trust your night out on the town proved worth the security risk.'

'Had its moments.' I reached out and speared another dim sum parcel with my fork, not looking at either of my companions. Wardani had in any case retreated behind her sunlenses the moment she sat down, and Schneider was brooding intently on the dregs in his coffee cup. The conversation had not been sparkling so far. 'Sit down, help yourself.'

'Thank you.' Hand hooked out a chair and seated himself. On closer inspection, he looked a little tired around the eyes. 'I've already had lunch. Mistress Wardani, the primary components from your hardware list are here. I'm having them brought up to your suite.'

The archaeologue nodded and turned her head upward to the sun. When it became apparent that this was going to be the full extent of her response, Hand turned his attention to me and cranked up an eyebrow. I shook my head slightly.

Don't ask.

'Well. We're about ready to recruit, lieutenant, if you—'

'Fine.' I washed down the dim sum with a short swallow of tea and got up. The atmosphere around the table was getting to me. 'Let's go.'

No one said anything. Schneider didn't even look up, but Wardani's blacked-out sunlenses tracked my retreat across the terrace like the blank faces of a sentry gun sensor.

We rode down from the roof in a chatty elevator which named each floor for us as we passed it and outlined a few of Mandrake's current projects on the way. Neither of us spoke, and a scant thirty seconds later the doors recessed back on the low ceiling and raw fused-glass walls of the basement level. Iluminum strips cast a bluish light in the fusing and on the far side of the open space a blob of hard sunlight signalled an exit. Parked carelessly opposite the elevator doors, a nondescript straw-coloured cruiser was waiting.

'Thaisawasdi Field,' said Hand, leaning into the driver's compartment. 'The Soul Market.'

The engine note dialled up from idle to a steady thrum. We climbed in and settled back into the automould cushioning as the cruiser lifted and spun like a spider on a thread. Through the unpolarised glass of the cabin divider and past the shaven head of the driver, I watched the blob of sunlight expand as we rushed softly towards the exit. Then the light exploded around us in a hammering of gleam on metal, and we spiralled up into the merciless blue desert sky above Landfall. After the muted atmospheric shielding on the roof level, there was a slightly savage satisfaction to the change.

Hand touched a stud on the door and the glass polarised blue.

'You were followed last night,' he said matter of factly.

I glanced across the compartment at him. 'What for? We're on the same side, aren't we?'

'Not by us.' He made an impatient gesture. 'Well, yes, by us, by overhead, of course, that's how we spotted them. But I'm not talking about that. This was low-tech stuff. You and Wardani came home separated from Schneider – which incidentally wasn't all that intelligent – and you were shadowed. One on Schneider, but he peeled off, presumably as soon as he saw Wardani wasn't coming out. The others went with you as far as Find Alley, just out of sight of the bridge.'

'How many?'

'Three. Two full human, one battle-tech cyborg by the way it moved.'

'Did you pick them up?'

'No.' Hand rapped one lightly closed fist against the window. 'The duty machine only had protect-and-retrieve parameters. By the time we were notified, they'd gone to ground near the Latimer canal head and by the time we *got* there, they were gone. We looked, but . . .'

He spread his hands. The tiredness around the eyes was making some sense. He'd been up all night trying to safeguard his investment.

'What are you grinning about?'

'Sorry. Just touched. Protect and retrieve, huh?'

'Ha ha.' He fixed me with a stare until my grin showed some signs of ebbing. 'So, is there something you want to tell me?'

I thought briefly of the camp commandant and his current-stunned mumblings about an attempt to rescue Tanya Wardani. I shook my head.

'Are you certain?'

'Hand, be serious. If I'd known someone was shadowing me, do you think they'd be in any better state now than Deng and his goons?'

'So who were they?'

'I thought I just told you I didn't know. Street scum, maybe?'

He gave me a pained look. 'Street scum following a Carrera's Wedge uniform?'

'OK, maybe it was a manhood thing. Territorial. You've got some gangs in Landfall, haven't you?'

'Kovacs, please. You be serious. If you didn't notice them, how likely is it they were that low-grade?'

I sighed. 'Not very.'

'Precisely. So who else is trying to carve themselves a slice of artefact pie?'

'I don't know,' I admitted gloomily.

The rest of the flight passed in silence.

Finally, the cruiser banked about and I tipped a glance out of the window. We were spiralling down towards what looked like a sheet of dirty ice littered with used bottles and cans. I frowned and recalibrated for scale.

'Are these the original—?'

Hand nodded. 'Some of them, yes. The big ones. The rest are impounds, stuff from when the bottom fell out of the artefact market. Soon as you can't pay your landing slot, they grab your haulage and grav-lift it out here until you do. Of course, with the way the market went, hardly anyone bothered even trying to pay off what they owed, so the Port Authority salvage crews went in and decommissioned them with plasma cutters.'

We drifted in over the nearest of the grounded colony barges. It was like floating across a vast felled tree. Up at one end, the thrust assemblies that had propelled the vessel across the gulf between Latimer and Sanction IV were spread like branches, crushed to the landing field underneath and fanned stiffly against the hard blue sky above. The barge would never lift again, had in fact never been intended for more than a one-way trip. Assembled in orbit around Latimer a century ago, built only for the long blast across interstellar space and a single planetfall at journey's end, she would have burnt out her antigrav landing system coming down. The detonation of the final touchdown repulsor jets would have fused the desert sand beneath into an oval of glass that would eventually be extended by engineers to join the similar ovals left by other barges and so create Thaisawasdi Field, to serve the fledgling colony for the first decade of its life.

By the time the corporates got round to building their own private fields and the associated complexes, the barges would have been gutted, used initially to live out of, then as a ready source of refined alloys and hardware to build from. On Harlan's World, I'd been inside a couple of the original Konrad Harlan fleet, and even the decks had been cannibalised, carved back to multilevelled ridges of metal clinging to the inner curve of the hull. Only the hulls themselves were ever left intact, out of some bizarre quasi-reverence of the kind that in earlier ages got successive generations to give up their lives to build cathedrals.

The cruiser crossed the spine of the barge and slid down the curve of the hull to a soft landing in the pool of shadow cast by the grounded vessel. We climbed out into sudden cool and a quiet broken only by the whisper of a breeze across the glass plain and, faintly, the human sounds of commerce from within the hull.

'This way.' Hand nodded at the curving wall of alloy before us, and strode in towards a triangular cargo vent near ground level. I caught myself scanning the edifice for possible sniper points, shrugged off the reflex irritably and went after him. The wind swept detritus obligingly out of my way in little knee-high swirls.

Close up, the cargo vent was huge, a couple of metres across at its apex and wide enough at base to permit the passage of a trolleyed marauder bomb fuselage. The loading ramp that led up to the entrance had doubled as a hatch when the barge was in flight and now it squatted on massive hydraulic haunches that hadn't worked in decades. At the top the vent was flanked with carefully blurred holographic images that might have been either Martians or angels in flight.

'Dig art,' said Hand disparagingly. Then we were past them and into the vaulted gloom beyond.

It was the same feeling of decayed space that I'd seen on Harlan's World, but where the Harlan fleet hulks had been preserved with museum sobriety, this space was filled with a chaotic splatter of colour and sound. Stalls built from bright primary plastics and wire were cabled and epoxied seemingly at random up the curve of the hull and across what remained of the principal decks, giving the impression that a colony of poisonous mushrooms had infected the original structure. Sawn-off sections of companionway and ladders of welded support struts linked it all together. Here and there more holographic art lent extra flare to the glow of lamps and illuminum strips. Music wailed and basslined unpredictably from hull-mounted speakers the size of crates. High above it all, someone had punched metre-width holes in the hull alloy so that beams of solid sunlight blasted through the gloom at tall angles.

At the impact point of the closest beam stood a tall, raggedly dressed figure, sweat-beaded black face turned up to the light as if it were a warm shower. There was a battered black top hat jammed on his head and an equally well used long black coat draped across his gaunt frame. He heard our steps on the metal and pivoted, arms held cruciform.

'Ah, gentlemen.' The voice was a prosthetic bubbling, emitted by a rather obvious leech unit stapled to the scarred throat. 'You are just in time. I am Semetaire. Welcome to the Soul Market.'

Up on the axial deck, we got to watch the process begin.

As we stepped out of the cage elevator, Semetaire moved aside and gestured with one rag-feathered arm.

'Behold,' he said.

Out on the deck, a tracked cargo loader was backing up with a small skip held high in its lifting arms. As we watched, the skip tilted forward and something started to spill over the lip, cascading onto the deck and bouncing up again with a sound like hail stones.

Cortical stacks.

It was hard to tell without racking up the neurachem vision, but most of them looked too bulky to be clean. Too bulky, and too whitish-yellow with the fragments of bone and spinal tissue that still clung to the metal. The skip hinged further back, and the spillage became a rush, a coarse white-noised outpouring of metallic shingle. The cargo loader continued to backtrack, laying a thick, spreading trail of the stuff. The hailstorm built to a quick drumming fury, then choked up as the continuing cascade of stacks was soaked up by the mounds that had already fallen.

The skip up-ended, emptied. The sound stopped.

'Just in,' observed Semetaire, leading us around the spillage. 'Mostly from the Suchinda bombardment, civilians and regular forces, but there are bound to be some rapid deployment casualties as well. We're picking them up all over the east. Someone misread Kemp's ground cover pretty badly.'

'Not for the first time,' I muttered.

'Nor the last, we hope.' Semetaire crouched down and scooped up a double handful of cortical stacks. The bone clung to them in patches, like yellow-stained rime. 'Business has rarely been this good.'

Something scraped and rattled in the dimly lit cavern. I looked up sharply, chasing the sound.

All the way round the extended mound, traders were moving in with shovels and buckets, elbowing at each other for a better place at the digging. The shovel blades made a grating, scraping sound as they bit in, and each flung shovel-load rattled in the buckets like gravel.

For all the competition for access, I noticed they gave Semetaire a wide berth. My eyes turned back to the top-hatted figure crouched in front of me and his scarred face split in a huge grin as if he could feel my gaze. Enhanced peripherals, I guessed and watched as, still smiling gently, he opened his fingers and let the stacks trickle back into the pile. When his hands were empty again, he brushed the palms off against each other and stood.

'Most sell by gross weight,' he murmured. 'It is cheap and simple. Talk with them if you will. Others scan out the civilians for their customers, the chaff from the military wheat, and the price is still low. Perhaps this will be sufficient for your needs. Or perhaps you need Semetaire.'

'Get to the point,' said Hand curtly.

Beneath the battered top hat, I thought the eyes narrowed fractionally, but whatever was in that tiny increment of anger never made it into the rag-wrapped black man's voice. 'The point,' he said courteously, 'is as it always is. The point is what you desire. Semetaire sells only what those who come to him desire. What do *you* desire, Mandrake man? You and your Wedge wolf?'

I felt the mercury shiver of the neurachem go through me. I was not wearing my uniform. Whatever this man was racked with, it was more than enhanced peripherals.

Hand said something in a hollow-syllabled language I didn't recognise, and made a small sign with his left hand. Semetaire stiffened.

'You are playing a dangerous game,' said the Mandrake exec quietly. 'And the charade is at an end. Is that understood?'

Semetaire stood immobile for a moment, and then his grin broke out again. With both hands he reached symmetrically into his ragged coat, and found himself looking down the barrel of a Kalashnikov interface gun from a range of about five centimetres. My left hand had put the weapon there without conscious thought.

'Slowly,' I suggested.

'There is no problem here, Kovacs.' Hand's voice was mild, but his eyes were still locked with Semetaire's. 'The family ties have been established now.'

Semetaire's grin said that wasn't so, but he withdrew his hands from under the coat slowly enough. Gripped delicately in each palm was what looked like a live gunmetal crab. He looked from one set of gently flexing segmented legs to the other and then back down the barrel of my gun. If he was afraid, it didn't show.

'What is it you desire, company man?'

'Call me that again, and I might be forced to pull this trigger.'

'He's not talking to you, Kovacs.' Hand nodded minimally at the Kalashnikov and I stowed it. 'Spec ops, Semetaire. Fresh kills, nothing over a month. And we're in a hurry. Whatever you've got on the slab.'

Semetaire shrugged. 'The freshest are here,' he said, and tossed the two crab remotes down on the mound of stacks, where they commenced spidering busily about, picking up one tiny metal cylinder after another in delicate mandibular arms, holding each one beneath a blue glowing lens and then discarding it. 'But if you are pressed for time . . .'

He turned aside and led us to a sombrely-appointed stall where a thin woman, as pale as he was dark, hunched over a workstation, stressblasting bone fragments from a shallow tray of stacks. The tiny high-pitched fracturing sound as the bone came off ran a barely audible counterpoint to the bass-throated bite, crunch, rattle of the prospectors' shovels and buckets behind us.

Semetaire spoke to the woman in the tongue Hand had used earlier and she unwound herself languidly from amongst the cleaning tools. From a shelf at the back of the stall, she lifted a dull metal canister about the size of a surveillance drone and carried it out to us. Holding it up for inspection, she tapped with one overlong black painted fingernail at a symbol engraved in the metal. She said something in the language of echoing syllables.

I glanced at Hand.

'The chosen of Ogon,' he said, without apparent irony. 'Protected in iron for the master of iron, and of war. Warriors.'

He nodded and the woman set down the canister. From one side of the workstation she brought a bowl of perfumed water with which she rinsed her hands and wrists. I watched, fascinated, as she laid newly wet fingers on the lid of the canister, closed her eyes and intoned another string of cadenced sounds. Then, she opened her eyes and twisted the lid off.

'How many kilos do you want?' asked Semetaire, incongruously pragmatic against the backdrop of reverence.

Hand reached across the table and scooped a handful of stacks out of the canister. They gleamed silvery clean in the cup of his hand.

'How much are you going to gut me?'

'Seventy-nine fifty the kilo.'

The exec grunted. 'Last time I was here, Pravet charged me forty-seven fifty, and he was apologetic about it.'

'That's a dross price and you know it, company man.' Semetaire shook his head, smiling. 'Pravet deals with unsorted product, and he doesn't even clean it most of the time. If you want to spend your valuable corporate time picking bone tissue off a pile of civilian and standard conscript stacks, then go and haggle with Pravet. These are selected warrior class, cleaned and anointed, and they are worth what I ask. We should not waste each other's time in this way.'

'Alright.' Hand weighed the palmful of capsuled lives. 'You've got your expenses to think about. Sixty thousand flat. And you know I'll be back sometime.'

'Sometime.' Semetaire seemed to be tasting the word. 'Sometime, Joshua Kemp may put Landfall to the nuclear torch. Sometime, company man, we may all be dead.'

'We may indeed.' Hand tipped the stacks back into the canister. They made a clicking sound, like dice falling. 'And some of us sooner than others, if we go round making anti-Cartel statements about Kempist victory. I could have you arrested for that, Semetaire.'

The pale woman behind the workstation hissed and raised a hand to trace symbols in the air, but Semetaire snapped something at her and she stopped.

'Where would be the point in arresting me?' he asked smoothly, reaching into the canister and extracting a single gleaming stack. 'Look at this. Without me, you'd only have to fall back on Pravet. Seventy.'

'Sixty-seven fifty, and I'll make you Mandrake's preferred supplier.'

Semetaire rolled the stack between his fingers, apparently musing. 'Very well,' he said finally. 'Sixty-seven fifty. But that price comes with a set minimum. Five kilos.'

'Agreed.' Hand produced a credit chip holo-engraved with the Mandrake insignia. As he gave it to Semetaire, he grinned unexpectedly. 'I was here for ten, anyway. Wrap them up.'

Semetaire tossed the stack back into the canister. He nodded at the pale woman, and she brought out a concave weighing plate from beneath the workstation. Tilting the canister and reaching inside with a reverent hand, she scooped out the stacks a palmful at a time and laid them gently in the curve of the plate. Ornate violet digits evolved in the air above the mounting pile.

Out of the corner of my eye I caught a glimpse of movement near ground level, and turned hurriedly to face it.

'A find,' said Semetaire lightly, and grinned.

One of the crab-legged remotes had returned from the pile and, having reached Semetaire's foot, was working its way steadily up his trouser leg. When it reached the level of his belt, he plucked it off and held it still while, with the other hand, he prised something from the thing's mandibles. Then he tossed the little machine away. It drew in its limbs as it sensed the freefall and when it hit the deck, it was a featureless grey ovoid that bounced and rolled to a quick halt. A moment later, the limbs extended cautiously. The remote righted itself and scuttled off about its master's business.

'Ahhh, look.' Semetaire was rubbing the tissue-flecked stack between his fingers and thumb, still grinning. 'Look at that, Wedge Wolf. Do you see? Do you see how the new harvest begins?'

CHAPTER THIRTEEN

The Mandrake AI read the stack-stored soldiers we'd bought as three-dimensional machine-code data, and instantly wrote off a third as irretrievably psychologically damaged. Not worth talking to. Resurrected into virtuality, all they'd do would be scream themselves hoarse.

Hand shrugged it off.

'That's about standard,' he said. 'There's always some wastage, whoever you buy from. We'll run a psychosurgery dream sequencer on the others. That should give us a long shortlist without having to actually wake any of them up. Those are the want parameters.'

I picked up the hardcopy from the table and glanced through it. Across the conference room, the damaged soldiers' data scrolled down on the wall screen in two-dimensional analogue.

'Experience of high-rad combat environments?' I looked up at the Mandrake exec. 'Is this something I should know about?'

'Come on, Kovacs. You already do.'

'I.' The flash would reach into the mountains. Would chase the shadows out of gullies that hadn't seen light so harsh in geological eons. 'Had hoped it wouldn't turn out that way.'

Hand examined the table top as if it needed resheening. 'We needed the peninsula cleared,' he said carefully. 'By the end of the week it will be. Kemp's pulling back. Call it serendipity.'

Once, on reconaissance along a ridge on the slumped spine of Dangrek, I'd seen Sauberville sparkling far off in the late afternoon sun. There was too much distance for detail – even with the neurachem racked up to maximum the city looked like a silver bracelet, flung down at the water's edge. Remote, and unconnected with anything human.

I met Hand's eyes across the table.

'So we're all going to die.'

He shrugged. 'It seems unavoidable, doesn't it? Going in that soon after the blast. I mean, we can use clone stock with high tolerance for the new recruits, and antirad medication will keep us all functional for the time it takes, but in the long run . . .'

'Yeah, well in the long run I'll be wearing out a designer sleeve in Latimer City.'

'Quite.'

'What kind of rad-tolerant sleeves you have in mind?'

Another shrug. 'Don't know for sure, I'll have to talk to bioware. Maori stock, probably. Why, want one?'

I felt the Khumalo bioplates twitch in the flesh of my palms, as if angry, and shook my head.

'I'll stick with what I've got, thanks.'

'You don't trust me?'

'Now you come to mention it, no. But that isn't it.' I jabbed a thumb at my own chest. 'This is Wedge custom. Khumalo Biosystems. They don't build better for combat than this stuff.'

'And the anti-rad?'

'It'll hold up long enough for what we have to do. Tell me something, Hand. What are you offering the new recruits long-term? Aside from a new sleeve that may or may not stand up to the radiation? What do they get when we're done?'

Hand frowned at the question. 'Well. Employment.'

'They had that. Look where it got them.'

'Employment *in Landfall*.' For some reason the derision in my voice seemed to be chewing at him. Or maybe something else was. 'Contracted security staff for Mandrake, guaranteed for the duration of the war or five years, whichever lasts longer. Does that meet your Quellist, Man-of-the-Downtrodden, Anarchist scruples?'

I raised an eyebrow.

'Those are three *very* tenuously connected philosophies, Hand, and I don't really subscribe to any of them. But if you're asking, does it sound like a good alternative to being dead, I'd say so. If it were me, I'd probably want in at that price.'

'A vote of confidence.' Hand's tone was withering. 'How reassuring.'

'Provided, of course, I didn't have friends and relatives in Sauberville. You might want to check for that in the back-data.'

He looked at me. 'Are you trying to be funny?'

'I can't think of anything very funny about wiping out an entire city.' I shrugged. 'Just now, anyway. Maybe that's just me.'

'Ah, so this is a moral qualm rearing its ugly head, is it?'

I smiled thinly. 'Don't be absurd, Hand. I'm a soldier.'

'Yes, it might be as well to remember that. And don't take your surplus feelings out on me, Kovacs. As I said before, I am not actually calling in the strike on Sauberville. It is merely opportune.'

'Isn't it just.' I tossed the hardcopy back across the table, trying not to wish it was a fused grenade. 'So let's get on with it. How long to run this dream sequencer?'

According to the psychosurgeons, we act more in keeping with our true selves in a dream than in any other situation, including the throes of orgasm and the moment of our deaths. Maybe that explains why so much of what we do in the real world makes so little sense.

It certainly makes for fast psychevaluation.

The dream sequencer, combined in the heart of the Mandrake AI with the want parameters and a Sauberville-related background check, went through the remaining seven kilos of functional human psyche in less than four hours. It gave us three hundred and eighty-seven possibles, with a high probability core of two hundred and twelve.

'Time to wake them up,' said Hand, flipping through profiles on screen and yawning. I felt my jaw muscles flexing in unwilling sympathy.

Perhaps out of mutual mistrust, neither of us had left the conference room while the sequencer ran, and after edging round the subject of Sauberville a bit more, we hadn't had that much to say to each other either. My eyes were itchy from watching the data scrolldown and not much else, my limbs twitched with the desire for some physical exertion and I was out of cigarettes. The impulse to yawn fought for control of my face.

'Have we really got to talk to all of them?'

Hand shook his head. 'No, we really haven't. There's a virtual version of me in the machine with some psychosurgeon peripherals wired in. I'll send it in to bring back the best dozen and a half. That's if you trust me that far.'

I gave it up and yawned, finally, cavernously.

'Trust. Enabled. You want to get some air and a coffee?'

We left for the roof.

Up on top of the Mandrake Tower, the day was inking out to a desert indigo dusk. In the east, stars poked through the vast expanse of darkening Sanction IV sky. At the western horizon, it seemed as though the last of the sun's juice was being crushed from between thin strips of cloud by the weight of the settling night. The shields were way down, letting in most of the evening's warmth and a faint breeze out of the north.

I glanced around at the scattering of Mandrake personnel in the roof garden Hand had chosen. They formed pairs or small groups at the bars and tables and talked in modulated, confident tones that carried. Amanglic corporate standard sewn with the sporadic local music of Thai and French. No one appeared to be paying us any attention.

The language mix reminded me.

'Tell me, Hand.' I broke the seal on a new pack of Landfall Lights and drew one to life. 'What was that shit out at the market today? That language the three of you were speaking, the left-handed gestures?'

Hand tasted his coffee and set it down. 'You haven't guessed?'

'Voodoo?'

'You might put it that way.' The pained look on the exec's face told me he wouldn't put it that way in a million years. 'Though properly speaking it hasn't been called that for several centuries. Neither was it called that back at the origin. Like most people who don't know, you're oversimplifying.'

'I thought that was what religion was. Simplification for the hard of thinking.'

He smiled. 'If that is the case, then the hard of thinking seem to be in a majority, do they not?'

'They always are.'

'Well, perhaps.' Hand drank more coffee and regarded me over the cup. 'You really claim to have no God? No higher power? The Harlanites are mostly Shintoists, aren't they? That, or some Christian offshoot?'

'I'm neither,' I said flatly.

'Then you have no refuge against the coming of night? No ally when the immensity of creation presses down on the spine of your tiny existence like a stone column a thousand metres tall?'

'I was at Innenin, Hand.' I knocked ash off the cigarette and gave him back his smile, barely used. 'At Innenin, I heard soldiers with columns about that tall on their backs screaming for a whole spectrum of higher powers. None of them showed up that I noticed. Allies like that I can live without.'

'God is not ours to command.'

'Evidently not. Tell me about Semetaire. That hat and coat. He's playing a part, right?'

'Yes.' There was a cordial distaste leaking into Hand's voice now. 'He has adopted the guise of Ghede, in this case the lord of the dead—'

'Very witty.'

'—in an attempt to dominate the weaker-minded among his competitors. He is probably an adept of sorts, not without a certain amount of influence in the spirit realm, though certainly not enough to call up that particular personage. I am somewhat more.' He offered me a slight smile. 'Accredited, shall we say. I was merely making that clear. Presenting my credentials, you might say, and establishing the fact that I found his act in poor taste.'

'Strange this Ghede hasn't got around to making the same point, isn't it?'

Hand sighed. 'Actually, it's very likely that Ghede, like you, sees the humour of the situation. For a Wise One, he is very easily amused.'

'Really.' I leaned forward, searching his face for some trace of irony. 'You believe this shit, right? I mean, seriously?'

The Mandrake exec watched me for a moment, then he tipped back his head and gestured at the sky above us.

'Look at that, Kovacs. We're drinking coffee so far from Earth you have to work hard to pick out Sol in the night sky. We were carried here on a wind that blows in a dimension we cannot see or touch. Stored as dreams in the mind of a machine that thinks in a fashion so far in advance of our own brains it might as well carry the name of god. We have been resurrected into bodies not our own, grown in a secret garden outwith the body of any mortal woman. These are the *facts* of our existence, Kovacs. How, then, are they different, or any less mystical, than the belief that there is another realm where the dead live in the company of beings so far beyond us we *must* call them gods?'

I looked away, oddly embarrassed by the fervour in Hand's voice. Religion is funny stuff, and it has unpredictable effects on those who use it. I stubbed out my cigarette and chose my words with care.

'Well, the difference is that the facts of our existence weren't dreamed up by a bunch of ignorant priests centuries before anyone had left the Earth's surface or built anything resembling a machine. I'd say that on balance that makes them a better fit than your spirit realm for whatever reality we find out here.'

Hand smiled, apparently unoffended. He seemed to be enjoying himself. 'That is a local view, Kovacs. Of course, all the remaining churches have their origins in pre-industrial times, but faith is metaphor, and who knows how the data behind these metaphors has travelled, from where and for how long. We walk amidst the ruins of a civilisation that apparently had godlike powers thousands of years before we could walk upright. Your own world, Kovacs, is encircled by angels with flaming swords—'

'Whoa.' I lifted my hands, palms out. 'Let's damp down the metaphor core for a moment. Harlan's World has a system of orbital battle platforms that the Martians forgot to decommission when they left.'

'Yes.' Hand gestured impatiently. 'Orbitals built of some substance that resists every attempt to scan it, orbitals with the power to strike down a city or a mountain, but who forbear to destroy anything save those vessels that try to ascend into the heavens. What else is that but an angel?'

'It's a fucking machine, Hand. With programmed parameters that probably have their basis in some kind of planetary conflict—'

'Can you be sure of that?'

He was leaning across the table now. I found myself mirroring his posture as my own intensity stoked.

'Have you ever been to Harlan's World, Hand? No, I thought not. Well I grew up there and I'm telling you the orbitals are no more mystical than any other Martian artefact—'

'What, no more mystical than the songspires?' His voice dropped to a hiss. 'Trees of stone that sing to the rising and setting sun? No more mystical than a gate that opens like a bedroom door onto—'

He stopped abruptly and glanced around, face flushing with the near indiscretion. I sat back and grinned at him.

'Admirable passion, for someone in a suit that expensive. So you're trying to sell me the Martians as voodoo gods. Is that it?'

'I'm not trying to sell you anything,' he muttered, straightening up. 'And no, the Martians fit quite comfortably into this world. We don't need recourse to the places of origin to explain them. I'm just trying to show you how limited your world view is without an acceptance of wonder.'

I nodded.

'Very good of you.' I stabbed a finger at him. 'Just do me a favour, Hand. When we get where we're going, keep this shit stowed, will you. I'm going to have enough to worry about without you weirding out on me.'

'I believe only what I have seen,' he said stiffly. 'I have seen Ghede and Carrefour walk amongst us in the flesh of men, I have heard their voices speak from the mouths of the hougan, I have *summoned* them.'

'Yeah, right.'

He looked at me searchingly, offended belief melting slowly into something else. His voice loosened and flowed down to a murmur. 'This is strange, Kovacs. You have a faith as deep as mine. The only thing I wonder is why you need so badly not to believe.'

That sat between us for almost a minute before I touched it. The noise from surrounding tables faded out and even the wind out of the north seemed to be holding its breath. Then I leaned forward, speaking less to communicate than to dispel the laser-lit recall in my head.

'You're wrong, Hand,' I said quietly. 'I'd love to have access to all this shit you believe. I'd love to be able to summon someone who's responsible for this fuck-up of a creation. Because then I'd be able to kill them. Slowly.'

Back in the machine, Hand's virtual self worked the long shortlist down to eleven. It took nearly three months to do it. Run at the AI's top capacity of three hundred and fifty times real time, the whole process was over shortly before midnight.

By that time, the intensity of the conversation up on the roof had mellowed, first into an exchange of experiential reverie, a kind of rummaging around in the things we had seen and done that tended to support our individual world views, and thence to increasingly vague observations on life threaded onto long mutual silences as we stared beyond the ramparts of the tower and out into the desert night. Hand's pocket bleep broke into the powered-down mood like a note shattering glass.

We went down to look at what we had, blinking in the suddenly harsh lights inside the tower and yawning. Less than an hour later, as midnight turned over and the new day began, we turned off Hand's virtual self and uploaded ourselves into the machine in his place.

Final selection.

CHAPTER FOURTEEN

In recall, their faces come back to me.

Not the faces of the beautiful rad-resistant Maori combat sleeves they wore up to Dangrek and the smoking ruins of Sauberville. Instead, I see the faces they owned before they died. The faces Semetaire claimed and sold back into the chaos of the war. The faces they remembered themselves as, the faces they presented in the innocuous hotel-suite virtuality where I first met them.

The faces of the dead.

Ole Hansen:

Ludicrously pale Caucasian, cropped hair like snow, eyes the calm blue of the digit displays on medical equipment in non-critical mode. Shipped in whole from Latimer with the first wave of cryocapped UN reinforcements, back when everyone thought Kemp was going to be a six-month pushover.

'This had better not be another desert engagement.' There were still patches of sunscorched red across his forehead and cheekbones. 'Because if it is, you can just put me back in the box. That cellular melanin itches like fuck.'

'It's cold where we're going,' I assured him. 'Latimer City winter at warmest. You know your team is dead?'

A nod. 'Saw the flash from the 'copter. Last thing I remember. It figures. Captured marauder bomb. I told them to just blow the motherfucker where it lay. You can't talk those things round. Too stubborn.'

Hansen was part of a crack demolitions unit called the Soft

Touch. I'd heard of them on the Wedge grapevine. They had a reputation for getting it right most of the time. Had had.

'You going to miss them?'

Hansen turned in his seat and looked across the virtual hotel room to the hospitality unit. He looked back at Hand.

'May I?'

'Help yourself.'

He got up and went to the forest of bottles, selected one and poured amber liquid into a tumbler until it was brim full. He raised the drink in our direction, lips tight and blue eyes snapping.

'Here's to the Soft Touch, wherever their fragmented fucking atoms may be. Epitaph: they should have listened to fucking orders. They'd fucking be here now.'

He poured the drink down his throat in a single smooth motion, grunted deep in his throat and tossed the glass away across the room underhand. It hit the carpeted floor with an undramatic thump and rolled to the wall. Hansen came back to the table and sat down. There were tears in his eyes, but I guess that was the alcohol.

'Any other questions?' he asked, voice ripped.

Yvette Cruickshank:

A twenty-year-old, face so black it was almost blue, bone structure that belonged somewhere on the forward profile of a high-altitude interceptor, a dreadlocked mane gathered up the height of a fist before it spilled back down, hung with dangerous-looking steel jewellery and a couple of spare quickplant plugs, coded green and black. The jacks at the base of her skull showed three more.

'What are those?' I asked her.

'Linguapack, Thai and Mandarin, Ninth Dan Shotokan,' she fingered her way up the braille-tagged feathers in a fashion that suggested she could probably rip and change blind and under fire. 'Advanced Field Medic.'

'And the ones in your hair?'

'Satnav interface and concert violin.' She grinned. 'Not much call for that one recently, but it keeps me lucky.' Her face fell with comic abruptness that made me bite my lip. 'Kept.'

'You've requested rapid deployment posts seven times in the last year,' said Hand. 'Why is that?'

She gave him a curious look. 'You already asked me that.'

'Different me.'

'Oh, I get it. Ghost in the machine. Yeah, well, like I said before. Closer focus, more influence over combat outcomes, better toys. You know, you smiled more the last time I said that.'

Jiang Jianping:

Pale Asiatic features, intelligent eyes with a slightly inward cast, and a light smile. You had the impression that he was contemplating some subtly amusing anecdote he'd just been told. Aside from the callused edges of his hands and a looseness of stance below his black coveralls, there was little to hint at his trade. He looked more like a slightly weary teacher than someone who knew fifty-seven separate ways to make a human body stop working.

'This expedition,' he murmured, 'is presumably not within the general ambit of the war. It is a commercial matter, yes?'

I shrugged. 'Whole war's a commercial matter, Jiang.'

'You may believe that.'

'So may you,' said Hand severely. 'I am privy to government communiques at the highest level, and I'm telling you. Without the Cartel, the Kempists would have been in Landfall last winter.'

'Yes. That is what I was fighting to prevent.' He folded his arms. 'That is what I *died* to prevent.'

'Good,' said Hand briskly. 'Tell us about that.'

'I have already answered this question. Why do you repeat it?' The Mandrake exec rubbed at his eye.

'That wasn't me. It was a screening construct. There hasn't been time to review the data so, please.'

'It was a night assault in the Danang plain, a mobile relay station for the Kempists' marauder-bomb management system.'

'You were part of that?' I looked at the ninja in front of me with new respect. In the Danang theatre, the covert strikes on Kemp's communications net were the only real success the government could claim in the last eight months. I knew soldiers whose lives had been saved by the operation. The propaganda channels had still been trumpeting the news of strategic victory about the time my platoon and I were getting shot to pieces up on the Northern Rim.

'I was honoured enough to be appointed cell commander.'

Hand looked at his palm, where data was scrolling down like some mobile skin disease. Systems magic. Virtual toys.

'Your cell achieved its objectives, but you were killed when they pulled out. How did that happen?'

'I made a mistake.' Jiang enunciated the words with the same distaste he had pronounced Kemp's name.

'And what was that?' No one could have given the Mandrake exec points for tact.

'I believed the automated sentry systems would deactivate when the station was blown. They did not.'

'Oops.'

He flicked a glance at me.

'My cell could not withdraw without cover. I stayed behind.'

Hand nodded. 'Admirable.'

'It was my error. And it was a small price to pay to halt the Kempist advance.'

'You're not a big Kemp fan, are you, Jiang?' I kept my tone careful. It looked as if we'd got a believer here.

'The Kempists preach a revolution,' he said scornfully, 'But what will change if they take power on Sanction IV?'

I scratched my ear. 'Well, there'll be a lot more statues of Joshua Kemp in public places, I imagine. Apart from that, probably not much.'

'Exactly. And for this he has sacrificed how many hundreds of thousands of lives?'

'Hard to say. Look, Jiang, we're not Kempists. If we get what we want, I can promise you there'll be a big renewed interest in making sure Kemp gets nowhere near power on Sanction IV. Will that do?'

He placed his hands flat on the table and studied them for a while.

'Do I have an alternative?' he asked.

Ameli Vongsavath:

A narrow, hawk-nosed face the colour of tarnished copper. Hair in a tidy pilot cut that was growing out, henna streaking black. At the back, tendrils of it almost covered the silvered sockets that would take the flight symbiote cables. Beneath the left eye, black tattooed cross-hatching marked the cheekbone where the dataflow filaments would go in. The eye above was a liquid crystal grey, mismatched with the dark brown of the right-hand pupil.

'Hospital stock,' she said, when her augmented vision noticed where I was looking. 'I took some fire over Bootkinaree Town last year, and it blew out the dataflow. They patched me up in orbit.'

'You flew back out with blown datafeeds?' I asked sceptically. The overload would have shattered every circuit in her cheekbone and scorched tissue for half a handsbreadth in every direction. 'What happened to your autopilot?'

She grimaced. 'Fried.'

'So how did you run the controls in that state?'

'I shut down the machine and flew it on manual. Cut back to basic thrust and trim. This was a Lockheed Mitoma – their controls still run manually if you do that.'

'No, I meant how did you run the controls with the state *you* were in.'

'Oh.' She shrugged. 'I have a high pain threshold.'

Right.

Luc Deprez:

Tall and untidy, sandy blond hair grown longer than made sense for a battlefield, and in nothing you'd call a style. Face made up of sharp Caucasian angles, long bony nose, lantern jaw, eyes a curious shade of green. Sprawled at ease in the virtual chair, head tilted to one side as if he couldn't quite make us out in this light.

'So.' He acquired my Landfall Lights from the table with a long arm and shook one out of the packet. 'You going to tell me something about this gig?'

'No,' said Hand. 'It's confidential until you're on board.'

A throaty chuckle amidst smoke as he puffed the cigarette to life. 'That's what you said last time. And like I said to you last time, who the hell am I going to tell, man. You don't want to hire me, I'm going straight back into the tin can, right?'

'Nonetheless.'

'Alright. So you want to ask me something?'

'Tell us about your last covert assault tag,' I suggested.

'That's confidential.' He surveyed our unsmiling faces for a moment. 'Hey, that was a joke. I already told your partner all about it. Didn't he brief you?'

I heard Hand make a compressed sound.

'Ah, that was a construct,' I said hurriedly. 'We're hearing this for the first time. Run through it again for us.'

Deprez shrugged. 'Sure, why not? Was a hit on one of Kemp's sector commanders. Inside his cruiser.'

'Successful?'

He grinned at me. 'I would say so. The head, you know. It came off.'

'I just wondered. You being dead and all.'

'That was bad luck. The fuck's blood was deterrent toxin-loaded. Slow-acting. We didn't find out until we were airborne and heading out.'

Hand frowned. 'You got splashed?'

'No, man.' A pained expression flitted across the angular face. 'My partner, she caught the spray when the carotid went. Right in the eyes.' He plumed smoke at the ceiling. 'Too bad, she was our pilot.'

'Ah.'

'Yeah. We flew into the side of a building.' He grinned again. 'That was *fast*-acting, man.'

Markus Sutjiadi:

Beautiful with an uncanny geometric perfection of feature that could have sat alongside Lapinee somewhere in the net. Eyes almond in shade and shape, mouth a straight line, face tending towards an inverted isosceles triangle, blunted at its corners to provide the solid chin and wide forehead, straight black hair plastered down. Features curiously immobile, as if drugged into detachment. A sense of energy conserved, of waiting. The face of a global pin-up who'd played too much competition poker recently.

'Boo!' I couldn't resist it.

142

The almond eyes barely flickered.

'There are serious charges outstanding against you,' said Hand with a reproachful glance in my direction.

'Yes.'

We all waited for a moment, but Sutjiadi clearly didn't think there was any more to say on the subject. I started to like him.

Hand threw out a hand like a conjurer, and a screen evolved into the air just beyond his splayed fingers. *More* fucking system magic. I sighed and watched as a head and shoulders in a uniform like mine evolved beside a downscroll of biodata. The face was familiar.

'You murdered this man,' Hand said coldly. 'Would you like to explain why?'

'No.'

'He doesn't have to,' I gestured at the face on the screen. 'Dog Veutin gets a lot of people that way. I'm just interested to know *how* you managed to kill him.'

This time, the eyes lost some of their flatness, and his gaze glanced briefly off my Wedge insignia, confused.

'I shot him in the back of the head.'

I nodded. 'Shows initiative. Is he really dead?'

'Yes. I used a Sunjet on full charge.'

Hand system-magicked the screen away with a snap of his fingers. 'Your brig shuttle may have been shot out of the sky, but the Wedge think your stack probably survived. There's a reward posted for anyone who turns it up. They still want you for formal execution.' He looked sideways at me. 'As I understand it that tends to be a pretty unpleasant business.'

'Yeah, it is.' I'd seen a couple of these object lessons early on in my career with the Wedge. They took a long time.

'I have no interest in seeing you handed over to the Wedge,' said Hand. 'But I cannot risk this expedition on a man who will carry insubordination to these extremes. I need to know what happened.'

Sutjiadi was watching my face. I gave him the faintest hint of a nod.

'He ordered my men decimated,' he said tightly.

I nodded again, to myself this time. Decimation was, by all accounts, one of Veutin's favourite forms of liaison with local troops.

'And why was that?'

'Oh for fuck's sake, Hand,' I turned in my seat. 'Didn't you hear him? He was ordered to decimate his command, and he didn't want to. That kind of insubordination, I can live with.'

'There may be factors which—'

'We're wasting time,' I snapped, and turned back to Sutjiadi. 'Given the same situation again, is there anything you'd do differently?'

'Yes.' He showed me his teeth. I'm not sure I'd call it a grin. 'I'd have the Sunjet on wide beam. That way I'd have half-cooked his whole squad, and they wouldn't have been in any condition to arrest me.'

I tipped a glance back at Hand. He was shaking his head, one hand up to his eyes.

Sun Liping:

Dark Mongol eyes shelved in epicanthic folds on high, broad cheekbones. A mouth poised in a faint downturn that might have been the aftermath of rueful laughter. Fine lines in the tanned skin and a solid fall of black hair draped over one shoulder and held firmly in place by a big silver static field generator. An aura of calm, equally unshakeable.

'You killed yourself?' I asked doubtfully

'So they tell me.' The downturned lips amped up to a crooked grimace. 'I remember pulling the trigger. It's gratifying to know my aim doesn't deteriorate under pressure.'

The slug from her sidearm had gone in under the right jaw line, ploughed directly through the centre of the brain and blown an admirably symmetrical hole in the top of her head on its way out.

'Hard to miss at that range,' I said with experimental brutality.

The calm eyes never flinched.

'I understand it can be done,' she said gravely.

Hand cleared his throat. 'Would you like to tell us *why* you did it?'

She frowned. 'Again?'

'That,' said Hand through slightly gritted teeth, 'was a debriefing construct, not me.'

'Oh.'

The eyes slanted sideways and up, searching, I guessed, for a retina-wired peripheral scroll down. The virtuality had been written not to render internal hardware, except in Mandrake personnel, but she showed no surprise at a lack of response so maybe she was just remembering it the old-fashioned way.

'It was a squadron of automated armour. Spider tanks. I was trying to undermine their response parameters, but there was a viral booby trap wired into the control systems. A Rawling variant, I believe.' The mild grimace again. 'There was very little time to take stock, as you can probably imagine, so I can't be sure. In any event, there was no time to jack out; the primary baffles of the virus had already welded me in. In the time I had before it downloaded fully, I could only come up with the one option.'

'Very impressive,' said Hand.

When it was done, we went back up to the roof to clear our heads. I leaned on a parapet and looked out over the curfewed quiet of Landfall while Hand went off to find some coffee. The terraces behind me were deserted, chairs and tables scattered like some hieroglyphic message left for orbital eyes. The night had cooled off while we were below, and the breeze made me shiver. Sun Liping's words came back to me.

Rawling variant.

It was the Rawling virus that had killed the Innenin beachhead. Had made Jimmy de Soto claw out his own eye before he died. State-of-the-art back then, cheap off-the-rack military surplus now. The only viral software Kemp's hard-pressed forces could afford.

Times change, but market forces are forever. History unreels, the real dead stay that way.

The rest of us get to go on.

Hand came back apologetically with machine-coffee canisters. He handed me mine and leaned on the parapet at my side.

'So what do you think?' he asked after a while.

'I think it tastes like shit.'

He chuckled. 'What do you think of our team?'

'They'll do.' I sipped at the coffee and brooded on the city below.

'I'm not overhappy about the ninja, but he's got some useful skills and he seems prepared to get killed in the line of duty, which is always a big advantage in a soldier. How long to prep the clones?'

'Two days. Maybe a little less.'

'It'll be twice that before these people are up to speed in a new sleeve. Can we do the induction in virtual?'

'I see no reason why not. The MAI can spin out hundred per cent accurate renderings for each clone from the raw data in the biolab machines. Running at three-fifty times real, we can give the whole team a full month in their new sleeves, on site in the Dangrek construct, all inside a couple of hours, real time.'

'Good,' I said, and wondered why it didn't feel that way.

'My own reservations are with Sutjiadi. I am not convinced that a man like that can be expected to take orders well.'

I shrugged. 'So give him the command.'

'Are you serious?'

'Why not? He's qualified for it. He's got the rank, and he's had the experience. Seems to have loyalty to his men.'

Hand said nothing. I could sense his frown across the half metre of parapet that separated us.

'What?'

'Nothing.' He cleared his throat. 'I had just. Assumed. You would want the command yourself.'

I saw the platoon again as the smart shrapnel barrage erupted overhead. Lightning flash, explosions, and then the fragments, skipping and hissing hungrily through the quicksilver flashing curtain of the rain. Crackling of blaster discharge in the background, like something ripping.

Screams.

What was on my face didn't feel like a smile, but evidently it was.

'What's so funny?'

'You've read my file, Hand.'

'Yes.'

'And you still thought I wanted the command. Are you fucking insane?'

CHAPTER FIFTEEN

The coffee kept me awake.

Hand went to bed or whatever canister he crawled into when Mandrake wasn't using him, and left me staring at the desert night. I searched the sky for Sol and found it glimmering in the east at the apex of a constellation the locals called the Thumb Home. Hand's words drifted back through me.

. . . So far from earth you have to work hard to pick out Sol in the night sky. We were carried here on a wind that blows in a dimension we cannot see or touch. Stored as dreams in the mind of a machine . . .

I shook it off, irritably.

It wasn't like I'd been born there. Earth was no more home to me than Sanction IV, and if my father had ever pointed Sol out to me in between bouts of drunken violence, I had no memory of it. Any significance that particular point of light had for me, I'd got off a disc. And from here, you couldn't even see the star that Harlan's World orbited.

Maybe that's the problem.

Or maybe it was just that I'd been there, to the legendary home of the human race, and now, looking up, I could imagine, a single astronomical unit out from the glimmering star, a world in spin, a city by the sea dropping away into darkness as night came on, or rolling back up and into the light, a police cruiser parked somewhere and a certain police lieutenant drinking coffee not much better than mine and maybe thinking . . .

That's enough, Kovacs.

For your information, the light you're watching arrive left fifty years before she was even born. And that sleeve you're fantasising about is in its sixties by now, if she's even wearing it still. Let it go.

Yeah, yeah.

I knocked back the dregs of the coffee, grimaced as it went down cold. By the look of the eastern horizon, dawn was on its way, and I had a sudden crushing desire not to be here when it arrived. I left the coffee carton standing sentinel on the parapet, and picked my way back through the scattered chairs and tables to the nearest elevator terminal.

The elevator dropped me the three floors to my suite and I made it along the gently curving corridor without meeting anyone. I was pulling the retina cup out of the door on its saliva-thin cable when the sound of footfalls in the machined quiet sent me back against the opposite wall, right hand reaching for the single interface gun I still carried from habit tucked into the back of my waistband.

Spooked.

You're in the Mandrake Tower, Kovacs. Executive levels. Not even dust gets up here without authorisation. Get a fucking grip, will you.

'Kovacs?'

Tanya Wardani's voice.

I swallowed and pushed myself away from the wall. Wardani rounded the curve of the corridor and stood looking at me with what seemed like an unusual proportion of uncertainty in her stance.

'I'm sorry, did I scare you?'

'No.' Reaching again for the retina cup, which had backreeled into the door when I went for the Kalashnikov.

'Have you been up all night?'

'Yes.' I applied the cup to my eye and the door folded back. 'You?'

'More or less. I tried to get some sleep a couple of hours ago, but . . .' she shrugged. 'Too keyed up. Are you all done?'

'With the recruiting?'

'Yes.'

'Yes.'

'How are they?'

'Good enough.'

The door made an apologetic chiming sound, drawing attention to the lack of entry effected so far.

'Are you—'

'Do you—' I gestured.

'Thanks.' She moved, awkwardly, and stepped in ahead of me.

The suite lounge was walled in glass that I'd left at semi-opaque when I went out. City lights specked the smoky surface like deep-fry caught glowing in a Millsport trawler's nets. Wardani halted in the middle of the subtly furnished living space and turned about.

'I—'

'Have a seat. The mauve ones are all chairs.'

'Thanks, I still can't quite get used to—'

'State of the art.' I watched as she perched on the edge of one of the modules, and it tried in vain to lift and shape itself around her body. 'Want a drink?'

'No. Thanks.'

'Pipe?'

'God, no.'

'So how's the hardware?'

'It's good.' She nodded, more to herself than anyone. 'Yes. Good enough.'

'Good.'

'You think we're nearly ready?'

'I—' I pushed away the flash-rip behind my eyes and crossed to one of the other seats, making a performance of settling into it. 'We're waiting for developments up there. You know that.'

'Yes.'

A shared quiet.

'Do you think they'll do it?'

'Who? The Cartel?' I shook my head. 'Not if they can help it. But Kemp might. Look, Tanya. It may not even happen. But whether it does or not, there's nothing any of us can do about it. It's too late for that kind of intervention now. Way war works. Abolition of the individual.'

'What's that? Some kind of Quellist epigram?'

I smiled. 'Loosely paraphrased, yes. You want to know what Quell had to say about war? About all violent conflict?'

She made a restless motion. 'Not really. OK, sure. Tell me. Why not? Tell me something I haven't heard before.'

'She said wars are fought over hormones. Male hormones, largely. It's not about winnning or losing at all, it's about hormonal discharge. She wrote a poem about it, back before she went underground. Let's see—'

I closed my eyes and thought back to Harlan's World. A safe house in the hills above Millsport. Stolen bioware stacked in a corner, pipes and post-op celebration wreathing the air. Idly arguing politics with Virginia Vidaura and her crew, the infamous Little Blue Bugs. Quellist quotes and poetry bantered back and forth.

'You in pain?'

I opened my eyes and shot her a reproachful glance. 'Tanya, this stuff was mostly written in Stripjap. That's a Harlan's World trade tongue – gibberish to you. I'm trying to remember the Amanglic version.'

'Well, it looks painful. Don't knock yourself out on my account.'

I held up a hand. 'Goes like this:

> *Male-sleeved;*
> *Stop up your hormones*
> *Or spend them in moans*
> *Of other calibre*
> *(We'll reassure you – the load is large enough)*

> *Blood-pumped*
> *Pride in your prowess*
> *Will fail you, fuck you*
> *And everything you touch*
> *(You'll reassure us – the price was small enough)*'

I sat back. She sniffed.

'Bit of an odd stance for a revolutionary. Didn't she lead some kind of bloody uprising? Fight to the death against Protectorate tyranny, or something?'

'Yeah. Several kinds of bloody uprising, in fact. But there's no evidence she actually died. She disappeared in the last battle for Millsport. They never recovered a stack.'

'I don't really see how storming the gates of this Millsport gels with that poem.'

I shrugged. 'Well, she never really changed her views on the roots of violence, even in the thick of it. Just realised it couldn't be avoided, I guess. Changed her actions instead, to suit the terrain.'

'That's not much of a philosophy.'

'No, it isn't. But Quellism was never very big on dogma. About the only credo Quell ever subscribed to was *Face the Facts*. She wanted that on her tomb. *Face the Facts*. That meant dealing with them creatively, not ignoring them or trying to pretend they're just some historical inconvenience. She always said you can't control a war. Even when she was starting one.'

'Sounds a little defeatist to me.'

'Not at all. It's just recognition of the danger. Facing the facts. Don't start wars if you can possibly avoid it. Because once you do, it's out of any sane control. No one can do anything except try to survive while it runs its hormonal course. Hold on to the rod and ride it out. Stay alive, and wait for the discharge.'

'Whatever.' She yawned and looked out of the window. 'I'm not very good at waiting, Kovacs. You'd think being an archaeologue would have cured me of that, wouldn't you?' A shaky little laugh. 'That, and. The camp—'

I stood up abruptly. 'Let me get you that pipe.'

'No.' She hadn't moved, but her voice was nailed down solid. 'I don't need to forget anything, Kovacs. I need—'

She cleared her throat.

'I need you to do something for me. With me. What you did to me. Before, I mean. What you did has.' She looked down at her hands. 'Had an impact I didn't. Didn't expect.'

'Ah.' I sat down again. 'That.'

'Yes, that.' There was a flicker of anger in her tone now. 'I suppose it makes sense. It's an emotion-bending process.'

'Yes, it is.'

'Yes, it is. Well, there's one particular emotion I need bending back into place now, and I don't really see any other way to do that than by fucking you.'

'I'm not sure that—'

'I don't care,' she said violently. 'You changed me. You *fixed* me.' Her voice quietened. 'I suppose I should be grateful, but that isn't how it feels. I don't feel grateful, I feel *fixed*. You've created this. Imbalance in me, and I want that part of me back.'

'Look, Tanya, you aren't really in any condition—'

'Oh, that.' She smiled thinly. 'I appreciate I'm not exactly sexually attractive right now, except maybe—'

'Wasn't what I meant—'

'To a few freaks who like starved pubescents to fuck. No, we'll need to *fix* that. We need to go virtual for this.'

I struggled to shake off a numbing sense of unreality. 'You want to do this *now*?'

'Yes, I do.' Another sliced-off smile. 'It's interfering with my sleep patterns, Kovacs. And right now I need my sleep.'

'Do you have somewhere in mind?'

'Yes.' It was like a children's game of dare.

'So where is that exactly?'

'Downstairs.' She got up and looked down at me. 'You know, you ask a lot of questions for a man that's about to get laid.'

Downstairs was a floor about midway up the tower which the elevator announced as a recreational level. The doors opened onto the unpartitioned space of a fitness centre, machines bulking insect-like and menacing in the unlit gloom. Towards the back, I spotted the tilted webs of a dozen or so virtualink racks.

'We doing this out here?' I asked uncomfortably.

'No. Closed chambers at the back. Come *on*.'

We passed through the forest of stilled machines, lights flickering up above and amongst them, then flickering out again as we moved on. I watched the process out of a neurasthenic grotto that had been growing up around me like coral since before I came down from the roof. Too much virtuality will do that to you sometimes. There's this vague feeling of abrasion in the head when you disconnect, a disquieting sense that reality isn't quite sharp enough any more, a waxing and waning fuzziness that might be what the edge of madness feels like.

The cure for this definitely is *not* more virtual time.

There were nine closed chambers, modular blisters swelling out of the end wall under their respective numbers. Seven and eight were cracked open, spilling low orange light around the line of the hatch. Wardani stopped in front of seven and the door hinged outward. The orange light expanded pleasantly in the gap, tuned into soft hypnomode. No dazzle. She turned to look back at me.

'Go ahead,' she said. 'Eight is slaved to this one. Just hit "consensual" on the menu pad.'

And she disappeared into the warm orange glow.

Inside module eight, someone had seen fit to cover the walls and roofing with empathist psychogram art, which in the hypnomode lighting seemed little more than a random set of fishtail swirls and spots. Then again, that's what most empathist stuff looks like to me in any light. The air was just the right side of warm and beside the automould couch there was a complicated spiral of metal to hang clothes.

I stripped off and settled on the automould, pulled down the headgear and swiped the flashing consensual diamond as the displays came online. I just remembered to knock out the physical feedback baffle option before the system kicked in.

The orange light appeared to thicken, taking on a foggy substance through which the psychogram swirls and dots swam like complex equations or maybe some kind of pond life. I had a moment to wonder if the artist had intended either of those comparisons – empathists are a weird lot – and then the orange was fading and shredding away like steam, and I stood in an immense tunnel of black vented metal panels, lit only by lines of flashing red diodes that receded to infinity in both directions.

In front of me, more of the orange fog boiled up out of a vent and shredded into a recognisably female form. I watched fascinated as Tanya Wardani began to emerge from the general outline, made at first entirely of flickering orange smoke, then seemingly veiled in it from head to foot, then clad only in patches, and then, as these tore away, clad in nothing at all.

Glancing down at myself, I saw I was similarly naked.

'Welcome to the loading deck.'

Looking up again, my first thought was that she had already gone to work on herself. Most constructs load on self-images held in the memory, with subroutines to beat anything too delusional – you end up looking pretty much the way you do in reality, less a couple of kilos and maybe plus a centimetre or two. The version of Tanya Wardani I was looking at didn't have those kind of discrepancies – it was more a general sheen of health that she didn't yet have back in the real world, or perhaps just the lack of a similar, more grimy sheen of *unhealth*. The eyes were less sunken, the cheek and collar bones less pronounced. Under the slightly pouched breasts, the ribs were there, but fleshed far past what I'd imagined below her draped clothing.

'They're not big on mirrors in the camp,' she said, maybe reading something in my expression. 'Except for interrogation. And after a while you try not to see yourself in windows walking past. I probably still look a lot worse than I think I do. Especially after that instant fix you loaded into me.'

I couldn't think of anything even remotely appropriate to say.

'You on the other hand . . .' She stepped forward and, reaching out low, caught me by the prick. 'Well, let's see what you've got here.'

I was hard almost instantly.

Maybe it was something written into the protocols of the system, maybe just too long without the release. Or maybe there was some unclean fascination in anticipating the use of this body with its lightly accented marks of privation. Enough to hint artfully at abuse, not enough to repel. *Freaks who like starved pubescents to fuck?* No telling how a combat sleeve might be wired at this level. Or any male sleeve, come to that. Dig down into the blood depths of hormonal bedrock, where violence and sex and power grow fibrously entwined. It's a murky, complicated place down there. No telling what you'll drag up once you start excavating.

'That's good,' she breathed, abruptly close to my ear. She had not let go. 'But I don't rate this much. You've not been looking after yourself, soldier.'

Her other hand spread wide and scraped up my belly from the roots of my prick to the arc of my ribcage. Like a carpenter's sanding glove, planing back the layering of flab that had begun to thicken over my sleeve's tank-grown abdominal musculature. I glanced down, and saw with a slight visceral shock that some of the flab really had started to plane off, fading out with the motion of her flattened palm. It left a warm feeling threaded through the muscle beneath, like whisky going down.

Sy-system magic, I managed through the spasm as she tugged hard at me with the gripping hand and repeated the upward smoothing gesture with the other.

I lifted my own hands towards her, and she skipped back.

'Uh-uh.' She took another step away. 'I'm not ready yet. Look at me.'

She lifted both hands and cupped her breasts. Pushed upward with the heels of her palms, then let them fall back, fuller, larger. The nipples – had one of them been broken before? – swollen dark and conical like chocolate sheathing on the copper skin.

'Like that?' she asked.

'Very much.'

She repeated the open-handed grasping motion, topping it with a circular massaging action. When she let go this time, her breasts were well on their way to the dimensions of one of Djoko Roespinoedji's gravity-defying concubines. She reached back and did something similar to her buttocks, turning to show me the cartoon rounding she'd given them. She bent forward and pulled the cheeks apart.

'Lick me,' she said, with sudden urgency.

I went down on one knee and pressed my face into the crease, spearing forward with my tongue, working at the tight whorl of closed sphincter. I wrapped an arm around one long thigh to steady myself and with the other hand I reached up and found her already wet. The ball of my thumb sank into her from the front as my tongue worked deeper from the rear, both rubbing soft synchronised circles amid her insides. She grunted, somewhere at the base of her throat, and we

Shifted

Into liquid blue. The floor was gone, and most of the gravity with it. I thrashed and lost my thumbhold. Wardani twisted languidly around and fastened to me like belaweed around a rock. The fluid was not water; it had left our skins slick against each other, and I could breath it as well as if it were tropical air. I gasped my lungs full of it as Wardani slithered down, biting at my chest and stomach, and finally laid hands and mouth on my hard-on.

I didn't last long. Floating in the infinite blue while Tanya Wardani's newly pneumatic breasts pressed against my thighs and her nipples traced up and down on my oiled skin and her mouth sucked and her curled fingers pumped, I had just enough time to notice a light source above us before my neck muscles started to tauten, cranking my head back, and the twitching messages along my nerves gathered together for a final climactic rush.

There was a scratch replay vibrato effect built into the construct. My orgasm went on for over thirty seconds.

As it tailed off, Tanya Wardani floated up past me, hair spread around her face, threads of semen blown out amidst bubbles from the corners of her grin. I struck out and grabbed one passing thigh, dragged her back into range.

She flexed in the water analogue as my tongue sank into her, and more bubbles ran out of her mouth. I caught the reverberation of her moan through the fluid like the sympathetic vibration of jet engines in the pit of my stomach, and felt myself stiffening in response. I pressed my tongue down harder, forgetting to breathe and then discovering I didn't actually need to for a long time. Wardani's writhing grew more urgent and she crooked her legs around my back to anchor herself in place. I cupped her buttocks and squeezed, pushing my face into the folds of her cunt, then slid my thumb back inside her and recommenced the soft circular motion in counterpoint to the spiralling of my tongue. She gripped my head in both hands and crushed my face against her. Her writhings became thrashings, her moans a sustained shout that filled my ears like the sound of surf overhead. I sucked. She stiffened, and screamed, and then shuddered for minutes.

We drifted to the surface together. An astronomically unlikely red giant sun was sinking at the horizon, bathing the suddenly normalised water around us in stained-glass light. Two moons sat high in the eastern sky and behind us waves broke on a white sand beach fringed by palms.

'Did you. Write this?' I asked, treading water and nodding at the view.

'Hardly.' She wiped water out of her eyes and slicked back her hair with both hands. 'It's off the rack. I checked out what they had this afternoon. Why, you like it?'

'So far. But I have a feeling that sun is an astronomical impossibility.'

'Yeah, well, breathing underwater's not overly realistic either.'

'I didn't get to breathe.' I held my hands above the water in claws, miming the grip she'd had on my head, and pulled a suffocated face. 'This bring back any memories?'

To my amazement, she flushed scarlet. Then she laughed, splashed water in my face and struck out for the shore. I trod water for a moment, laughing too, and then went after her.

The sand was warm, powder fine and system-magically unwilling to stick to wet flesh. Behind the beach, coconuts fell sporadically from the palms and, unless collected, broke down into fragments which were carried away by tiny jewel-coloured crabs.

We fucked again at the water's edge, Tanya Wardani seated astride my cock, cartoon ass bedded soft and warm on my crossed legs. I buried my face in her breasts, settled hands at her hips and lifted her gently up and down until the shuddering started in her again, caught me like a contagious fever and ran through us both. The scratch replay subroutine had a resonance system built in that cycled the orgasm back and forth between us like an oscillating signal, swamping and ebbing for what felt like forever.

It was love. Perfect passion compatibility, trapped, distilled and amped up almost beyond bearing.

'You knock out the baffles?' she asked me, a little breathlessly, after.

'Of course. You think I want to go through all this and *still* come out swilling full of semen and sex hormones?'

'*Go through?*' She lifted her head from the sand, outraged.

I grinned back. 'Sure. This is for *your* benefit, Tanya. I wouldn't be here other— Hoy, no throwing sand.'

'Fucking—'

'Look—'

I fended off the fistful of sand with one arm and pushed her into the surf. She went over backwards, laughing. I stood up in a ludicrous Micky Nozawa fighting stance, while she picked herself up. Something out of *Siren Fist Demons*.

'Don't try to lay your profane hands on me, woman.'

'Looks to me like you want to have hands laid on you,' she said, shaking back her hair and pointing.

It was true. The sight of the system magic-enhanced body, beaded with water, had the signals flickering through my nerve endings again, and my glans was already filling up with blood like a ripening plum in time-lapse fast-forward sequence.

I gave up the guard, and glanced around the construct. 'You know, off the rack or not, this is some good shit, Tanya.'

'Last year's *CyberSex Down* seal of approval, apparently.' She shrugged. 'I took a chance. You want to try the water again? Or, apparently there's this waterfall thing back through the trees.'

'Sounds good to me.'

On the way past the front line of palms with their huge phallic trunks lifting like dinosaur necks off the sand, I scooped up a newly fallen coconut. The crabs scattered with comic speed, scuttling for burrows in the sand from which they poked cautious eyestalks. I turned the coconut over in my hands. It had landed with a small chunk already torn out of the green shell, exposing soft, rubbery flesh beneath. Nice touch. I punctured the inner membrane with my thumb and tipped it back like a gourd. The milk inside was improbably chilled.

Another nice touch.

The forest floor beyond was conveniently clear of sharp debris and insects. Water poured and splashed somewhere with attention-grabbing clarity. An obvious path led through the palm trunks towards the sound. We walked, hand in hand, beneath rainforest foliage filled with brightly-coloured birds and small monkeys making suspiciously harmonic noises.

The waterfall was a two-tier affair, pouring down in a long plume into a wide basin, then tumbling through rocks and rapids to another smaller pool where the drop was less. I arrived slightly ahead of her and stood on wet rocks at the edge of the second pool, arms akimbo, looking down. I repressed a grin. The moment was cleared for her to push me in, trembling with the potential.

Nothing.

I turned to look at her, and saw she was trembling slightly.

'Hoy, Tanya.' I took her face between my hands. 'Are you OK? What's the matter?'

But I knew what the *motherfucking* matter was.

Because, Envoy techniques or not, healing is a complex, creeping process, and it'll glitch on you as soon as your back's turned.

The *motherfucking* camp.

The low-key arousal fled, leaching out of my system like saliva from a mouthful of lemon. The fury sheeted up through me.

The *motherfucking* war.

If I'd had Isaac Carrera and Joshua Kemp there, in the middle of all that edenic beauty, I'd have torn their entrails out with my bare hands, knotted them together and kicked them into the pool to drown.

Can't drown in this water, sneered the part of me that would never shut down, the smug Envoy control. *You can breathe in this water.*

Maybe men like Kemp and Carrera couldn't.

Yeah, right.

So instead, I caught Tanya Wardani around the waist, and crushed her against me, and jumped for us both.

CHAPTER SIXTEEN

I came out of it with an alkaline smell in my nostrils and my belly sticky with fresh semen. My balls ached as if they'd been kicked. Over my head, the display had cleared to standby. A time-check pulsed in one corner. I'd been under less than two minutes, real time.

I sat up groggily.

'Fuck. Me.' I cleared my throat, and looked around. Fresh self-moistening towelling hung from a roll behind the automould, presumably with just this in mind. I tore off a handful and wiped myself down, still trying to blink the virtuality out of my eyes.

We'd fucked in the waterfall pool, languid underwater once Wardani's trembling had passed.

We'd fucked again on the beach.

We'd fucked back up on the loading deck, a last-chance-grabbed-at-leaving sort of thing.

I tore off more towel, wiped my face and rubbed at my eyes. I dressed slowly, stowed the smart gun, wincing as it prodded down from my waistband into my tender groin. I found a mirror on the wall of the chamber and peered into it, trying to sort out what had happened to me in there.

Envoy psychoglue.

I'd used it on Wardani without really thinking about it, and now she was up and walking around. That was what I'd wanted. The dependency whiplash was an almost inevitable side-effect, but so what? It was the kind of thing that didn't much matter in the usual Envoy run of things – as likely as not you were in combat with other things to worry about, often you'd moved on by the time it became a problem the subject had to deal with. What didn't generally happen was the kind of restorative purging Wardani had prescribed for herself and then gone after.

I couldn't predict how that would work.

I'd never known it to happen before. Never even *seen* it before.

I couldn't work out what she'd made me feel in turn.

And I wasn't learning anything new looking at myself in the mirror.

I built a shrug and a grin, and walked out of the chamber into the pre-dawn gloom among the stilled machines. Wardani was waiting outside, by one of the open-rig webs and

Not alone.

The thought jarred through my soggy nervous system, painfully sluggish, and then the unmistakeable spike-and-ring configuration at the projection end of a Sunjet was pushed against the back of my neck.

'You want to avoid any sudden moves, chum.' It was a strange accent, an equatorial twang to it even through the voiceprint distorter. 'Or you and your girlfriend here are going to be wearing no heads.'

A professional hand snaked round my waist, plucked the Kalashnikov from its resting place and tossed it away across the room. I heard the muffled clunk as it hit the carpeted floor and slid.

Try to pinpoint it.

Equatorial accent.

Kempists.

I looked over at Wardani, her oddly limp-hanging arms, and the figure who held a smaller hand blaster to her nape. He was dressed in the form-fitting black of a stealth assault suit and masked with clear plastic that moved in random waves over his face, distorting the features continually, except for two little watchful blue-tinted windows over the eyes.

There was a pack on his back that had to carry whatever intrusion hardware they'd used to get in here. Had to be a biosigns imaging set, counterfeed code sampler and securisys sandbagger in there, minimum.

High fucking tech.

'You guys are *so* dead,' I said, trying for amused calm.

'*Extra* funny, chum.' The one who'd taken me tugged at my arm and pulled me around so I was looking down the ramping chute of the Sunjet. Same dress code, same running plastic mask. Same black pack. Two more clone-identical forms bulked behind him, watching opposite ends of the room. Their Sunjets were cradled low, deceptively casual. My enthusiasm for the odds collapsed like a set of unplugged LED displays.

Play for time.

'Who sent you guys?'

'See,' said the spokesman, voice squelching in and out of focus. 'It's rigged this way. Her we want, you're just carbon walking. Limit that mouth, maybe we lift you too, just for tidiness. Keep gritting me, I'll make a mess just to see your Envoy grey cells fly. Am I coming through?'

I nodded, desperately trying to mop up the post-coital languor that had drenched my system. Shifting my stance slightly . . .

Aligning from memory . . .

'Good, then let's have your arms.' He dropped his left hand to his belt and produced a contact stunner. The aim of the Sunjet never wavered in the right-hand grip. The mask flexed in an approximation of a smile. 'One at a time, of course.'

I raised my left arm and held it out to him. Flexed my right hand behind me, riding out the sense of impotent fury, so the palm rippled.

The little grey device came down on my wrist, charged light winking. He had to shift the Sunjet, of course, or the dead weight of my arm was going to come down on it like a club when the stunner fired . . .

Now. So low even the neurachem barely picked it out. A thin whine through the conditioned air.

The stunner fired.

Painless. Cold. A localised version of what it felt like to get shot with a beam stunner. The arm flopped like a dead fish, narrowly missing the Sunjet despite its new alignment. He twitched slightly aside, but it was a relaxed move. The mask grinned.

'That's good. Now the other one.'

I smiled and shot him—

Grav microtech – a weapons engineering breakthrough from the house of Kalashnikov.

—from the hip. Three times across the chest, hoping to drill clean through whatever armour he was wearing and into the backpack. Blood—

Across short distances, the Kalashnikov AKS91 interface gun will lift and fly direct to an implanted bioalloy home plate.

—drenched the stealth suit, tickled my face with backblown spray. He staggered, Sunjet wagging like an admonishing finger. His colleagues—

Almost silent, the generator delivers total capacity in a ten-second burst.

—hadn't worked it out yet. I fired high at the two behind him, probably hit one of them somewhere. They rolled away, grabbing cover. Return fire crackled around me, nowhere close.

I came around, dragging the numbed arm like a shoulder bag, looking for Wardani and her captor.

'Fucking don't, man, I'll—'

And shot through the writhing plastic of the mask.

The slug punched him back a clean three metres, into the spidery arms of a climbing machine, where he hung, slumped and used up.

Wardani dropped to the ground, bonelessly. I threw myself down, chased by fresh Sunjet fire. We landed nose to nose.

'You OK?' I hissed.

She nodded, cheek pressed flat to the floor, shoulders twitching as she tried to move her stunned arms.

'Good. Stay there.' I flailed my own numbed limb around and searched the machine jungle for the two remaining Kempists.

No sign. Could be fucking anywhere. Waiting for a clear shot. *Fuck this.*

I lined up on the crumpled form of the squad leader, on the backpack. Two shots blew it apart, fragments of hardware jumping out of the exit holes in the fabric.

Mandrake security woke up.

Lights seared. Sirens shrieked from the roof, and an insectile storm of nanocopters issued from vents on the walls. They swooped over us, blinked glass bead eyes and passed us by. A few metres over, a flight of them rained laser fire down amidst the machines.

Screams.

An abortive Sunjet blast carving wildly through the air. The nanocopters it touched flamed and spun out like burning moths. The laser fire from the others redoubled, chickling.

Screams powering down to sobbing. The sickly stench of charred flesh made it across in ribbons to where I lay. It was like a homecoming.

The nanocopter swarm broke up, drifting away disinterestedly. A couple threw down parting rays as they left. The sobbing stopped.

Silence.

Beside me, Wardani eeled her knees under her, but could not get upright. No upper body strength in her recovering body. She looked wildly across at me. I propped myself up on my working arm, then levered myself to my feet.

'Stay there. I'll be back.'

I went reflexively to check on the corpses, ducking stray nanocopters.

The masks had frozen in rictus smiles, but faint ripples still ran through the plastic at intervals. As I watched the two the copters had killed, something fizzled under each head and smoke spiralled up.

'Oh, shit.'

I ran back to the one I'd shot in the face, the one caught upright in the machine, but it was the same story. The base of the skull had already charred black and ragged, and the head was listing slightly against one of the climbing machine's struts. Missed in the storm of fire from the nanocopters. Below the neat hole I'd put in the centre of the mask, the mouth grinned at me with plastic insincerity.

'Fuck.'

'*Kov*acs.'

'Yeah, sorry.' I stowed the smart gun and pulled Wardani unceremoniously to her feet. At the end of the room, the elevator opened and spilled out a squad of armed security.

I sighed. 'Here we go.'

They spotted us. The squad captain cleared her blaster.

'Remain still! Raise your hands!'

I lifted my working arm. Wardani shrugged.

'I'm not pissing about here, folks!'

'We're injured,' I called back. 'Contact stunners. And everyone else is dead, extremely. The bad guys had stack blowout failsafes. It's all over. Go wake Hand up.'

Hand took it quite well, considering. He got them to turn over one of the corpses and crouched beside it, poking at the charred spinal cord with a metal stylus.

'Molecular acid canister,' he said thoughtfully. 'Last year's Shorn Biotech. I didn't realise the Kempists had these yet.'

'They've got everything you've got, Hand. They've just got a lot less of it, that's all. Read your Brankovitch. "Trickledown in War-based Markets".'

'Yes, thank you, Kovacs.' Hand rubbed at his eyes. 'I already have a doctorate in Conflict Investment. I don't really need the gifted amateur reading list. What I would like to know, however, is what you two were doing down here at this time of the morning.'

I exchanged a look with Wardani. She shrugged.

'We were fucking,' she said.

Hand blinked.

'Oh,' he said. 'Already.'

'What's that supposed t—'

'Kovacs, please. You're giving me a headache.' He got up and nodded at the head of the forensic squad who was hovering nearby. 'OK, get them out of here. See if you can get a tissue match for those scrapes we took out of Find Alley and the canal head. File c221mh, central clearing'll let you have the codes.'

We all watched as the dead were loaded onto ground-effect gurneys and escorted to the elevators. Hand just caught himself returning the stylus to his jacket, and handed it to the last of the retreating forensic squad. He brushed the ends of his fingers absently against each other.

'Someone wants you back, Mistress Wardani,' he said. 'Someone with resources. I suppose that in itself ought to reassure me as to the value of our investment in you.'

Wardani made a faint, ironic bow.

'Someone with wires to the inside too,' I added sombrely. 'Even with a backpack full of intrusion gear, there's no way they got in here without help. You've got leakage.'

'Yes, so it would appear.'

'Who did you send to check out those shadows we brought back from the bar night before last?'

Wardani looked at me, alarmed.

'Someone followed us?'

I gestured at Hand. 'So he says.'

'Hand?'

'Yes, Mistress Wardani, that is correct. You were followed as far as Find Alley.' He sounded very tired, and the glance he shot at me was defensive. 'It was Deng, I think.'

'Deng? Are you serious? Shit, how long do you guys give line-of-duty casualties before you jam them back into a sleeve?'

'Deng had a clone on ice,' he snapped back. 'That's standard policy for security operations managers, and he got a virtual week of counselling and full-impact recreational leave before he was downloaded. He was fit for duty.'

'Was he? Why don't you call him?'

I was remembering what I'd said to him in the ID&A construct. *The men and women you work for would sell their own children into a brothel if it meant getting their hands on what I showed them tonight. And alongside that, my friend, you. Don't. Matter.*

Just killed is a fragile state of mind for the uninitiated. It makes you susceptible to suggestion. And Envoys are past masters at persuasion.

Hand had his audio phone open.

'Wake up Deng Zhao Jun please.' He waited. 'I see. Well, try that then.'

I shook my head.

'That good old spit-in-the-sea-that-nearly-drowned-you bravado, eh Hand? Barely over the death trauma, and you're throwing him back into action *on a related case?* Come on, put the phone away. He's gone. He's sold you out and skipped with the loose change.'

Hand's jaw knotted, but he kept the phone at his ear.

'Hand, I practically *told* him to do it.' I met the sideways-flung disbelief in his eyes. 'Yeah, go ahead. Blame me, if it makes you feel better. I told him Mandrake didn't give a shit about him, and you went ahead and proved it by cutting a deal with us. And then you put him on watchdog detail, just to rub it in.'

'I did not assign Deng, god*damn you Kovacs.*' He was hanging onto his temper by shreds, biting down on it. His hand was white-knuckled on the phone. 'And you had *no business* telling him anything. Now, shut the *fuck* up. *Yes*, yes this is Hand.'

He listened. Spoke controlled monosyllables acid-etched with frustration. Snapped the phone closed.

'Deng left the tower in his own transport early last night. He disappeared in the Old Clearing House mall a little before midnight.'

'Just can't get the staff these days, eh?'

'Kovacs.' The exec snapped out his hand, as if physically holding me at arm's length. His eyes were hard with mastered anger. 'I don't want to hear it. Alright? I don't. Want to hear it.'

I shrugged.

'No one ever does. That's why this sort of thing keeps on happening.' Hand breathed out, compressed.

'I am not going to debate employment law with you, Kovacs, at five in the fucking morning.' He turned on his heel. 'You two had better get your act together. We download into the Dangrek construct at nine.'

I looked sideways at Wardani, and caught a smirk. It was childishly contagious and it felt like hands linking behind the Mandrake exec's back.

Ten paces off, Hand stopped. As if he'd sensed it.

'Oh.' He turned to face us. 'By the way. The Kempists airburst a marauder bomb over Sauberville an hour ago. High yield, hundred per cent casualties.'

I caught the flare of white in Wardani's eye as she snatched her gaze away from mine. She stared at the lower middle distance. Mouth clamped.

Hand stood there and watched it happen.

'Thought you'd both like to know that,' he said.

CHAPTER SEVENTEEN

Dangrek.

The sky looked like old denim, faded blue bowl ripped with threads of white cloud at high altitude. Sunlight filtered through, bright enough to make me narrow my eyes. Warm fingers of it brushed over exposed portions of my skin. The wind had risen a little since last time, buffeting from the west. Little black drifts of fallout dusted off the vegetation around us.

At the headland, Sauberville was still burning. The smoke crawled up into the old denim sky like the wipings of heavily oiled fingers.

'Proud of yourself, Kovacs?'

Tanya Wardani muttered it in my ear as she walked past me to get a better look from further up the slope. It was the first thing she'd said to me since Hand broke the news.

I went after her.

'You've got a complaint about this, you'd better go register it with Joshua Kemp,' I told her when I caught up. 'And anyway, don't act like this is new. You knew it was coming like everybody else.'

'Yes, I'm just a little gorged on it right now.'

It was impossible to get away from. Screens throughout the Mandrake Tower had run it non-stop. Bright pinhead-to-bladder flash in silence, reeled in on some military documentary team's cameras, and then the sound. Gabbled commentary over a rolling thunder and the spreading mushroom cloud. Then the lovingly freeze-frame-advanced replays.

The MAI had gobbled it up and incorporated it for us. Wiped that irritating grey fuzz indeterminacy from the construct.

'Sutjiadi, get your team deployed.'

It was Hand's voice, drumming through the induction rig speaker. A loose exchange of military shorthand followed and in irritation I yanked the speaker away from its resting place behind my ear. I ignored the footfalls of someone tramping up the slope behind us and focused on the locked posture of Tanya Wardani's head and neck.

'I guess it was quick for them,' she said, still staring out at the headland.

'Like the song says. Nothing faster.'

'Mistress Wardani.' It was Ole Hansen, some echo of the arc-light intensity from his original blue eyes somehow burning through the wide-set dark gaze of his new sleeve. 'We'll need to see the demolition site.'

She choked back something that might have been a laugh, and didn't say the obvious thing.

'Sure,' she said instead. 'Follow me.'

I watched the two of them pick their way down the other side of the slope towards the beach.

'Hoy! Envoy guy!'

I turned unwillingly, and spotted Yvette Cruickshank navigating her Maori sleeve uncertainly up the slope towards me, Sunjet slung flat across her chest and a set of ranging lenses pushed up on her head. I waited for her to reach me, which she did without tripping in the long grass more than a couple of times.

'How's the new sleeve?' I called as she stumbled for the second time.

'It's—' She shook her head, closed the gap and started again, voice lowered back to normal. ''s a fraction strange, know what I mean?'

I nodded. My first re-sleeve was more than thirty subjective years in my past, objectively close to two centuries ago, but you don't forget. The initial re-entry shock never really goes away.

'Bit fucking *pallid*, too.' She pinched up the skin on the back of her hand and sniffed. 'How come I couldn't get some fine black cover like yours?'

'I didn't get killed,' I reminded her. 'Besides, once the radiation starts to bite, you're going to be glad. What you're wearing there needs about half the dosage I'll be taking to stay operational.'

She scowled. 'Still going to get us all in the end, though, isn't it.'

'It's only a sleeve, Cruickshank.'

'That's right, just give me some of that Envoy *cool*.' She barked a laugh and upended her Sunjet, gripping the short, thick barrel disconcertingly in one slim hand. Squinting up from the discharge channel and directly at me, she asked, 'Think you could go for a white-girl sleeve like this then?'

I considered. The Maori combat sleeves were long on limb and broad in the chest and shoulders. A lot of them, like this one, were pale-skinned, and being fresh out of the clone tanks accentuated the effect, but faces ran to high cheekbones, wide spaced eyes and flaring lips and noses. *White-girl sleeve* seemed a little harsh. And even inside the shapeless battlefield chameleochrome coveralls . . .

'You going to look like that,' Cruickshank remarked, 'you'd better be buying something.'

'Sorry. Just giving the question my full consideration.'

'Yeah. Skip it. I wasn't that worried. You were operational around here, weren't you?'

'A couple of months back.'

'So what was it like?'

I shrugged. 'People shooting at you. Air full of pieces of fast-moving metal looking for a home. Pretty standard stuff. Why?'

'I heard the Wedge got a pasting. That true?'

'It certainly looked that way from where I was standing.'

'So how come Kemp suddenly decides, from a position of strength, to cut and nuke?'

'Cruickshank.' I started and then stopped, unable to think of a way to get through the armour plate of youth she was wearing. She was twenty-two, and like all twenty-two year olds she thought she was the immortal focal point of this universe. Sure she'd been killed, but so far all that had done was prove the immortal part. It would not have occurred to her that there might be a world view in which what she saw was not only marginal but almost wholly irrelevant.

She was waiting for an answer.

'Look,' I said finally. 'No one told me what we were fighting for up here, and from what we got out of the prisoners we interrogated, I'd say they didn't know either. I gave up expecting this war to make sense a while ago, and I'd advise you to do the same if you plan on surviving much more of it.'

She raised an eyebrow, a mannerism that she hadn't quite got nailed in her new sleeve.

'So you don't know, then.'

'No.'

'Cruickshank!' Even with my own induction rig unhooked, I heard the tinny crash of Markus Sutjiadi's voice over the comlink. 'You want to get down here and work for a living like the rest of us?'

'Coming, cap.' She pulled a mouth-down face in my direction and started back down the slope. A couple of steps down, she stopped and turned back.

'Hey, Envoy guy.'

'Yeah?'

'That stuff about the Wedge taking a pasting? Wasn't a crit, OK. Just what I heard.'

I felt myself grinning at the carefully deployed sensitivity.

'Forget it, Cruickshank. Couldn't give a shit. I'm more bent out of shape you didn't like me drooling on you.'

'Oh.' She grinned back. 'Well, I guess I did ask.' Her gaze dropped to my crotch and she crossed her eyes for effect. 'What about I get back to you on that one?'

'Do that.'

The induction rig buzzed against my neck. I stuck it back in place and hooked up the mike.

'Yeah, Sutjiadi?'

'If it's not too much trouble, *sir*,' the irony dripped off the last word, 'would you mind leaving my soldiers alone while they deploy?'

'Yeah, sorry. Won't happen again.'

'Good.'

I was about to disconnect when Tanya Wardani's voice came across the net in soft expletives.

'Who's that?' snapped Sutjiadi. 'Sun?'

'I don't *fucking* believe this.'

'It's Mistress Wardani, sir.' Ole Hansen came in, laconically calm, over the muttered curses from the archaeologue. 'I think you'd better all get down here and take a look at this.'

I raced Hand to the beach and lost by a couple of metres. Cigarettes and damaged lungs don't count in a virtuality, so it must have been concern for Mandrake's investment that drove him. Very commendable. Still not attuned to their new sleeves, the rest of the party fell behind us. We reached Wardani alone.

We found her in much the same position she'd taken up facing the rockfall last time we'd been in the construct. For a moment, I couldn't see what she was looking at.

'Where's Hansen?' I asked stupidly.

'He went in,' she said, waving a hand forward. 'For what it's worth.'

Then I saw it. The pale bite-marks of recent blasting, gathered around a two-metre fissure opened in the fall, and a path winding out of sight beyond.

'Kovacs?' There was a brittle lightness to the query in Hand's tone.

'I see it. When did you update the construct?'

Hand stalked closer to examine the blasting marks. 'Today.'

Tanya Wardani nodded to herself. 'High-orbit satellite geoscan, right?'

'That's correct.'

'Well.' The archaeologue turned away and reached in her coat pocket for cigarettes. 'We aren't going to find anything out here then.'

'Hansen!' Hand cupped his hands and shouted into the fissure, the induction rig he was wearing apparently forgotten.

'I hear you.' The demolition expert's voice came thrumming back on the rig, detached and edged with a smirk. 'There's nothing back here.'

'Of course there isn't,' commented Wardani, to nobody in particular.

'. . . some kind of circular clearing, about twenty metres across, but the rocks look strange. Kind of fused.'

'That's improvisation,' said Hand impatiently into the rig mike. 'The MAI's guessing at what's in there.'

'Ask him if there's anything in the middle,' said Wardani, kindling her cigarette against the breeze off the sea.

Hand relayed the query. The answer crackled back over the set.

'Yeah, some kind of central boulder, maybe a stalagmite.'

Wardani nodded. 'That's your gate,' she said. 'Probably old echo-sounding data the MAI reeled in from some flyby area recon a while ago. It's trying to map the data with what it can see from the orbital view, and since it's got no reason to believe there's anything in there but rocks—'

'Someone's been here,' said Hand, jaw set.

'Well yes.' Wardani blew out smoke and pointed. 'Oh, and there's that.'

Anchored in the shallows a few hundred metres along the beach, a small, battered-looking trawler wagged back and forth in a longshore current. Her nets spilled over the side like something escaping.

The sky whited out.

It wasn't quite as rough a ride as the ID&A set had been, but still, the abrupt return to reality impacted on my system like a bath of ice, chilling extremities and sending a shiver deep through the centre of my guts. My eyes snapped open on the expensive empathist psychogram art.

'Oh, nice,' I grumbled, sitting up in the soft lighting and groping around for the 'trodes.

The chamber door hinged outward on a subdued hum. Hand stood in the doorway, clothing still fully not closed up, limned from behind by the brightness of normal lights. I squinted at him.

'Was that *really* necessary?'

'Get your shirt on, Kovacs.' He was closing his own at the neck as he spoke. 'We've got things to do. I want to be on the peninsula by this evening.'

'Aren't you overreacting a li—'

He was already turning away.

'Hand, the recruits aren't used to those sleeves yet. Not by a long way.'

'I left them in there.' He flung the words back over his shoulder. 'They can have another ten minutes – that's two days virtual time. Then we download them for real and *leave*. If someone's up at Dangrek ahead of us, they're going to be very sorry.'

'If they were there when Sauberville went down,' I shouted after him, suddenly furious. 'They're probably *already* very sorry. Along with everyone else.'

I heard his footsteps, receding up the corridor. Mandrake Man, shirt closed up, suit settling onto squared shoulders, moving forward. Enabled. About Mandrake's heavy-duty business, while I sat barechested in a puddle of my own unfocused rage.

PART THREE
Disruptive Elements

The difference between virtuality and life is very simple. In a construct you know everything is being run by an all-powerful machine. Reality doesn't offer this assurance, so it's very easy to develop the mistaken impression that you're in control.

Quellcrist Falconer *Ethics on the Precipice*

CHAPTER EIGHTEEN

There is no subtle way to deploy an IP vessel across half a planet. So we didn't try.

Mandrake booked us a priority launch and landing parabola with the Cartel's suborbital traffic arm, and we flew out to an anonymous landing field on the outskirts of Landfall just as the heat was leaching out of the afternoon. There was a shiny new Lockheed Mitoma IP assault ship dug into the concrete, looking like nothing so much as a smoked glass scorpion someone had ripped the fighting claws off. Ameli Vongsavath grunted in approval when she saw it.

'Omega series,' she said to me, mainly because I happened to be standing next to her when we climbed out of the cruiser. She was fixing her hair reflexively as she spoke, twisting the thick black strands up and clear of the flight symbiote sockets at her nape, pegging the loosely gathered bun in place with static clips. 'You could fly that baby right down Incorporation Boulevard and not even scorch the trees. Put plasma torpedoes through the front door of the Senate House, stand on your tail and be in orbit before they blew.'

'For example,' I said dryly. 'Of course, with those mission objectives, you'd be a Kempist, which means you'd be flying some beaten-up piece of shit like a Mowai Ten. Right, Schneider?'

Schneider grinned. 'Yeah, doesn't bear thinking about.'

'What doesn't bear thinking about?' Yvette Cruickshank wanted to know. 'Being a Kempist?'

'No, flying a Mowai,' Schneider told her, eyes flickering up and down the frame of her Maori combat sleeve. 'Being a Kempist's not so bad. Well, apart from all the pledge singing.'

Cruickshank blinked. 'You were really a Kempist?'

'He's joking,' I said, with a warning glance at Schneider. There was no political officer along this time, but Jiang Jianping at least seemed to have strong feelings about Kemp, and there was no telling how many other members of the team might share them. Stirring up potential animosities just to impress well-shaped women didn't strike me as all that smart.

Then again, Schneider hadn't had his hormones wrung out in virtual that morning, so maybe I was just being unduly balanced about the whole thing.

One of the Lock Mit's loading hatches hinged up. A moment later Hand appeared in the entrance in neatly pressed combat chameleochrome, now smoky grey against the prevalent hue of the assault ship. The change from his usual corporate attire was so complete it jarred, for all that everyone else was similarly dressed.

'Welcome to the fucking cruise,' muttered Hansen.

We cleared for dust-off five minutes before Mandrake's authorised launch envelope opened. Ameli Vongsavath put the flight plan to bed in the Lock Mit's datacore, powered up the systems and then to all appearances went to sleep. Jacked in at nape and cheekbone, eyes shuttered down, she lay back in her borrowed Maori flesh like the cryocapped princess in some obscure Settlement Years fairytale. She'd scored perhaps the darkest, slimmest built of the sleeves, and the datacables stood out against her skin like pale worms.

Sidelined in the co-pilot's seat, Schneider cast longing glances at the helm.

'You'll get your chance,' I told him.

'Yeah, when?'

'When you're a millionaire on Latimer.'

He shot me a resentful glance and put one booted foot up on the console in front of him.

'Ha fucking ha.'

Below her closed eyes, Ameli Vongsavath's mouth quirked. It must have sounded like an elaborate way of saying *not in a million years*. None of the Dangrek crew knew about the deal with Mandrake. Hand had introduced us as consultants, and left it at that.

'You think it'll go through the gate?' I asked Schneider, trying to extract him from his sulk.

He didn't look up at me. 'How the hell would I know?'

'Just w—'

'Gentlemen,' Ameli Vongsavath had still not opened her eyes. 'Do you think I could have a little pre-swim quiet in here please?'

'Yeah, shut up Kovacs,' said Schneider maliciously. 'Why don't you get back with the passengers?'

Back in the main cabin, the seats on either side of Wardani were taken by Hand and Sun Liping, so I crossed to the opposing side and dropped into the space next to Luc Deprez. He gave me a curious glance and then went back to examining his new hands.

'Like it?' I asked him.

He shrugged. 'It has a certain splendour. But I am not used to being so *bulky*, you know.'

'You'll settle into it. Sleeping helps.'

The curious look again. 'You know this for certain then. What kind of consultant are you exactly?'

'Ex-Envoy.'

'Really?' He shifted in the seat. 'That's a surprise. You will have to tell me about this.'

I caught echoes of his movement from other seats, where I'd been overheard. Instant notoriety. Just like being back in the Wedge.

'Long story. And not very interesting.'

'We are now one minute from launch,' Ameli Vongsavath's voice came through the intercom, sardonic, 'I'd like to take this opportunity to officially welcome you aboard the fast assault launch *Nagini* and to warn you that if you are not now secured to a seat, I cannot guarantee your physical integrity for the next fifteen minutes.'

There was a scrabble of activity along the two lines of seats. Grins broke out among those who had already webbed in.

'I think she exaggerates,' remarked Deprez, smoothing the webbing bond tabs unhurriedly into unity on the harness's chest plate. 'These vessels have good compensators.'

'Well, you never know. Might catch some orbital fire on the way through.'

'That's right, Kovacs.' Hansen grinned across at me. 'Look on the positive side.'

'Just thinking ahead.'

'Are you afraid?' asked Jiang suddenly.

'Regularly. You?'

'Fear is an inconvenience. You must learn to suppress it. That is what it is to be a committed soldier. To abandon fear.'

'No, Jiang,' said Sun Liping gravely. 'That is what it is to be dead.'

The assault ship tilted suddenly, and weight smashed down on my guts and chest. Blood-drained limbs. Crushed-out breath.

'Jesus fucking Christ,' said Ole Hansen through his teeth.

It slacked off, presumably when we got orbital and some of the power Ameli Vongsavath had rammed into the lifters was allowed back into the onboard grav system. I rolled my head sideways to look at Deprez.

'Exaggerates, huh?'

He spotted blood from his bitten tongue onto his knuckle and looked at it critically. 'I would call that exaggeration, yes.'

'Orbital status attained,' Vongsavath's voice confirmed. 'We have approximately six minutes of safe transit under the Landfall High Orbit Geosynch Umbrella. After that we're exposed, and I'll be throwing some evasive curves, so keep those tongues tucked up safe.'

Deprez nodded glumly and held up his blood-spotted knuckle. Laughter down the gangway.

'Hey, Hand,' said Yvette Cruickshank. 'How come the Cartel doesn't just put up five, six of those HOGs, wide-spaced, and finish this war?'

Further down the opposite row, Markus Sutjiadi smiled very slightly, but said nothing. His eyes flickered towards Ole Hansen.

'Hey, Cruickshank.' The demolitions expert could have been speaking on Sutjiadi's cue. His tone was withering. 'Can you even *spell* marauder? You got any idea what kind of target a HOG makes from shallow space?'

'Yeah.' Cruickshank came back stubborn. 'But most of Kemp's marauders are on the ground now, and with the geosynchs in place . . .'

'Try telling that to the inhabitants of Sauberville,' Wardani told her, and the comment dragged a comet tail of quiet across the discussion. Glances shuttled back and forth up the gangway like slug-thrower shells chambering.

'That attack was ground launched, Mistress Wardani,' said Jiang finally.

'Was it?'

Hand cleared his throat. 'In point of fact, the Cartel are not entirely sure how many of Kemp's missile drones are still deployed off-planet—'

'No shit,' grunted Hansen.

'—but to attempt high-orbit placement of any substantial platform at this stage would not be sufficiently—'

'Profitable?' asked Wardani.

Hand gave her an unpleasant smile. 'Low risk.'

'We're about to leave the Landfall HOG umbrella,' said Ameli Vongsavath over the intercom, tour-guide calm. 'Expect some kinks.'

I felt a subtle increase in pressure at my temples as power diverted from the onboard compensators. Vongsavath getting ready for aerobatics around the curve of the world and down through re-entry. With the HOG setting behind us, there would be no more paternal corporate presence to cushion our fall back into the war zone. From here on in, we were out to play on our own.

They exploit, and deal, and shift ground constantly, but for all that you can get used to them. You can get used to their gleaming company towers and their nanocopter security, their cartels and their HOGs, their stretched-over-centuries unhuman patience and their assumed inheritance of godfather status for the human race. You can get so you're grateful for the there-but-for-the-grace-of-God relief of whatever little flange of existence they afford you on the corporate platform. You can get so it seems eminently preferable to a cold gut-swooping drop into the human chaos waiting below.

You can get so you're grateful.

Got to watch out for that.

'Over the rim,' said Ameli Vongsavath from the cockpit.

We dropped.

With the onboard comp running at combat minimum, it felt like the start of a grav jump, before the harness kicks in. My guts lifted to the base of my ribcage and the back of my eyeballs tickled. The neurachem fizzled sullenly to unwanted life and the bioalloy plates in my hands shivered. Vongsavath must have nailed us to the floor of Mandrake's landing envelope and piled on everything the main drives would give her, hoping to beat any distant early-warned Kempist anti-incursion systems that might have decoded the flight path from Cartel traffic transmissions.

It seemed to work.

We came down in the sea about two kilometres off the Dangrek coast, Vongsavath using the water to crash cool re-entry surfaces in approved military fashion. In some places, environmental pressure groups have got violent over this kind of contamination, but somehow I doubted anyone on Sanction IV would be up for it. War has a soothing, simplifying effect on politics that must hit the politicians like a betathanatine rush. You don't have to balance the issues any more, and you can justify anything. Fight and win, and bring the victory home. Everything else whites out, like the sky over Sauberville.

'Surface status attained,' intoned Vongsavath. 'Preliminary sweeps show no traffic. I'm going for the beach on secondaries, but I'd like you to stay in your seats until advised otherwise. Commander Hand, we have a needlecast squirt from Isaac Carrera you might like to have a look at.'

Hand traded glances with me. He reached back and touched the seat mike.

'Run it on the discreet loop. Mine, Kovacs, Sutjiadi.'

'Understood.'

I pulled down the headset and settled the discreet reception mask over my face. Carrera came online behind the shrill warble of unravelling scrambler codes. He was in combat coveralls and a recently gelled wound was livid across his forehead and down one cheek. He looked tired.

'This is Northern Rim Control to incoming FAL 931/4. We have your flight plan and mission filed but must warn you that under current circumstances we cannot afford ground or close detail aerial support. Wedge forces have fallen back to the Masson lake system where we are holding a defensive stance until the Kempist offensive has been assessed and its consequences correlated. A full-scale jamming offensive is expected in the wake of the bombing, so this is probably the last time you'll be able to communicate effectively with anyone outside the blast zone. Additional to these strategic considerations, you should be aware that the Cartel have deployed experimental nanorepair systems in the Sauberville area. We cannot predict how these systems will react to unexpected incursions. Personally,' he leaned forward in the screen, 'my advice would be to withdraw on secondary drives as far as Masson and wait until I can order a reprise front back-up to the coast. This shouldn't involve a delay of any more than two weeks. Blast research,' a ripple of distaste passed across his face, as if he had just caught the odour of something rotting in his wounds, 'is hardly a priority worthy of the risks you are running, whatever competitive advantage your masters may hope to gain from it. A Wedge incoming code is attached, should you wish to avail yourself of the fallback option. Otherwise, there is nothing I can do for you. Good luck. Out.'

I unmasked and pushed back the headset. Hand was watching me with a faint smile tucked into one corner of his mouth.

'Hardly a Cartel-approved perspective. Is he always that blunt?'

'In the face of client stupidity, yes. It's why they pay him. What's this about experimental—'

Hand made a tiny shutdown gesture with one hand. Shook his head.

'I wouldn't worry about it. Standard Cartel scare line. It keeps unwanted personnel out of the no-go zones.'

'Meaning you called it in that way?'

Hand smiled again. Sutjiadi said nothing, but his lips tightened. Outside, the engine note shrilled.

'We're on the beach,' said Ameli Vongsavath. 'Twenty-one point seven kilometres from the Sauberville crater. Pictures, anybody?'

CHAPTER NINETEEN

Clotted white.

For fragments of a second, standing in the hatch of the *Nagini* and staring across the expanse of sand, I thought it had been snowing.

'Gulls,' said Hand knowledgeably, jumping down and kicking at one of the clumps of feathers underfoot. 'Radiation from the blast must have got them.'

Out on the tranquil swells, the sea was strewn with mottled white flotsam.

When the colony barges first touched down on Sanction IV – and Latimer, and Harlan's World for that matter – they were, for many local species, exactly the cataclysm they must have sounded like. Planetary colonisation is invariably a destructive process, and advanced technology hasn't done much more than sanitise that process so that humans are guaranteed their customary position on top of whatever ecosystem they are raping. The invasion is all-pervasive and, from the moment of the barges' initial impact, inevitable.

The massive ships cool slowly, but already there is activity within. Serried ranks of clone embryos emerge from the cryotanks and are loaded with machine care into rapid-growth pods. A storm of engineered hormones rages through the pod nutrients, triggering the burst of cell development that will bring each clone to late adolescence in a matter of months. Already the advance wave, grown in the latter stages of the interstellar flight, is being downloaded with the minds of the colony elite, decanted and awoken to take up their established place in the brand new order. It's not quite the golden land of opportunity and adventure that the chroniclers would have you believe.

Elsewhere in the hull, the real damage is being done by the environmental modelling machines.

Any self-respecting effort at colonisation brings along a couple of these eco-AIs. After the early catastrophes on Mars and Adoracion, it became rapidly apparent that attempting to graft a sliced sample of the terrestrial ecosystem onto an alien environment was no elephant ray hunt. The first colonists to breathe the newly terraformed air on Mars were all dead in a matter of days, and a lot of those who'd stayed inside died fighting swarms of a voracious little beetle that no one had ever seen before. Said beetle turned out to be the very distant descendant of a species of terrestrial dustmite that had done rather too well in the ecological upheaval occasioned by the terraforming.

So. Back to the lab.

It was another two generations before the Martian colonists finally got to breathe untanked air.

On Adoracion, it was worse. The colony barge *Lorca* had left several decades before the Martian debacle, built and hurled at the nearest of the habitable worlds indicated on the Martian astrogation charts with the bravado of a Molotov cocktail hurled at a tank. It was a semi-desperate assault on the armoured depths of interstellar space, an act of technological defiance in the face of the oppressive physics that govern the cosmos and an act of equally defiant faith in the newly decoded Martian archives. By all accounts, pretty much everyone thought it would fail. Even those who contributed their copied consciousnesses to the colony's datastack and their genes to the embryo banks were less than optimistic about what their stored selves would encounter at journey's end.

Adoracion, as its name suggests, must have seemed like a dream come true. A green and orange world with approximately the same nitrogen/oxygen mix as Earth and a more user-friendly land-to-sea ratio. A plant-life base that could be eaten by the herds of cloned livestock in the belly of the *Lorca* and no obvious predators that couldn't be easily shot. Either the colonists were a pious lot or arriving on this new Eden pushed them that way, because the first thing they did upon disembarkation was build a cathedral and give thanks to God for their safe deliverance.

A year passed.

Hypercasting was still in its infancy back then, barely able to carry the simplest of messages in coded sequence. The news that came filtering back down the beams to Earth was like the sound of screams from a locked room in the depths of an empty mansion. The two ecosystems had met and clashed like armies on a battlefield from which there was no retreat. Of the million-odd colonists aboard the *Lorca*, over seventy per cent died within eighteen months of touchdown.

Back to the lab.

These days we've got it down to a fine art. Nothing organic leaves the hull until the eco-modeller has the whole host ecosystem down. Automated probes go out and prowl the new globe, sucking in samples. The AI digests the data, runs a model against a theoretical terrestrial presence at a couple of hundred times real-world speed and flags the potential clashes. For anything that looks like a problem it writes a solution, genetech or nanotech, and from the correlated whole, generates a settlement protocol. With the protocol laid down, everyone goes out to play.

Inside the protocols for the three dozen or so Settled Worlds, you find certain advantageous terrestrial species cropping up time and time again. They are the success stories of planet Earth – tough, adaptive evolutionary athletes to a creature. Most of them are plants, microbes and insects, but among the supersized animals there are a few that stand out. Merino sheep, grizzly bears and seagulls feature at the top of the list. They're hard to wipe out.

The water around the trawler was clogged with the white feathered corpses. In the unnatural stillness of the shoreline, they muffled the faint lapping of wavelets on the hull even further.

The ship was a mess. It drifted listlessly against its anchors, the paint on the Sauberville side scorched to black and bare metal glints by the wind from the blast. A couple of windows had blown out at the same time and it looked as if some of the untidy pile of nets on deck had caught and melted. The angles of the deck winch were similarly charred. Anyone standing outside would probably have died from third-degree burns.

There were no bodies on deck. We knew that from the virtuality.

'Nobody down here either,' said Luc Deprez, poking his head out of the mid-deck companionway. 'Nobody has been aboard for months. Maybe a year. Food everywhere has been eaten by the bugs and the rats.'

Sutjiadi frowned. 'There's food out?'

'Yeah, lots of it.' Deprez hauled himself out of the companionway and seated himself on the coaming. The bottom half of his chameleochrome coveralls stayed muddy dark for a second before it adjusted to the sunlit surroundings. 'Looks like a big party, but no one stayed around to do the clearing up.'

'I've had parties like that,' said Vongsavath.

Below, the unmistakeable whoosh-sizzle of a Sunjet. Sutjiadi, Vongsavath and I tensed in unison. Deprez grinned.

'Cruickshank is shooting the rats,' he said. 'They are quite large.'

Sutjiadi put up his weapon and looked up and down the deck, marginally more relaxed than when we'd come aboard. 'Estimates, Deprez. How many were there?'

'Rats?' Deprez's grin widened. 'It is hard to tell.'

I repressed a smile of my own.

'Crew,' said Sutjiadi with an impatient gesture. 'How many crew, *sergeant?*'

Deprez shrugged, unimpressed by the rank-pulling. 'I am not a chef, *captain*. It is hard to tell.'

'I used to be a chef,' said Ameli Vongsavath unexpectedly. 'Maybe I'll go down and look.'

'You stay here.' Sutjiadi stalked to the side of the trawler, kicking a seagull corpse out of his way. 'Starting now, I'd like a little less humour out of this command and a little more application. You can start by getting this net hauled up. Deprez, you go back down and help Cruickshank get rid of the rats.'

Deprez sighed and set aside his Sunjet. From his belt he pulled an ancient-looking sidearm, chambered a round and sighted on the sky with it.

'My kind of work,' he said cryptically, and swung back down the companionway, gun hand held high over his head.

The induction rig crackled. Sutjiadi bent his head, listening. I fitted my own disconnected rig back in place.

'. . . is secured.' It was Sun Liping's voice. Sutjiadi had given her command of the other half of the team and sent them up the beach with Hand, Wardani and Schneider, whom he clearly regarded as civilian irritations at best, liabilities at worst.

'Secured how?' he snapped.

'We've set up perimeter sentry systems in an arc above the beach. Five-hundred-metre-wide base-line, hundred-and-eighty-degree sweep. Should nail anything incoming from the interior or along the beach in either direction.' Sun paused for a moment, apologetic. 'That's line-of-sight only, but it's good for several kilometres. It's the best we can do.'

'What about the uh, the mission objective?' I broke in. 'Is it intact?'

Sutjiadi snorted. 'Is it there?'

I shot him a glance. Sutjiadi thought we were on a ghost hunt. Envoy-enhanced gestalt scanning read it in his demeanour like screen labelling. He thought Wardani's gate was an archaeologue fantasy, overhyped from some vague original theory to make a good pitch to Mandrake. He thought Hand had been sold a cracked hull, and corporate greed had gobbled up the concept in a stampede to be first on the scene of any possible development option. He thought there was going to be some serious indigestion once the team arrived on site. He hadn't said as much in the construct briefing, but he wore his lack of conviction like a badge throughout.

I couldn't really blame him. By their demeanour, about half of the team thought the same. If Hand hadn't been offering such crazy back-from-the-dead war-exemption contracts, they probably would have laughed in his face.

Not much more than a month ago, I'd nearly done the same to Schneider myself.

'Yes, it's here.' There was something peculiar in Sun's voice. As far as I could tell, she hadn't ever been one of the doubters, but now her tone bordered on awe. 'It's. Like nothing I've ever seen.'

'Sun? Is it open?'

'Not as far as we are aware, Lieutenant Kovacs, no. I think you had better speak to Mistress Wardani if you want details.'

I cleared my throat. 'Wardani? You there?'

'Busy.' Her voice was taut. 'What did you find on the boat?'

'Nothing yet.'

'Yeah, well. Same here. Out.'

I glanced over at Sutjiadi again. He was focused on the middle distance, new Maori face betraying nothing. I grunted, tugged the rig off and went to find out how the deck winch worked. Behind me, I heard him calling in a progress report from Hansen.

The winch turned out not much different to a shuttle loader, and with Vongsavath's help, I got the mechanism powered up before Sutjiadi was finished on the comlink. He wandered over just in time to see the boom swing out smoothly and lower the manigrab for the first haul.

Dragging in the nets proved another story. It took us a good twenty minutes to get the hang of it, by which time the rat hunt was over and Cruickshank and Deprez had joined us. Even then, it was no joke manoeuvring the cold, soaking-heavy drapes of net over the side and onto the deck in some sort of order. None of us were fishermen, and it was clear that there were some substantial skills involved in the process that we didn't have. We slipped and fell over a lot.

It turned out worth it.

Tangled in the last folds to come aboard were the remains of two corpses, naked apart from the still shiny lengths of chain that weighted them down at the knees and chest. The fish had picked them down to bone and skin that looked like torn oilcloth wrapping. Their eyeless skulls lolled together in the suspended net like the heads of drunks, sharing a good joke. Floppy necks and wide grins.

We stood looking up at them for a while.

'Good guess,' I said to Sutjiadi.

'It made sense to look.' He stepped closer and looked speculatively up at the naked bones. 'They've been stripped, and threaded into the net. Arms and legs, and the ends of the two chains. Whoever did this didn't want them coming up. Doesn't make much sense. Why hide the bodies when the ship is here drifting for anyone to come out from Sauberville and take for salvage?'

'Yeah, but nobody did,' Vongsavath pointed out.

Deprez turned and shaded his eyes to look at the horizon, where Sauberville still smouldered. 'The war?'

I recalled dates, recent history, calculated back. 'Hadn't come this far west a year ago, but it was cutting loose down south.' I nodded towards the twists of smoke. 'They would have been scared. Not likely to come across here for anything that might draw orbital fire. Or something maybe mined to suck in a remote bombardment. Remember Bootkinaree Town?'

'Vividly,' said Ameli Vongsavath, pressing fingers to her left cheekbone.

'That was about a year ago. Would have been all over the news. That bulk carrier down in the harbour. There wouldn't have been a civilian salvage team on the planet working after that.'

'So why hide these guys at all?' asked Cruickshank.

I shrugged. 'Keeps them out of sight. Nothing for aerial surveillance to reel in and sniff over. Bodies *might* have triggered a local investigation back then. Back before things really got out of hand in Kempopolis.'

'Indigo City,' said Sutjiadi pointedly.

'Yeah, don't let Jiang hear you calling it that.' Cruickshank grinned. 'He already jumped down my throat for calling Danang a terror strike. And I meant it as a fucking compliment!'

'Whatever.' I rolled my eyes. 'The point is, without bodies this is just a fishing boat someone hasn't been back for. That doesn't attract much attention in the run-up to a global revolution.'

'It does if the boat was hired in Sauberville.' Sutjiadi shook his head. 'Bought even, it's still local interest. Who were those guys? Isn't that old Chang's trawler out there? Come on, Kovacs, it's only a couple of dozen kilometres.'

'There's no reason to assume this boat's local.' I gestured out at the placid ocean. 'On this planet you could sail a boat like this one all the way up from Bootkinaree and never spill your coffee.'

'Yeah, but you could hide the bodies from aerial surveillance by chucking them down into the galley with the rest of the mess,' objected Cruickshank. 'It doesn't add up.'

Luc Deprez reached up and shifted the net slightly. The skulls bobbed and leaned. 'The stacks are gone,' he said. 'They were put in the water to hide the rest of their identity. Faster than leaving them for the rats, I think.'

'Depends on the rats.'

'Are you an expert?'

'Maybe it was a burial,' offered Ameli Vongsavath.

'In a *net*?'

'We're wasting time,' said Sutjiadi loudly. 'Deprez, get them down, wrap them up and put them somewhere the rats can't get at them. We'll run a post mortem with the autosurgeon back on the *Nagini* later. Vongsavath and Cruickshank, I want you to go through this boat from beak to backside. Look for anything that might tell us what happened here.'

'That's stem to stern, sir,' said Vongsavath primly.

'Whatever. Anything that might tell us something. The clothing that came off these two maybe or . . .' He shook his head, irritable with the awkward new factors. 'Anything. Anything at all. Get on with it. Lieutenant Kovacs, I'd like you to come with me. I want to check on our perimeter defences.'

'Sure.' I scooped up the lie with a slight smile.

Sutjiadi didn't want to check on the perimeter. He'd seen Sun and Hansen's résumés, just like me. They didn't need their work checking.

He didn't want to see the perimeter.

He wanted to see the gate.

CHAPTER TWENTY

Schneider had described it to me, several times. Wardani had sketched it for me once in a quiet moment at Roespinoedji's. An imaging shop on the Angkor Road had run up a 3-D graphic from Wardani's input for the Mandrake pitch. Later, Hand had the Mandrake machines blow up the image to a full-scale construct we could walk around in virtual.

None of it came close.

It stood in the man-made cavern like some vertically stretched vision from the Dimensionalist school, some element out of the nightmare technomilitary landscapes of Mhlongo or Osupile. There was a gaunt *foldedness* to the structure, like six or seven ten-metre tall vampire bats crushed back to back in a defensive phalanx. There was none of the passive openness that the word 'gate' suggested. In the soft light filtering down through chinks in the rocks above, the whole thing looked hunched and waiting.

The base was triangular, about five metres on a side, though the lower edges bore less resemblance to a geometric shape than to something that had grown down into the ground like tree roots. The material was an alloy I'd seen in Martian architecture before, a dense black-clouded surface that would feel like marble or onyx to the touch but always carried a faint static charge. The technoglyph panelling was dull green and ruby, mapped in odd, irregular waves around the lower section, but never rising higher than a metre and a half from the ground. Towards the top of this limit, the symbols seemed to lose both coherence and strength – they thinned out, grew less well defined and even the style of the engraving seemed more hesitant. It was as if, Sun said later, the Martian technoscribes were afraid to work too close to what they had created on the plinth above.

Above, the structure folded rapidly in on itself as it rose, creating a series of compressed black alloy angles and upward leading edges that ended in a short spire. In the long splits between the folds, the black clouding on the alloy faded to a dirty translucence and inside this, the geometry seemed to continue folding in on itself in some indefinable way which was painful to look at for too long.

'Believe it now?' I asked Sutjiadi, as he stood beside me, staring. He didn't respond for a moment, and when he did there was the same slight numbness in his voice that I'd heard from Sun Liping over the comlink.

'It is not still,' he said quietly. 'It feels. In motion. Like turning.'

'Maybe it is.' Sun had come up with us, leaving the rest of the team down by the *Nagini*. No one else seemed overkeen to spend time either in or near the cavern.

'It's supposed to be a hyperspatial link,' I said, moving sideways in an attempt to break the hold the thing's alien geometry was exerting. 'If it maintains a line through to wherever, then maybe it moves in hyperspace, even when it's shut down.'

'Or maybe it cycles,' Sun suggested. 'Like a beacon.'

Unease.

I felt it course through me at the same time as I spotted it in the twitch across Sutjiadi's face. Bad enough that we were pinned down here on this exposed tongue of land without the added thought that the thing we had come to unlock might be sending off 'come and get me' signals in a dimension we as a species had only the vaguest of handles on.

'We're going to need some lights in here,' I said.

The spell broke. Sutjiadi blinked hard and looked up at the falling rays of light. They were greying out with perceptible speed as evening advanced across the sky outside.

'We'll have it blasted out,' he said.

I exchanged an alarmed glance with Sun.

'Have what blasted?' I asked cautiously.

Sutjiadi gestured. 'The rock. *Nagini* runs a front-mounted ultravibe battery for ground assault. Hansen should be able to clear the whole thing back this far without putting a scratch on the artefact.'

Sun coughed. 'I don't think Commander Hand will approve that, sir. He ordered me to bring up a set of Angier lamps before dark. And Mistress Wardani has asked for remote monitoring systems to be installed so she can work direct on the gate from—'

'Alright, lieutenant. Thank you.' Sutjiadi looked around the cavern once more. 'I'll talk to Commander Hand.'

He strode out. I glanced at Sun and winked.

'That's a conversation I want to hear,' I said.

Back at the *Nagini*, Hansen, Schneider and Jiang were busy erecting the first of the rapid deployment bubblefabs. Hand was braced in one corner of the assault ship's loading hatch, watching a cross-legged Wardani sketch something on a memoryboard. There was an unguarded fascination in his expression that made him look suddenly younger.

'Some problem, captain?' he asked, as we came up the ramp.

'I want that thing,' said Sutjiadi, jerking a thumb back over his shoulder, 'out in the open. Where we can watch it. I'm having Hansen 'vibe-blast the rocks out of the way.'

'Out of the question.' Hand went back to watching what the archaeologue was doing. 'We can't risk exposure at this stage.'

'Or damage to the gate,' said Wardani sharply.

'Or damage to the gate,' agreed the executive. 'I'm afraid your team are going to have to work with the cavern as it is, captain. I don't believe there's any risk involved. The bracing the previous visitors put in appears to be solid.'

'I've seen the bracing,' said Sutjiadi. 'Bonding epoxy is not a substitute for a permanent structure, but that's—'

'Sergeant Hansen seemed quite impressed with it.' Hand's urbane tone was edged with irritation. 'But if you are concerned, please feel free to reinforce the current arrangement in any way you see fit.'

'I was going to say,' Sutjiadi said evenly, 'that the bracing is beside the point. I am not concerned with the risks of collapse. I am urgently concerned with what is in the cavern.'

Wardani looked up from her sketching.

'Well that's good, captain,' she said brightly. 'You've gone from polite disbelief to urgent concern in less than twenty-four hours real time. What exactly are you concerned about?'

Sutjiadi looked uncomfortable.

'This artefact,' he said. 'You claim it's a gate. Can you give me any guarantees that nothing will come through it from the other side?'

'Not really, no.'

'Do you have any idea *what* might come through?'

Wardani smiled. 'Not really, no.'

'Then I'm sorry, Mistress Wardani. It makes military sense to have the *Nagini*'s main weaponry trained on it at all times.'

'This is not a military operation, captain.' Hand was working on ostentatiously bored now. 'I thought I made that clear during briefing. You are part of a commercial venture, and the specifics of our commerce dictate that the artefact cannot be exposed to aerial view until it is contractually secured. By the terms of the Incorporation Charter, that will not become the case until what is on the other side of the gateway is tagged with a Mandrake ownership buoy.'

'And if the gate chooses to open before we are ready, and something hostile comes through it?'

'Something hostile?' Wardani set aside her memoryboard, apparently amused. 'Something such as what?'

'You would be in a better position than I to evaluate that, Mistress Wardani,' said Sutjiadi stiffly. 'My concern is simply for the safety of this expedition.'

Wardani sighed.

'They weren't vampires, captain,' she said wearily.

'I'm sorry?'

'The Martians. They weren't vampires. Or demons. They were just a technologically advanced race with wings. That's all. There's nothing on the other side of that thing,' she stabbed a finger in the general direction of the rocks, 'that we won't be able to build ourselves in a few thousand years. If we can get a lock on our militaristic tendencies, that is.'

'Is that intended as an insult, Mistress Wardani?'

'Take it any way you like, captain. We are, all of us, already, dying slowly of radiation poisoning. A couple of dozen kilometres in that direction a hundred thousand people were vaporised yesterday. By soldiers.' Her voice was starting to rise, trembling at base. 'Anywhere else on about sixty per cent of this planet's land mass, your chances of an early, violent death are excellent. At the hands of soldiers. Elsewhere, the camps will kill you with starvation or beatings if you step out of political line. This service too, brought to us by soldiers. Is there something else I can add to clarify my reading of militarism for you?'

'Mistress Wardani.' Hand's voice held a tight strain I hadn't heard before. Below the ramp, Hansen, Schneider and Jiang had stopped what they were doing and were looking over towards the raised voices. 'I think we're getting off the point. We were discussing security.'

'Were we?' Wardani forced a shaky laugh, and her voice evened out. 'Well, captain. Let me put it to you that in the seven decades I have been a qualified archaeologue, I have never come across evidence to suggest that the Martians had anything more unpleasant to offer than what men like you have already unleashed across the face of Sanction IV. Excluding the small matter of the fallout from Sauberville, you are probably safer sitting in front of that gate than anywhere else in the northern hemisphere at the moment.'

There was a small silence.

'Maybe you want to train the *Nagini*'s main guns on the entrance to the cavern,' I suggested. 'Same effect. In fact, with the remote monitoring in place, it'll be better. If the monsters with half-metre fangs turn up, we can collapse the tunnel on them.'

'A good point.' Seemingly casual, Hand moved to position himself carefully in the hatch between Wardani and Sutjiadi. 'That seems the best compromise, does it not, captain?'

Sutjiadi read the executive's stance and took the hint. He threw a salute and turned on his heel. As he went down the ramp past me, he glanced up. He didn't quite have his previous immobility of feature down with the new Maori face. He looked betrayed.

You find innocence in the strangest places.

At the base of the ramp he caught one of the gull corpses with his foot and stumbled slightly. He kicked the clump of feathers away from him in a spray of turquoise sand.

'Hansen,' he snapped tightly. 'Jiang. Get all of this shit off the beach. I want it cleared back two hundred metres from the ship on all sides.'

Ole Hansen raised an eyebrow and slotted an ironic salute in beside it. Sutjiadi wasn't looking – he'd already stalked away towards the water's edge.

Something wasn't right.

Hansen and Jiang used the drives from two of the expedition's grav bikes to blow the gull corpses back in a skirling knee-high storm front of feathers and sand. In the space they cleared around the *Nagini*, the encampment took rapid shape, speeded up by the return of Deprez, Vongsavath and Cruickshank from the trawler. By the time it was fully dark, five bubblefabs had sprouted from the sand in a rough circle around the assault ship. They were uniform in size, chameleochrome-coated and featureless apart from small illuminum numerals above each door. Each 'fab was equipped to sleep four in twin bunk rooms, separated by a central living space but two of the units had been assembled in a non-standard configuration with half the bedspace, one to serve as a general meeting room and the other as Tanya Wardani's lab.

I found the archaeologue there, still sketching.

The hatch was open, freshly lasered out and hinged back on epoxy welding that still smelled faintly of resin. I touched the chime pad and leaned in.

'What do you want?' she asked, not looking up from what she was doing.

'It's me.'

'I know who it is, Kovacs. What do you want?'

'An invitation over the threshold?'

She stopped sketching and sighed, still not looking up.

'We're not in virtual any more, Kovacs. I—'

'I wasn't looking for a fuck.'

She hesitated, then met my gaze levelly. 'That's just as well.'

'So do I get to come in?'

'Suit yourself.'

I ducked through the entrance and crossed to where she was sitting, picking my way among the litter of hardcopy sheets the memoryboard had churned out. They were all variations on a theme – sequences of technoglyphs with scrawled annotation. As I watched, she put a line through the current sketch.

'Getting anywhere?'

'Slowly.' She yawned. 'I don't remember as much as I thought. Going to have to redo some of the secondary configs from scratch again.'

I propped myself against a table edge.

'So how long do you reckon?'

She shrugged. 'A couple of days. Then there's testing.'

'How long for that?'

'The whole thing, primaries and secondaries? I don't know. Why? Your bone marrow starting to itch already?'

I glanced through the open door to where the fires in Sauberville cast a dull red glow on the night sky. This soon after the blast, and this close in, the elemental exotics would be out in force. Strontium 90, iodine 131 and all their numerous friends, like a 'methed-up party of Harlan family heirs crashing wharfside Millsport with their chittering bright enthusiasm. Wearing their unstable subatomic jackets like swamp panther skin, and wanting into everywhere, every cell they could fuck up with their heavily jewelled presence.

I twitched despite myself.

'I'm just curious.'

'An admirable quality. Must make soldiering difficult for you.'

I snapped open one of the camp chairs stacked beside the table and lowered myself into it. 'I think you're confusing curiosity with empathy.'

'Really?'

'Yes, really. Curiosity's a basic monkey trait. Torturers are full of it. Doesn't make you a better human being.'

'Well, I suppose you'd know.'

It was an admirable riposte. I didn't know if she'd been tortured in the camp – in the momentary flare of anger I hadn't cared – but she never flinched as the words came out.

'Why are you behaving like this, Wardani?'

'I told you we're not in virtual any more.'

'No.'

I waited. Eventually she got up and went across to the back wall of the compartment, where a bank of monitors for the remote gear showed the gate from a dozen slightly different angles.

'You'll have to forgive me, Kovacs,' she said heavily. 'Today I saw a hundred thousand people murdered to clear the way for our little venture, and I know, *I know*, we didn't do it, but it's a little too convenient for me not to feel responsible. If I go for a walk, I know there are little bits of them blowing around in the wind out there. And that's without those heroes of the revolution you killed so efficiently this morning. I'm sorry, Kovacs. I have no training at this sort of thing.'

'You won't want to talk about the two bodies we fished out of the trawl nets, then.'

'Is there something to talk about?' She didn't look round.

'Deprez and Jiang just got through with the autosurgeon. Still no idea what killed them. No trace of trauma in any of the bone structure, and there's not a great deal else left to work from.' I moved up beside her, closer to the monitors. 'I'm told there are tests we can do with bone at cellular level, but I have a feeling they aren't going to tell us anything either.'

That got her looking at me.

'Why?'

'Because whatever killed them has something to do with this.' I tapped the glass of a monitor where the gate loomed close up. 'And this is like nothing any of us have seen before.'

'You think something came through the gate at the witching hour?' she asked scornfully. 'The vampires got them?'

'*Something* got them,' I said mildly. 'They didn't die of old age. Their stacks are gone.'

'Doesn't that rule out the vampire option? Stack excision is a peculiarly human atrocity, isn't it?'

'Not necessarily. Any civilisation that could build a hyperportal must have been able to digitise consciousness.'

'There's no actual evidence for that.'

'Not even common sense?'

'Common sense?' The scorn was back in her voice. 'The same common sense that said a thousand years ago that *obviously* the sun goes round the earth, just *look* at it? The common sense that Bogdanovich appealed to when he set up hub theory? Common sense is anthropocentric, Kovacs. It assumes that because this is the way human beings turned out, it has to be the way any intelligent technological species would turn out.'

'I've heard some pretty convincing arguments along those lines.'

'Yeah, haven't we all,' she said shortly. 'Common sense for the common herd, and why bother to feed them anything else. What if Martian ethics didn't permit re-sleeving, Kovacs? Ever think of that? What if death means you've proved yourself unworthy of life? That even if you could be brought back, you have no *right* to it.'

'In a technologically advanced culture? A starfaring culture? This is bullshit, Wardani.'

'No, it's a theory. Function-related raptor ethics. Ferrer and Yoshimoto at Bradbury. And at the moment, there's very little hard evidence around to disprove it.'

'Do *you* believe it?'

She sighed and went back to her seat. 'Of course I don't believe it. I'm just trying to demonstrate that there's more to eat at this party than the cosy little certainties human science is handing round. We know almost nothing about the Martians, and that's after hundreds of years of study. What we think we know could be proved completely wrong at any moment, easily. Half of the things we dig up, we have no idea what they are, and we still sell them as fucking coffee-table trinkets. Right now, someone back on Latimer has probably got the encoded secret of a faster-than-light drive mounted on their fucking living-room wall.' She paused. 'And it's probably upside down.'

I laughed out loud. It shattered the tension in the 'fab. Wardani's face twitched in an unwilling smile.

'No, I mean it,' she muttered. 'You think, just because I can open this gate, that we've got some kind of handle on it. Well, we haven't. You can't assume anything here. You can't think in human terms.'

'OK, fine.' I followed her back to the centre of the room and reclaimed my own seat. In fact, the thought of a human stack being retrieved by some kind of Martian gate commando, the thought of that personality being downloaded into a Martian virtuality and what that might do to a human mind, was making my spine crawl. It was an idea I would have been just as happy never to have come up with. 'But you're the one who's beginning to sound like a vampire story now.'

'I'm just warning you.'

'OK, I'm warned. Now tell me something else. How many other archaeologues knew about this site?'

'Outside of my own team?' She considered. 'We filed with central processing in Landfall, but that was before we knew what it was. It was just listed as an obelisk. Artefact of Unknown Function, but like I said, AUFs are practically every second thing we dig up.'

'You know Hand says there's no record of an object like this in the Landfall registry.'

'Yeah, I read the report. Files get lost, I guess.'

'Seems a little too convenient to me. And files may get lost, but not files on the biggest find since Bradbury.'

'I told you, we filed it as an AUF. An obelisk. *Another* obelisk. We'd already turned up a dozen structural pieces along this coast by the time we found this one.'

'And you never updated? Not even when you knew what it was?'

'No.' She gave me a crooked smile. 'The Guild has always given me a pretty hard time about my Wycinski-esque tendencies, and a lot of the Scratchers I took on got tarred by association. Cold-shouldered by colleagues, slagged off in academic journals. The usual conformist stuff. When we realised what we'd found, I think we all felt the Guild could wait until we were ready to make them eat their words in style.'

'And when the war started, you buried it for the same reasons?'

'Got it in one.' She shrugged. 'It might sound childish now, but at the time we were all pretty angry. I don't know if you'd understand that. How it feels to have every piece of research you do, every theory you come up with, rubbished because you once took the wrong side in a political dispute.'

I thought briefly back to the Innenin hearings.

'It sounds familiar enough.'

'I think.' She hesitated. 'I think there was something else as well. You know the night we opened the gate for the first time, we went crazy. Big party, lots of chemicals, lots of talk. Everyone was talking about full professorships back on Latimer; they said I'd be made an honorary Earth scholar in recognition of my work.' She smiled. 'I think I even made an acceptance speech. I don't remember that stage of the evening too well, never did, even the next morning.'

She sighed and rid herself of the smile.

'Next morning, we started to think straight. Started to think about what was really going to happen. We knew that if we filed, we'd lose control. The Guild would fly in a Master with all the right political affiliations to take charge of the project, and we'd be sent home with a pat on the back. Oh, we'd be back from the academic wilderness of course, but only at a price. We'd be allowed to publish, but only after careful vetting to make sure there wasn't too much Wycinski in the text. There'd be work, but not on an independent basis. Consultancy,' she pronounced the word as if it tasted bad, 'on someone else's projects. We'd be well paid, but paid to keep quiet.'

'Better than not getting paid at all.'

A grimace. 'If I'd wanted to work second shovel to some smooth-faced politically-appropriate fuck with half my experience and qualifications, I could have gone to the plains like everybody else. The whole reason I was out here in the first place was because I wanted my own dig. I wanted the chance to prove that something I believed in was right.'

'Did the others feel that strongly?'

'In the end. In the beginning, they signed up with me because they needed the work and at the time no one else was hiring Scratchers. But a couple of years living with contempt changes you. And they were young, most of them. That gives you energy for your anger.'

I nodded.

'Could that be who we found in the nets?'

She looked away. 'I suppose so.'

'How many were there on the team? People who could have come back here and opened the gate?'

'I don't know. About half a dozen of them were actually Guild-qualified, there were probably two or three of those who could have. Aribowo. Weng, maybe. Techakriengkrai. They were all good. But on their own? Working backwards from our notes, working together?' She shook her head. 'I don't *know*, Kovacs. It was. A different time. A team thing. I've got no idea how any of those people would perform under different circumstances. Kovacs, I don't even know how *I'll* perform any more.'

A memory of her beneath the waterfall flickered, unfairly, off the comment. It coiled around itself in my guts. I groped after the thread of my thoughts.

'Well, there'll be DNA files for them in the Guild archives at Landfall.'

'Yes.'

'And we can run a DNA match from the bones—'

'Yes, I *know*.'

'—but it's going to be hard to get through and access data in Landfall from here. And to be honest, I'm not sure what purpose it'll serve. I don't much care who they are. I just want to know how they ended up in that net.'

She shivered.

'If it's them,' she began, then stopped. 'I don't want to know who it is, Kovacs. I can live without that.'

I thought about reaching for her, across the small space between our chairs, but sitting there she seemed suddenly as gaunt and folded as the thing we had come here to unlock. I couldn't see a point of contact anywhere on her body that would not make my touch seem intrusive, overtly sexual or just ridiculous.

The moment passed. Died.

'I'm going to get some sleep,' I said, standing up. 'You probably better do the same. Sutjiadi's going to want a crack-of-dawn start.'

She nodded vaguely. Most of her attention had slipped away from me. At a guess, she was staring down the barrel of her own past.

I left her alone amidst the litter of torn technoglyph sketches.

CHAPTER TWENTY-ONE

I woke up groggy with either the radiation or the chemicals I'd taken to hold it down. There was grey light filtering through the bubblefab's dormitory window and a dream scuttling out the back of my head half seen . . .

Do you see, Wedge Wolf? Do you see?

Semetaire?

I lost it to the sound of enthusiastic teeth-cleaning from the bathroom niche. Twisting my head, I saw Schneider towelling his hair dry with one hand while he scrubbed vigorously at his gums with a powerbrush held in the other.

'Morning,' he frothed.

'Morning.' I propped myself upright. 'What time is it?'

'Little after five.' He made an apologetic shrug and turned to spit in the basin. 'Wouldn't be up myself, but Jiang is out there bouncing around in some martial arts frenzy, and I'm a light sleeper.'

I cocked my head and listened. From beyond the canvasynth flap, the neurachem brought me the clear sounds of hard breathing and loose clothing snapping repeatedly taut.

'Fucking psycho,' I grumbled.

'Hey, he's in good company on this beach. I thought it was a requirement. Half the people you recruited are fucking psychos.'

'Yeah, but Jiang's the only one with insomnia, it appears.' I stumbled upright, frowning at the time it was taking for the combat sleeve to get itself properly online. Maybe this was what Jiang Jianping was fighting. Sleeve damage is an unpleasant wake-up call and, however subtly it manifests itself, a harbinger of eventual mortality. Even with the faint twinges that come with the onset of age, the message is flashing numeral clear. Limited time remaining. Blink, blink.

Rush/snap!

'*Haiii!!!*'

'Right.' I pressed my eyeballs hard with finger and thumb. 'I'm awake now. You finished with that brush?'

Schneider handed the powerbrush over. I stabbed a new head from the dispenser, pushed it to life and stepped into the shower niche.

Rise and shine.

Jiang had powered down somewhat by the time I stepped, dressed and relatively clear-headed, through the dormitory flap to the central living space. He stood rooted, swivelling slightly from side to side and weaving a slow pattern of defensive configurations around him. The table and chairs in the living space had been cleared to one side to make room, and the main exit from the 'fab was bound back. Light streamed into the space from outside, tinged blue from the sand.

I got a can of military-issue amphetamine cola from the dispenser, pulled the tab and sipped, watching.

'Was there something?' Jiang asked, as his head shifted in my direction behind a wide sweeping right-arm block. Sometime the previous night he'd razored the Maori sleeve's thick dark hair back to an even two centimetres all over. The face the cut revealed was big-boned and hard.

'You do this every morning?'

'Yes.' The syllable came out tight. Block, counterstrike, groin and sternum. He was very fast when he wanted to be.

'Impressive.'

'Ne*cessary*.' Another death blow, probably to the temple, and delivered out of a combination of blocks that telegraphed retreat. Very nice. 'Every skill must be practised. Every act rehearsed. A blade is only a *blade* when it cuts.'

I nodded. 'Hayashi.'

The patterns slowed fractionally.

'You have read him?'

'Met him once.'

Jiang stopped and looked at me narrowly. 'You *met* Toru Hayashi?'

'I'm older than I look. We deployed together on Adoracion.'

'You are an Envoy?'

'Was.'

For a moment, he seemed unsure what to say. I wondered if he thought I was joking. Then he brought his arms forward, sheathed his right fist at chest height in the cup of his left hand and bowed slightly over the grasp.

'Takeshi-san, if I offended you with my talk of fear yesterday, I apologise. I am a fool.'

'No problem. I wasn't offended. We all deal with it different ways. You planning on breakfast?'

He pointed across the living space to where the table had been pushed back to the canvasynth wall. There was fresh fruit piled on a shallow bowl and what looked like slices of rye bread.

'Mind if I join you?'

'I would be. Honoured.'

We were still eating when Schneider came back from wherever he'd been for the last twenty minutes.

'Meeting in the main 'fab,' he said over his shoulder, disappearing into the dormitory. He emerged a minute later. 'Fifteen minutes. Sutjiadi seems to think everyone should be there.'

He was gone again.

Jiang was half to his feet when I put out a hand and gestured him back to his seat.

'Take it easy. He said fifteen minutes.'

'I wish to shower and change,' said Jiang, a little stiffly.

'I'll tell him you're on your way. Finish your breakfast, for Christ's sake. In a couple of days from now it'll make you sick to the stomach just to swallow food. Enjoy the flavours while you can.'

He sat back down with a strange expression on his face.

'Do you mind, Takeshi-san, if I ask you a question?'

'Why am I no longer an Envoy?' I saw the confirmation in his eyes. 'Call it an ethical revelation. I was at Innenin.'

'I have read about it.'

'Hayashi again?'

He nodded.

'Yeah, well, Hayashi's account is pretty close, but he wasn't there. That's why he comes off ambiguous about the whole thing. Didn't feel fit to judge. I was there, and I'm eminently fit to judge. They fucked us. No one's too clear on whether they actually *intended* to or not, but I'm here to tell you that doesn't matter. My friends died – really died – when there was no need. That's what counts.'

'Yet, as a soldier, surely you must—'

'Jiang, I don't want to disappoint you, but I try not to think of myself as a soldier any more. I'm trying to evolve.'

'Then what do you consider yourself?' His voice stayed polite, but his demeanour had tightened and his food was forgotten on his plate. 'What have you evolved into?'

I shrugged. 'Difficult to say. Something better, at any rate. A paid killer, maybe?'

The whites of his eyes flared. I sighed.

'I'm sorry if that offends you, Jiang, but it's the truth. You probably don't want to hear it, most soldiers don't. When you put on that uniform, you're saying in effect that you resign your right to make independent decisions about the universe and your relation-ship to it.'

'That is *Quellism*.' He all but reared back from the table as he said it.

'Maybe. That doesn't stop it being true.' I couldn't quite work out why I was bothering with this man. Maybe it was something about his ninja calm, the way it begged to be shattered. Or maybe it was just being woken up early by his tightly controlled killing dance. 'Jiang, ask yourself, what are you going to do when your superior officer orders you to plasma-bomb some hospital full of injured children?'

'There are certain actions—'

'No!' The snap in my own voice surprised me. 'Soldiers don't get to make those kinds of choices. Look out the window, Jiang. Mixed in with that black stuff you see blowing around out there, there's a thin coating of fat molecules that used to be people. Men, women, children, all vaporised by some soldier under orders from some superior officer. Because they were in the way.'

'That was a Kempist action.'

'Oh, *please*.'

'I would not carry out—'

'Then you're no longer a soldier, Jiang. Soldiers follow orders. Regardless. The moment you refuse to carry out an order, you're no longer a soldier. You're just a paid killer trying to renegotiate your contract.'

He got up.

'I am going to change,' he said coldly. 'Please present my apologies to Captain Sutjiadi for the delay.'

'Sure.' I picked up a kiwi fruit from the table and bit through the skin. 'See you there.'

I watched him retreat to the other dormitory, then got up from the table and wandered out into the morning, still chewing the furred bitterness of the kiwi skin amidst the fruit.

Outside, the camp was coming slowly to life. On my way to the assembly 'fab I spotted Ameli Vongsavath crouched under one of the *Nagini*'s support struts while Yvette Cruickshank helped her lift part of the hydraulic system clear for inspection. With Wardani bunking in her lab, the three remaining females had ended up sharing a 'fab, whether by accident or design I didn't know. None of the male team members had tried for the fourth bunk.

Cruickshank saw me and waved.

'Sleep well?' I called out.

She grinned back. 'Like the fucking dead.'

Hand was waiting at the door to the assembly 'fab, the clean angles of his face freshly shaven, the chameleochrome coveralls immaculate. There was a faint tang of spice in the air that I thought might come from something on his hair. He looked so much like a net ad for officer training that I could cheerfully have shot him in the face as soon as said good morning.

'Morning.'

'Good morning, lieutenant. How did you sleep?'

'Briefly.'

Inside, three-quarters of the space was given over to the assembly hall, the rest walled off for Hand's use. In the assembly space, a dozen memoryboard-equipped chairs had been set out in an approximate ring and Sutjiadi was busy with a map projector, spinning up a table-sized central image of the beach and surroundings, punching in tags and making notes on his own chair's board. He looked up as I came in.

'Kovacs, good. If you've got no objections, I'm going to send you out on the bike with Sun this morning.'

I yawned. 'Sounds like fun.'

'Yes, well that isn't the primary purpose. I want to string a secondary ring of remotes a few kilometres back to give us a response edge, and while Sun's doing that she can't be watching her own ass. You get the turret duty. I'll have Hansen and Cruickshank start at the north end and swing inland. You and Sun go south, do the same thing.' He gave me a thin smile. 'See if you can't arrange to meet somewhere in the middle.'

I nodded.

'Humour.' I took a seat and slumped in it. 'You want to watch that, Sutjiadi. Stuff's addictive.'

Up on the seaward slopes of Dangrek's spine, the devastation at Sauberville was clearer. You could see where the fireball had blasted a cavity into the hook at the end of the peninsula and let the sea in, changing the whole shape of the coastline. Around the crater, smoke was still crawling into the sky, but from up here you could make out the myriad tiny fires that fed the flow, dull red like the beacons used to flag potential flashpoints on a political map.

Of the buildings, the city itself, there was nothing left at all.

'You've got to hand it to Kemp,' I said, mostly to the wind coming in off the sea, 'he doesn't mess about with decision-making by committee. There's no bigger picture with this guy. Soon as it looks like he's losing, bam! He just calls in the angelfire.'

'Sorry?' Sun Liping was still engrossed in the innards of the sentry system we had just planted. 'You talking to me?'

'Not really.'

'Then you were talking to yourself?' Her brows arched over her work. 'That's a bad sign, Kovacs.'

I grunted and shifted in the gunner's saddle. The grav bike was canted at an angle on the rough grass, mounted Sunjets cranked down to maintain a level bead on the landward horizon. They twitched from time to time, motion trackers chasing the wind through the grass or maybe some small animal that had somehow managed not to die when the blast hit Sauberville.

'Alright, we're done.' Sun closed up the inspection hatch and stood back, watching the turret reel drunkenly to its feet and turn to face the mountains. It firmed up as the ultravibe battery snicked out of the upper carapace, as if it suddenly recalled its purpose in life. The hydraulic system settled it into a squat that took the bulk of the body below line of sight for anyone coming up this particular ridge. A fairweather sensor crept out of the armour below the gun segment and flexed in the air. The whole machine looked absurdly like a starved frog in hiding, testing the air with one especially emaciated foreleg.

I chinned the contact mike.

'Cruickshank, this is Kovacs. You paying attention?'

'Nothing but.' The rapid deployment commando came back laconic. 'Where you at, Kovacs?'

'We have number six fed and watered. Moving on to site five. We should have line of sight on you soon. Make sure you keep your tags where they can be read.'

'Relax, will you? I do this for a living.'

'That didn't save you last time, did it?'

I heard her snort. 'Low blow, man. Low blow. How many times you been dead anyway, Kovacs?'

'A few,' I admitted.

'So.' Her voice rose derisively. 'Shut the fuck up.'

'See you soon, Cruickshank.'

'Not if I get you in my sights first. Out.'

Sun climbed aboard the bike.

'She likes you,' she said over her shoulder. 'Just for your information. Ameli and I spent most of last night hearing what she'd like to do to you in a locked escape pod.'

'Good to know. You weren't sworn to secrecy then?'

Sun fired up the motors and the wind shield snipped shut around us. 'I think,' she said meditatively, 'the idea was that one of us would tell you as soon as possible. Her family are from the Limon Highlands back on Latimer, and from what I hear the Limon girls don't mess about when they want something plugging in.' She turned to look at me. 'Her choice of words, not mine.'

I grinned.

'Of course she'll need to hurry,' Sun went on, busying herself with the controls. 'In a few days none of us'll have any libido left worth talking about.'

I lost the grin.

We lifted and coasted slowly along the seaward side of the ridge. The grav bike was a comfortable ride, even weighed down with loaded panniers, and with the wind screen on, conversation was easy.

'Do you think the archaeologue can open the gate as she claims?' Sun asked.

'If anyone can.'

'If anyone can,' she repeated thoughtfully.

I thought about the psychodynamic repairs I had done on Wardani, the bruised interior landscape I had had to open up, peeling it back like bandaging that had gone septic and stiffened into the flesh beneath. And there at the core, the tightly wired centredness that had allowed her to survive the damage.

She had wept when the opening took hold, but she cried wide-eyed, like someone fighting the weight of drowsiness, blinking the tears out of her eyes, hands clenched into fists at her sides, teeth gritted.

I woke her up, but she brought herself back.

'Scratch that,' I said. 'She can do it. No question.'

'You show remarkable faith.' There was no criticism in Sun's voice that I could hear. 'Strange in a man who works so hard at burying himself beneath the weight of disbelief.'

'It isn't faith,' I said shortly. 'It's knowledge. There's a big difference.'

'Yet I understand Envoy conditioning provides insights that readily transform the one into the other.'

'Who told you I was an Envoy?'

'You did.' This time I thought I could detect a smile in Sun's voice. 'Well, at least, you told Deprez, and I was listening.'

'Very astute of you.'

'Thank you. Is my information accurate then?'

'Not really, no. Where did you hear it?'

'My family is originally from Hun Home. There, we have a Chinese name for the Envoys.' She made a short string of tightly sung syllables. 'It means One who makes Facts from Belief.'

I grunted. I'd heard something similar on New Beijing a couple of decades ago. Most of the colonial cultures have built myths around the Envoys at one time or another.

'You sound unimpressed.'

'Well, it's a bad translation. What the Envoys have is just an intuition enhancement system. You know. You're going out, it's not a bad day but you take a jacket on impulse. Later it rains. How does that work?'

She looked over her shoulder, one eyebrow cocked. 'Luck?'

'Could be luck. But what's more likely is that systems in your mind and body that you're not aware of measure the environment at some subconscious level and just occasionally manage to squirt the message through all the superego programming. Envoy training takes that and refines it so your superego and subconscious get along better. It's nothing to do with belief, it's just a. A sense of something underlying. You make the connections and from that you can assemble a skeleton model of the truth. Later on, you go back and fill in the gaps. Gifted detectives have been doing it for centuries unaided. This is just the superamped version.' Suddenly I was tired of the words coming out of my mouth, the glib flow of human systems specs that you could wrap yourself in to escape the emotional realities of what you did for a living. 'So tell me, Sun. How did you get from Hun Home to here?'

'Not me, my parents. They were contract biosystems analysts. They came here on the needlecast when the Hun Home cooperatives bought into settling Sanction IV. Their personalities, I mean. DHF'd into custom-grown clones from Sino stock on Latimer. All part of the deal.'

'Are they still here?'

She hunched her shoulders slightly. 'No. They retired to Latimer several years ago. The settlement contract paid very well.'

'You didn't want to go with them?'

'I was born on Sanction IV. This is my home.' Sun looked back at me again. 'I imagine you have a problem understanding that.'

'Not really. I've seen worse places to belong.'

'Really?'

'Sure. Sharya for one. *Right! Go right!*'

The bike dipped and banked. Admirable responses from Sun in her new sleeve. I shifted in my saddle, scanning the hillscape. My hands went to the flying grips of the mounted Sunjet set and jerked it down to manual height. On the move it wasn't much good as an automated weapon without some very careful programming and we hadn't had time for that.

'There's something moving out there.' I chinned the mike. 'Cruickshank, we've got movement across here. Want to join the party?'

The reply crisped back. 'On our way. Stay tagged.'

'Can you see it?' asked Sun.

'If I could see it, I'd have shot it. What about the scope?'

'Nothing so far.'

'Oh, *that's* good.'

'I think . . .' We crested a hillock and Sun's voice came back, cursing, by the sound of it, in Mandarin. She booted the bike sideways and swung about, creeping up another metre from the ground. Peering down over her shoulder, I saw what we'd been looking for.

'What the *fuck* is that?' I whispered.

On another scale, I might have thought I was looking at a recently hatched nest of the bio-engineered maggots they use for cleaning wounds. The grey mass that writhed on the grass below us had the same slick-wet consistency and self-referential motion, like a million microscopic pairs of hands washing themselves and each other. But there would have been enough maggots here for every wound inflicted on Sanction IV in the last month. We were looking at a sphere of seething activity over a metre across, pushed gently about on the hillside like a gas-filled balloon. Where the shadow of the bike fell across it, bulges formed on the surface and bulked upwards, bursting like blisters with a soft popping and falling back into the substance of the main body.

'Look,' said Sun quietly. 'It likes us.'

'What the fuck is it?'

'I didn't know the first time you asked me.'

She nudged the bike back to the slope we'd just crested, and put us down. I lowered the Sunjet discharge channels to focus on our new playmate.

'Do you think this is far enough away?' she asked.

'Don't worry,' I said grimly. 'If it even twitches this way, I'm going to blast it apart on general principles. Whatever it is.'

'That strikes me as unsophisticated.'

'Yeah, well. Just call me Sutjiadi.'

The thing, whatever it was, seemed to have calmed down now we no longer cast a shadow on its surface. The internal writhing motion went on, but there was no sign of a coordinated lateral move in our direction. I leaned on the Sunjet mounting and watched, wondering briefly if we weren't somehow still back in the Mandrake construct, looking at another probability dysfunction like the grey cloud that had obscured Sauberville while its fate was still undecided.

A dull droning reached my ears.

'Here come the blam blam crew.' I scanned the ridge northward, spotted the other bike and neurachem'd a close-up. Cruickshank's hair bannered out against the sky from her perch behind the weaponry. They had the windscreen powered back to a driver's cone for speed. Hansen drove hunched forward into it, intent. I was surprised at the warm rush the sight kicked off inside me.

Wolf gene splice, I registered irritably. *Never shake it.*

Good old Carrera. Never misses a trick, the old bastard.

'We should 'cast this back to Hand,' Sun was saying. 'The Cartel archives may have something on it.'

Carrera's voice drifted through my mind.

the Cartel have deployed

I looked back at the seething grey mass with new eyes.

Fuck.

Hansen brought the bike to a juddering halt alongside us and leaned on the handlebars. His brow furrowed.

'Wha—'

'We don't know what the fuck it is,' Sun broke in tartly.

'Yes we do,' I said.

CHAPTER TWENTY-TWO

Hand looked impassively at the projected image for a long moment after Sun froze the film. No one else was looking at the holodisplay any more. Seated in the ring, or crowding in at the bubblefab's door, they were looking at him.

'Nanotech, right?' Hansen said it for everyone.

Hand nodded. His face was a mask, but to the Envoy-tuned senses I had deployed, the anger came smoking off him in waves.

'*Experimental* nanotech,' I said. 'I thought that was a standard scare line, Hand. Nothing to worry about.'

'It usually is,' he said evenly.

'I've worked with military nanosystems,' said Hansen. 'And I've never seen anything like that.'

'No, you wouldn't have.' Hand loosened slightly and leaned forward to gesture at the holodisplay. 'This is new. What you're looking at here is a null configuration. The nanobes have no specific programming to follow.'

'So what are they doing?' asked Ameli Vongsavath.

Hand looked surprised. 'Nothing. They are doing nothing, Mistress Vongsavath. Exactly that. They feed off the radiation from the blast, they reproduce at a modest rate and they. Exist. Those are the only designed parameters.'

'Sounds harmless,' said Cruickshank dubiously.

I saw Sutjiadi and Hansen exchange glances.

'Harmless, certainly, as things stand now.' Hand hit a stud on his chair's board and the frozen image vanished. 'Captain, I think it's best if we wrap this up for now. Would I be right in assuming the sensors we have strung should warn us of any unforeseen developments ahead of time?'

Sutjiadi frowned.

'Anything that moves will show up,' he agreed. 'But—'

'Excellent. Then we should all get back to work.'

A murmur ran round the briefing circle. Someone snorted. Sutjiadi snapped icily for quiet. Hand stood up and pushed through the flap to his quarters. Ole Hansen jerked his chin after the executive, and a ripple of supportive muttering broke out. Sutjiadi reprised his shut-the-fuck-up frost, and started handing out tasks.

I waited it out. The members of the Dangrek team drifted out in ones and twos, the last of them ushered out by Sutjiadi. Tanya Wardani hovered briefly at the door to the bubblefab on her way out, looking in my direction, but Schneider said something in her ear and the two of them followed the general flow. Sutjiadi gave me a hard stare when he saw I was staying, but he walked away. I gave it another couple of minutes, then got up and went to the flap of Hand's quarters. I touched the chime and walked in.

Hand was stretched out on his camp bed, staring at the ceiling. He barely looked in my direction.

'What do you want, Kovacs?'

I snapped out a chair and sat in it. 'Well, less tinsel than you're currently deploying would be a start.'

'I don't believe I've told any lies to anyone recently. And I try to keep track.'

'You haven't told much truth either. Not to the grunts anyway, and with spec ops, I think that's a mistake. They aren't stupid.'

'No, they aren't stupid.' He said it with the detachment of a botanist labelling specimens. 'But they're paid, and that's as good or better.'

I examined the side of my hand. 'I've been paid too, but that won't stop me ripping your throat out if I find you're trying to tinsel me.'

Silence. If the threat bothered him, it didn't show.

'So,' I said at last, 'you going to tell me what's going on with the nanotech?'

'Nothing is *going on*. What I told Mistress Vongsavath was

accurate. The nanobes are in a null configuration because they are doing precisely nothing.'

'Come on, Hand. If they're doing nothing, then what are you so bent out of shape about?'

He stared at the ceiling of the bubblefab for a while. He seemed fascinated by the dull grey lining of the bubblefab's ceiling. I was on the point of getting up and hauling him bodily off the bed, but something in the Envoy conditioning held me in place. Hand was working through something.

'Do you know,' he murmured, 'the great thing about wars like this?'

'Keeps the population from thinking too hard?'

A faint smile flitted across his face.

'The potential for innovation,' he said.

The assertion seemed to give him sudden energy. He swung his feet off the bed and sat up, elbows on knees, hands clasped. His eyes bored into mine.

'What do you think of the Protectorate, Kovacs?'

'You're joking, right?'

He shook his head. 'No games. No entrapment. What's the Protectorate to you?'

'*The skeletal grip of a corpse's hand round eggs trying to hatch?*'

'Very lyrical, but I didn't ask you what Quell called it. I asked what you think.'

I shrugged. 'I think she was right.'

Hand nodded.

'Yes,' he said simply. 'She was right. The human race has straddled the stars. We've plumbed the insides of a dimension we have no senses to perceive in order to do it. We've built societies on worlds so far apart that the fastest ships we have would take half a millennium to get from one side of our sphere of influence to the other. And you know how we did all that?'

'I think I've heard this speech.'

'The corporations did it. Not governments. Not politicians. Not this fucking joke Protectorate we pay lip service to. Corporate planning gave us the vision, corporate investment paid for it, and corporate employees built it.'

'Let's hear it for the corporations.' I patted my palms together, half a dozen dry strokes.

Hand ignored it. 'And when we were done, what happened? The UN came and they muzzled us. They stripped us of the powers they'd awarded us for the diaspora. They levied their taxes again, they rewrote their protocols. They *castrated* us.'

'You're breaking my heart, Hand.'

'You're not funny, Kovacs. Do you have any idea what technological advances we might have made by now if that muzzle hadn't gone back on. Do you know how *fast* we were during the diaspora?'

'I've read about it.'

'In spaceflight, in cryogenics, in bioscience, in machine intelligence.' He ticked them off on bent-back fingers. 'A century of advances in less than a decade. A global tetrameth rush for the entire scientific community. And it all stopped with the Protectorate protocols. We'd have fucking faster-than-light spaceflight by now if they hadn't stopped us. Guaranteed.'

'Easy to say now. I think you're omitting a few inconvenient historical details, but that's not really the point. You're trying to tell me the Protectorate has unwritten the protocols for you, just so you can get this little war won at speed?'

'In essence, yes.' His hands made shaping motions in the space between his knees. 'It's not official, of course. No more than all those Protectorate dreadnoughts that aren't officially anywhere near Sanction IV. But unofficially, every member of the Cartel has a mandate to push war-related product development to the hilt, and then further.'

'And that's what's squirming around out there? Pushed-to-the-hilt nanoware?'

Hand compressed his lips. 'SUS-L. Smart Ultra Short-Lived nanobe systems.'

'Sounds promising. So what does it do?'

'I don't know.'

'Oh for f—'

'No.' He leaned forward. 'I *don't* know. None of us do. It's a new front. They're calling it OPERNS. Open Programme, Environmentally-Reactive Nanoscale Systems.'

'The OPERN System? That's just *so* fucking cute. And it's a weapon?'

'Of course it is.'

'So how does it work?'

'Kovacs, you don't listen.' There was a dreary kind of enthusiasm building in his voice now. 'It's an evolving system. *Smart* evolution. No one knows what it does. Try to imagine what might have happened to life on earth if DNA molecules could think in some rudimentary way – imagine how fast evolution might have got us to where we are now. Now speed that up by a factor of a million or more because when they say Short-Lived they mean it. Last time I was briefed on the project they had each generation down to less than a four-minute lifespan. What does it do? Kovacs, we're only just starting to map what it *can* do. They've modelled it in high-speed MAI-generated constructs, and it comes out different every time. Once it built these robot guns like grasshoppers, the size of a spider tank but they could jump seventy metres into the air and come down firing accurately. Another time it turned into a spore cloud that dissolved carbon bond molecules on contact.'

'Oh. Good.'

'It shouldn't take that turn out here – there's not the density of military personnel for it to be an evolutionarily selective trait.'

'But it could do pretty much anything else.'

'Yes.' The Mandrake exec looked at his hands. 'I would imagine so. Once it goes active.'

'And how long have we got before that happens?'

Hand shrugged. 'Until it disturbs Sutjiadi's sentry systems. As soon as they fire on it, it starts evolving to cope.'

'And if we go blast it now? Because I know that's going to be Sutjiadi's vote.'

'With what? If we use the UV in the *Nagini*, it'll just be ready for the sentry systems that much faster. If we use something else, it'll evolve around that and probably go up against the sentries that much tougher and smarter. It's *nanoware*. You can't kill nanobes individually. And some always survive. Fuck, Kovacs, eighty per cent kill rate is what our labs work off as an evolutionary ideal. It's the principle of the thing. Some survive, the toughest motherfuckers, and those are the ones that work out how to beat you next time around. *Anything*, anything at all you do to kick it out of the null configuration just makes things worse.'

'There must be some way to shut it down.'

'Yes, there is. All you need are the project termination codes. Which I don't have.'

The radiation or the drugs, whatever it was, I felt suddenly tired. I stared at Hand through gritted up eyes. Nothing to say that wouldn't be a rant along the lines of Tanya Wardani's tirade against Sutjiadi the night before. Waste of warm air. You can't talk to people like that. Soldiers, corporate execs, politicians. All you can do is kill them, and even that rarely makes things any better. They just leave their shit behind, and someone else to carry on.

Hand cleared his throat. 'If we're lucky, we'll be out of here before it gets very far advanced.'

'If Ghede is on our side, don't you mean?'

He smiled. 'If you like.'

'You don't believe a word of that shit, Hand.'

The smile wiped away. 'How would you know what I believe?'

'OPERNS. SUS-L. You know the acronyms. You know the construct-run results. You know this fucking programme hardware and soft. Carrera warned us about nanotech deployment, you didn't blink. And now suddenly you're pissed-off and scared. Something doesn't fit.'

'That's unfortunate.' He started to get up. 'I've told you as much as I'm going to, Kovacs.'

I beat him to his feet and drew one of the interface guns, right-handed. It clung to my palm like something feeding.

'Sit down.'

He looked at the levelled gun—

'Don't be ridiculou—'

—then at my face, and his voice dried up.

'Sit. Down.'

He lowered himself carefully back to the bed. 'If you harm me, Kovacs, you've lost everything. Your money on Latimer, your passage offworld—'

'From the sound of it, I don't look much like collecting at the moment anyway.'

'I'm backed up, Kovacs. Even if you kill me, it's a wasted bullet. They'll re-sleeve me in Landfall and—'

'Have you ever been shot in the stomach?'

His eyes snapped to mine. He shut up.

'These are high-impact fragmentation slugs. Close-quarters anti-personnel load. I imagine you saw what they did to Deng's crew. They go in whole and they come out like monomol shards. I shoot you in the gut and it'll take you the best part of a day to die. Whatever they do with your stored self, you'll go through that here and now. I died that way once, and I'm telling you, it's something you want to avoid.'

'I think Captain Sutjiadi might have something to say about that.'

'Sutjiadi will do what I tell him, and so will the others. You didn't make any friends in that meeting, and they don't want to die at the hands of your evolving nanobes any more than I do. Now suppose we finish this conversation in a civilised fashion.'

I watched him measure the will in my eyes, in my gathered stance. He'd have some diplomatic psychosense conditioning, some learned skill at gauging these things, but Envoy training has a built-in capacity to deceive that leaves most corporate bioware standing. Envoys project pure from a base of synthetic belief. At that moment, I didn't even know myself whether I was going to shoot him or not.

He read real intent. Or something else cracked. I saw the moment cross his face. I put up the smart gun. I didn't know which way it would have gone. You very often don't. Being an Envoy is like that.

'This doesn't go outside the room,' he said. 'I'll tell the others about SUS-L, but the rest we keep at this level. Anything else will be counterproductive.'

I raised an eyebrow. 'That bad?'

'It would appear,' he spoke slowly, as if the words tasted bad. 'That I have overextended myself. We've been set up.'

'By?'

'You wouldn't know them. Competitors.'

I seated myself again. 'Another corporation?'

He shook his head. 'OPERNS is a Mandrake package. We bought in the SUS-L specialists freelance, but the project is Mandrake's. Sealed up tight. These are execs inside Mandrake, jockeying for position. Colleagues.'

The last word came out like spit.

'You got a lot of colleagues like that?'

That raised a grimace. 'You don't make friends in Mandrake, Kovacs. Associates will back you as far as it pays them to. Beyond that, you're dead in the water if you trust anyone. Comes with the territory. I'm afraid I have miscalculated.'

'So they deploy the OPERN systems in the hope you won't come back from Dangrek. Isn't that kind of short-sighted? In view of why we're here, I mean?'

The Mandrake exec spread his hands. 'They don't know why we're here. The data's sealed in the Mandrake stack, my access only. It will have cost them every favour they own just to find out I'm down here in the first place.'

'If they're looking to take you down here . . .'

He nodded. 'Yeah.'

I saw new reasons why he wouldn't want to take a bullet out here. I revised my estimate of the face-down. Hand hadn't cracked, he'd calculated.

'So how safe is your remote storage?'

'From outside Mandrake? Pretty much impregnable. From inside?' He looked at his hands. 'I don't know. We left in a hurry. The security codes are relatively old. Given time.'

He shrugged.

'Always about time, huh?'

'We could always pull back,' I offered. 'Use Carrera's incoming code to withdraw.'

Hand smiled tightly.

'Why do you think Carrera gave us that code? Experimental nanotech is locked up under Cartel protocols. In order to deploy it, my enemies would have to have influence at War Council level. That means access to the authorisation codes for the Wedge and anyone else fighting on the Cartel side. Forget Carrera. Carrera's in their pocket. Even if it wasn't at the time Carrera gave it out, the incoming code is just a missile tag waiting to go operative now.' The tight smile again. 'And I understand the Wedge generally hit what they're shooting at.'

'Yeah.' I nodded. 'Generally, they do.'

'So.' Hand got up and walked to the window flap opposite his bed. 'Now you know it all. Satisfied?'

I thought it through.

'The only thing that gets us out of here in one piece is . . .'

'That's right.' He didn't look away from the window. 'A transmission detailing what we've found and the serial number of the claim buoy deployed to mark it as Mandrake property. Those are the only things that'll put me back into the game at a level high enough to trump these *infidels*.'

I sat there for a while longer, but he seemed to have finished, so I got up to leave. He still didn't look at me. Watching his face, I felt an unlooked-for twinge of sympathy for him. I knew what miscalculation felt like. At the exit flap, I paused.

'What is it?' he asked.

'Maybe you'd better say some prayers,' I told him. 'Might make you feel better.'

CHAPTER TWENTY-THREE

Wardani worked herself grey.

She attacked the gate's impassive folded density with a focus that bordered on fury. She sat for hours at a time, sketching glyphs and calculating their likely relation to each other. She speed-loaded technoglyph sequencing into the dull grey instant-access datachips, working the deck like a jazz pianist on tetrameth. She fired it through the assembly of synthesiser equipment around the gate and watched with arms wrapped tightly around herself as the control boards sparked holographic protest at the alien protocols she imposed. She scanned the glyph panelling on the gate through forty-seven separate monitors for the scraps of response that might help her with the next sequence. She faced the lack of coherent animation the glyphs threw back at her with jaw set, and then gathered her notes and tramped back down the beach to the bubblefab to start all over again.

When she was there, I stayed out of the way and watched her hunched figure through the 'fab flap from a vantage point on the loading hatch of the *Nagini*. Close-focus neurachem reeled in the image and gave me her face intent over the sketchboard or the chiploader deck. When she went to the cave, I stood amidst the chaos of discarded technoglyph sketching on the floor of the bubblefab and watched her on the wall of monitors.

She wore her hair pulled severely back, but strands got out and rioted on her forehead. One usually made it down the side of her face, and left me with a feeling I couldn't put in place.

I watched the work, and what it did to her.

Sun and Hansen watched their remote-sentry board, in shifts.

Sutjiadi watched the mouth of the cave, whether Wardani was working there or not.

The rest of the crew watched half-scrambled satellite broadcasts. Kempist propaganda channels when they could get them, for the laughs, government programming when they couldn't. Kemp's personal appearances drew jeers and mock shootings of the screen, Lapinee recruitment numbers drew applause and chant-alongs. Somewhere along the line, the spectrum of response got blurred into a general irony and Kemp and Lapinee started getting each other's fanmail. Deprez and Cruickshank drew beads on Lapinee whenever she cropped up, and the whole crew had Kemp's ideological speeches down, chanting along with full body language and demagogue gestures. Mostly, whatever was on kick-fired much-needed laughter. Even Jiang joined in with the pale flicker of a smile now and then.

Hand watched the ocean, angled south and east.

Occasionally, I tipped my head back to the splatter of starfire across the night sky, and wondered who was watching us.

Two days in, the remotes drew first blood on a nanobe colony.

I was vomiting up my breakfast when the ultravibe battery cut loose. You could feel the thrum in your bones and the pit of your stomach, which didn't help much.

Three separate pulses. Then nothing.

I wiped my mouth clean, hit the bathroom niche's disposal stud and went out onto the beach. The sky was nailed down grey to the horizon, only the persistent smouldering of Sauberville to mar it. No other smoke, no rinsed-out splash of fireglow to signify machine damage.

Cruickshank was out in the open, Sunjet unlimbered, staring up into the hills. I crossed to where she stood.

'You feel that?'

'Yeah.' I spat into the sand. My head was still pulsing, either from the heaving or the ultravibe fire. 'Looks like we've engaged.'

She glanced sideways at me. 'You OK?'

'Threw up. Don't look so smug. Couple of days, you'll be at it yourself.'

'Thanks.'

The gut-deep thrum again, sustained this time. It slopped through my insides. Collateral discharge, the spreading, non-specific recoil from the directed narrowcast wave the battery was throwing down. I gritted my teeth and closed my eyes.

'That's the bead,' said Cruickshank. 'The first three were tracking shots. Now it's locked on.'

'Good.'

The thrum leached out. I bent over and tried to snort one nostril clear of the little clots of vomit that were still lodged at the back of my nasal passages. Cruickshank looked on with interest.

'Do you mind?'

'Oh. Sorry.' She looked away.

I blasted the other nostril clear, spat again and searched the horizon. Still nothing on the skyline. Little flecks of blood in the snot and vomit clots at my feet. Sense of something coming apart.

Fuck.

'Where's Sutjiadi?'

She pointed towards the *Nagini*. There was a mobile crank ramp under the assault ship's nose and Sutjiadi stood on it with Ole Hansen, apparently discussing some aspect of the vessel's forward battery. A short distance up the beach, Ameli Vongsavath sat on a low dune and watched. Deprez, Sun and Jiang were either still at breakfast in the ship's galley, or off doing something to kill the waiting.

Cruickshank shaded her eyes and looked at the two men on the ramp.

'I think our captain's been looking forward to this,' she said reflectively. 'He's been rubbing up against that big bunch of guns every day since we got here. Look, he's smiling.'

I trudged across to the ramp, riding out slow waves of nausea. Sutjiadi saw me coming and crouched down on the edge. No trace of the alleged smile.

'It seems our time has run out.'

'Not yet. Hand said it'll take the nanobes a few days to evolve suitable responses to the ultravibe. I'd say we're about halfway.'

'Then let's hope your archaeologue friend is similarly advanced. Have you talked to her recently?'

'Has anybody?'

He grimaced. Wardani hadn't been very communicative since the news about the OPERN system broke. At mealtimes, she ate for fuel and left. She shot down attempts at conversation with monosyllabic fire.

'I'd appreciate a status report,' said Sutjiadi.

'On it.'

I went up the beach via Cruickshank, trading a Limon handshake she'd shown me as I passed. It was applied reflex, but it gusted a little smile across my face and the sickness in my guts receded a fraction. Something the Envoys taught me. Reflex can touch some odd, deep places.

'Talk to you?' asked Ameli Vongsavath when I reached her vantage point.

'Yeah, I'll be back down here in a moment. Just want to check on our resident driven woman.'

It didn't get much of a smile.

I found Wardani slumped in a lounger at one side of the cave, glowering at the gate. Playback sequences flickered on the filigree screens stretch-deployed over her head. The datacoil weaving at her side was cleared, motes of data circling forlornly at the top left corner where she had left them minimised. It was an unusual configuration – most people crush the display motes flat to the projection surface when they're done – but either way it was the electronic equivalent of sweeping an arm across your desk and dumping the contents all over the floor. On the monitors, I'd watched her do it time and again, the exasperated gesture made somehow elegant by the reversed, upward sweep. It was something I liked watching.

'I'd rather you didn't ask the obvious question,' she said.

'The nanobes have engaged.'

She nodded. 'Yeah, felt it. What's that give us, about three or four days?'

'Hand said four at the outside. So don't feel like you're under any kind of pressure here.'

That got a wan smile. Evidently I was warming up.

'Getting anywhere?'

'That's the obvious question, Kovacs.'

'Sorry.' I found a packing case and perched on it. 'Sutjiadi's getting twitchy though. He's looking for parameters.'

'I guess I'd better stop pissing about and just open this thing, then.'

I mustered a smile of my own. 'That'd be good, yeah.'

Quiet. The gate sucked my attention.

'It's there,' she muttered. 'The wavelengths are right, the sound and vision glyphs check out. The maths works, that is, as far as I *understand* the maths, it works. I've backed up from what I know should happen, extrapolated, this is what we did last time, near as I can remember. It *should* fucking work. I'm missing something. Something I've forgotten. Maybe something I had.' Her face twitched. 'Battered out of me.'

There was a hysterical snap in her voice as she shut up, an edge cutting back along the line of memories she couldn't afford. I scrambled after it.

'If someone's been here before us, could they have changed the settings in some way?'

She was silent for a while. I waited it out. Finally, she looked up.

'Thanks.' She cleared her throat. 'Uh. For the vote of confidence. But you know, it's kind of unlikely. Millions to one unlikely. No, I'm pretty sure I've just missed something.'

'But it is possible?'

'It's *possible*, Kovacs. Anything's possible. But realistically, no. No one human could have done that.'

'Humans opened it,' I pointed out.

'Yeah. Kovacs, a *dog* can open a door if it stands tall enough on its hind legs. But when was the last time you saw a dog take the hinges off a door and rehang it?'

'Alright.'

'There's an order of competence here. Everything we've learnt to do with Martian technology – reading the astrogation charts, activating the storm shelters, riding that metro system they found on Nkrumah's Land – these are all things any ordinary adult Martians could do in their sleep. Basic tech. Like driving a car or living in a house. *This.*' She gestured at the hunched spire on the other side of her battery of instruments. 'This is the pinnacle of their technology. The only one we've found in five hundred years of scratching around on more than thirty worlds.'

'Maybe we're just looking in the wrong places. *Pawing shiny plastic packing while we tread underfoot the delicate circuitry it once protected.*'

She shot me a hard look. 'What are you, a Wycinski convert?'

'I did some reading in Landfall. Not easy finding copies of his later stuff, but Mandrake has a pretty eclectic set of datastacks. According to what I saw, he was pretty convinced the whole Guild search protocol is fucked.'

'He was bitter by the time he wrote that. It isn't easy to be a certified visionary one day and a purged dissident the next.'

'He predicted the gates, didn't he?'

'Pretty much. There were hints in some of the archive material his teams recovered at Bradbury. A couple of references to something called the Step Beyond. The Guild chose to interpret that as a lyrical poet's take on hypercast technology. Back then we couldn't tell what we were reading. Epic poetry or weather reports, it all looked the same and the Guild were just happy if we could squeeze some raw meaning out. The Step Beyond as a translation of hypercaster was meaning snatched from the jaws of ignorance. If it referred to some piece of technology no one had ever seen, that was no use to anybody.'

A swelling vibration spanned the cave. Dust filtered down from around the makeshift bracing. Wardani tipped a glance upward.

'Uh-oh.'

'Yeah, better keep an eye on that. Hansen and Sun both reckon it'll stand reverberations a lot closer than the sentries on the inner ring, but then.' I shrugged. 'Both of them have made at least one fatal mistake in the past. I'll get a ramp in here and check the roof isn't going to fall on you in your moment of triumph.'

'Thanks.'

I shrugged again. 'In everyone's interests, really.'

'That's not what I meant.'

'Oh.' I gestured, suddenly feeling clumsy. 'Look, you opened this thing before. You can do it again. Just a matter of time.'

'Which we don't have.'

'Tell me,' I looked, Envoy-rapid, for some way to disrupt the spiralling gloom in her voice. 'If this really is the pinnacle of Martian technology, how come your team were able to crack it in the first place? I mean . . .?'

I lifted my hands in appeal.

She cracked another weary smile, and I wondered suddenly how hard the radiation poisoning and the chemical counterbalance were hitting her.

'You still don't get it, do you Kovacs? These aren't humans we're talking about. They didn't think the way we do. Wycinski called it peeled-back democratic technoaccess. It's like the storm shelters. Anyone could access them – any Martian, that is – because, well, what's the *point* of building technology that some of your species might have trouble accessing?'

'You're right. That isn't human.'

'It's one of the reasons Wycinski got into trouble with the Guild in the first place. He wrote a paper on the storm shelters. The science behind the shelters is actually quite complicated, but they'd been built in such a way that it didn't matter. The control systems were rendered back to a simplicity even we could operate. He called it a clear indication of species-wide unity, and he said it demonstrated that the concept of a Martian imperium tearing itself apart in a colonial war was just so much bullshit.'

'Just didn't know when to shut up, huh?'

'That's one way of putting it.'

'So what was he arguing? A war against another race? Somebody we haven't run up against yet?'

Wardani shrugged. 'That, or they just pulled out of this region of the galaxy and went somewhere else. He never really went far down either line of reasoning. Wycinski was an iconoclast. He was more concerned with tearing down the idiocies the Guild had already perpetrated than with constructing his own theories.'

'That's a surprisingly stupid way to behave for someone so bright.'

'Or surprisingly brave.'

'That's one way of putting it.'

Wardani shook her head. 'Whatever. The point is, all the technology we've discovered that we understand, we can work.' She gestured at the banks of equipment ranged around the gate. 'We have to synthesise the light from a Martian throat gland, and the sonics we think they produced, but if we *understand it*, we can make it work. You asked how come we were able to crack it last time. It was designed that way. Any Martian needing to get through this gate could open it. And that means, given this equipment and enough time, we can too.'

The flickers of fight sparked beneath the words. She was back up. I nodded slowly, then slid off the packing case.

'You going?'

'I've got to talk to Ameli. You need anything?'

She looked at me strangely. 'Nothing else, thanks.' She straightened up a little in the lounger. 'I've got a couple more sequences to run through here, then I'll be down to eat.'

'Good. See you then. Oh,' I paused on my way out. 'What shall I say to Sutjiadi? I need to tell him something.'

'Tell him I'll have this gate open inside two days.'

'Really?'

She smiled. 'No, probably not. But tell him anyway.'

Hand was busy.

The floor of his quarters was traced about with an intricate pattern in poured sand, and scented smoke drifted from black candles set at the four corners of the room. The Mandrake exec was seated cross-legged and in some kind of trance at one end of the sand tracery. His hands held a shallow copper bowl into which one slashed thumb dripped blood. A carved bone token lay in the centre of the bowl, ivory flecked with red where the blood had trickled down.

'What the fuck are you doing, Hand?'

He surfaced from the trance and fury spasmed across his face. '*I told Sutjiadi no one was to disturb me.*'

'Yeah, he told me that. Now what the fuck are you doing?'

The moment hung. I read Hand. The body language said he was yawing close to violence, which was fine by me. Dying slowly was making me twitchy and keen to do harm. Any sympathy I'd had for him a couple of days back was fast evaporating.

Maybe he read me too. He made a downward spiral motion with his left hand, and the tension in his face smoothed out. He set the bowl aside and licked the surplus blood off his thumb.

'I wouldn't expect you to understand, Kovacs.'

'Let me guess.' I looked around at the candles. The smell of their incense was dark and acrid. 'You're calling up a little supernatural help to get us out of this mess.'

Hand reached back and snuffed the nearest of the candles without getting up. His Mandrake mask was back in place, his voice even. 'As usual, Kovacs, you approach what you do not understand with all the sensitivity of a chimpanzee troop. Suffice it to say there are rituals that must be honoured if any relationship with the spirit realm is to be fruitful.'

'I think I can grasp that, just about. You're talking about a pay-off system. Quid pro quo. A little blood for a handful of favours. Very commercial, Hand, very *corporate*.'

'What do you want, Kovacs?'

'An intelligent conversation. I'll wait outside.'

I stepped back through the flap, surprised at a slight trembling that had set in in my hands. Probably unhandled feedback from the biocircuits in my palm plates. They were as twitchy as racing dogs at the best of times, intensely hostile to any incursions on their processing integrity, and they probably weren't handling the radiation any better than the rest of my body.

Hand's incense sat at the back of my throat like fragments of wet cloth. I coughed it out. My temples pulsed. I grimaced and made chimpanzee noises. Scratched under my arms. Cleared my throat and coughed again. I settled into a chair in the briefing circle and examined one of my hands. Eventually, the trembling stopped.

It took the Mandrake exec about five minutes to clear away his paraphernalia and he emerged looking like a close-to-functional version of the Matthias Hand we were used to seeing around camp. There were blue smears under each eye and his skin had an underlying greyish pallor, but the distance I had seen in the eyes of other men dying of radiation sickness was not there. He had it locked down. There was only the slow seeping knowledge of imminent mortality, and that you had to look for with Envoy eyes.

'I'm hoping this is *very* important, Kovacs.'

'I'm hoping it's not. Ameli Vongsavath tells me the *Nagini*'s onboard monitoring system shut itself down last night.'

'What?'

I nodded. 'Yeah. For about five or six minutes. It isn't difficult to do – Vongsavath says you can convince the system it's part of a standard overhaul. So, no alarms.'

'Oh, Damballah.' He looked out at the beach. 'Who else knows?'

'You do. I do. Ameli Vongsavath does. She told me, I've told you. Maybe you can tell Ghede, and he'll do something about it for you.'

'Don't start with me, Kovacs.'

'It's time for a management decision, Hand. I figure Vongsavath has to be clean – there was no reason for her to tell me about this otherwise. I *know* I'm clean, and I'm guessing you are too. Outside of that, I wouldn't like to say who else we can trust.'

'Has Vongsavath checked the ship?'

'She says, as well as she can without take-off. I was thinking more about the equipment in the hold.'

Hand closed his eyes. 'Yeah. Great.'

He was picking up my speech patterns.

'From a security perspective, I'd suggest Vongsavath takes the two of us up, ostensibly for a check on our nanosized friends. She can run the system checks while we go through the manifest. Call it late this afternoon – that's a credible gap since the remotes kicked in.'

'Alright.'

'I'd also suggest you start carrying one of these where it can't be seen.' I showed him the compact stunner Vongsavath had given me. 'Cute, isn't it? Navy standard issue apparently, out of the *Nagini*'s cockpit emergency box. In case of mutiny. Minimal consequences if you fuck up and shoot the wrong guy.'

He reached for the weapon.

'Uh-uh. Get your own.' I dropped the tiny weapon back into my jacket pocket. 'Talk to Vongsavath. She's tooled up, too. Three of us ought to be enough to stop anything before it gets started.'

'Right.' He closed his eyes again, pressed thumb and forefinger to the inner corners of his eyes. 'Right.'

'I know. It feels like someone really doesn't want us to get through that gate, doesn't it. Maybe you're burning incense to the wrong guys.'

Outside, the ultravibe batteries cut loose again.

CHAPTER TWENTY-FOUR

Ameli Vongsavath put us five kilometres up, flew about for a while and then kicked on the holding auto. The three of us crowded the cockpit and crouched around the flight display holo like hunter gatherers around a fire, waiting. When none of the *Nagini*'s systems had catastrophically failed three minutes later, Vongsavath pushed out a breath she seemed to have been holding since we stationed.

'Probably never was anything to worry about,' she said without much conviction. 'Whoever's been playing around in here isn't likely to want to die with the rest of us, whatever else they might want to achieve.'

'That,' I said gloomily, 'all depends on the level of your commitment.'

'You're thinking Ji—'

I put a finger to my lips. 'No names. Not yet. Don't shape your thoughts ahead of time. And besides, you might want to consider that all our saboteur would really need is a little faith in their recovery team. We'd all still be stack-intact if this thing fell out of the sky, wouldn't we.'

'Unless the fuel cells were mined, yes.'

'There you are, then.' I turned to Hand. 'Shall we?'

It didn't take long to find the damage. When Hand cracked the seal on the first high-impact shielded canister in the hold, the fumes that boiled out were enough to drive us both back up the hatch onto the crew deck. I slapped the emergency isolate panel and the hatch dropped and locked with a solid thump. I rolled onto my back on the deck, eyes streaming, hacking a cough that dug claws in the bottom of my lungs.

'Holy. *Fuck*.'

Ameli Vongsavath darted into view. 'Are you guys—'

Hand waved her back, nodding weakly.

'Corrosion grenade,' I wheezed, wiping at my eyes. 'Must have just tossed it in and locked up after. What was in HIS One, Ameli?'

'Give me a minute.' The pilot went back into the cockpit to run the manifest. Her voice floated back through. 'Looks like medical stuff, mostly. Back-up plugins for the autosurgeon, some of the anti-radiation drugs. Both ID&A sets, one of the major trauma mobility suits. Oh, and one of the Mandrake declared ownership buoys.'

I nodded at Hand.

'Figures.' I pushed myself into a sitting position against the curve of the hull. 'Ameli, can you check where the other buoys are stored. And let's get the hold vented before we open this hatch again. I'm dying fast enough, without that shit.'

There was a drink dispenser on the wall above my head. I reached up, tugged a couple of cans free and tossed one to Hand.

'Here. Something to wash your alloy oxides down with.'

He caught the can and coughed out a laugh. I grinned back.

'So.'

'So.' He popped the can. 'Whatever leakage we had back in Landfall seems to have followed us here. Or do you think someone from outside crept into the camp last night and did this?'

I thought about it. 'It's stretching credibility. With the nanoware on the prowl, a two-ring sentry system, and lethal-dose radiation blanketing the whole peninsula, they'd have to be some kind of psychotic with a mission.'

'The Kempists who got into the Tower at Landfall would fit that description. They were carrying stack burnouts, after all. Real death.'

'Hand, if *I* was going up against the Mandrake Corporation, I'd probably fit myself with one of those. I'm sure your counterintelligence arm have some really *lovely* interrogation software.'

He ignored me, following up his train of thought.

'Sneaking aboard the *Nagini* last night wouldn't be a hard reprise for anyone who can crack the Mandrake Tower.'

'No, but it's more likely we've got leakage in the house.'

'Alright, let's assume that. Who? Your crew or mine?'

I tipped my head in the direction of the cockpit hatch and raised my voice.

'Ameli, you want to kick on the auto and get in here. I'd hate you to think we're talking about you behind your back.'

There was a very brief pause, and Ameli Vongsavath appeared in the hatchway, looking slightly uncomfortable.

'Already on,' she said. 'I, uh, I was listening anyway.'

'Good.' I gestured her forward. 'Because logic dictates that right now you're the only person we can really trust.'

'Thank you.'

'He said logic dictates.' Hand's mood hadn't improved since I hauled him out of prayers. 'There are no compliments going down here, Vongsavath. You told Kovacs about the shutdown; that pretty much clears you.'

'Unless I was just covering myself for when someone opened that canister and discovered my sabotage anyway.'

I closed my eyes. 'Ameli . . .'

'Your crew or mine, Kovacs.' The Mandrake exec was getting impatient. 'Which is it?'

'My crew?' I opened my eyes and stared at the labelling on my can. I'd already run this idea through a couple of times since Vongsavath's revelation, and I thought I had the logic sorted. 'Schneider probably has the flyer skills to shut down the onboard monitors. Wardani probably doesn't. And in either case someone would have had to come up with a better offer than.' I stopped and glanced towards the cockpit. 'Than Mandrake has. That's hard to imagine.'

'It's been my experience that enough political belief will short-circuit material benefit as a motivation. Could either of them be Kempists?'

I thought back down the line of my association with Schneider

I'm not going to fucking watch anything like that ever again. I'm out, whatever it takes

and Wardani

Today I saw a hundred thousand people murdered . . . if I go for a walk, I know there are little bits of them blowing around in the wind out there

'I don't see it, somehow.'

'Wardani was in an internment camp.'

'Hand, a quarter of the fucking population of this planet is in internment camps. It isn't difficult to get membership.'

Maybe my voice wasn't as detached as I'd tried for. He backed up.

'Alright, *my* crew,' he glanced apologetically at Vongsavath. 'They were randomly selected, and they've only been downloaded back into new sleeves a matter of days. It's not likely that the Kempists could have got to them in that time.'

'Do you trust Semetaire?'

'I trust him not to give a shit about anything beyond his own percentage. And he's smart enough to know Kemp can't win this war.'

'I suspect *Kemp's* smart enough to know Kemp can't win this war, but it isn't interfering with his belief in the fight. Short-circuits material benefit, remember?'

Hand rolled his eyes.

'Alright, *who?* Who's your money on?'

'There is another possibility you're not considering.'

He looked across at me. 'Oh, please. Not the half-metre fang stuff. Not the Sutjiadi song.'

I shrugged. 'Suit yourself. We've got two unexplained corpses, stacks excised, and whatever else happened to them, it looks like they were part of an expedition to open the gate. Now we're trying to open the gate and,' I jabbed a thumb at the floor, 'we get this. Separate expeditions, months, maybe a year apart. The only common link is what's on the other side of the gate.'

Ameli Vongsavath cocked her head. 'Wardani's original dig didn't seem to have any problems, right?'

'Not that they noticed, no.' I sat up straighter, trying to box the flow of ideas between my hands. 'But who knows what kind of timescale this thing reacts on. Open it once, you get noticed. If you're tall and bat-winged, no problem. If you're not, it sets off some kind of . . . I don't know, some kind of slow-burning airborne virus, maybe.'

Hand snorted. 'Which does what exactly?'

'I don't know. Maybe it gets inside your head and. Fucks you up. Makes you psychotic. Makes you murder your colleagues, chop their stacks out and bury them under a net. Makes you destroy expeditionary equipment.' I saw the way they were both looking at me. 'Alright, I *know*. I'm just spinning examples here. But think about it. Out there, we've got a nanotech system that evolves its own fighting machines. Now we built that. The human race. And the human race is several thousand years behind the Martians at a *conservative* estimate. Who knows what kind of defensive systems they could have developed and left lying around.'

'Maybe this is just my commercial training, Kovacs, but I find it hard to believe in a defence mechanism that takes a year to kick in. I mean, *I* wouldn't buy shares in it, and I'm a caveman compared to the Martians. Hypertechnology, I *think*, presupposes hyperefficiency.'

'You *are* a fucking caveman, Hand. For one thing, you see everything, including efficiency, in terms of profit. A system doesn't have to produce external benefits to be efficient, it just has to *work*. For a weapons system, that's doubly true. Take a look out the window at what's left of Sauberville. Where's the profit in that?'

Hand shrugged. 'Ask Kemp. He did it.'

'Alright then, think about this. Five or six centuries ago, a weapon like the one that levelled Sauberville would have been useless for anything except deterrence. Nuclear warheads scared people back then. Now we throw them around like toys. We know how to clean up after them, we have coping strategies that make their actual use viable. To get deterrent effect, we have to look at genetic or maybe nanoware weapons. That's us, that's where we are. So it's safe to assume that the Martians had an even bigger problem if they ever went to war. What could they possibly use for deterrence?'

'Something that turns people into homicidal maniacs?' Hand looked sceptical. 'After a year? Come on.'

'But what if you can't stop it,' I said softly.

It grew very quiet. I looked at them both in turn and nodded.

'What if it comes through a hyperlink like that gate, fries the behavioural protocols in any brain it runs into, and eventually infects everything on the other side? It wouldn't matter how slow it was, if it was going to eat the entire planet's population in the end.'

'Eva—' Hand saw where it was going and shut up.

'You can't evacuate, because that just spreads it to wherever you go. You can't do anything except seal off the planet and watch it die, maybe over a generation or two, but without. Fucking. Remission.'

The quiet came down again like a drenched sheet, draping us with its chilly folds.

'You think there's something like that loose on Sanction IV?' asked Hand finally. 'A behavioural virus?'

'Well it *would* explain the war,' said Vongsavath brightly, and all three of us barked unlooked-for laughter.

The tension shattered.

Vongsavath dug out a pair of emergency oxygen masks from the cockpit crash kit, and Hand and I went back down to the hold. We cracked the remaining eight canisters and stood well back.

Three were corroded beyond repair. A fourth had partial damage – a faulty grenade had wrecked about a quarter of the contents. We found fragments of casing, identifiable as *Nagini* armoury stock.

Fuck.

A third of the anti-radiation chemicals. Lost.

Back-up software for half the mission's automated systems. Trashed.

One functional buoy left.

Back on the cabin deck, we grabbed seats, peeled off the masks and sat in silence, thinking it through. The Dangrek team as a high-impact canister, sealed tight with spec ops skills and Maori combat sleeves.

Corrosion within.

'So what are you going to tell the rest?' Ameli Vongsavath wanted to know.

I traded glances with Hand.

'Not a thing,' he said. 'Not a fucking thing. We keep this between the three of us. Write it off to an accident.'

'Accident?' Vongsavath looked startled.

'He's right, Ameli.' I stared into space, worrying at it. Looking for the splinters of intuition that might give me an answer. 'There's no percentage in airing this now. We just have to live with it until we get to the next screen. Say it was powerpack leakage. Mandrake skimping on military surplus past its sell-by date. They ought to believe that.'

Hand did not smile. I couldn't really blame him.

Corrosion within.

CHAPTER TWENTY-FIVE

Before we landed, Ameli Vongsavath ran surveillance on the nanocolonies. We played it back in the conference room.

'Are those webs?' someone asked.

Sutjiadi dialled the magnifier up to full. He got grey cobwebbing, hundreds of metres long and tens wide, filling the hollows and creases beyond the reach of the remote UV batteries. Angular things like four-legged spiders crawled about in the mesh. There was the suggestion of more activity, deeper in.

'That is fast work,' said Luc Deprez, around a mouthful of apple. 'But to me it looks defensive.'

'For the moment,' Hand agreed.

'Well, let's keep it that way.' Cruickshank looked belligerently round the circle. 'We've sat still long enough for this bullshit. I say we haul out one of our MAS mortars and drop a case of frag shells into the middle of that stuff right now.'

'They'll just learn to deal with it, Yvette.' Hansen was staring into space as he said it. We appeared to have sold the powerpack leakage story successfully, but the drop to a single remaining buoy still seemed to have hit Hansen curiously hard. 'They'll learn and adapt on us again.'

Cruickshank made an angry gesture. 'Let them learn. It buys us more time, doesn't it?'

'That sounds like sense to me.' Sutjiadi stood up. 'Hansen, Cruickshank. As soon as we've eaten. Plasma core, fragmentation load. I want to see that stuff burning from here.'

Sutjiadi got what he wanted.

After a hurried early-evening meal in the *Nagini*'s galley, everyone spilled out onto the beach to see the show. Hansen and Cruickshank set up one of the mobile artillery systems, fed Ameli Vongsavath's aerial footage into the ranging processer and then stood back while the weapon lobbed plasma-cored shells up over the hills into the nanocolonies and whatever they were evolving beneath their webbed cocoons. The landward horizon caught fire.

I watched it from the deck of the trawler with Luc Deprez, leant on the rail and sharing a bottle of Sauberville whisky we'd found in a locker on the bridge.

'Very pretty,' said the assassin, gesturing at the glow in the sky with his glass. 'And very crude.'

'Well, it's a war.'

He eyed me curiously. 'Strange point of view for an Envoy.'

'Ex-Envoy.'

'Ex-Envoy, then. The Corps has a reputation for subtlety.'

'When it suits them. They can get pretty unsubtle when they want to. Look at Adoracion. Sharya.'

'Innenin.'

'Yeah, Innenin too.' I looked into the dregs of my drink.

'Crudity is the problem, man. This war could have been over a year ago with a little more subtlety.'

'You reckon?' I held up the bottle. He nodded and held out his glass.

'For sure. Put a wet team into Kempopolis, and ice that fuck. War. Over.'

'That's simplistic, Deprez.' I poured refills. 'He's got a wife, children. A couple of brothers. All good rallying points. What about them?'

'Them too, of course.' Deprez raised his glass. 'Cheers. Probably, you'd have to kill most of his chiefs of staff as well, but so what. It's a night's work. Two or three squads, coordinated. At a total cost of. What?'

I knocked back the first of the new drink, and grimaced. 'Do I look like an accountant?'

'All I know is that for what it costs to put a couple of wet-ops squads into the field, we could have finished this war a year ago. A few dozen people really dead, instead of this mess.'

'Yeah, sure. Or we could just deploy the smart systems on both sides and evacuate the planet until they fight themselves to a standstill. Machine damage, and no loss of human life at all. Somehow I don't see them doing that either.'

'No,' said the assassin sombrely. 'That *would* cost too much. Always cheaper to kill people than machines.'

'You sound kind of squeamish for a covert ops killer, Deprez. If you don't mind me saying so.'

He shook his head.

'I know what I am,' he said. 'But it is a decision I have taken, and something I'm good at. I saw the dead of both sides at Chatichai – there were boys and girls among them, not old enough to be legally conscripted. This was not their war, and they did not deserve to die in it.'

I thought briefly of the Wedge platoon I'd led into hostile fire a few hundred kilometres south west of here. Kwok Yuen Yee, hands and eyes ripped away by the same smart shrapnel blast that had taken Eddie Munharto's limbs and Tony Loemanako's face. Others, less lucky. Hardly innocents, any of them, but they hadn't been asking to die either.

Out on the beach, the barrage of mortar fire stopped. I narrowed my eyes on the figures of Cruickshank and Hansen, indistinct now in the gathering gloom of evening, and saw that they were standing the weapon down. I drained my glass.

'Well, that's that.'

'Do you think it will work?'

I shrugged. 'Like Hansen says. For a while.'

'So they learn our explosive projectile capacity. Probably they also learn to resist beam weapons – the heat effects are very similar. And they are already learning our UV capacity from the sentries. What else do we have?'

'Sharp sticks?'

'Are we close to opening the gate?'

'Why ask me? Wardani's the expert.'

'You seem. Close to her.'

I shrugged again and stared out over the rail in silence. Evening was creeping in across the bay, tarnishing the surface of the water as it came.

'Are you staying out here?'

I held the bottle up to the darkening sky and the banked red glow below. It was still more than half full.

'No reason to leave yet that I can see.'

He chuckled. 'You do realise that we are drinking a collector's item there. It may not taste like it, but that stuff will be worth money now. I mean.' He gestured over his shoulder at where Sauberville used to be. 'They aren't going to be making any more.'

'Yeah.' I rolled over on the rail and faced across the deck towards the murdered city. I poured another glass full and raised it to the sky. 'So here's to them. Let's drink the fucking bottle.'

We said very little after that. Conversation slurred and slowed down as the level in the bottle sank and night solidified around the trawler. The world closed down to the deck, the bulk of the bridge and a cloud-shrouded miser's handful of stars. We left the rail and sat on the deck, propped against convenient points of superstructure.

At some point, out of nowhere, Deprez asked me:

'Were you grown in a tank, Kovacs?'

I lifted my head and focused on him. It was a common misconception about the Envoys, and 'tankhead' was an equally common term of abuse on half a dozen worlds I'd been needlecast to. Still, from someone in spec ops . . .

'No, of course not. Were you?'

'Of course I fucking was not. But the Envoys—'

'Yeah, the Envoys. They push you to the wall, they unpick your psyche in virtual and they rebuild you with a whole lot of conditioned shit that in your saner moments you'd probably rather not have. But most of us are still real-world human. Growing up for real gives you a base flexibility that's pretty much essential.'

'Not really.' Deprez wagged a finger. 'They could generate a construct, give it a virtual life at speed and then download into a clone. Something like that wouldn't even have to *know* it hadn't had a real upbringing. You could *be* something like that for all you know.'

I yawned. 'Yeah, yeah. So could you, for that matter. So could we all. It's something you live with every time you get re-sleeved, every time you get DHF'd, and you know how I know they haven't done that to me?'

'How?'

'Because there's no *way* they'd programme an upbringing as fucked up as mine. It made me sociopathic from an early age, sporadically and violently resistant to authority and emotionally unpredictable. Some fucking clone warrior that makes me, Luc.'

He laughed and, after a moment, so did I.

'It brings you to think, though,' he said, laughter drying up.

'What does?'

He gestured around. 'All this. This beach, so calm. This quiet. Maybe it's all some military construct, man. Maybe it's a place to shunt us while we're dead, while they decide where to decant us next.'

I shrugged. 'Enjoy it while it lasts.'

'You would be happy like that? In a construct?'

'Luc, after what I've seen in the last two years, I'd be happy in a waiting zone for the souls of the damned.'

'Very romantic. But I am talking about a military virtuality.'

'We differ over terms.'

'You consider yourself damned?'

I downed more Sauberville whisky and grimaced past the burn. 'It was a joke, Luc. I'm being funny.'

'Ah. You should warn me.' He leaned forward suddenly. 'When did you first kill someone, Kovacs?'

'If it's not a personal question.'

'We may die on this beach. Really die.'

'Not if it's a construct.'

'Then what if we are damned, as you say?'

'I don't see that as a reason to unburden my soul to you.'

Deprez pulled a face. 'We'll talk about something else, then. Are you fucking the archaeologue?'

'Sixteen.'

'What?'

'Sixteen. I was sixteen. That's closer to eighteen, earth standard. Harlan's World orbits slower.'

'Still very young.'

I considered. 'Nah, it was about time. I'd been running with the gangs since I was fourteen. I'd come close a couple of times already.'

'It was a gang killing?'

'It was a mess. We tried to rip off a tetrameth dealer, and he was tougher than we'd expected. The others ran, I got caught up.' I looked at my hands. 'Then I was tougher than he expected.'

'Did you take his stack?'

'No. Just got out of there. I hear he came looking for me when he got re-sleeved, but I'd joined up by then. He wasn't connected enough to fuck with the military.'

'And in the military they taught you how to inflict real death.'

'I'm sure I would have got around to it anyway. What about you? You have a similarly fucked run-up at this stuff?'

'Oh no,' he said lightly. 'It's in my blood. Back on Latimer, my family name has historic links to the military. My mother was a colonel in the Latimer IP marines. Her father was a navy commodore. I have a brother and a sister, both in the military.' He smiled in the gloom, and his clone-new teeth gleamed. 'You might say we were bred for it.'

'So how does covert ops sit with your historic military family history? They disappointed you didn't end up with a command? If that's not a personal question.'

Deprez shrugged. 'Soldier's a soldier. It is of little importance how you do your killing. At least, that is what my mother maintains.'

'And your first?'

'On Latimer.' He smiled again, remembering. 'I wasn't much older than you, I suppose. During the Soufriere Uprising, I was part of a reconnaissance squad across the swamplands. Walked around a tree and bam!' He brought fist and cupped hand together. 'There he was. I shot him before I realised it. It blasted him back ten metres and cut him in two pieces. I saw it happen and in that moment I did not understand what had happened. I did not understand that I had shot this man.'

'Did you take his stack?'

'Oh, yes. We had been instructed. Recover all fatalities for interrogation, leave no evidence.'

'That must have been fun.'

Deprez shook his head.

'I was sick,' he admitted. 'Very sick. The others in my squad laughed at me, but the sergeant helped me do the cutting. He also cleaned me up and told me not to worry about it too much. Later there were others, and I, well, I became accustomed.'

'And good at it.'

He met my gaze, and the confirmation of that shared experience sparked.

'After the Soufriere campaign, I was decorated. Recommended for covert duties.'

'You ever run into the Carrefour Brotherhood?'

'Carrefour?' He frowned. 'They were active in the troubles further south. Bissou and the cape – do you know it?'

I shook my head.

'Bissou was always their home ground, but who they were fighting for was a mystery. There were Carrefour hougans running guns to the rebels on the cape – I know, I killed one or two myself – but we had some working for us as well. They supplied intelligence, drugs, sometimes religious services. A lot of the rank-and-file soldiers were strong believers, so getting a hougan blessing before battle was a good thing for any commander to do. Have you had dealings with them?'

'A couple of times in Latimer City. More by reputation than actual contact. But Hand is a hougan.'

'Indeed.' Deprez looked abruptly thoughtful. 'That is very interesting. He does not. *Behave* like a man of religion.'

'No, he doesn't.'

'It will make him. Less predictable.'

'Hoy. Envoy guy.' The shout came from under the port rail, and in its wake I caught the murmur of motors. 'You aboard?'

'Cruickshank?' I looked up from my musing. 'That you, Cruickshank?'

Laughter.

I stumbled upright and went to the rail. Peering down, I made out Schneider, Hansen and Cruickshank, all crammed onto one grav bike and hovering. They were clutching bottles and other party apparatus, and from the erratic way the bike held station, the party had started a while ago back on the beach.

'You'd better come aboard before you drown,' I said.

The new crew came with music attached. They dumped the sound system on the deck and the night lit up with Limon Highland salsa. Schneider and Hansen put together a tower pipe and powered it up at base. The smoke fumed off fragrant amidst the hung nets and masting. Cruickshank passed out cigars with the ruin-and-scaffold label of Indigo City.

'These are banned,' observed Deprez, rolling one between his fingers.

'Spoils of war.' Cruickshank bit the end off her own cigar and lay back across the deck with it still in her mouth. She turned her head to light up from the glowing base of the tower pipe, and hinged back up from the waist without apparent effort. She grinned at me as she came upright. I pretended I hadn't been staring with glazed fascination down the length of her outstretched Maori frame.

'Al*right*,' she said, commandeering the bottle from me. '*Now* we're running interference.'

I found a crumpled pack of Landfall Lights in a pocket, and lit my cigar from the ignition patch.

'This was a quiet party until you turned up.'

'Yeah, right. Two old dogs comparing kills, was it?'

The cigar smoke bit. 'So where did you steal these from, Cruickshank?'

'Armoury supply clerk at Mandrake, just before we left. And I didn't steal anything, we have an arrangement. He's meeting me in the gun room.' She shuttled her eyes ostentatiously up and aside, checking a retinal time display. 'In about an hour from now. So. *Were* you two old dogs comparing kills?'

I glanced at Deprez. He quelled a grin.

'No.'

'That's good.' She plumed smoke skyward. 'I got enough of that shit in Rapid Deployment. Bunch of brainless assholes. I mean,

Samedi's sake, it's not like killing people is *hard*. We've all got the capacity. Just a case of shedding the shakes.'

'And refining your technique, of course.'

'You taking the piss out of me, Kovacs?'

I shook my head and drained my glass. There was something sad about watching someone as young as Cruickshank take all the wrong turns you took a handful of subjective decades back.

'You're from Limon, yes?' Deprez asked.

'Highlander, born and bred. Why?'

'You must have had some dealings with Carrefour then.'

Cruickshank spat. Quite an accurate shot, under the bottom of the rail and overboard. 'Those fuckers. Sure, they came around. Winter of '28. They were up and down the cable trails, converting and, when that didn't work, burning villages.'

Deprez threw me a glance.

I said it. 'Hand's ex-Carrefour.'

'Doesn't show.' She blew smoke. 'Fuck, why should it? They look just like regular human beings 'til it's time for worship. You know for all the shit they pile on Kemp,' she hesitated and glanced around with reflexive caution. On Sanction IV, checking for a political officer was as ingrained as checking your dosage meter. 'At least he won't have the Faith on his side of the fence. Publicly expelled them from Indigo City, I read about that back in Limon, before the blockade came down.'

'Well, God,' said Deprez dryly. 'You know, that's a lot of competition for an ego the size of Kemp's.'

'I heard all Quellism is like that. No religion allowed.'

I snorted.

'Hey.' Schneider pushed his way into the ring. 'Come on, I heard that too. What was that Quell said? *Spit on the tyrant God if the fucker tries to call you to account?* Something like that?'

'Kemp's no fucking Quellist,' said Ole Hansen from where he was slumped against the rail, pipe in one trailing hand. He handed the stem to me with a speculative look. 'Right, Kovacs?'

'It's questionable. He borrows from it.' I fielded the pipe and drew on it, balancing the cigar in my other hand. The pipe smoke slunk into my lungs, billowing over the internal surfaces like a cool

251

sheet being spread. It was a subtler invasion than the cigar, though maybe not as subtle as the Guerlain Twenty had been. The rush came on like wings of ice unfurling through my ribcage. I coughed and stabbed the cigar in Schneider's direction. 'And that quote is bullshit. Neo-Quellist fabricated crap.'

That caused a minor storm.

'Oh, come *on*—'

'*What?*'

'It was her deathbed speech, for Samedi's sake.'

'Schneider, she never died.'

'Now *there*,' said Deprez ironically, 'is an article of faith.'

Laughter splashed around me. I hit the pipe again, then passed it across to the assassin.

'Alright, she never died *that we know of*. She just disappeared. But you don't get to make a deathbed speech without a deathbed.'

'Maybe it was a valediction.'

'Maybe it was bullshit.' I stood up, unsteadily. 'You want the quote, I'll give you the quote.'

'Yeahhh!!!'

'Alright!!'

They scooted back to give me room.

I cleared my throat. '*I have no excuses*, she said. This is from the Campaign Diaries, not some bullshit invented deathbed speech. She was retreating from Millsport, fucked over by their microbombers, and the Harlan's World authorities were all over the airwaves, saying God would call her to account for the dead on both sides. She said *I have no excuses, least of all for God. Like all tyrants, he is not worthy of the spit you would waste on negotiations. The deal we have is infinitely simpler – I don't call him to account, and he extends me the same courtesy*. That's exactly what she said.'

Applause, like startled birds across the deck.

I scanned faces as it died down, gauging the irony gradient. To Hansen, the speech seemed to have meant something. He sat with his gaze hooded, sipping thoughtfully at the pipe. At the other end of the scale, Schneider chased the applause with a long whistle and leaned on Cruickshank with painfully obvious sexual intent. The

Limon Highlander glanced sideways and grinned. Opposite them, Luc Deprez was unreadable.

'Give us a poem,' he said quietly.

'Yeah,' jeered Schneider. 'A war poem.'

Out of nowhere, something short-circuited me back to the perimeter deck of the hospital ship. Loemanako, Kwok and Munharto, gathered round, wearing their wounds like badges. Unblaming. Wolf cubs to the slaughter. Looking for me to validate it all and lead them back out to start again.

Where were my excuses?

'I never learnt her poetry,' I lied, and walked away along the ship's rail to the bow, where I leaned and breathed the air as if it was clean. Up on the landward skyline, the flames from the bombardment were already dying down. I stared at it for a while, gaze flipping focus from the glow of the fire to the embers at the end of the cigar in my hand.

'Guess that Quellist stuff goes deep.' It was Cruickshank, settling beside me against the rail. 'No joke if you're from the H World, huh?'

'It isn't that.'

'No?'

'Nah. She was a fucking psycho, Quell. Probably caused more real death singlehanded than the whole Protectorate marine corps in a bad year.'

'Impressive.'

I looked at her and couldn't stop myself smiling. I shook my head. 'Oh, Cruickshank, *Cruickshank*.'

'What?'

'You're going to remember this conversation one day, Cruickshank. Someday, about a hundred and fifty years from now, when you're standing on my side of the interface.'

'Yeah, right, old man.'

I shook my head again, but couldn't seem to shake the grin loose. 'Suit yourself.'

'Well, yeah. Been doing that since I was eleven.'

'Gosh, almost a whole decade.'

'I'm twenty-two, Kovacs.' She was smiling as she said it, but only to herself, gazing down at the black and starlight dapple of the water below us. There was an edge on her voice that didn't match the smile. 'Got five years in, three of them in tactical reserve. Marine induction, I graded ninth in my class. That's out of more than eighty inductees. I took seventh in combat proficiency. Corporal's flashes at nineteen, squad sergeant at twenty-one.'

'Dead at twenty-two.' It came out harsher than I'd meant.

Cruickshank drew a slow breath. 'Man, you are in a *shitty* mood. Yeah, dead at twenty-two. And now I'm back in the game, just like everybody else around here. I'm a big girl, Kovacs, so how 'bout you cut out the little-sister crap for a while.'

I raised an eyebrow, more at the sudden realisation that she was right than anything else.

'Whatever you say. Big girl.'

'Yeah, I saw you looking.' She drew hard on her cigar and plumed the smoke out towards the beach. 'So what do you say, old man? Are we going to get it on before the fallout takes us down? Seize the moment?'

Memories of another beach cascaded through my head, dinosaur-necked palms leaning up over white sand and Tanya Wardani moving in my lap.

'I don't know, Cruickshank. I'm not convinced this is the time and place.'

'Gate got you spooked, huh?'

'That wasn't what I meant.'

She waved it away. 'Whatever. You think Wardani can open that thing?'

'Well, she did before, by all accounts.'

'Yeah, but she looks like shit, man.'

'Well, I guess that's military internment for you, Cruickshank. You should try it some time.'

'Back off, Kovacs.' There was a studied boredom to her voice that woke an updraft of anger inside me. 'We don't work the camps, man. That's government levy. Strictly home-grown.'

Riding the updraft. 'Cruickshank, you don't know a *fucking* thing.'

She blinked, missed a beat, and then came back balanced again, little wisps of hurt almost fanned away with heavy cool.

'Well, uh, I *know* what they say about Carrera's Wedge. Ritual execution of prisoners is what I hear. Very messy, *by all accounts*. So maybe you want to make sure you're clamped to the cable before you start throwing your weight about with me, huh?'

She turned back to the water. I stared at her profile for a while, feeling my way around the reasons I was losing control, and not liking them much. Then I leaned on the rail next to her.

'Sorry.'

'Skip it.' But she flinched away along the rail as she said it.

'No, really. I'm sorry. This place is killing me.'

An unwilling smile curled her lip.

'I mean it. I've been killed before, more times than you'd believe,' I shook my head. 'It's just, it never took this long before.'

'Yeah. Plus you're abseiling after the archaeologue, right?'

'Is it that obvious?'

'It is now.' She examined her cigar, pinched the glowing end off and tucked the rest into a breast pocket. 'I don't blame you. She's smart, she's got her head wrapped around stuff that's just ghost stories and math to the rest of us. Real mystic chick. I can see the appeal.'

She looked around.

'Surprise you, huh?'

'A little.'

'Yeah, well. I may be a grunt, but I know Once in a Lifetime when I see it. That thing we've got back there, it's going to change the way we see things. You can feel that when you look at it. Know what I mean?'

'Yes, I do.'

'Yeah.' She gestured out to where the beach glowed pale turquoise beyond the darkened water. 'I know it. Whatever else we do after this, looking through that gate is going to be the thing that makes us who we are for the rest of our lives.'

She looked at me.

'Feels weird, you know. It's like, I died. And now I've come back, and I have to face this moment. I don't know if it should scare me.

But it doesn't. Man, I'm looking forward to it. I can't wait to see what's on the other side.'

There was an orb of something warm building in the space between us. Something that fed on what she was saying and the look on her face and a deeper sense of time rushing away around us like rapids.

She smiled once more, smeared across her face in a hurry, and then she turned away.

'See you there, Kovacs,' she murmured.

I watched her walk the length of the boat and rejoin the party without a backward glance.

Nice going, Kovacs. Could you be any more heavy-handed?

Extenuating circumstances. I'm dying.

You're all, dying, Kovacs. All of you.

The trawler shifted in the water, and I heard netting creak overhead. My mind flickered back to the catch we'd hauled aboard. Death hung in the folds, like a Newpest geisha in a hammock. Set against the image, the little gathering at the other end of the deck seemed suddenly fragile, at risk.

Chemicals.

That old Altered Significance shuffle of too many chemicals tubing through the system. Oh, and that fucking wolf splice again. Don't forget that. Pack loyalty, just when you least need it.

No matter, I will have them all. The new harvest begins.

I closed my eyes. The nets whispered against each other.

I have been busy in the streets of Sauberville, but—

Fuck off.

I pitched my cigar over the rail, turned and walked rapidly to the main companionway.

'Hoy, Kovacs?' It was Schneider, looking glassily up from the pipe. 'Where you going, man?'

'Call of nature,' I slurred back over my shoulder and braced my way down the companionway rails a wrist-jarring half metre at a time. At the bottom I collided with an idly swinging cabin door in the gloom, fought it off with a sodden ghost of the neurachem and lurched into the narrow space behind.

Illuminum tiles with badly-fitted cover plates let out thin right-angled lines of radiance along one wall. It was just enough to make out detail with natural vision. Frame bed, moulded up from the floor as part of the original structure. Storage racks opposite. Desk and work deck alcoved in at the far end. For no reason, I took the three steps required to reach the end of the cabin and leaned hard on the horizontal panel of the desk, head down. The datadisplay spiral awoke, bathing my lowered features in blue and indigo light. I closed my eyes and let the light wash back and forth across the darkness behind my eyelids. Whatever had been in the pipe flexed its serpent coils inside me.

Do you see, Wedge Wolf? Do you see how the new harvest begins?

Get the fuck out of my head, Semetaire.

You are mistaken. I am no charlatan, and Semetaire is only one of a hundred names . . .

Whoever you are, you're looking for an antipersonnel round in the face.

But you brought me here.

I don't think so.

I saw a skull, lolling at a rakish angle in the nets. Sardonic amusement grinning from blackened, eaten-back lips.

I have been busy in the streets of Sauberville, but I am finished there now. And there is work for me here.

Now you're *mistaken. When I want you, I'll come looking for you.*

Kovacs-vacs-vacs-vacs-vacs . . .

I blinked. The datadisplay ripped light across my open eyes. Someone moved behind me.

I straightened up and stared into the bulkhead above the desk. The dull metal threw back blue from the display. Light caught on a thousand tiny dents and abrasions.

The presence behind me shifted—

I drew breath.

—Closer—

And spun, murderous.

'Shit, Kovacs, you want to give me a heart attack?'

Cruickshank was a step away, hands on her hips. The datadisplay glow picked out the uncertain grin on her face and the unseamed shirt beneath her chameleochrome jacket.

The breath gusted out of me. My adrenalin surge collapsed.

'Cruickshank, what the fuck are you doing down here?'

'Kovacs, what the fuck are *you* doing here? You said a call of nature. What are you planning to do, piss on the datacoil there?'

'What did you follow me down here for?' I hissed. 'You going to *hold* it for me?'

'I don't know. That what you like, Kovacs? You a digital man? That your thing?'

I closed my eyes for a moment. Semetaire was gone, but the thing in my chest was still coiling languidly through me. I opened my eyes again, and she was still there.

'You going to talk like that, Cruickshank, you'd better be buying.'

She grinned. One hand brushed with apparent casualness at the unseamed opening of her shirt, thumb hooking in and slipping the fabric back to reveal the breast beneath. She looked down at her own recently acquired flesh as if entranced by it. Then she brought her fingers back to brush the nipple, flicking back and forth at it until it had stiffened.

'I look like I'm only looking, Envoy guy?' she asked lazily.

She looked up at me and it got pretty frantic after that. We closed and her thigh slid between mine, warm and hard through the soft cloth of the coveralls. I pushed her hand away from her breast and replaced it with my own. The closure became a clinch, both of us looking down at the exposed nipple squeezed between us, and what my fingers were doing to it. I could hear her breath starting to scrape as her own hand unclasped my waistband and slid inside. She cupped the end of my cock and kneaded at it with thumb and palm.

We fell sideways onto the bedshelf in a tangle of clothing and limbs. A salt damp and mustiness rose almost visibly around us on impact. Cruickshank threw out one booted foot and kicked the cabin door closed. It shut with a clang that must have been heard all the way back up to the party on deck. I grinned into Cruickshank's hair.

'Poor old Jan.'

'Huh?' She turned from what she was doing to my prick for a moment.

'I think, *ahhhh*, I think this is going to piss him off. He's been drifting after you since we left Landfall.'

'Listen, with legs like these, *anyone* with a male heterosex gene code is going to be drifting after me. I wouldn't,' she started to stroke, paced a pair of seconds apart. 'Read. Anything. Into it.'

I drew breath. 'OK, I won't.'

'Good. Anyway,' she lowered one breast towards the head of my prick and began to rub slow circles around the nipple with my glans. 'He's probably got his hands full with the archaeologue.'

'*What?*'

I tried to sit up. Cruickshank pushed me back down absently, most of her still focused on the rubbing friction of glans on breast.

'Nah, you just stay there till I'm finished with you. I wasn't going to tell you this, but seeing as,' she gestured at what she was doing. 'Well, I guess you can deal with it. Seen the two of them sloping off together a couple of times now. And Schneider always comes back with this big shit-eating grin, so I figure, you know.' She shrugged, and went back to the timed strokes. 'Well, he's not a. Bad looking. Guy for a. Whiteboy and. Wardani, well. She'd probably. Take whatever. She can get. You liking this, Kovacs?'

I groaned.

'Thought so. You guys.' She shook her head. 'Standard porn-construct stuff. Never fails.'

'You come here, Cruickshank.'

'Ah-ah. No way. Later. I want to see your face when you want to come and I don't let you.'

She had working against her the alcohol and the pipe, impending radiation poisoning, Semetaire rustling around in the back of my head and now the thought of Tanya Wardani in Schneider's embrace – still Cruickshank had me there in less than ten minutes with the combination of hard strokes and soft brushstrokes across her breasts. And when she got me there, she pulled me back from the brink three times with pleased, excited sounds in her throat, before finally masturbating me rapidly and violently to a climax that spattered us both with semen.

The release was like something being unplugged in my head. Wardani and Schneider, Semetaire and impending death all went with it, blown out of my skull through my eyes with the force of the orgasm. I went limp in the narrow bed-space and the cabin beyond spun away into distant irrelevance.

When I felt something again, it was the smooth brush of Cruickshank's thigh as she swung herself astride my chest and seated herself there.

'Now, Envoy guy,' she said, reaching down for my head with both hands. 'Let's see you pay that off.'

Her fingers laced across the back of my head and she held me to the budding folds of flesh like a nursing mother, rocking gently. Her cunt was hot and wet on my mouth and the juices that pooled and slipped out of her tasted of bitter spice. There was a scent to her like delicately burnt wood and a sound in the back of her throat like a saw blade rubbing back and forth. I could feel the tension welling up in the long muscles of her thighs as her climax built, and towards the end she lifted fractionally from her seat on my chest and began tilting her pelvis back and forth in a blind echo of coitus. The cage of fingers nursing my head between her thighs made tiny flexing motions, as if she was losing her grip on the last handhold over an abyss. The noise in her throat became a tight and urgent panting, sawing towards a hoarse cry.

You don't lose me that easily, Wedge Wolf

Cruickshank rose on her haunches, muscles locked up rigid, and yelled her orgasm into the damp air of the cabin.

Not that easily

She shuddered and sank back, crushing the air out of me. Her fingers let go and my head dropped back to the clammy sheets.

I am locked in and

'Now,' she said, reaching back along my body. 'Let's see what we . . . Oh.'

You couldn't miss the surprise in her voice, but she hid the attendant disappointment well. I was semi-erect in her hand, an unreliable hard-on bleeding back to the muscles my body thought it needed to fight or run from the thing in my head.

Yes. Do you see how the new harvest begins. You can run, but—
Get the FUCK out of my head.

I propped myself up on my elbows, feeling the shutdown settling over my face in tight masking bands. The fire we'd lit in the cabin was guttering out. I tried for a smile and felt Semetaire take it away from me.

'Sorry about that. I guess. This dying thing's getting to me sooner than I thought.'

She shrugged. 'Hey, Kovacs. The words *just physical* were never truer than right here and now. Don't give yourself a hard time about it.'

I winced.

'Oh shit, I'm sorry.' It was the same comically crestfallen expression I'd seen on her face in the construct interview. Somehow, on the Maori sleeve it was funnier still. I chuckled, grabbed at the glimmer of laughter offered. Grabbed and grinned harder.

'Ahhh,' she said, feeling the change. 'Want to try anyway? Won't take much, I'm all wet inside.'

She slid back and arched over me. In the faint glow from the datacoil, I fixed my gaze on the juncture of her thighs with a kind of desperation and she fed me into herself with the confidence of someone chambering a round.

The heat and pressure and the long, tensed body riding me were the fragments I used to keep going, but it still wasn't what you'd call great sex. I slipped free a couple of times and my problems became hers as the obvious lack of abandonment braked her excitement back to not much more than methodical technical expertise and a determination to get this done.

Do you see how—

I flailed down the voice in the back of my head and brought some determination of my own to match that of the woman I was joined to. For a while it was work, attention to posture and tight smiles. Then I pushed a thumb into her mouth, let her moisten it and used it to find her clitoris in the crux of her spread legs. She took my other hand and pressed it onto her breast, and not long after she found an orgasm of sorts.

I didn't, but in the grinning, sweat-soaked kiss we shared after she had come, that didn't seem to matter so much.

It wasn't great sex, but it slammed the door on Semetaire for a while. And later, when Cruickshank pulled her clothes back together and went back up on deck, to cheers and applause from the rest of the party, I stayed in the gloom waiting for him, and he still chose not to show.

It was the closest thing to a victory that I ever enjoyed on Sanction IV.

CHAPTER TWENTY-SIX

Consciousness hit me in the head like a freak fighter's claw. I flinched from the impact and rolled over in the bedshelf, trying to crawl back into sleep, but the movement brought with it a rolling wave of nausea. I stopped the vomit in its tracks with an effort of will and propped myself up on one elbow, blinking. Daylight was boring a blurry hole through the gloom above my head from a porthole I hadn't noticed the night before. At the other end of the cabin, the datacoil wove its tireless spiral from the emanator on the desk to the shelved systems data in the top left-hand corner. Voices came through the bulkhead behind me.

Check functionality. I heard Virginia Vidaura's admonitions from the Envoy training modules. *It's not injury you're concerned with, it's damage. Pain you can either use or shut down. Wounds matter only if they cause structural impairment. Don't worry about the blood; it isn't yours. You put this flesh on a couple of days ago, and you'll be taking it off again soon if you can manage not to get killed first. Don't worry about wounds; check your functionality.*

My head felt as if someone was sawing it in half from the inside. Waves of feverish sweat spread down through me, apparently from a point on the back of my scalp. The floor of my stomach had climbed and was nestling somewhere at the base of my throat. My lungs hurt in an obscure, misted way. It felt as if I'd been shot with the stunner in my jacket pocket, on a not particularly low beam.

Functionality!

Thanks Virginia.

Hard to tell how much of this was hangover and how much was dying. Hard to care. I worked myself cautiously into a sitting position on the edge of the shelf and noticed for the first time that I'd fallen asleep more or less in my clothes. I searched my pockets, turned up the battlefield medic's gun and the anti-radiation capsules. I weighed the transparent plastic tubes in one hand and thought about it. The shock of injection was very likely going to make me vomit.

A deeper trawl through my pockets finally turned up a stick of military-issue painkillers. I snapped one loose, held it between finger and thumb and looked at it for a moment, then added a second. Conditioned reflex took the controls as I checked the delivery muzzle of the medic's gun, cleared the breech and loaded the two crystal-filled capsules nose to tail. I snapped the slide and the gun made a high-pitched scaling whine as the magnetic field charged.

My head twinged. An excruciating hard-under-soft sensation that made me, for some reason, think of the flecks of systems data floating in the corner of the coil at the other end of the room.

The charged light winked redly at me from the gun. Inside the breech, inside the capsules, the military-format crystal shards would be aligned, sharp-edged ends pointing down the barrel like a million poised daggers. I pushed the muzzle against the crook of my elbow and squeezed the trigger.

The relief was instant. A soft red rush through my head, wiping the pain away in smudges of pink and grey. Wedge issue. Nothing but the very best for Carrera's wolves. I smirked to myself, stoned on the endorphin boost, and groped for the anti-radiation capsules.

Feeling pretty fucking functional now, Virginia.

Dumped out the shredded painkiller caps. Reloaded with anti-rad, snapped the slide.

Look at yourself, Kovacs. A dying, disintegrating set of cells, woven back together with chemical thread.

That didn't sound like Virginia Vidaura, so it might have been Semetaire, creeping back from last night's retreat. I pushed the observation to the back of my mind and focused on function.

You put this flesh on a couple of days ago, and you'll be taking it off again soon . . .

Yeah, yeah.

Waited out the rising whine. Waited for the red-eyed wink.

Shot.
Pretty fucking functional.

Clothing arranged in something approaching fastened order, I followed the sound of the voices to the galley. Everyone from the party was gathered there, with the notable exception of Schneider, and breakfast was in progress. I got a brief round of applause as I made my appearance. Cruickshank grinned, bumped hips with me and handed me a mug of coffee. By the look of her pupils, I wasn't the only one who'd been at the mil-issue medicine pack.

'What time did you guys wind up?' I asked, seating myself.

Ole Hansen consulted his retinal display. "bout an hour ago. Luc here offered to cook. I went back to the camp for the stuff.'

'What about Schneider?'

Hansen shrugged and forked food into his mouth. 'Went with, but then he stayed. Why?'

'No reason.'

'Here.' Luc Deprez slid an omelette-laden plate in front of me. 'Refuel.'

I tried a couple of mouthfuls, but couldn't develop any enthusiasm for it. I wasn't feeling any definable pain, but there was a sickly instability underlying the numbness that I knew had set in at a cellular level. I hadn't had any real appetite for the last couple of days, and it had been getting increasingly hard to hold food down early in the morning. I cut up the omelette and pushed the pieces around the plate, but in the end I left most of it.

Deprez pretended not to notice, but you could tell he was hurt.

'Anyone notice if our tiny friends are still burning?'

'There's smoke,' said Hansen. 'But not much of it. You not going to eat that?'

I shook my head.

'Give it here.' He grabbed my plate and scraped it onto his own. 'You really must have overdone the local hooch last night.'

'I'm dying, Ole,' I said irritably.

'Yeah, maybe it's that. Or the pipe. My father told me once, never mix alcohol and whiff. Fucks you up.'

A comset chime sounded from the other end of the table.

Someone's discarded induction rig left on broadcast. Hansen grunted, and reached for the set with his free hand. He held it to his ear.

'Hansen. Yeah.' He listened. 'Alright. Five minutes.' He listened again, and a thin smile appeared on his face. 'Right, I'll tell them. Ten minutes. Yeah.'

He tossed the set back among the plates and grimaced.

'Sutjiadi?'

'Got it in one. Going to fly a recon over the nanocolonies. Oh yeah.' His grin came back. 'And the man says *don't* turn off your fucking rigs if you don't want to log a fucking *disciplinary*.'

Deprez chuckled. 'Is that a fucking quote?'

'No. Fucking paraphrase.' Hansen tossed his fork across his plate and stood up. 'He didn't say disciplinary, he called it a DP9.'

Running a platoon is a tricky job at the best of times. When your crew are all way-past-lethal spec ops prima donnas who've been killed at least once, it must be a nightmare.

Sutjiadi wore it well.

He watched without expression as we filed into the briefing room and found seats. The memoryboard on each seat had been set with a foil of edible painkillers, bent and stood on end. Someone whooped above the general murmur when they saw the drugs, then quietened down as Sutjiadi looked in their direction. When he spoke, his voice could have belonged to a restaurant mandroid recommending wine.

'Anyone here who still has a hangover had better deal with it now. One of the outer-ring sentry systems is down. There's no indication of how.'

It got the desired reaction. The murmur of conversation damped out. I felt my own endorphin high dip.

'Cruickshank and Hansen, I want you to take one of the bikes and go check it out. Any sign of activity, any activity *at all*, you veer off and get straight back here. Otherwise, I want you to recover any wreckage on site and bring it back for analysis. Vongsavath, I want the *Nagini* powered up and ready to lift at my command. Everybody else, arm yourselves and stay where you can be found. And wear your rigs at all times.' He turned to Tanya Wardani, who was slumped in a chair at the back of the room, wrapped in her coat and masked with sunlenses. 'Mistress Wardani. Any chance of an estimated opening time.'

'Maybe tomorrow.' She gave no sign that she was even looking at him behind the lenses. 'With luck.'

Someone snorted. Sutjiadi didn't bother to track it.

'I don't need to remind you, Mistress Wardani, that we are under threat.'

'No. You don't.' She unfolded herself from the chair and drifted for the exit. 'I'll be in the cave.'

The meeting broke up in her wake.

Hansen and Cruickshank were gone less than half an hour.

'Nothing,' the demolitions specialist told Sutjiadi when they got back. 'No debris, no scorching, no signs of machine damage. In fact,' he looked back over his shoulder, back to where they'd searched, 'no sign the fucking thing was ever there in the first place.'

The tension in the camp notched higher. Most of the spec ops team, true to their individual callings, retreated into moody quiet and semi-obsessive examinations of the weapons they were skilled with. Hansen unpacked the corrosion grenades and studied their fuses. Cruickshank stripped down the mobile artillery systems. Sutjiadi and Vongsavath disappeared into the cockpit of the *Nagini*, followed after a brief hesitation by Schneider. Luc Deprez sparred seriously with Jiang Jianping down by the waterline, and Hand retreated into his bubblefab, presumably to burn some more incense.

I spent the rest of the morning seated on a rock ledge above the beach with Sun Liping, hoping the residues from the night before would work their way out of my system before the painkillers did. The sky over us had the look of better weather. The previous day's nailed-down grey had broken apart on reefs of blue arrowing in from the west. Eastward, the smoke from Sauberville bent away with the evacuating cloud cover. Vague awareness of the hangover that waited beyond the curtain of endorphins lent the whole scene an undeservedly mellow tone.

The smoke from the nanocolonies that Hansen had seen was

gone altogether. When I mentioned the fact to Sun, she just shrugged. I wasn't the only one feeling irrationally mellow, it seemed.

'Any of this worry you at all?' I asked her.

'This situation?' She appeared to think about it. 'I've been in more danger, I think.'

'Of course you have. You've been dead.'

'Well, yes. But that wasn't what I meant. The nanosystems are a concern, but even if Matthias Hand's fears are well founded, I don't imagine they will evolve anything capable of pulling the *Nagini* out of the sky.'

I thought about the grasshopper robot guns Hand had mentioned. It was one of many details he had chosen not to pass on to the rest of the team when he briefed them on the OPERN system.

'Do your family know what you do for a living?'

Sun looked surprised. 'Yes, of course. My father recommended the military. It was a good way of getting my systems training paid for. They always have money, he told me. Decide what you want to do, and then get them to pay you to do it. Of course, it never occurred to him that there'd be a war here. Who would have thought it, twenty years ago?'

'Yeah.'

'And yours?'

'My what? My father? Don't know, haven't seen him since I was eight. Nearly forty years ago, subjective time. More than a century and a half, objective.'

'I'm sorry.'

'Don't be. My life got radically better when he left.'

'Don't you think he'd be proud of you now?'

I laughed. 'Oh, yeah. Absolutely. He was always a big fan of violence, my old man. Season ticket holder to the freak fights. 'Course, he had no formal training himself, so he always had to make do with defenceless women and children.' I cleared my throat. 'Anyway, yeah. He'd be proud of what I've done with my life.'

Sun was quiet for a moment.

'And your mother?'

I looked away, trying to remember. The downside of Envoy total recall is that memories of everything before the conditioning tend to seem blurry and incomplete by comparison. You accelerate away from it all, like lift-off, like launch. It was an effect I'd craved at the time. Now, I wasn't sure. I couldn't remember.

'I think she was pleased when I enlisted,' I said slowly. 'When I came home in the uniform, she had a tea ceremony for me. Invited everyone on the block. I guess she was proud of me. And the money must have helped. There were three of us to feed – me and two younger sisters. She did what she could after my father left, but we were always broke. When I finished basic, it must have tripled our income. On Harlan's World, the Protectorate pays its soldiers pretty well – it has to, to compete with the yakuza and the Quellists.'

'Does she know you are here?'

I shook my head.

'I was away too much. In the Envoys, they deploy you everywhere except your home world. There's less danger of you developing some inconvenient empathy with the people you're supposed to be killing.'

'Yes.' Sun nodded. 'A standard precaution. It makes sense. But you are no longer an Envoy. Did you not return home?'

I grinned mirthlessly.

'Yeah, as a career criminal. When you leave the Envoys, there isn't much else on offer. And by that time my mother was married to another man, a Protectorate recruiting officer. Family reunion seemed. Well, inappropriate.'

Sun said nothing for a while. She seemed to be watching the beach below us, waiting for something.

'Peaceful here, isn't it?' I said, for something to say.

'At a certain level of perception.' She nodded. 'Not, of course, at a cellular level. There is a pitched battle being fought there, and we are losing.'

'That's right, cheer me up.'

A smile flitted across her face. 'Sorry. But it's hard to think in terms of peace when you have a murdered city on one hand, the pent-up force of a hyperportal on the other, a closing army of nanocreatures somewhere just over the hill and the air awash with lethal-dose radiation.'

'Well, now that you put it like that . . .'

The smile came back. 'It's my training, Kovacs. I spend my time interacting with machines at levels my normal senses can't perceive. When you do that for a living, you start to see the storm beneath the calm everywhere. Look out there. You see a tideless ocean, sunlight falling on calm water. It's peaceful, yes. But under the surface of the water, there are millions of creatures engaged in a life-and-death struggle to feed themselves. Look, most of the gull corpses are gone already.' She grimaced. 'Remind me not to go swimming. Even the sunlight is a solid fusillade of subatomic particles, blasting apart anything that hasn't evolved the appropriate levels of protection, which of course every living thing around here has because its distant ancestors died in their millions so that a handful of survivors could develop the necessary mutational traits.'

'All peace is an illusion, huh? Sounds like something a Renouncer monk would say.'

'Not an illusion, no. But it is relative, and *all* of it, all peace, has been paid for somewhere, at some time, by its opposite.'

'That's what keeps you in the military, is it?'

'My contract is what keeps me in the military. I have another ten years to serve, minimum. And if I'm honest,' she shrugged, 'I'll probably stay on after that. The war will be over by then.'

'Always more wars.'

'Not on Sanction IV. Once they've crushed Kemp, there'll be a clampdown. Strictly police actions from then on. They'll never let it get out of hand like this again.'

I thought about Hand's exultation at the no-holds-barred licensing protocols Mandrake were currently running on, and I wondered.

Aloud, I said, 'A police action can get you killed just as dead as a war.'

'I've been dead. And now look at me. It wasn't so bad.'

'Alright, Sun.' I felt a wavefront of new weariness wash through me, turning my stomach and hurting my eyes. 'I give up. You're one tough motherfucker. You should be telling this stuff to Cruickshank. She'd eat it up.'

'I do not think Yvette Cruickshank needs any encouragement. She is young enough to be enjoying this for itself.'

'Yeah, you're probably right.'

'And if I appear a *tough motherfucker* to you, it was not my intention. But I am a career soldier, and it would be foolish to build resentment against that choice. It *was* a choice. I was not conscripted.'

'Yeah, well these days that's. . . .' The edge ebbed out of my voice as I saw Schneider drop from the forward hatch of the *Nagini* and sprint up the beach. 'Where's he going?'

Below us, from under the angle of the ledge we were seated on, Tanya Wardani emerged. She was walking roughly seaward, but there was something odd about her gait. Her coat seemed to shimmer blue down one side in granular patches that looked vaguely familiar.

I got to my feet. Racked up the neurachem.

Sun laid a hand on my arm. 'Is she—'

It was sand. Patches of damp turquoise sand from the inside of the cavern. Sand that must have clung when—

She crumpled.

It was a graceless fall. Her left leg gave out as she put it down and she pivoted round and downwards around the buckling limb. I was already in motion, leaping down from the ledge in a series of neurachem-mapped footholds, each one good only for momentary bracing and then on to the next before I could slip. I landed in the sand about the same time Wardani completed her fall and was at her side a couple of seconds before Schneider.

'I saw her fall when she came out of the cave,' he blurted as he reached me.

'Let's get her—'

'I'm *fine*.' Wardani turned over and shook off my arm. She propped herself up on an elbow and looked from Schneider to me and back. I saw, abruptly, how haggard she had become. 'Both of you, I'm fine. Thanks.'

'So what's going on?' I asked her quietly.

'What's going on?' She coughed and spat in the sand, phlegm

streaked with blood. 'I'm dying, just like everyone else in this neighbourhood. That's what's going on.'

'Maybe you'd better not do any more work today,' said Schneider hesitantly. 'Maybe you should rest.'

She shot him a quizzical look, then turned her attention to getting up.

'Oh, yeah.' She heaved herself upright and grinned. 'Forgot to say. I opened the gate. Cracked it.'

I saw blood in the grin.

CHAPTER TWENTY-SEVEN

'I don't see anything,' said Sutjiadi.

Wardani sighed and walked to one of her consoles. She hit a sequence of screen panels and one of the stretch-filigrees eased down until it stood between us and the apparently impenetrable spike of Martian technology in the centre of the cavern. Another screen switch and lamps seated in the corners of the cavern went incandescent with blue.

'There.'

Through the stretchscreen, everything was bathed in cool violet light. In the new colour scheme, the upper edges of the gate flickered and ran with gobs of brilliance that slashed through the surrounding glow like revolving biohazard cherries.

'What is that?' asked Cruickshank at my back.

'It's a countdown,' said Schneider with dismissive familiarity. He'd seen this before. 'Right, Tanya.'

Wardani smiled weakly and leaned on the console.

'We're pretty sure the Martians saw further into blue than we do. A lot of their visual notation seems to refer to bands in the ultraviolet range.' She cleared her throat. 'They'd be able to see this unaided. And what it's saying, more or less, is: stand clear.'

I watched, fascinated. Each blob seemed to ignite at the peak of the spire and then separate and drip rapidly along the leading edges to the base. At intervals along the drip down, the lights fired bursts off themselves into the folding that filled the splits between the edges. It was hard to tell, but if you tracked the trajectory of these offbursts, they seemed to be travelling a long way into the cramped geometry of each crack, a longer distance than they had any right to in three-dimensional space.

'Some of it becomes visual later,' said Wardani. 'The frequency scales down as we get nearer to the event. Not sure why.'

Sutjiadi turned aside. In the splashes of rendered light through the filigree screen, he looked unhappy.

'How long?' he asked.

Wardani lifted an arm and pointed along the console to the scrambling digits of a countdown display. 'About six hours, standard. A little less now.'

'Samedi's sake, that is *beautiful*,' breathed Cruickshank. She stood at my shoulder and stared entranced at the screened spike and what was happening to it. The light passing over her face seemed to have washed her features of every emotion but wonder.

'We'd better get that buoy up here, captain.' Hand was peering into the explosions of radiance with an expression I hadn't seen since I surprised him at worship. 'And the launching frame. We'll need to fire it across.'

Sutjiadi turned his back on the gate. 'Cruickshank. *Cruickshank!*'

'Sir.' The Limon woman blinked and looked at him, but her eyes kept tugging back towards the screen.

'Get back down to the *Nagini* and help Hansen prep the buoy for firing. And tell Vongsavath to get a launch and landing mapped for tonight. See if she can't break through some of this jamming and transmit to the Wedge at Masson. Tell them we're coming out.' He looked across at me. 'I'd hate to get shot down by friendly fire at this stage.'

I glanced at Hand, curious to see how he'd handle this one.

I needn't have worried.

'No transmissions just yet, captain.' The executive's voice was a study in absent detachment – you would have sworn he was absorbed in the gate countdown – but under the casual tone there was the unmistakeable tensile strength of an order given. 'Let's keep this on a need-to-know basis until we're actually ready to go home. Just get Vongsavath to map the parabola.'

Sutjiadi wasn't stupid. He heard the cabling buried in Hand's voice and shot me another look, questioning.

I shrugged, and weighed in on the side of Hand's deception. What are Envoys for, after all?

'Look at it this way, Sutjiadi. If they knew you were on board, they'd probably shoot us down anyway, just to get to you.'

'Carrera's Wedge,' said Hand stiffly, 'will do no such thing while they are under contract to the Cartel.'

'Don't you mean the government?' jeered Schneider. 'I thought this war was an internal matter, Hand.'

Hand shot him a weary look.

'Vongsavath.' Sutjiadi had chinned his mike to the general channel. 'You there?'

'In place.'

'And the rest of you?'

Four more voices thrummed in the induction mike at my ear. Hansen and Jiang taut with alertness, Deprez laconic and Sun somewhere in between.

'Map a launch and landing. Here to Landfall. We expect to be out of here in another seven hours.'

A round of cheers rang through the induction mike at my ear.

'Try to get some idea of what the suborbital traffic's like along the curve, but maintain transmission silence until we lift. Is that clear?'

'Silent running,' said Vongsavath. 'Got it.'

'Good.' Sutjiadi nodded at Cruickshank, and the Limon woman loped out of the cavern. 'Hansen, Cruickshank's coming down to help prep the claim buoy. That's all. The rest of you, stay sharp.' Sutjiadi unlocked his posture slightly and turned to face the archaeologue. 'Mistress Wardani, you look ill. Is there anything remaining for you to do here?'

'I—' Wardani sagged visibly over the console. 'No, I'm done. Until you want the damned thing closed again.'

'Oh, that won't be necessary,' Hand called out from where he stood to one side of the gate, looking up at it with a distinctly proprietorial air. 'With the buoy established, we can notify the Cartel and bring in a full team. With Wedge support, I imagine we can render this a ceasefire zone' – he smiled – 'rather rapidly.'

'Try telling that to Kemp,' said Schneider.

'Oh, we will.'

'In any case, Mistress Wardani.' Sutjiadi's tone was impatient. 'I suggest you return to the *Nagini* as well. Ask Cruickshank to jack her field medic programme and look you over.'

'Well, thanks.'

'I beg your pardon.'

Wardani shook her head and propped herself upright. 'I thought one of us should say it.'

She left without a backward glance. Schneider looked at me, and after a moment's hesitation, went after her.

'You've got a way with civilians, Sutjiadi. Anyone ever tell you that?'

He stared at me impassively. 'Is there some reason for you to stay?'

'I like the view.'

He made a noise in his throat and looked back at the gate. You could tell he didn't like doing it, and with Cruickshank gone, he was letting the feeling leak out. There was a gathered stiffness about his stance as soon as he faced the device, something akin to the tension you see in bad fighters before a bout.

I put up a flat hand in clear view, and after a proper pause I slapped him lightly on the shoulder.

'Don't tell me this thing scares you, Sutjiadi. Not the man who faced down Dog Veutin and his whole squad. You were my hero for a while, back there.'

If he thought it was funny, he kept it to himself.

'Come on, it's a *machine*. Like a crane, like a.' I groped about for appropriate comparisons. 'Like a machine. That's all it is. We'll be building these ourselves in a few centuries. Take out the right sleeve insurance, you might even live to see it.'

'You're wrong,' he said distantly. 'This isn't like anything human.'

'Oh shit, you're not going to get mystical on me, are you?' I glanced across to where Hand stood, suddenly feeling unfairly ganged-up on. 'Of *course* it isn't like anything human. Humans didn't build it, the Martians did. But they're just another race.

276

Smarter than us maybe, further ahead than us maybe, but that doesn't make them gods or demons, does it? Does it?'

He turned to face me. 'I don't know. Does it?'

'Sutjiadi, I swear you're beginning to sound like that moron over there. This is *technology* you're looking at.'

'No.' He shook his head. 'This is a threshold we're about to step over. And we're going to regret it. Can't you feel that? Can't you feel the. The *waiting* in it?'

'No, but I can feel the waiting in me. If this thing creeps you out so much, can we go and do something constructive.'

'That would be good.'

Hand seemed content to stay and gloat over his new toy, so we left him there and made our way back along the tunnel. Sutjiadi's jitters must have sparked across to me somehow though, because as the first twist took us out of sight of the activated gate, I had to admit that I felt something on the back of my neck. It was the same feeling you sometimes get when you turn your back on weapons systems you know are armed. No matter that you're tagged safe, you know that the thing at your back has the power to turn you into small shreds of flesh and bone, and that despite all the programming in the world, *accidents happen*. And friendly fire kills you just as dead as the unfriendly kind.

At the entrance, the bright, diffuse glare of daylight waited for us like some inversion of the dark, compressed thing within.

I shook the thought loose irritably.

'You happy now?' I enquired acidly, as we stepped out into the light.

'I'll be happy when we've deployed the buoy and put a hemisphere between us and that thing.'

I shook my head. 'I don't get you, Sutjiadi. Landfall's built within sniper fire of six major digs. This whole planet is riddled with Martian ruins.'

'I'm from Latimer, originally. I go where they tell me.'

'Alright, Latimer. They're not short on ruins either. Jesus, every fucking world we've colonised belonged to them once. We've got their charts to thank for being out here in the first place.'

'Exactly.' Sutjiadi stopped dead and swung on me with the closest thing I'd seen to true emotion on his face since he'd lost the tussle over blasting the rockfall away from the gate. '*Exactly*. And you want to know what that means?'

I leaned back, surprised by the sudden intensity. 'Yeah, sure. Tell me.'

'It means we shouldn't be out here, Kovacs.' He was speaking in a low, urgent voice I hadn't heard him use before. 'We don't belong here. We're not *ready*. It's a stupid fucking mistake that we stumbled onto the astrogation charts in the first place. Under our own steam, it would have taken us thousands of years to find these planets and colonise them. We *needed* that time, Kovacs. We needed to *earn* our place in interstellar space. Instead we got out here bootstrapping ourselves on a dead civilisation we don't understand.'

'I don't think—'

He trampled the objection down. 'Look at how long it's taken the archaeologue to open that gate. Look at all the half-understood scraps we've depended on to come this far. *We're pretty sure the Martians saw further into blue than we do.*' He mimicked Wardani savagely. 'She's got no idea, and neither does anyone else. We're *guessing*. We have no idea what we're doing, Kovacs. We wander around out here, nailing our little anthropomorphic certainties to the cosmos and whistling in the dark, but the truth is we haven't the faintest fucking idea what we're doing. We shouldn't be out here at all. We do not *belong* here.'

I pushed out a long breath.

'Well. Sutjiadi.' I looked at ground and sky in turn. 'You'd better start saving for a needlecast to Earth. Place is a shithole, of course, but it's where we're from. We sure as hell belong *there*.'

He smiled a little, rearguard cover for the emotion now receding from his face as the mask of command slid back on.

'It's too late for that,' he said quietly. 'Much too late for that.'

Down by the *Nagini*, Hansen and Cruickshank were already stripping down the Mandrake claim buoy.

CHAPTER TWENTY-EIGHT

It took Cruickshank and Hansen the best part of an hour to prep the Mandrake claim buoy, mostly because Hand came down out of the cave and insisted on running three full systems checks before he was satisfied with the device's ability to do the job.

'Look,' said Hansen irritably, as they powered up the locational computer for the third time. 'It snaps onto starfield occlusion, and once it's patterned the trace, there's nothing short of a dark body event going to tear it loose. Unless this starship of yours habitually makes itself invisible, there's no problem.'

'That isn't impossible,' Hand told him. 'Run the mass detector back-up again. Make sure it fires up on deployment.'

Hansen sighed. At the other end of the two-metre buoy, Cruickshank grinned.

Later, I helped her carry the launch cradle down from the *Nagini*'s hold and bolt the thing together on its garish yellow tracks. Hansen finished the last of the systems checks, slapped panels shut along the conical body and patted the machine affectionately on one flank.

'All ready for the Big Deep,' he said.

With the launch cradle assembled and working, we enlisted Jiang Jianping's help and lifted the buoy gently into place. Originally designed to be deployed through a torpedo tube, it looked vaguely ridiculous crouched on the tiny tracked cradle, as if it might tip over on its nose at any moment. Hansen ran the tracks back and forth, then round in a couple of circles to check mobility, then snapped the remote off, pocketed it and yawned.

'Anyone want to see if we can catch a Lapinee spot?' he asked.

I checked my retinal time display, where I'd synchronised a stopwatch function to the countdown in the cave. A little over four hours to go. Behind the flaring green numerals in the corner of my vision, I saw the buoy's nose twitch and then pivot forward over the rolled front of the cradle tracks. It bedded in the sand with a solid little thump. I glanced over at Hansen and grinned.

'Oh for Samedi's sake,' said Cruickshank when she saw where we were looking. She stalked over to the cradle. 'Well don't just stand there grinning like a bunch of idiots, help me—'

She ripped apart.

I was closest, already turning to answer her call for help. Later, recalling in the sick numbness of the aftermath, I saw/remembered how the impact split her from just above the hip bone, sawed upwards in a careless back-and-forth scribble and tossed the pieces skywards in a fountain of blood. It was spectacular, like some kind of total body gymnast's trick gone wrong. I saw one arm and a fragment of torso hurled up over my head. A leg spun past me and the trailing edge of the foot caught me a glancing blow across the mouth. I tasted blood. Her head climbed lazily into the sky, rotating, whipping the long hair and a ragged tail of neck and shoulder flesh end over end like party streamers. I felt the patter of more blood, hers this time, falling like rain on my face.

I heard myself scream, as if from a very long distance. Half the word *no*, torn loose of its meaning.

Beside me, Hansen dived after his discarded Sunjet.

I could see

Yells from the *Nagini*.

the thing

Someone cut loose with a blaster.

that did it.

Around the launch cradle, the sand seethed with activity. The thick, barbed cable that had ripped Cruickshank open was one of a half dozen, pale grey and shimmering in the light. They seemed to exude a droning sound that itched in my ears.

They laid hold of the cradle and tore at it. Metal creaked. A bolt tore free of its mountings and whirred past me like a bullet.

The blaster discharged again, joined by others in a ragged chorus of crackling. I saw the beams lance through the thing in the sand and leave it unchanged. Hansen trod past me, Sunjet cuddled to his shoulder, still firing. Something clicked into place.

'*Get back!*' I screamed at him. '*Get the fuck back!*'

The Kalashnikovs filled my fists.

Too late.

Hansen must have thought he was up against armouring, or maybe just rapidity of evasive motion. He'd spread his beam to beat the latter and was closing to up the power. The General Systems Sunjet (Snipe) Mark Eleven will cut through tantalum steel like a knife through flesh. At close range, it vaporises.

The cables might have glowed a little in places. Then the sand under his feet erupted and a fresh tentacle whiplashed upward. It shredded his legs to the knee in the time it took me to lower the smart guns halfway to the horizontal. He screamed shrilly, an animal sound, and toppled, still firing. The Sunjet turned sand to glass in long, shallow gouges around him. Short, thick cables rose and fell like flails over his trunk. His screaming jerked to a halt. Blood gouted lumpily, like the froth of lava you see in the caldera of a volcano.

I walked in, firing.

The guns, the interface guns, like rage extended in both hands. Biofeed from the palm plates gave me detail. High impact, fragmentation load, magazines full to capacity. The vision I had, outside my fury, found structure in the writhing thing before me and the Kalashnikovs punched solid fire at it. The biofeed put my aim in place with micrometre precision.

Lengths of cable chopped and jumped, dropping to the sand and flopping there like landed fish.

I emptied both guns.

They spat out their magazines and gaped open, eagerly. I pounded the butts against my chest. The harness loader delivered, the gun butts sucked the fresh clips in with slick magnetic clicks. Heavy again, my hands whipped out, left and right, seeking, sighting.

The killing cables were gone, chopped off. The others surged at me through the sand and died, cut to pieces like vegetables under a chef's knife.

I emptied again.

Reloaded.

Emptied.

Reloaded.

Emptied.

Reloaded.

Emptied.

Reloaded.

Emptied.

And beat my chest repeatedly, not hearing as the harness clicked empty at me. The cables around me were down to a fringe of feebly waving stumps. I threw away the emptied guns and seized a random length of steel from the wrecked launch cradle. Up over my head, and down. The nearest crop of stumps shivered apart. Up. Down. Fragments. Splinters. Up. Down.

I raised the bar, and saw Cruickshank's head looking up at me.

It had fallen face up on the sand, long, tangled hair half obscuring the wide open eyes. Her mouth was open, as if she was going to say something, and there was a pained expression frozen across her features.

The buzzing in my ears had stopped.

I dropped my arms.

The bar.

My gaze, to the feebly twitching lengths of cable around me.

In the sudden, cold flooding return of sanity, Jiang was at my side.

'Get me a corrosion grenade,' I said, and my voice was unrecognisable in my own ears.

The *Nagini* held station, three metres above the beach. Solid-load machine guns were mounted at the opened loading hatches on both sides. Deprez and Jiang crouched behind each weapon, faces painted pale by the backglow from the tiny screens of the remote sensing sights. There had been no time thus far to arm the automated systems.

The hold behind them was piled with hastily recovered items from the bubblefabs. Weaponry, food canisters, clothing; whatever could be swept up and carried at the run under the watchful gaze of the machine-gun cover. The Mandrake claim buoy lay at one end of the hold, curved body shifting slightly back and forth on the metal deck as Ameli Vongsavath made tiny adjustments to the *Nagini*'s holding buoyancy. At Matthias Hand's insistence, it had been the first item recovered from the suddenly perilous flat expanse of turquoise sand below us. The others obeyed him numbly.

The buoy was very likely wrecked. The conical casing was scarred and torn open along its length. Monitor panels had been ripped off their hinges and the innards extruded like the shredded ends of entrails, like the remains of—

Stop that.

Two hours remaining. The numerals flared in my eye.

Yvette Cruickshank and Ole Hansen were aboard. The human remains retrieval system, itself a grav-lift robot, had floated delicately back and forth above the gore-splattered sand, vacuumed up what it could find, tasted and tested for DNA, and then regurgitated separately into two of the half dozen tasteful blue body bags sprouting from the tubes at its rear. The separation and deposit process made sounds that reminded me of vomiting. When the retrieval robot was done, each bag was snapped free, laser sealed at the neck and bar-coded. Stone-faced, Sutjiadi carried them one at a time to the corpse locker at the back of the hold and stowed them. Neither bag seemed to contain anything even remotely human shaped.

Neither of the cortical stacks had been recovered. Ameli Vongsavath was scanning for traces, but the current theory was that the nanobes cannibalised anything non-organic to build the next generation. No one could find Hansen and Cruickshank's weapons either.

I stopped staring a hole in the corpse locker hatch and went upstairs.

On the crew deck, in the aft cabin, a sample length of nanobe cable lay sealed in permaplastic under the eye of Sun Liping's microscope. Sutjiadi and Hand crowded behind her. Tanya Wardani leaned in a corner, arms hugged around herself, face locked. I sat down, well away from all of them.

'Take a look.' Sun glanced round at me, and cleared her throat. 'It's what you said.'

'Then I don't need to look.'

'You're saying these are the nanobes?' asked Sutjiadi, incredulous. 'Not—'

'The gate isn't even fucking open, Sutjiadi.' I could hear the fraying in my own voice.

Sun peered again into the microscope's screen. She seemed to have found an obscure form of refuge there.

'It's an interlocking configuration,' she said. 'But the components don't actually touch. They must be related to each other purely through field dynamics. It's like a, I don't know, a very strong electromagnetic muscle system over a mosaic skeleton. Each nanobe generates a portion of the field and that's what webs it in place. The Sunjet blast just passes through it. It might vaporise a few individual nanobes in the direct path of the beam, although they do seem to be resistant to very high temperatures, but anyway that's not enough to damage the overall structure and, sooner or later, other units shift in to replace the dead cells. The whole thing's organic.'

Hand looked down at me curiously. 'You knew this?'

I looked at my hands. They were still trembling slightly. Beneath the skin of my palms, the bioplates flexed restlessly.

I made an effort to hold it down.

'I worked it out. In the firefight.' I stared back up at him. Peripherally noticed that Wardani was looking at me too. 'Call it Envoy intuition. The Sunjets don't work, because we've already subjected the colonies to high-temperature plasma fire. They've evolved to beat it, and now they've got conferred immunity to beam weapons.'

'And the ultravibe?' Sutjiadi was talking to Sun.

She shook her head. 'I've passed a test blast across it and nothing happens. The nanobes resonate inside the field, but it doesn't damage them. Less effect than the Sunjet beam.'

'Solid ammunition's the only thing that works,' said Hand thoughtfully.

284

'Yeah, and not for much longer.' I got up to leave. 'Give them some time, they'll evolve past that too. That, and the corrosion grenades. I should have saved them for later.'

'Where are you going, Kovacs?'

'If I were you, Hand, I'd get Ameli to lift us a little higher. Once they learn not everything that kills them lives on the ground, they're likely to start growing longer arms.'

I walked out, trailing the advice like clothing discarded on the way to bed and long sleep. I found my way more or less at random back down to the hold, where it seemed the automated targeting systems on the machine guns had been enabled. Luc Deprez stood on the opposite side of the hatch to his weapon, smoking one of Cruickshank's Indigo City cigars and staring down at the beach three metres below. At the far end of the deck, Jiang Jianping was seated cross-legged in front of the corpse locker. The air was stiff with the uncomprehending silence that serves males as a function of grief.

I slumped against a bulkhead and squeezed my eyes closed. The countdown flared in the sudden darkness behind my eyelids. One hour, fifty-three minutes. Counting down.

Cruickshank flickered through my head. Grinning, focused on a task, smoking, in the throes of orgasm, shredded into the sky—

Stop that.

I heard the brush of clothing near me and looked up. Jiang was standing in front of me.

'Kovacs.' He crouched to my level and started again. 'Kovacs, I am sorry. She was a fine sol—'

The interface gun flashed out in my right hand and the barrel punched him in the forehead. He sat down backwards with the shock.

'Shut *up* Jiang.' I clamped my mouth shut and drew a breath. 'You say one more *fucking* word and I'll paint Luc with your brains.'

I waited, the gun at the end of my arm feeling as if it weighed a dozen kilos. The bioplate hung onto it for me. Eventually, Jiang got to his feet and left me alone.

One hour fifty. It pulsed in my head.

CHAPTER TWENTY-NINE

Hand called the meeting formally at one hour and seventeen minutes. Cutting it fine, but then maybe he was letting everybody air their feelings informally first. There'd been shouting from the upper deck pretty much since I left. Down in the hold, I could hear the tone of it but not, without applying the neurachem, the substance. It seemed to have been going on for a long time.

From time to time, I heard people come and go in the hold, but none of them came near me and I couldn't muster the energy or the interest to look up. The only person not giving me a wide berth, it seemed, was Semetaire.

Did I not tell you there was work for me here?

I closed my eyes.

Where is my antipersonnel round, Wedge Wolf? Where is your flamboyant fury now, when you need it?

I don't—

Are you looking for me now?

I don't do that shit no more.

Laughter, like the gravel of cortical stacks pouring from a skip.

'Kovacs?'

I looked up. It was Luc Deprez.

'I think you had better come upstairs,' he said.

Over our heads, the noise seemed to have quietened down.

'We are *not*,' said Hand quietly, looking around the cabin, 'I repeat, *not* leaving here without staking a Mandrake claim on the other side of that gate. Read the terms of your contracts. The phrasing *every available avenue of opportunity* is paramount and omnipresent.

Whatever Captain Sutjiadi orders you to do now, you will be executed and returned to the soul dumps if we leave without exploring those avenues. Am I making myself clear?'

'No, you're not,' shouted Ameli Vongsavath through the connecting hatch from the cockpit. 'Because the only avenue I can see is carrying a fucked marker buoy up the beach by hand and trying to throw it bodily through the gate on the off-chance it might still work. That doesn't sound to me like an opportunity for anything except suicide. These things take your stack.'

'We can scan for the nanobes—' But angry voices trampled Hand down. He raised his hands over his head in exasperation. Sutjiadi snapped for quiet, and got it.

'We are soldiers.' Jiang spoke unexpectedly into the sudden lull. 'Not Kempist conscripts. This is not a fighting chance.'

He looked around, seeming to have surprised himself as much as anyone else.

'When you sacrificed yourself on the Danang plain,' Hand said, 'you knew you had no fighting chance. You gave up your life. That's what I'm buying from you now.'

Jiang looked at him with open disdain. 'I gave my life for the soldiers under my command. Not for commerce.'

'Oh, Damballah.' Hand tipped his eyes to the ceiling. 'What do you think this war is about, you stupid fucking grunt? Who do you think *paid* for the Danang assault? Get it through your head. You are fighting for *me*. For the corporates and their puppet fucking government.'

'Hand.' I stepped off the hatch ladder and into the centre of the cabin. 'I think your sales technique's flagging. Why don't you give it a rest?'

'Kovacs, I am not—'

'Sit down.' The words tasted like ashes across my tongue, but there must have been something more substantial in them, because he did it.

Faces turned expectantly in my direction.

Not this again.

'We're not going anywhere,' I said. 'We can't. I want out of here as much as any of you, but we can't. Not until we've placed the buoy.'

I waited out the surf of objections, profoundly disinterested in quelling them. Sutjiadi did it for me. The quiet that followed was thin.

I turned to Hand.

'Why don't you tell them who deployed the OPERN system? Tell them why.'

He just looked at me.

'Alright. *I'll* tell them.' I looked round at all the watching faces, feeling the quiet harden and thicken as they listened. I gestured at Hand. 'Our sponsor here has a few home-grown enemies back in Landfall who'd quite like him not to come back. The nanobes are their way of trying to ensure he doesn't. So far that hasn't worked, but back in Landfall they don't know that. If we lift out of here, they will know, and I doubt we'll make the first half of the launch curve before something pointed comes looking for us. Right, Matthias?'

Hand nodded.

'And the Wedge code?' asked Sutjiadi. 'That counts for nothing?'

More gabbled queries boiled over in the wake of his question.

'What Wedge co—'

'Is that an incoming ID? Thanks for the—'

'How come we didn't—'

'Shut up, all of you.' To my amazement, they did. 'Wedge command transmitted an incoming code for our use in an emergency. You weren't made aware of it because,' I felt a smile form on my mouth like a scab, 'you didn't need to know. You didn't matter enough. Well, now you know, and I guess it might seem like a guarantee of safe passage. Hand, you want to explain the fallacy there?'

He looked at the ground for a moment, then back up. There seemed to be something firming in his eyes.

'Wedge Command are answerable to the Cartel,' he said with the measure of a lecturer. 'Whoever deployed the OPERN system nanobes would have needed some form of Cartel sanction. The same channels will provide them with the authorisation codes Isaac

288

Carrera operates under. The Wedge are the most likely candidates to shoot us down.'

Luc Deprez shifted lazily against a bulkhead. 'You're Wedge, Kovacs. I don't believe they will murder one of their own. They're not known for it.'

I tipped a glance at Sutjiadi. His face tightened.

'Unfortunately,' I said. 'Sutjiadi here is wanted for the murder of a Wedge officer. My association with him makes me a traitor. All Hand's enemies have to do is provide Carrera with a crew list for the expedition. It'll short-circuit any influence I have.'

'You could not bluff? I understood the Envoys were famous for that.'

I nodded. 'I might try that. But the odds aren't good, and there is an easier way.'

That cut across the low babble of dispute.

Deprez inclined his head. 'And that is?'

'The only thing that gets us out of here in one piece is deployment of the buoy, or something like it. With a Mandrake flag on the starship, all bets are off and we're home free. Anything less can be read as a bluff or, even if they believe what we've found, Hand's pals can swoop in here and deploy their own buoy after we're dead. We have to transmit a claim confirmation to beat that option.'

It was a moment that held so much tension, the air seemed to wobble, rocking like a chair pushed onto its back legs. They were all looking at me. They were all *fucking* looking at me.

Please, not this again.

'The gate opens in an hour. We blast the surrounding rock off with the ultravibe, we fly through the gate and we deploy the fucking buoy. Then we go home.'

The tension erupted again. I stood in the chaos of voices and waited, already knowing how the surf would batter itself out. They'd come round. They'd come round because they'd see what Hand and I already knew. They'd see it was the only loophole, the only way back for us all. And anyone who didn't see it that way—

I felt a tremor of wolf splice go through me, like a snarl.

Anyone who didn't see it that way, I'd shoot.

For someone whose speciality was machine systems and electronic disruption, Sun turned out to be remarkably proficient with heavy artillery. She test-fired the ultravibe battery at a handful of targets up and down the cliffs, and then had Ameli Vongsavath float the *Nagini* up to less than fifty metres off the cave entrance. With the forward re-entry screens powered up to fend off the debris, she opened fire on the rockfall.

It made the sound of wire ends scratched across soft plastic, the sound of Autumn Fire beetles feeding on belaweed at low tide, the sound of Tanya Wardani removing the spinal bone from Deng Zhao Jun's cortical stack in a Landfall fuck hotel. It was all of these chirruping, chittering, screeching sounds, mixed and amped to doomsday proportions.

It was a sound like the world splintering apart.

I watched it on a screen down in the hold, with the two automated machine guns and the corpse locker for company. There wasn't space for an audience in the cockpit anyway, and I didn't feel like staying in the crew cabin with the rest of the living. I sat on the deck and stared disconnected at the images, rock changing colour with shocking vividness as it crazed and shattered under pressures of plate-tectonic magnitude, then the rushing collapse of the shards as they hurried downward, turned to dense clouds of powder before they could escape the ultravibe beams probing back and forth in the debris. I could feel a vague discomfort in the pit of my stomach from the backwash. Sun was firing on low intensity and shielding in the weapons pod kept the worst of the ultravibe blast damped down aboard the *Nagini*. But still the shrill scream of the beam and the pittering screeches of the tortured rock clawed their way in through the two open hatches and screwed into my ears like surgery.

I kept seeing Cruickshank die.

Twenty-three minutes.

The ultravibe shut down.

The gate emerged from the devastation and billowing dust like a tree through a blizzard. Wardani had told me it wouldn't be harmed by any weapon she knew of, but Sun had still programmed the *Nagini*'s weapon systems to cease fire as soon as they had visual.

Now, as the dust clouds began to drift away, I saw the tangled remnants of the archaeologue's equipment, torn and flung apart by the final seconds of the ultravibe blast. It was hard to believe the dense integrity of the artefact bulking above the debris.

A tiny feather of awe brushed down my spine, a sudden recollection of what I was looking at. Sutjiadi's words came back to me.

We do not belong here. We are not ready.

I shrugged it off.

'Kovacs?' From the sound of Ameli Vongsavath's voice over the induction rig, I wasn't the only one with the elder civilisation jitters.

'Here.'

'I'm closing the deck hatches. Stand clear.'

The machine-gun mounts slid smoothly backward into the body of the deck and the hatches lowered, shutting out the light. A moment later, the interior lighting flickered on, cold.

'Some movement.' Sun said warningly. She was on the general channel, and I heard the succession of sharp indrawn breaths from the rest of the crew.

There was a slight jolt as Vongsavath shifted the *Nagini* up a few more metres. I steadied myself against the bulkhead and, despite myself, looked down at the deck under my feet.

'No, it's not under us.' It was as if Sun had been watching me. 'It's, I think it's going for the gate.'

'Fuck, Hand. How much of this thing is there?' Deprez asked.

I could almost see the Mandrake exec's shrug.

'I'm not aware of any limits on the OPERN system's growth potential. It may have spread under the whole beach for all I know.'

'I think that's unlikely,' said Sun, with the calm of a lab technician in mid-experiment. 'The remote sensing would have found something that large. And besides, it has not consumed the other sentry robots, which it would if it were spreading laterally. I suspect it opened a gap in our perimeter and then flowed through in linear—'

'Look,' said Jiang. 'It's there.'

On the screen over my head, I saw the arms of the thing emerge from the rubble-strewn ground around the gate. Maybe it had already tried to come up under the foundation and failed. The cables were a good two metres from the nearest edge of the plinth when they struck.

'Here we fucking go,' said Schneider.

'No, wait.' This was Wardani, a soft gleam in her voice that could almost have been pride. 'Wait and see.'

The cables seemed to be having trouble getting a grip on the material the gate was made of. They lashed down, then slid off as if oiled. I watched the process repeat itself a half dozen times, and then drew a sharp breath as another, longer arm erupted from the sand, flailed upward a half dozen metres and wrapped around the lower slopes of the spire. If the same limb had come up under the *Nagini*, it could have dragged us out of the sky comfortably.

The new cable flexed and tightened.

And disintegrated.

At first, I thought Sun had disregarded my instructions and opened fire again with the ultravibe. Then recollection caught up. The nanobes were immune to vibe weapons.

The other cables were gone as well.

'Sun? What the fuck happened?'

'I am attempting to ascertain exactly that.' Sun's machine associations were starting to leak into her speech patterns.

'It turned it off,' Wardani said simply.

'Turned what off?' asked Deprez.

And now I could hear the smile in the archaeologue's voice. 'The nanobes exist in an electromagnetic envelope. That's what binds them together. The gate just turned off the field.'

'Sun?'

'Mistress Wardani appears to be correct. I can detect no electromagnetic activity anywhere near the artefact. And no motion.'

The faint hiss of static on the induction rig as everyone digested the confirmation. Then Deprez's voice, thoughtful.

'And we're supposed to fly through that thing?'

Considering what had gone before and what was to come on the other side, zero hour at the gate was remarkably undramatic. At two and a half minutes to zero, the dripping blobs of ultraviolet we'd seen through Wardani's filigree screen became slowly visible as liquid purple lines playing up and down along the outer edges of the spire. In the daylight, the display was no more impressive than a landing beacon by dawn light.

At eighteen seconds, something seemed to happen along the recessed foldings, something like wings being shaken.

At nine seconds a dense black dot appeared without any fuss at the point of the spire. It was shiny, like a single drop of high-grade lubricant, and it appeared to be rolling around on its own axis.

Eight seconds later, it expanded with unhurried smoothness to the base of the spire, and then beyond. The plinth disappeared, and then the sand to a depth of about a metre.

In the globe of darkness, stars glimmered.

PART FOUR
Unexplained Phenomena

Anyone who builds satellites we can't shoot down needs to be taken seriously and, if they ever come back for their hardware, be approached with caution. That's not religion, it's common sense.

Quellcrist Falconer *Metaphysics for Revolutionaries*

CHAPTER THIRTY

I don't like hard space. It fucks with your head.

It's not anything physical. You can make more mistakes in space than at the bottom of the ocean, or in a toxic atmosphere like Glimmer Five's. You can get away with far more in a vacuum, and on occasion I have done. Stupidity, forgetfulness and panic will not get you killed with the same implacable certainty as they will in less forgiving environments. But it isn't that.

The Harlan's World orbitals sit five hundred kilometres out and will shoot down anything that masses more than a six-seater helicopter as soon as look at it. There have been some notable exceptions to this behaviour, but so far no one has been able to work out what caused them. As a result, Harlanites don't go up in the air much, and vertigo is as common as pregnancy. The first time I wore a vacuum suit, courtesy of the Protectorate marines and aged eighteen, my entire mind turned to ice and looking down through the infinite emptiness, I could hear myself whimpering deep in the back of my throat. It looked like a *very* long way to fall.

Envoy conditioning gives you a handle on most kinds of fear, but you're still aware of what scares you because you feel the weight of the conditioning coming online. I've felt that weight every single time. In high orbit over Loyko during the Pilots' Revolt, deploying with Randall's vacuum commandos around Adoracion's outer moon, and once, in the depths of interstellar space, playing a murderous game of tag with members of the Real Estate Crew around the hull of the hijacked colony barge *Mivtsemdi*, falling endlessly along her trajectory, light years from the nearest sun. The *Mivtsemdi* firefight was the worst. It still gives me the occasional nightmare.

The *Nagini* slithered through the gap in three-dimensional space the gate had peeled back, and hung amidst nothing. I let out the same breath we'd all been holding since the assault ship began inching towards the gate, got out of my seat and walked forward to the cockpit, bouncing slightly in the adjusted grav-field. I could already see the starfield on the screen, but I wanted a genuine view through the toughened transparencies of the assault ship's nose. It helps to see your enemy face to face, to sense the void out there a few centimetres from the end of your nose. It helps you to know where you are to the animal roots of your being.

It's strictly against the rules of spaceflight to open connecting hatches during entry into hard space, but no one said anything, even when it must have been clear where I was going. I got a strange look from Ameli Vongsavath as I stepped through the hatch, but she didn't say anything either. Then again, she was the first pilot in the history of the human race to effect an instantaneous transfer from a planetary altitude of six metres to the middle of deep space, so I suspect she had other things on her mind.

I stared forward, past her left shoulder. Stared *down*, and felt my fingers curl tight on the back of Vongsavath's seat.

Fear confirmed.

The old shift in the head, like pressure doors locking sections of my brain up under diamond bright illumination. The conditioning.

I breathed.

'You're going to stay, you might want to sit down,' said Vongsavath, busy with a buoyancy monitor that had just started gibbering at the sudden lack of a planet beneath us.

I clambered to the co-pilot's seat and lowered myself into it, looking for the webbing straps.

'See anything?' I asked with elaborate calm.

'Stars,' she said shortly.

I waited for a while, getting used to the view, feeling the itch at the outer corners of my eyes as instinct-deep reflexes pulled my peripheral vision backwards, looking for some end to the intense lack of light.

'So how far out are we?'

Vongsavath punched up figures on the astrogation set.

'According to this?' She whistled low. 'Seven hundred and eighty-odd million klicks. Believe that?'

It put us just inside the orbit of Banharn, the solitary and rather unimpressive gas giant that stood sentinel on the outer edges of the Sanction system. Three hundred million kilometres further in on the ecliptic was a circling sea of rubble, too extensive to be called a belt, that had for some reason never got round to coalescing into planetary masses. A couple of hundred million kilometres the other side of that was Sanction IV. Where we'd been about forty seconds ago.

Impressive.

Alright, a stellar-range needlecast can put you on the other side of so many kilometres you run out of places to put the zeroes in less time than that. But you have to be digitised first, and then you have to be downloaded into a new sleeve at the other end, and all that takes time and technology. It's a *process*.

We hadn't been through a process, or at least nothing humanly recognisable as such. We'd just bumped across a line. Given inclination and a vacuum suit, I could literally have stepped across that line.

Sutjiadi's sense of *not belonging* came and touched me again at the nape of the neck. The conditioning awoke and damped it out. The wonder along with the fear.

'We've stopped,' murmured Vongsavath, to herself more than me. 'Something soaked up our acceleration. You'd expect some. Holy. God.'

Her voice, already low, sank to a whisper on the last two words and seemed to decelerate the way the *Nagini* apparently had. I looked up from the figures she'd just maximised on the display, and my first thought, still scrabbling around in a planet-bound context, was that we had cruised into a shadow. By the time I remembered that there were no mountains out here, and not much in the way of sunlight to be obscured anyway, the same chilly shock that Vongsavath must have been feeling hit me.

Over our heads, the stars were sliding away.

They disappeared silently, swallowed with terrifying speed by the vast, occluding bulk of something hanging, it seemed, only metres above the overhead viewports.

'That's it,' I said, and a small cold shiver ran through me as I said it, as if I'd just completed an obscure summoning.

'Range . . .' Vongsavath shook her head. 'It's nearly five kilometres off. That makes it—'

'Twenty-seven kilometres across,' I read out the data myself. 'Fifty-three long. External structures extending . . .'

I gave up.

'Big. Very big.'

'Isn't it.' Wardani's voice came from right behind me. 'See the crenellation at the edge. Each of those bites is nearly a kilometre deep.'

'Why don't I just sell seats in here,' snapped Vongsavath. 'Mistress Wardani, will you please return to the cabin and sit down.'

'Sorry,' murmured the archaeologue. 'I was just—'

Sirens. A spaced scream, slashing at the air in the cockpit.

'Incoming,' yelled Vongsavath, and kicked the *Nagini* on end.

It was a manoeuvre that would have hurt in a gravity well, but with only the ship's own grav field exerting force, it felt more like an experia special effect, an Angel wharf-conjuror's trick with holoshift.

Vacuum combat fragments:

I saw the missile coming, falling end over end towards the right side viewports.

I heard the battle systems reporting for duty in their cosily enthusiastic machine voices.

Shouts from the cabin behind me.

I started to tense. The conditioning broke in heavily, forced me into impact-ready limpness—

Just a minute.

'That can't be right,' said Vongsavath suddenly.

You don't see missiles in space. Even the ones *we* can build move too fast for a human eye to track effectively.

'No impact threat,' observed the battle computer, sounding slightly disappointed. 'No impact threat.'

'It's barely moving.' Vongsavath punched up a new screen, shaking her head. 'Axial velocity at . . . Ah, that's just *drift*, man.'

'Those are still machined components,' I said, pointing at a small spike in the red section of the spectrum scan. 'Circuitry, maybe. It ain't a rock. Not just a rock, anyway.'

'It's not active, though. Totally inert. Let me run the—'

'Why don't you just bring us round and back up,' I made a quick calculation in my head. 'About a hundred metres. It'll be practically sitting out there on the windscreen. Kick on the external lights.'

Vongsavath locked onto me with a look that somehow managed to combine disdain with horror. It wasn't exactly a flight manual recommendation. More importantly, she probably still had the adrenalin chop sloshing about in her system the same as me. It's apt to make you grumpy.

'Coming about,' she said finally.

Outside the viewports, the environment lighting ignited.

In a way, it wasn't such a great idea. The toughened transparent alloy of the viewports would have been built to vacuum combat spec, which means stopping all but the most energetic micrometeorites without much more than surface pitting. Certainly it wasn't about to be ruined by bumping into something adrift. But the thing that came bumping up over the nose of the *Nagini* made an impact anyway.

Behind me, Tanya Wardani shrieked, a short, quickly-locked-up sound.

Scorched and ruptured though it was by the extremes of cold and the absence of pressure outside, the object was still recognisable as a human body, dressed for summer on the Dangrek coast.

'Holy God,' whispered Vongsavath, again.

A blackened face peered sightlessly in at us, empty eye sockets masked in trailing strands of exploded, frozen tissue. The mouth below was all scream, as silent now as it would have been when its owner tried to find a voice for the agony of dissolution. Beneath a ludicrously loud summer shirt, the body was swollen by a bulk that I guessed were the ruptured intestines and stomach. One clawed hand bumped knuckles on the viewport. The other arm was jerked back, over the head. The legs were similarly flexed, forward and back. Whoever it was had died flailing at the vacuum.

Died falling.

Behind me, Wardani was sobbing quietly.

Saying a name.

We found the rest of them by suit beacons, floating at the bottom of a three-hundred-metre dimple in the hull structure and clustered around what appeared to be a docking portal. There were four, all wearing cheap pull-on vacuum suits. From the look of it, three had died when their air supply ran out, which according to suit specs would have taken about six to eight hours. The fourth one hadn't wanted to wait that long. There was a neat five-centimetre hole melted through the suit's helmet from right to left. The industrial laser cutter that had done the damage was still tethered to the right hand at the wrist.

Vongsavath sent out the manigrab-equipped EVA robot once again. We watched the screens in silence as the little machine collected each corpse in its arms and bore it back to the *Nagini* with the same gentle deftness of touch it had applied to the blackened and ruptured remains of Tomas Dhasanapongsakul at the gate. This time, with the bodies enfolded in the white wrap of their vacuum suits, it could almost have been footage of a funeral run in reverse. The dead carried back out of the deep, and consigned to the *Nagini*'s ventral airlock.

Wardani could not cope. She came down to the hold deck with the rest of us while Vongsavath blew the inner hatch on the airlock from the flight deck. She watched Sutjiadi and Luc Deprez bring the vacuum-suited bodies up. But when Deprez broke the seals of the first helmet and lifted it off the features beneath, she uttered a choked sob and spun away to the far corner of the hold. I heard her retching. The acid reek of vomit stung the air.

Schneider went after her.

'You know this one too?' I asked redundantly, staring down at the dead face. It was a woman in a mid-forties sleeve, eyes wide and accusatory. She was frozen solid, neck protruding stiffly from the ring of the suit aperture, head lifting rigidly clear of the deck. The heating elements of the suit must have taken a while longer to give out than the air supply, but if this woman was part of the same team that we'd found in the trawl net, she'd been out here for at least a year. They don't make suits with that kind of survivability.

Schneider answered for the archaeologue. 'It's Aribowo. Pharintorn Aribowo. Glyph specialist on the Dangrek dig.'

I nodded at Deprez. He unsealed the other helmets and detached them. The dead stared up at us in a line, heads lifted as if in the midst of some group abdominal workout. Aribowo and three male companions. Only the suicide's eyes were closed, features composed in an expression of such peace that you wanted to check again for the slick, cauterised hole this man had bored through his own skull.

Looking at him, I wondered what I would have done. Seeing the gate slam shut behind me, knowing at that moment that I was going to die out here in the dark. Knowing, even if a fast rescue ship were dispatched immediately to these exact coordinates, that rescue would come months too late. I wondered if I would have had the courage to wait, hanging in the infinite night, hoping against hope for some miracle to occur.

Or the courage not to.

'That's Weng,' Schneider had come back and was hovering at my shoulder. 'Can't remember his other name. He was some kind of glyph theorist too. I don't know the others.'

I glanced across the deck to where Tanya Wardani was huddled against the hull wall, arms wrapped around herself.

'Why don't you leave her alone?' hissed Schneider.

I shrugged. 'OK. Luc, you'd better go back down into the lock and get Dhasanapongsakul bagged before he starts to drip. Then the rest of them. I'll give you a hand. Sun, can we get the buoy overhauled? Sutjiadi, maybe you can help her. I'd like to know if we're actually going to be able to deploy the fucking thing.'

Sun nodded gravely.

'Hand, you'd better start thinking of contingencies, because if the buoy's fucked, we're going to need an alternative plan of action.'

'Wait a minute.' Schneider looked genuinely scared for the first time since I'd met him. 'We're *staying* around here. After what happened to these people, we're *staying*?'

'We don't know what happened to these people, Schneider.'

'Isn't it obvious? The gate isn't stable, it shut down on them.'

'That's bullshit, Jan.' There was an old strength trickling through the rasp in Wardani's voice, a tone that made something flare up in my stomach. I looked back at her, and she was on her feet again, wiping her face clean of the tears and vomit specks with the heel of one palm. 'We opened it last time, and it stood for days. There's no instability in the sequencing I ran, then or now.'

'Tanya.' Schneider looked suddenly betrayed. He spread his hands wide. 'I mean—'

'I don't know what happened here, I don't know what,' she squeezed out the words, '*fucked. Up.* Glyph sequences Aribowo used, but it isn't going to happen to us. I know what I am doing.'

'With respect, Mistress Wardani,' Sutjiadi looked around at the assembled faces, gauging support. 'You've admitted that our knowledge of this artefact is incomplete. I fail to see how you can guarantee—'

'I am a Guild Master.' Wardani stalked back towards the lined up corpses, eyes flaring. It was as if she was furious with them all for getting killed. 'This woman was not. Weng Xiaodong. Was not. Tomas Dhasanapongsakul. Was not. These people were *Scratchers*. Talented, maybe, but that is *not* enough. I have over seventy years of experience in the field of Martian archaeology, and if I tell you that the gate is stable, then *it is* stable.'

She glared around her, eyes bright, corpses at her feet. No one seemed disposed to argue the point.

The poisoning from the Sauberville blast was gathering force in my cells. It took longer to deal with the bodies than I'd expected, certainly longer than it ought have taken any ranking officer in Carrera's Wedge, and when the corpse locker hinged slowly shut afterwards, I felt wrung out.

Deprez, if he felt the same, wasn't showing it. Maybe the Maori sleeves were holding up according to spec. He wandered across the hold to where Schneider was showing Jiang Jianping some kind of trick with a grav harness. I hesitated for a moment, then turned away and headed for the ladder to the upper deck, hoping to find Tanya Wardani in the forward cabin.

Instead, I found Hand, watching the vast bulk of the Martian starship roll past below us on the cabin's main screen.

'Takes some getting used to, huh?'

There was a greedy enthusiasm in the executive's voice as he gestured at the view. The *Nagini*'s environment lights provided illumination for a few hundred metres in all directions, but as the structure faded away into the darkness, you were still aware of it, sprawling across the starfield. It seemed to go on forever, curving out at odd angles and sprouting appendages like bubbles about to burst, defying the eye to put limits on the darkness it carved out. You stared and thought you had the edge of it; you saw the faint glimmer of stars beyond. Then the fragments of light faded or jumped and you saw that what you thought was starfield was just an optical trick on the face of more bulking shadow. The colony hulks of the Konrad Harlan fleet were among the largest mobile structures ever built by human science, but they could have served this vessel as lifeboats. Even the Habitats in the New Beijing system didn't come close. This was a scale we weren't ready for yet. The *Nagini* hung over the starship like a gull over one of the bulk freighters that plied the Newpest to Millsport belaweed runs. We were an irrelevance, a tiny uncomprehending visitor along for the ride.

I dropped into the seat opposite Hand and swivelled it so that I faced the screen, feeling shivery in the hands and the spine. Shifting the corpses had been cold work, and when we bagged Dhasanapong-sakul the frozen strands of eye tissue branching like coral from his emptied sockets had broken off under the plastic, under the palm of my hand. I felt them give through the bag, I heard the brittle crickling noise they made.

That tiny sound, the little chirrup of death's particular consequences, had shunted aside most of my earlier awe at the massive dimensions of the Martian vessel.

'Just a bigger version of a colony barge,' I said. 'Theoretically, we could have built that big. It's just harder to accelerate all that mass.'

'Obviously not for them.'

'Obviously not.'

'So you think that's what it was? A colony ship?'

I shrugged, striving for a casualness I wasn't feeling. 'There are a limited number of reasons for building something this big. It's either hauling something somewhere, or you live in it. And it's hard to see why you'd build a habitat this far out. There's nothing here to study. Nothing to mine or skim.'

'It's hard to see why you'd park it here as well, if it is a colony barge.'

Crick-crickle.

I closed my eyes. 'Why do you care, Hand? When we get back, this thing's going to disappear into some corporate asteroid dock. None of us'll ever see it again. Why bother getting attached? You'll get your percentage, your bonus or whatever it is that powers you up.'

'You think I'm not curious?'

'I think you don't care.'

He said nothing after that, until Sun came up from the hold deck with the bad news. The buoy, it appeared, was irreparably damaged.

'It signals,' she said. 'And with some work, the drives can be re-engaged. It needs a new power core, but I believe I can modify one of the bike generators to do the job. But the locational systems are wrecked, and we do not have the tools or material to repair them. Without this, the buoy cannot keep station. Even the backwash from our own drives would probably kick it away into space.'

'What about deploying after we've fired our drives.' Hand looked from Sun to myself and back. 'Vongsavath can calculate a trajectory and nudge us forward, then drop the buoy when we're in. Ah.'

'Motion,' I finished for him. 'The residual motion it picks up from when we toss it is still going to be enough to make it drift away, right Sun?'

'That is correct.'

'And if we attach it?'

I grinned mirthlessly. 'Attach it? Weren't you there when the nanobes tried to attach themselves to the gate?'

'We'll have to look for a way,' he said doggedly. 'We are not going home empty-handed. Not when we've come this close.'

'You try welding to that thing out there and we won't be going home at all, Hand. You know that.'

'Then,' suddenly he was shouting at us. '*There has to be another solution.*'

'There is.'

Tanya Wardani stood in the hatch to the cockpit, where she had retreated while the corpses were dealt with. She was still pale from her vomiting, and her eyes looked bruised, but underlying it there was an almost ethereal calm I hadn't seen since we brought her out of the camp.

'Mistress Wardani.' Hand looked up and down the cabin, as if to check who else had witnessed the loss of cool. He pressed thumb and forefinger to his eyes. 'You have something to contribute?'

'Yes. If Sun Liping can repair the power systems of the buoy, we can certainly place it.'

'Place it where?' I asked.

She smiled thinly. 'Inside.'

There was a moment's silence.

'Inside,' I nodded at the screen, and the unreeling kilometres of alien structure. 'That?'

'Yes. We go in through the docking bay and leave the buoy somewhere secure. There's no reason to suppose the hull isn't radio-transparent, at least in places. Most Martian architecture is. We can test-broadcast anyway, until we find a suitable place.'

'Sun.' Hand was looking back at the screen, almost dreamily. 'How long would it take you to effect repairs on the power system?'

'About eight to ten hours. No more than twelve, certainly.' Sun turned to the archaeologue. 'How long will it take you, Mistress Wardani, to open the docking bay?'

'Oh,' Wardani gave us all another strange smile. 'It's already open.'

I only had one chance to speak to her before we prepared to dock. I met her on her way out of the ship's toilet facilities, ten minutes after the abrupt and dictatorial briefing Hand had thrown down for everyone. She had her back to me and we bumped awkwardly in the narrow dimensions of the entryway. She turned with a yelp and I saw there was a slight sweat still beading her forehead, presumably from more retching. Her breath smelt bad and stomach-acid odours crept out the door behind her.

She saw the way I was looking at her.

'What?'

'Are you alright?'

'No, Kovacs, I'm dying. How about you?'

'You sure this is a good idea?'

'Oh, not you as well! I thought we'd nailed this down with Sutjiadi and Schneider.'

I said nothing, just watched the hectic light in her eyes. She sighed.

'Look, if it satisfies Hand and gets us home again, I'd say yes, it is a good idea. And it's a damned sight safer than trying to attach a defective buoy to the hull.'

I shook my head.

'That's not it.'

'No?'

'No. You want to see the inside of this thing before Mandrake spirit it away to some covert dry dock. You want to own it, even if it's only for a few hours. Don't you.'

'You don't?'

'I think, apart from Sutjiadi and Schneider, we all do.' I knew Cruickshank would have – I could see the shine on her eyes at the thought of it. The awakening enthusiasm she'd had at the rail of the trawler. The same wonder I'd seen on her face when she looked at the activated gate countdown in the UV backwash. Maybe that was why I wasn't protesting beyond this muttered conversation amidst the curling odour of exhausted vomiting. Maybe this was something I owed.

'Well, then.' Wardani shrugged. 'What's the problem?'

'You know what the problem is.'

She made an impatient noise and moved to get past me. I stayed put.

'You want to get out of my way, Kovacs?' she hissed. 'We're five minutes off landing, and I need to be in the *cockpit*.'

'Why didn't they go in, Tanya?'

'We've been over—'

'That's bullshit, Tanya. Ameli's instruments show a breathable atmosphere. They found a way to open the docking system, or they found it already open. And then they waited out here to die while the air in their suits ran out. Why didn't they go in?'

'You were at the briefing. They had no food, they had—'

'Yeah, I heard you come up with metres and metres of wholecloth rationale, but what I didn't hear was anything that explains why four archaeologues would rather die in their spacesuits than spend their last hours wandering around the greatest archaeological find in the history of the human race.'

For a moment she hesitated, and I saw something of the woman from the waterfall. Then the feverish light flickered back on in her eyes.

'Why ask me? Why don't you just power up one of the ID&A sets, and fucking ask them? They're stack-intact, aren't they?'

'The ID&A sets are fucked, Tanya. Leak-corroded with the buoys. So I'm asking you again. Why didn't they go in?'

She was silent again, looking away. I thought I saw a tremor at the corner of one eye. Then it was gone, and she looked up at me with the same dry calm I'd seen in the camp.

'I don't know,' she said finally. 'And if we can't ask them, then there's only one other way to find out that I can think of.'

'Yeah.' I propped myself away from her wearily. 'And that's what this is about, isn't it. Finding out. Uncovering history. Carrying the fucking torch of human discovery. You're not interested in the money, you don't care who ends up with the property rights, and you certainly don't mind dying. So why should anybody else, right?'

She flinched, but it was momentary. She locked it down. And then she was turning away, leaving me looking at the pale light from the illuminum tile where she had been pressed.

CHAPTER THIRTY-ONE

It was like delirium.

I remember reading somewhere that when the archaeologues on Mars first got into the buried mausoleum spaces they later categorised as cities, a fair percentage of them went insane. Mental collapse was an occupational hazard of the profession back then. Some of the finest minds of the century were sacrificed in pursuit of the keys to Martian civilisation. Not broken and dragged down to raving insanity the way the archetypal antiheroes of experia horror flicks always end up. Not broken, just blunted. Worn down from the sharp edge of intellectual prowess to a slightly numb, slightly blurred distracted vagueness. They went that way in their dozens. Psychically abraded by the constant contact with the leavings of unhuman minds. The Guild spent them like surgical blades rammed against a spinning grindstone.

'Well, I suppose if you can *fly* . . .' said Luc Deprez, eyeing the architecture ahead without enthusiasm.

His stance telegraphed irritated confusion. I guessed he was having the same problem locking down potential ambush corners that I was. When the combat conditioning goes in that deep, not being able to do what they've trained you to itches like quitting nicotine. And spotting ambush in Martian architecture would have to be like trying to catch a Mitcham's Point slictopus with your bare hands.

From the ponderously overhanging lintel that led out of the docking bay, the internal structure of the ship burst up and around us like nothing I had ever seen. Groping after comparison, my mind came up with an image from my Newpest childhood. One spring out on the Deeps side of Hirata's Reef, I'd given myself a bad scare when the feed tube on my scrounged and patched scuba suit snagged on an outcrop of coral fifteen metres down. Watching oxygen explode out through the rupture in a riot of silver-bellied corpuscles, I'd wondered fleetingly what the storm of bubbles must look like from the inside.

Now I knew.

These bubbles were frozen in place, tinged mother-of-pearl shades of blue and pink where indistinct low-light sources glowed under their surfaces, but aside from that basic difference in longevity, they were as chaotic as my escaping air supply had been that day. There appeared to be no architectural rhyme or reason to the way they joined and merged into each other. In places the link was a hole only metres across. Elsewhere the curving walls simply broke their sweep as they met an intersecting circumference. At no point in the first space we entered was the ceiling less than twenty metres overhead.

'The floor's flat though,' murmured Sun Liping, kneeling to brush at the sheened surface underfoot. 'And they had – have – grav generators.'

'Origin of species.' Tanya Wardani's voice boomed slightly in the cathedric emptiness. 'They evolved in a gravity well, just like us. Zero g isn't healthy long-term, no matter how much fun it is. And if you have gravity, you need flat surfaces to put things down on. Practicality at work. Same as the docking bay back there. All very well wanting to stretch your wings, but you need straight lines to land a spaceship.'

We all glanced back at the gap we'd come through. Compared to where we stood now, the alien curvatures of the docking station had been practically demure. Long, stepped walls tapered outward like two-metre-fat sleeping serpents stretched out and laid not quite directly on top of each other. The coils wove just barely off a straight axis, as if even within the strictures of the docking station's purpose, the Martian shipwrights had not quite been able to restrain themselves from an organic flourish. There was no danger involved in bringing a docking vessel down through the increasing levels of atmospheric density held in by some mechanism in the stepped walls, but looking out to the sides, you still felt you were being lowered into the belly of something sleeping.

Delirium.

I could feel it brushing lightly at the upper extremities of my vision, sucking gently at my eyeballs and leaving me with a faintly swollen feeling behind the brow. A little like the cut-rate virtualities you used to get in arcades back when I was a kid, the ones where the construct wouldn't let your character look up more than a few degrees above the horizontal, even when that was where the next stage of the game was taking you. It was the same feeling here, the promise of a dull ache behind the eyes from constantly trying to see what was up there. An awareness of space overhead that you kept wanting to check on.

The curve on the gleaming surfaces around us put a tilt on it all, a vague sense that you were about to topple over sideways and that, in fact, toppled over and lying down might be the best stance to take in this gratingly alien environment. That this whole ridiculous structure was eggshell thin and ready to crack apart if you did the wrong thing, and that it might easily spill you out into the void.

Delirium.

Better get used to it.

The chamber was not empty. Skeletal arrangements of what looked like scaffolding loomed on the edges of the level floor space. I recalled holoshot images in a download I'd scanned as a child, Martian roosting bars, complete with virtually generated Martians roosting on them. Here, somehow, the emptiness of the bars gave each structure an eerie gauntness that did nothing for the creeping unease on the nape of my neck.

'They've been folded down,' murmured Wardani, staring upward. She looked puzzled.

At the lower curves of the bubble wall, machines whose functions I couldn't even guess at stood beneath the – apparently – tidied-away roost bars. Most of them looked spiny and aggressive, but when the archaeologue brushed past one, it did nothing more than mutter to itself and pettishly rearrange some of its spines.

Plastic rattle and swift scaling whine – armament deployed in every pair of hands across the hollow bell of the chamber.

'Oh, for God's sake.' Wardani barely spared us a backward glance. 'Loosen up, will you. It's asleep. It's a *machine*.'

I put up the Kalashnikovs and shrugged. Across the chamber Deprez caught my eye, and grinned.

'A machine for what?' Hand wanted to know.

This time the archaeologue did look round.

'I don't know,' she said tiredly. 'Give me a couple of days and a fully equipped lab team, maybe I could tell you. Right now, all I can tell you is that it's dormant.'

Sutjiadi took a couple of steps closer, Sunjet still raised. 'How can you tell that?'

'Because if it wasn't, we'd already be dealing with it on an interactive basis, believe me. Plus, can you see anybody with wingspurs rising a metre above their shoulders putting an active machine that close to a curved wall? I'm telling you, this whole place is powered down and packed up.'

'Mistress Wardani appears to be correct,' said Sun, pivoting about with the Nuhanovic survey set on her forearm raised. 'There is detectable circuitry in the walls, but most of it is inactive.'

'There must be something running all this.' Ameli Vongsavath stood with her hands in her pocket and stared up into the draughty heights at the centre of the chamber. 'We have breathable air. A bit thin, but it's warm. Come to that, this whole place has to be heated somehow.'

'Caretaker systems.' Tanya Wardani seemed to have lost interest in the machines. She wandered back to the group. 'A lot of the deeper buried cities on Mars and Nkrumah's Land had them too.'

'After this long?' Sutjiadi didn't sound happy.

Wardani sighed. She jerked a thumb at the docking bay entrance. 'It's not witchcraft, captain. You've got the same thing running the *Nagini* for us back there. If we all die, she'll sit there for a good few centuries waiting for someone to come back.'

'Yes, and if it's someone who doesn't have the codes, she'll blast them into soup. That doesn't reassure me, Mistress Wardani.'

'Well maybe that's the difference between us and the Martians. A little civilised sophistication.'

'And longer lasting batteries,' I said. 'This has all been here a lot longer than the *Nagini*'s good for.'

'What's the radio-transparency like?' asked Hand.

Sun did something to the Nuhanovic system she was wearing. The bulkier shoulder-mounted sections of the survey equipment flickered. Symbols evolved in the air over the back of her hand. She shrugged. 'It's not very good. I'm barely picking up the *Nagini*'s navigational beacon, and she's only on the other side of the wall. Shielding, I suppose. We are in a docking station, and close to the hull. I think we will need to move further in.'

I spotted a couple of alarmed glances flicker back and forth amongst the group. Deprez caught me watching and he smiled a little.

'So who wants to explore?' he asked softly.

'I don't think that's such a good idea,' said Hand.

I moved out from the instinctive defence huddle we'd all formed, stepped through the gap between two roost bars and reached up to the lip of the opening above and behind. Waves of tiredness and faint nausea shimmered through me as I hauled myself up, but by now I was expecting it and the neurachem locked it down.

The hollow beyond was empty. Not even dust.

'Maybe it's not such a good idea,' I agreed, dropping back. 'But how many human beings this side of the next millennium are going to get this chance? You need ten hours, right, Sun?'

'At the most.'

'And you reckon you can build us a decent map on that thing?' I gestured at the Nuhanovic set.

'Very probably. This *is* the best survey software money can buy.' She bowed briefly in Hand's direction. 'Nuhanovic smart systems. They don't build it better than this.'

I looked over to Ameli Vongsavath.

'And the *Nagini*'s weapon systems are powered up solid.'

The pilot nodded. 'Parameters I gave, she could stand off a full tactical assault with no help from us.'

'Well, then I'd say we've got a day-pass to the Coral Castle.' I glanced at Sutjiadi. 'Those of us that want it, that is.'

Looking around, I saw the idea taking hold. Deprez was already there, face and stance betraying his curiosity, but it was slowly filling up the rest of them too. Everywhere, heads were tilted back to take in the alien architecture, features ironed soft by wonder. Even Sutjiadi couldn't hold it off completely. The grim watchfulness he'd maintained since we breached the upper levels of the docking chamber's layered atmosphere field was melting into something less clamped down. The fear of the unknown was ebbing, cancelled out by something stronger and older.

Monkey curiosity. The trait I'd disparaged to Wardani when we arrived on the beach at Sauberville. The scampering, chittering jungle intelligence that would cheerfully scale the brooding figures of ancient stone idols and poke fingers into the staring eyesockets just to *see*. The bright obsidian desire to *know*. The thing that's dragged us out here, all the way from the grasslands of central Africa. The thing that one day'll probably put us somewhere so far out that we'll get there ahead of the sunlight from those central African days.

Hand stepped into the centre, poised in executive mode.

'Let's achieve some sense of priority here,' he said carefully. 'I sympathise with any wish you may all have to see some of this vessel – I would like to see it myself – but our major concern is to find a safe transmission base for the buoy. That we must do before anything else, and I suggest we do it as a single unit.' He turned to Sutjiadi. 'After that, we can detail exploratory parties. Captain?'

Sutjiadi nodded, but it was an uncharacteristically vague motion. Like the rest of us, he wasn't really paying attention at human frequencies any more.

If there'd been any lingering doubts about the Martian vessel's hulk status, a couple of hours in the frozen bubbles of its architecture was enough to cancel them out. We walked for over a kilometre, winding back and forth through the apparently random connections between chambers. In places the openings were more or less at floor level, but elsewhere they were cut high enough that Wardani or Sun had to power up the grav harnesses they were wearing and float up to peer through. Jiang and Deprez took point together, splitting and edging up to the entrance to each new chamber with quiet, symmetrical lethality.

We found nothing recognisably living.

The machines we came across ignored us, and no one seemed inclined to get close enough to elicit more of a reaction.

Increasingly, as we moved deeper into the body of the ship, we began to find structures that might by a stretch of the imagination be called corridors – long, bulbous spaces with egg-shaped entrances let in at either end. It looked like the same construction technique as the standard bubble chamber, modified to suit.

'You know what this whole thing is,' I told Wardani, while we waited for Sun to scout out another overhead opening. 'It's like aerogel. Like they built a basic framework and then just,' – I shook my head. The concept stubbornly resisted chiselling out into words – 'I don't know, just blew up a few cubic kilometres of heavy-duty aerogel base all over it, and then waited for it to harden.'

Wardani smiled wanly. 'Yeah, maybe. Something like that. That would put their plasticity science a little ahead of ours, wouldn't it. To be able to map and model foam data on this scale.'

'Maybe not.' I groped at the opening shape of the idea, feeling at its origami edges. 'Out here specific structure wouldn't matter. Whatever came out would do. And then you just fill the space with whatever you need. Drivers, environmental systems, you know, weapons . . .'

'Weapons?' She looked at me with something unreadable in her face. 'Does this have to be a warship?'

'No, it was an example. But—'

'Something in here,' said Sun over the comset. 'Some kind of tree or—'

What happened next was hard to explain.

I heard the sound coming.

I knew with utter certainty that I was going to hear it fractions of a second before the low chime floated down out of the bubble Sun was exploring. The knowledge was a solid sensation, heard like an echo cast backward against the slow decay of passing time. If it was the Envoy intuition, it was working at a level of efficiency I'd only previously run into in dreams.

'Songspire,' said Wardani.

I listened to the echoes fade, inverting the shiver of premonition I'd just felt, and suddenly wanted very much to be back on the other side of the gate, facing the mundane dangers of the nanobe systems and the fallout from murdered Sauberville.

Cherries and mustard. An inexplicable tangle of scents spilling down in the wake of the sound. Jiang raised his Sunjet.

Sutjiadi's normally immobile features creased.

'What *is* that?'

'Songspire,' I said, spinning matter-of-factness around my own creeping unease. 'Kind of Martian houseplant.'

I'd seen one once, for real, on Earth. Dug out of the Martian bedrock it had grown from over the previous several thousand years and plinthed as a rich man's objet d'art. Still singing when anything touched it, even the breeze, still giving out the cherry-and-mustard aroma. Not dead, not alive, not anything that could be categorised into a box by human science.

'How is it attached?' Wardani wanted to know.

'Growing out of the wall,' Sun's voice came back dented with a by now familiar wonder. 'Like some kind of coral . . .'

Wardani stepped back to give herself launch space and reached for the drives on her own grav harness. The quick whine of power-up stung the air.

'I'm coming up.'

'Just a moment, Mistress Wardani.' Hand glided in to crowd her. 'Sun, is there a way through up there?'

'No. Whole bubble's closed.'

'Then come back down.' He raised a hand to forestall Wardani. 'We do not have *time* for this. Later, if you wish, you may come back while Sun is repairing the buoy. For now, we must find a safe transmission base before anything else.'

A vaguely mutinous expression broke across the archaeologue's face, but she was too tired to sustain it. She knocked out the grav drivers again – downwhining machine disappointment – and turned away, something muttered and bitten off drifting back over her shoulder, almost as faint as the cherries and mustard from above.

She stalked a line away from the Mandrake exec towards the exit. Jiang hesitated a moment in her path, then let her by.

I sighed.

'Nice going, Hand. She's the closest thing we've got to a native guide in this.' I gestured around. 'Place, and you want to piss her off. They teach you that while you were getting your conflict investment doctorate? Upset the experts if you possibly can?'

'No,' he said evenly. 'But they taught me not to waste time.'

'Right.' I went after Wardani and caught up just inside the corridor leading out of the chamber. 'Hey, hold up. Wardani. Wardani, just chill out, will you. Man's an asshole, what are you going to do?'

'Fucking *merchant*.'

'Well, yeah. That too. But he is the reason we're here in the first place. Should never underestimate that mercantile drive.'

'What are you, a fucking economics philosopher now?'

'I'm.' I stopped. 'Listen.'

'No, I'm through with—'

'No, *listen*.' I held up a hand and pointed down the corridor. 'There. Hear that?'

'I don't hear . . .' Her voice trailed off as she caught it. By then, the Carrera's Wedge neurachem had reeled in the sound for me, so clear there could be no question.

Somewhere down the corridor, something was singing.

Two chambers further on, we found them. A whole bonsai songspire forest, sprouting across the floor and up the lower curve of a corridor neck where it joined the main bubble. The spires seemed to have broken through the primary structure of the vessel from the floor around the join, although there was no sign of damage at their roots. It was as if the hull material had closed around them like healing tissue. The nearest machine was a respectful ten metres off, huddled down the corridor.

The song the spires emitted was closest to the sound of a violin, but played with the infinitely slow drag of individual monofilaments across the bridge and to no melody that I could discern. It was a sound down at the lowest levels of hearing, but each time it swelled, I felt something tugging at the pit of my stomach.

'The air,' said Wardani quietly. She had raced me along the bulbous corridors and through the bubble chambers, and now she crouched in front of the spires, out of breath but shiny eyed. 'There must be convection through here from another level. They only sing on surface contact.'

I shook off an unlooked-for shiver.

'How old do you reckon they are?'

'Who knows?' She got to her feet again. 'If this was a planetary grav field, I'd say a couple of thousand years at most. But it isn't.' She took a step back and shook her head, hand cupping her chin, fingers pressed over her mouth as if to keep in a too-hasty comment. I waited. Finally the hand came away from her face and gestured, hesitant. 'Look at the branching pattern. They don't. They don't usually grow like this. Not this twisted.'

I followed her pointing finger. The tallest of the spires stood about chest high, spindly reddish black stone limbs snaking out of the central trunk in a profusion that did seem more exuberant and intricate than the growth I'd seen on the plinthed specimen back on earth. Surrounding it, other, smaller spires emulated the pattern, except that—

The rest of the party caught up, Deprez and Hand in the van. 'Where the hell have you. Oh.'

The faint singing from the spires crept up an almost imperceptible increment. Air currents stirred by the movement of bodies across the chamber. I felt a slight dryness in my throat at the sound it made.

'I'm just looking at these, if that's OK, Hand.'

'Mistress Wardani—'

I shot the exec a warning glance.

Deprez came up beside the archaeologue. 'Are they dangerous?'

'I don't know. Ordinarily, no, but—'

The thing that had been scratching for attention at the threshold of my consciousness suddenly emerged.

'They're growing towards each other. Look at the branches on the smaller ones. They all reach up and out. The taller ones branch in all directions.'

'That suggests communication of some sort. An integrated, self relating system.' Sun walked round the cluster of spires, scanning with the emissions tracer on her arm. 'Though, hmm.'

'You won't find any radiation,' said Wardani, almost dreamily. 'They suck it in like sponges. Total absorption of everything except red wave light. According to mineral composition, the surface of these things shouldn't be red at all. They ought to reflect right across the spectrum.'

'But they don't.' Hand made it sound as if he was thinking of having the spires detained for the transgression. 'Why is that, Mistress Wardani?'

'If I knew that, I'd be a Guild President by now. We know less about songspires than practically any other aspect of the Martian biosphere. In fact, we don't even know if you can rank them in the biosphere.'

'They grow, don't they?'

I saw Wardani sneer. 'So do crystals. That doesn't make them alive.'

'I don't know about the rest of you,' said Ameli Vongsavath, skirting the songspires with her Sunjet cocked at a semi-aggressive angle. 'But this looks to me like an infestation.'

'Or art,' murmured Deprez. 'How would we know?'

Vongsavath shook her head. 'This is a ship, Luc. You don't put your corridor art where you'll trip over it every time you walk through. Look at these things. They're all over the place.'

'And if you can fly through?'

'They'd still get in the way.'

'Collision Art,' suggested Schneider with a smirk.

'Alright, that's enough.' Hand waved himself some space between the spires and their new audience. Faint notes awoke as the motion brushed air currents against the red stone branches. The musk in the air thickened. 'We do not have—'

'Time for this,' droned Wardani. 'We must find a safe transmission base.'

Schneider guffawed. I bit back a grin and avoided looking in

Deprez's direction. I suspected that Hand's control was crumbling and I wasn't keen to push him over the edge at this point. I still wasn't sure what he'd do when he snapped.

'Sun,' the Mandrake exec's voice came out even enough. 'Check the upper openings.'

The systems specialist nodded and powered up her grav harness. The whine of the drivers cut in and then deepened as her bootsoles unstuck from the floor and she drifted upwards. Jiang and Deprez circled out, Sunjets raised to cover her.

'No way through here,' she called back down from the first opening.

I heard the change, and my eyes slanted back to the songspires. Wardani was the only one watching me and she saw my face. Behind Hand's back, her mouth opened in a silent question. I nodded at the spires and cupped my ear.

Listen.

Wardani moved closer, then shook her head.

Hissing. 'That's not poss—'

But it was.

The faint, violin-scraped sound of the song was modulating. Reacting to the constant underpinning drone of the grav drivers. That, or maybe the grav field itself. Modulating and, very faintly, strengthening.

Waking up.

CHAPTER THIRTY-TWO

We found Hand's safe transmission base four songspire clusters and about another hour later. By then we'd started to hook back towards the docking bay, following a tentative map that Sun's Nuhanovic scanners were building on her arm. The mapping software didn't like Martian architecture any more than I did, that much was apparent from the long pauses every time Sun loaded in a new set of data. But with a couple of hours' wandering behind us, and some inspired interfacing from the systems specialist, the programme was able to start making some educated guesses of its own about where we should be looking. Perhaps not surprisingly, it was dead right.

Climbing out of a massive spiralling tube whose gradient was too steep for human comfort, Sun and I staggered to a halt at the edge of a fifty-metre broad platform that was seemingly exposed to raw space on all sides. A crystal-clear open starfield curved overhead and down around us, interrupted only by the bones of a gaunt central structure reminiscent of a Millsport dockyard crane. The sense of exposure to the outside was so complete I felt my throat lock up momentarily in vacuum combat reflex at the sight. My lungs, still straining from the climb, flapped weakly in my chest.

I broke the reflex.

'Is that a forcefield?' I asked Sun, panting.

'No, it's solid.' She frowned over the forearm display. 'Transparent alloy, about a metre thick. That's very impressive. No distortion. Total direct visual control. Look, there's your gate.'

It stood in the starscape over our heads, a curiously oblong satellite of greyish-blue light creeping across the darkness.

'This has got to be the docking control turret,' Sun decided, patting her arm and turning slowly. 'What did I tell you. Nuhanovic smart mapping. They don't make it any bet—'

Her voice dried up. I looked sideways and saw how her eyes had widened, focused on something further ahead. Following her gaze to the skeletal structure at the centre of the platform, I saw the Martians.

'You'd better call the others up,' I said distantly.

They were hung over the platform like the ghosts of eagles tortured to death, wings spread wide, caught up in some kind of webbing that swung eerily in stray air currents. There were only two, one hoisted close to the highest extent of the central structure, the other not much above human head height. Moving warily closer, I saw that the webbing was metallic, strung with instrumentation whose purposes made no more overt sense than the machines we'd passed in the bubble chambers.

I passed another outcrop of songspires, most of them not much over knee height. They barely got a second glance. Behind me, I heard Sun yelling down the spiral to the rest of the party. Her raised voice seemed to violate something in the air. Echoes chased each other around the dome. I reached the lower of the two Martians, and stood beneath the body.

Of course, I'd seen them before. Who hasn't. You get input with this stuff from kindergarten upwards. The Martians. They've replaced the mythological creatures of our own picket-fenced earthbound heritage, the gods and demons we once used for the foundations of our legends. *Impossible to overestimate*, wrote Gretzky, back when he apparently still had some balls, *the sideswiping blow that this discovery dealt our sense of belonging in the universe, and our sense that the universe in some way belonged to us.*

The way Wardani laid it out for me, one desert evening on the balcony at Roespinoedji's warehouse:

Bradbury, 2089 pre-colonial reckoning. The founder-heroes of human antiquity are exposed for the pig-ignorant mall bullies they probably always were, as decoding of the first Martian data systems brings in evidence of a starfaring culture at least as old as the whole human race. The millennial knowledge out of Egypt and China starts to look like a ten-year-old child's bedroom datastack. The wisdom of the ages shredded at a stroke into the pipe-cooked musings of a bunch of canal-dive barflies. Lao Tzu, Confucius, Jesus Christ, Muhammed – what did these guys know? Parochial locals, never even been off the planet. Where were *they* when the Martians were crossing interstellar space.

Of course – *a sour grin out of one corner of Wardani's mouth* – established religion lashed back. The usual strategies. Incorporate the Martians into the scheme of things, scour the scriptures or make up some new ones, reinterpret. Failing that, lacking the grey matter for that much effort, just deny the whole thing as the work of evil forces and firebomb anyone who says otherwise. That ought to work.

But it didn't work.

For a while it looked as if it might. Upwelling hysteria brought sectarian violence and the recently established university departments of xenology frequently up in flames. Armed escorts for noted archaeologues and a fair few campus firefights between fundamentalists and the public order police. Interesting times for the student body . . .

Out of it all, the new faiths arose. Most of them not that much different to the old faiths by all accounts, and just as dogmatic. But underlying, or maybe floating uneasily atop, came a groundswell of secular belief in something that was a little harder to define than God.

Maybe it was the wings. A cultural archetype so deep – *angels, demons, Icarus and countless idiots like him off towers and cliffs until we finally got it right* – that humanity clung to it.

Maybe there was just too much at stake. The astrogation charts with their promise of new worlds we could just *go to*, assured of a terrestroid destination because, well, *it says so here*.

Whatever it was, you had to call it faith. It wasn't knowledge; the Guild wasn't that confident of its translation back then, and you don't launch hundreds of thousands of stored minds and clone embryos into the depths of interstellar space without something a lot stronger than a theory.

It was faith in the essential workability of the New Knowledge. In place of the terracentric confidence of human science and its ability to Work It All Out someday, a softer trust in the overarching edifice of Martian Knowledge that would, like an indulgent father, let us get out into the ocean and drive the boat for real. We were heading out the door, not as children grown and leaving home for the first time, but as toddlers gripping trustingly with one chubby fist at the talon of Martian civilisation. There was a totally irrational sense of safety and wrapped-up warmth to the whole process. That, as much as Hand's much vaunted economic liberalisation, was what drove the diaspora.

Three-quarters of a million deaths on Adoracion changed things. That, and a few other geopolitical shortcomings that cropped up with the rise of the Protectorate. Back on Earth, the old faiths slammed down, political and spiritual alike, iron-bound tomes of authority to live by. *We have lived loosely, and a price must be paid. In the name of stability and security, things must be run with a firm hand now.*

Of that brief flourishing of enthusiasm for all things Martian, very little remains. Wycinski and his pioneering team are centuries gone, hounded out of university posts and funding and in some cases actually murdered. The Guild has drawn into itself, jealously guarding what little intellectual freedom the Protectorate allows it. The Martians are reduced from anything approaching a full understanding to two virtually unrelated precipitates. On the one hand a textbook-dry series of images and notes, as much data as the Protectorate deems socially appropriate. Every child dutifully learns what they looked like, the splayed anatomy of their wings and skeleton, the flight dynamics, the tedious minutiae of mating and young-rearing, the reconstructions in virtual of their plumage and colouring, drawn from the few visual records we've managed to access or filled in with Guild guesses. Roost emblems, probable clothing. Colourful, easily digestible stuff. Not much sociology. Too poorly understood, too undefined, too volatile, and besides do people really want to bother themselves with all that . . .

'Knowledge tossed away,' she said, shivering a little in the desert chill.

'Wilful ignorance in the face of something we might have to work to understand.'

At the other end of the fractionating column the more esoteric elements gather. Weird religious offshoots, whispered legend and word of mouth from the digs. Here, something of what the Martians were to us once has remained – here, their impact can be described in murmured tones. Here they can be named as Wycinski once named them; *the New Ancients, teaching us the real meaning of that word. Our mysteriously absent winged benefactors, swooping low to brush the nape of our civilisation's neck with one cold wingtip, to remind us that six or seven thousand years of patchily recorded history isn't what they call ancient around* here.

This Martian was dead.

A long time dead, that much was apparent. The body had mummified in the webbing, wings turned parchment thin, head dried out to a long narrow skull whose beak gaped half open. The eyes were blackened in their backward-slashed sockets, half hidden by the draped membrane of the eyelids. Below the beak, the thing's skin bulged out in what I guessed must have been the throat gland. Like the wings, it looked paper-thin and translucent.

Under the wings, angular limbs reached across the webbing and delicate-looking talons grasped at instrumentation. I felt a tiny surge of admiration. Whatever this thing had been, it had died at the controls.

'Don't touch it,' snapped Wardani from behind me, and I became aware that I was reaching upward to the lower edge of the webbing frame.

'Sorry.'

'You will be, if the skin crumbles. There's an alkaline secretion in their subcutaneous fat layers that runs out of control when they die. Kept in balance by food oxidation during life, we think, but it's strong enough to dissolve most of a corpse, given a decent supply of water vapour.' As she spoke, she was moving around the webbing frame with the automatic caution of what must have been Guild training. Her face was utterly intent, eyes never shifting from the winged mummy above us. 'When they die like this, it just eats through the fat and dries out to a powder. Very corrosive if you breathe it in, or get it in your eyes.'

'Right.' I moved back a couple of steps. 'Thanks for the advance warning.'

She shrugged. 'I didn't expect to find them here.'

'Ships have crews.'

'Yeah, Kovacs, and cities have populations. We've still only ever found a couple of hundred intact Martian corpses in over four centuries of archaeology on three dozen worlds.'

'Shit like that in their systems, I'm not surprised.' Schneider had wandered over and was rubbernecking on the other side of the space below the webbing frame. 'So what happened to this stuff if they just didn't eat for a while?'

Wardani shot him an irritated glance. 'We don't know. Presumably the process would start up.'

'That must have hurt,' I said.

'Yes, I imagine it would.' She didn't really want to talk to either of us. She was entranced.

Schneider failed to take the hint. Or maybe he just needed the babble of voices to cover the huge stillness in the air around us and the gaze of the winged thing above us. 'How come they'd end up with something like that? I mean,' he guffawed, 'it's not exactly evolutionarily selective, is it? Kills you if you're hungry.'

I looked up at the desiccated, spreadeagled corpse again, feeling a fresh surge of the respect I'd first felt when I realised the Martians had died at their posts. Something indefinable happened in my head, something that my Envoy senses recognised as the intuitive shimmer at the edge of understanding.

'No, it's selective,' I realised as I spoke. 'It would have driven them. It would have made them the toughest motherfuckers in the sky.'

I thought I spotted a faint smile crossing Tanya Wardani's face. 'You should publish, Kovacs. That kind of intellectual insight.'

Schneider smirked.

'In fact,' the archaeologue said, falling into gentle lecture mode while she stared at the mummified Martian, 'the current evolutionary argument for this trait is that it helped keep crowded roosts hygienic. Vasvik and Lai, couple of years ago. Before that, most of the Guild agreed it would deter skin-feeding parasites and infection. Vasvik and Lai wouldn't actually dispute that, they're just jockeying for pole position. And, of course, there is the overarching toughest motherfuckers in the sky hypothesis, which a number of Guild Masters have elaborated, though none quite as elegantly as you, Kovacs.'

I tipped her a bow.

'Do you think we can get her down?' Wardani wondered aloud, standing back to get a better look at the cables the webbing frame depended from.

'Her?'

'Yeah. It's a roost guardian. See the spur on the wing. That bone ridge on back of the the skull. Warrior caste. They were all female as far as we know.' The archaeologue looked up at the cabling again. 'Think we can get this thing working?'

'Don't see why not.' I raised my voice to carry across the platform 'Jiang. You see anything like a winch on that side?'

Jiang looked upward, then shook his head.

'What about you, Luc?'

'Mistress Wardani!'

'Speaking of motherfuckers,' muttered Schneider. Matthias Hand was striding across to join the congregation beneath the spread-eagled corpse.

'Mistress Wardani, I hope you weren't thinking of doing anything other than look at this specimen.'

'Actually,' the archaeologue told him, 'we're looking for a way to winch it down. Got a problem with that?'

'Yes, Mistress Wardani, I have. This ship, and everything it contains, is the property of the Mandrake Corporation.'

'Not until the buoy sings, it isn't. That's what you told us to get us in here, anyway.'

Hand smiled thinly. 'Don't make an issue of this, Mistress Wardani. You've been well enough paid.'

'Oh, *paid*. I've been *paid*.' Wardani stared at him. '*Fuck* you, Hand.'

She stormed away across the platform and stood at its edge, looking out.

I stared at the Mandrake exec. 'Hand, what's the matter with you? I thought I told you to ease up on her. The architecture getting to you or something?'

I left him with the corpse and walked across to where Wardani stood with her arms wrapped tightly around her body and her head lowered.

'Not planning to jump, are you?'

She snorted. 'That piece of shit. He'd have a fucking corporate holofront on the gates of paradise if he ever found them.'

'Don't know about that. He's a pretty serious believer.'

'Yeah? Funny how it doesn't get in the way of his commercial life.'

'Yeah, well. Organised religion, you know.'

She snorted again, but there was a laugh in it this time and her posture unlocked a little.

'I don't know why I got so bent out of shape. I don't have the tools here to deal with organic remnants anyway. Let it stay up there. Who gives a shit?'

I smiled and placed a hand on her shoulder.

'You do,' I said gently.

The dome over our heads was as transparent to radio signals as it was to the visual spectrum. Sun ran a series of basic checks with the equipment she had, then we all trooped back to the *Nagini* and brought the damaged buoy up to the platform, together with three cases of tools Sun deemed likely to be useful. We stopped in every chamber, flagging the route with amber limpet cherries along the way, and painting the floor with illuminum paint, much to Tanya Wardani's chagrin.

'It'll wash off,' Sun Liping told her in a tone that suggested she didn't much care one way or the other.

Even with a couple of grav harnesses to ease the lifting, getting the buoy to its designated resting place was a long, hard job, made infuriating by the bubbling chaos of the ship's architecture. By the time we'd assembled everything on the platform – off to one side, at a discreet distance from the mummified original occupants – I was shattered. The radiation damage raging through my cells was getting beyond the power of the drugs to do anything about it.

I found a section of the central structure that wasn't directly below a corpse and propped myself against it, looking out at the starscape while my abused body did its best to stabilise my pulse and damp down the sickness in the pit of my guts. Out among the stars, the open gate winked at me as it rose over the platform's horizon. Further right, the nearest Martian tugged at an upper corner of my vision. I looked up and across to where the corpse peered down at me through shrouded eyes. I raised one finger to my temple in salute.

'Yeah. Be with you shortly.'

'I'm sorry?'

I rolled my head sideways and saw Luc Deprez standing a couple of metres away. In his rad-resistant Maori sleeve, he looked almost comfortable.

'Nothing. Communing.'

'I see.' From the expression on his face, it was pretty clear he didn't. 'I was wondering. Want to go for a look around?'

I shook my head.

'Maybe later. Don't let me stop you, though.'

He frowned, but he left me alone. I saw him leaving with Ameli Vongsavath in tow. Elsewhere on the platform, the rest of the party were gathered in small knots, talking in voices that didn't carry much. I thought I could hear the songspire cluster making faint counterpoint, but I wasn't up to focusing the neurachem. I felt an immense weariness come sliding down out of the starfield and the platform seemed to tilt away beneath me. I closed my eyes and drifted off into something that wasn't exactly sleep, but came equipped with all the disadvantages.

Kovacs . . .

Fucking Semetaire.

Do you miss your fragmented Limon Highlander?

Don't—

Do you wish she were here in one piece, eh? Or would you like the pieces of her squirming over you unattached?

My face twitched where her foot had smashed my lip as the nanobe cable hurled it past me.

Is there an appeal, hmmm? A segmented houri at your command. A hand here, a hand there. Curved handfuls of flesh. Consumer cut, so to speak. Soft, graspable flesh, Kovacs. Malleable. You could fill your hands with it. Mould it to you.

Semetaire, you're pushing me—

And unattached to any inconvenient independent will. Throw away the parts you have no use for. The parts that excrete, the parts that think beyond sensual use. The afterlife has many pleasures—

Leave me the fuck alone, Semetaire.

Why should I do that? Alone is cold, a gulf of coldness deeper than you looked upon from the hull of the Mivtsemdi. Why should I abandon you to that when you have been such a friend to me? Sent me so many souls.

Alright. That's it, motherfucker—

I snapped awake, sweating. Tanya Wardani was crouched a metre away, peering at me. Behind her, the Martian hung in mid-glide, staring blindly down like one of the angels in the Andric cathedral at Newpest.

'You OK, Kovacs?'

I pressed fingers against my eyes and winced at the ache the pressure caused.

'Not bad for a dead man, I suppose. You're not off exploring?'

'I feel like shit. Maybe later.'

I propped myself up a little straighter. Across the platform, Sun worked steadily on the buoy's exposed circuit plates. Jiang and Sutjiadi stood nearby, talking in low tones. I coughed. 'Limited amount of later round here. I doubt it'll take Sun the whole ten hours. Where's Schneider?'

'Went off with Hand. How come you're not doing the Coral Castle tour yourself?'

I smiled. 'You've never seen the Coral Castle in your life, Tanya. What are you talking about?'

She seated herself beside me, facing the starscape.

'Trying out my Harlan's World argot. Got a problem with that?'

'Fucking tourists.'

She laughed. I sat and enjoyed the sound until it died, and then we both sat for a while in a companionable quiet broken only by the sound of Sun's circuit soldering.

'Nice sky,' she said finally.

'Yeah. Answer me an archaeological question?'

'If you like.'

'Where did they go?'

'The Martians?'

'Yeah.'

'Well, it's a big cosmos. Who—'

'No, *these* Martians. The crew of this thing. Why leave something this big floating out here abandoned? It must have cost a planetary budget to build, even for them. It's functional, as near as we can tell. Heated, maintained atmosphere, working docking system. Why didn't they take it with them?'

'Who knows? Maybe they left in a hurry.'

'Oh, come—'

'No, I mean it. They pulled out of this whole region of space, or were wiped out, or wiped each other out. They left a lot of stuff. Whole cities of it.'

'Yeah. Tanya, you can't take a city away with you. Obviously you leave it. But this is a fucking starship. What could make them leave something like that behind?'

'They left the orbitals around Harlan's World.'

'Those are automated.'

'Well? So is this, to the extent of the maintenance systems.'

'Yes, but it was built for use by a crew. You don't have to be an archaeologue to see that.'

'Kovacs, why don't you go down to the *Nagini* and get some rest. Neither of us is up to exploring this place, and you're giving me a headache.'

'I think you'll find that's the radiation.'

'No, I—'

Against my chest, my discarded induction mike burred. I blinked down at it for a moment, then picked it up and fitted it.

'. . . just ly— . . . —ere,' said Vongsavath's voice, excited and laced heavily with static breakup. 'What-ver . . . was . . . don't thin— . . . died of starv . . .'

'Vongsavath, this is Kovacs. Back up a minute. Slow down and start again.'

'I said,' the pilot enunciated with heavy emphasis. 'Th— . . . 've found . . . ther body. A hu . . . body. Part . . . gang . . . —cked up at the dock . . . —ation. An— . . . looks li— . . . thing kill— . . . him.'

'Alright, we're on our way.' I struggled to my feet, forcing myself to speak at a pace Vongsavath might have a chance of understanding through the interference. 'Repeat. We are on our way. Stay put, back to back and don't move. And shoot any fucking thing you see.'

'What is it?' asked Wardani.

'Trouble.'

I looked around the platform and suddenly Sutjiadi's words came rolling back over me.

We shouldn't be out here at all.

Over my head, the Martian gazed blankly down at us. As far removed as any angel, and as much help.

CHAPTER THIRTY-THREE

He was lying in one of the bulbous tunnels, about a kilometre deeper into the body of the vessel, suited up and still largely intact. In the soft blue light from the walls, the features behind the faceplate were clearly shrunken onto the bones of the skull, but beyond that they didn't seem to have decomposed appreciably.

I knelt beside the corpse and peered at the sealed-in face.

'Doesn't look too bad, considering.'

'Sterile air supply,' said Deprez. He had his Sunjet cocked on his hip, and his eyes flickered constantly into the swollen roof-space overhead. Ten metres further on and looking slightly less comfortable with her weapon, Ameli Vongsavath prowled back and forth by the opening where the tunnel linked to the next bubble chamber. 'And anti-bacterials, if it's a halfway decent suit. Interesting. The tank's still a third full. Whatever he died of, it wasn't suffocation.'

'Any damage to the suit?'

'If there is, I cannot find it.'

I sat back on my heels. 'Doesn't make any sense. This air's breathable. Why suit up?'

Deprez shrugged. 'Why die in your suit on the outside of an open atmosphere lock? None of it makes any sense. I'm not trying any more.'

'Movement,' snapped Vongsavath.

I cleared the right-hand interface gun and joined her at the opening. The lower lip rose a little over a metre from the floor and curved upward like a wide smile before narrowing gradually up towards the roof on either side and finally closing in a tightly

334

rounded apex. There were two metres of clear cover on each side and space to crouch below the lip. It was a sniper's dream.

Deprez folded into the cover on the left, Sunjet stowed upright at his side. I crouched beside Vongsavath.

'Sounded like something falling,' murmured the pilot. 'Not this chamber, maybe the next.'

'Alright.' I felt the neurachem sliding coldly along my limbs, charging my heart. Good to know that, under the bone-deep weariness of the radiation poisoning, the systems were still online. And after grasping so long at shadows, fighting faceless nanobe colonies, the ghosts of the departed, human and not, the promise of solid combat was almost a pleasure.

Scratch almost. I could feel pleasure tickling up the walls of my stomach at the thought of killing something.

Deprez raised one hand from the projection ramp of his Sunjet. *Listen.*

This time I heard it – a stealthy scuffing sound across the chamber. I drew the other interface gun and settled into the cover of the raised lip. The Envoy conditioning squeezed the last of the tension out of my muscles and stowed it in coiled reflexes beneath a surface calm.

Something pale moved in a space on the other side of the next chamber. I breathed in and sighted on it.

Here we go.

'You there, Ameli?'

Schneider's voice.

I heard Vongsavath's breath hiss out about the same time as mine. She climbed to her feet.

'Schneider? What are you doing? I nearly shot you.'

'Well, that's fucking friendly.' Schneider appeared clearly in the opening and swung his leg over. His Sunjet was slung carelessly across one shoulder. 'We come rushing to the rescue, and you blow us away for our trouble.'

'Is it another archaeologue?' asked Hand, following Schneider through into the chamber. Incongruous in his right fist was a hand blaster. It was the first time, I realised, that I'd seen the executive armed since I'd known him. It didn't look right on him. It marred

335

his ninetieth-floor boardroom aura. It was inappropriate, a cracked front, jarring the way genuine battle coverage would in a Lapinee recruiting number. Hand was not a man who wielded weapons himself. Or at least not weapons as straightforward and grubby as a particle blaster.

Plus he's got a stunner tucked away in his pocket.

Recently powered up to combat readiness, the Envoy conditioning twinged uneasily.

'Come and have a look,' I suggested, masking my disquiet.

The two new arrivals crossed the open ground to us with a blasé lack of caution that screamed at my combat nerves. Hand leaned his hands on the lip of the tunnel entrance and stared at the corpse. His features, I suddenly saw, were ashen with the radiation sickness. His stance looked braced, as if he wasn't sure how much longer he could stand up. There was a tic at the corner of his mouth that hadn't been there when we touched down in the docking bay. Next to him, Schneider looked positively glowing with health.

I crushed out the flicker of sympathy. *Welcome to the fucking club, Hand. Welcome to ground level on Sanction IV.*

'He's suited up,' Hand said.

'Well spotted.'

'How did he die?'

'We don't know.' I felt another wave of weariness wash through me. 'And to be honest I'm not in the mood for an autopsy. Let's just get this buoy fixed, and get the fuck out of here.'

Hand gave me a strange look. 'We'll need to take him back.'

'Well, you can help me do it, then.' I walked back to the suited corpse and picked up one leg. 'Grab a foot.'

'You're going to drag him?'

'*We*, Hand. *We* are going to drag him. I don't think he'll mind.'

It took the best part of an hour to get the corpse back through the tortuous pipes and swooping chambers of the Martian vessel and aboard the *Nagini*. Most of that was taken up trying to locate the limpet cherries and illuminum arrows of our original mapping, but the radiation sickness took its toll along the way. At different points in the journey, Hand and I were taken with minor bouts of vomiting and had to give hauling the body over to Schneider and Deprez. Time emptying out for the final victims of Sauberville. I thought even Deprez, in his rad-resistant Maori sleeve, was starting to look ill as we fumbled the bulky suited burden through the last opening before the docking station. Now that I focused in the bluish light, Vongsavath too was starting to exhibit the same grey pallor and bruised eyes.

Do you see? whispered something that might have been Semetaire.

There seemed to be a huge, sickly sense of something waiting in the swollen heights of the ship's architecture, hovering on parchment-thin wings, and watching.

When we were done, I stood staring into the antiseptic violet glow of the corpse locker after the others had left. The tumbled, spacesuited figures within looked like a gaggle of overly padded null G crashball players, collapsed on top of each other when the field goes down and the house lights come up at the end of the match. The pouches containing the remains of Cruickshank, Hansen and Dhasanapongsakul were almost hidden from view.

Dying. . . .

Not dying yet. . . .

The Envoy conditioning, worrying at something not over, not resolved.

The Ground is for Dead People. I saw Schneider's illuminum tattoo like a beacon floating behind my eyes. His face, twisted unrecognisable with the pain of his injuries.

Dead people?

'Kovacs?' It was Deprez, standing in the hatch behind me. 'Hand wants us all back on the platform. We're taking food. You coming?'

'I'll catch you up.'

He nodded and dropped back to the floor outside. I heard voices and tried to blank them out.

Dying?

The Ground is

Motes of light circling like a datacoil display

The gate . . .

The gate, seen through the viewports of the *Nagini*'s cockpit . . .

The cockpit . . .

337

I shook my head irritably. Envoy intuition is an unreliable system at the best of times, and sinking fast from the weight of radiation poisoning isn't a great state to be in when you try to deploy it.

Not dying yet.

I gave up on trying to see the pattern and let the vagueness wash over me, seeing where it would take me.

The violet light of the corpse locker, beckoning.

The discarded sleeves within.

Semetaire.

By the time I got back to the platform, dinner was nearly over. Beneath the mummified hovering of the two Martians, the rest of the company were sitting around the stripped-down buoy on inflatable loungers, picking without much enthusiasm at the remains of tab-pull field ration pans. I couldn't really blame them – the way I was feeling, just the smell of the stuff made my throat close up. I choked a little on it, then hastily raised my hands as the sound brought a ripple of weapon-grabbing from the diners.

'Hey, it's me.'

Grumbling and guns discarded again. I made my way into the circle, looking for a seat. It was a lounger each, give or take. Jiang Jianping and Schneider had both seated themselves on the floor, Jiang cross-legged in a clear deck space, Schneider sprawled in front of Tanya Wardani's lounger with a proprietorial air that made my mouth twitch. I waved an offered pan away and seated myself on the edge of Vongsavath's lounger, wishing I felt a bit more up to this.

'What kept you?' asked Deprez.

'Been thinking.'

Schneider laughed. 'Man, that shit's *bad* for you. Don't do it. Here.' He rolled a can of amphetamine cola across the deck towards me. I stopped it with one boot. 'Remember what you told me back in the hospital? Don't fucking think, soldier – didn't you read your terms of enlistment?'

It raised a couple of half-hearted smiles. I nodded.

'When's he get here, Jan?'

'Huh?'

'I *said*,' I kicked the can back at him. His hand jumped out and snagged it, *very* fast. 'When's he get here?'

What conversation there was dropped out of the air like Konrad Harlan's one and only attempted gunship raid on Millsport. Particle-blasted down by the rattle of the can and the sudden silence that found it in Schneider's closed fist.

His right fist. His empty left was a little too slow, whipping out for a weapon fractions of a second after I had the Kalashnikov levelled on him. He saw, and froze up.

'Don't,' I told him.

At my side, I felt Vongsavath, still moving for the stunner in her pocket. I laid my free hand on her arm and shook my head slightly. Put some Envoy persuasion into my voice.

'No need, Ameli.'

Her arm dropped back to her lap. Peripheral scan told me everyone else was sitting this one out so far. Even Wardani. I eased slightly.

'When does he get here, Jan?'

'Kovacs, I don't know what the *fuck*—'

'Yeah, you do. When's he get here? Or don't you want both hands any more?'

'*Who?*'

'Carrera. When's he fucking get here, Jan. Last chance.'

'I don't—' Schneider's voice shrilled to an abrupt scream as the interface gun blew a hole through his hand and turned the can he was still holding into shredded metal. Blood and amphetamine cola splashed the air, curiously alike in colour. Flecks of it spotted Tanya Wardani's face and she flinched violently.

It's not a popularity contest.

'What's the matter, Jan?' I asked gently. 'That sleeve Carrera gave you not so hot on endorphin response?'

Wardani was on her feet, face unwiped. 'Kovacs, he's—'

'Don't tell me it's the same sleeve, Tanya. You fucked him, now and two years ago. You know.'

She shook her head numbly. 'The tattoo . . .' she whispered.

'The tattoo is new. Shiny new, even for illuminum. He got it

339

redone, along with some basic cosmetic surgery as part of the package. Isn't that right, Jan?'

The only thing that came out of Schneider was an agonised groaning. He held his shattered hand at arm's length, staring at it in disbelief. Blood dripped on the deck.

All I felt was tired.

'I figure you sold out to Carrera rather than go into virtual interrogation,' I said, still scanning peripherally for reactions among the crowd. 'Don't blame you really. And if they offered you a fresh combat sleeve, full rad/chem resist specs and custom trimmed, well there aren't many deals like that kicking about Sanction IV these days. And no telling how much dirty bombing both sides are going to do from now on in. Yeah, I'd have taken a deal like that.'

'Do you have any evidence of this?' asked Hand.

'Apart from the fact he's the only one of us still not going grey, you mean? Look at him, Hand. He's held up better than the Maori sleeves, and they're built for this shit.'

'I would not call that proof,' said Deprez thoughtfully. 'Though it is odd.'

'He's fucking *lying*,' gritted Schneider through his teeth. 'If anyone's running double for Carrera, it's Kovacs. For Samedi's sake, he's a *Wedge lieutenant*.'

'Don't push your luck, Jan.'

Schneider glared back at me, keening his pain. Across the platform, I thought I heard the songspires pick it up.

'Get me a fucking mediwrap,' he pleaded. 'Someone.'

Sun reached for her pack. I shook my head.

'No. First he tells us how long we've got before Carrera comes through the gate. We need to be ready.'

Deprez shrugged. 'Knowing this, are we not already ready?'

'Not for the Wedge.'

Wardani crossed wordlessly to where Sun stood and snatched the medipack from its fibregrip holster on the other woman's chest. 'Give me that. If you uniformed fucks won't do it, I will.'

She knelt at Schneider's side and opened the pack, spilling the entire contents across the floor as she searched for the wraps.

'The green tabbed envelopes,' said Sun helplessly. 'There.'

'Thank you,' gritted. She spared me a single glance. 'What are you going to do now, Kovacs? Cripple me too?'

'He would have sold us all out, Tanya. He has already.'

'You don't know that.'

'I know he somehow managed to survive two weeks aboard a restricted access hospital without any legitimate documentation. I know he managed to get into the officers' wards without a pass.'

Her face contorted. '*Fuck you*, Kovacs. When we were digging at Dangrek, he bluffed us a nine-week municipal power grant from the Sauberville authorities. With no fucking documentation.'

Hand cleared his throat.

'I would have thought—'

And the ship lit up around us.

It sheeted through the space under the dome, fragments of suddenly erupting light swelling to solid blocks of translucent colour spun around the central structure. Sparkling discharge spat through the air between the colours, lines of power shaken out like storm-torn sails ripped loose of rigging. Trailing fountains of the stuff poured down from the upper levels of expanding rotating light, splashing off the deck and awakening a deeper glow within the translucent surface where they hit. Above, the stars blotted out. At the centre, the mummified corpses of the Martians disappeared, shrouded in the evolving gale of radiance. There was a sound to it all, but less heard than felt through my light-soaked skin, a building thrum and quiver in the air that felt like the adrenalin rush at the start of combat.

Vongsavath touched my arm.

'Look outside,' she said urgently. For all she was at my side, it felt as if she was yelling through a howling wind. 'Look at the gate!'

I tipped my head back and threw the neurachem into seeing through the swirling currents of light to the crystal roof. At first, I couldn't understand what Vongsavath was talking about. I couldn't find the gate, and guessed it had to be somewhere on the other side of the ship, completing another orbit. Then I zeroed in on a vague blotch of grey, too dim to be . . .

And then I understood.

The storm of light and power raging around us was not confined to the air under the dome. Space around the Martian vessel was also seething to life. The stars had faded to dimly-seen gleamings through a curtain of something that stood hazed and shivering, kilometres beyond the orbit of the gate.

'It's a screen,' said Vongsavath with certainty. 'We're under attack.'

Over our heads, the storm was settling. Motes of shadow swam in the light now, here scattering to corners like shoals of startled silverfry seen in negative, elsewhere exploding in slow tumbling motion to take up station on a hundred different levels around the re-emerging corpses of the two Martians. Sequenced splinters of flashing colour flickered at the corners of attenuated fields in shades of pearl and grey. The overall thrumming subsided and the ship began to talk to itself in more defined syllables. Fluting notes echoed across the platform, interspersed with organ deep pulses of sound.

'This is—' My mind spun back to the narrow trawler cabin, the softly awake spiral of the datacoil, the motes of data swept to the top corner. 'This is a *datasystem*?'

'Well spotted.' Tanya Wardani stalked under the trailing skirts of radiance and pointed up to the pattern of shadow and light gathered around the two corpses. There was a peculiar exultation on her face. 'A little more extensive than your average desktop holo, isn't it. I imagine those two have the primary con. Shame they're not in any state to use it, but then I also imagine the ship is capable of looking after itself.'

'That depends on what's coming,' said Vongsavath grimly. 'Check out the upper screens. The grey background.'

I followed her arm. High up, near the curve of the dome a pearl surface ten metres across displayed a milky version of the starscape now dimmed by the shield outside.

Something moved there, shark-slim and angular against the stars.

'What the fuck is that?' asked Deprez.

'Can't you guess?' Wardani was almost shivering with the strength of whatever was slopping around inside her. She stood centre stage to us all. 'Look up. Listen to the ship. She's telling you what it is.'

The Martian datasystem was still talking, in no language anyone was equipped to understand, but with an urgency that required no translator. The splintered lights – *technoglyph numerals* jolted through me, almost as knowledge; *it's a countdown* – flashed over like digit counters tracking a missile. Querulous shrieks fluted up and down an unhuman scale.

'Incoming,' said Vongsavath, hypnotised. 'We're getting ready to engage with something out there. Automated battle systems.'

The *Nagini*—

I whipped around.

'Schneider,' I bellowed.

But Schneider was gone.

'Deprez,' I yelled it back over my shoulder, already on my way across the platform. 'Jiang. He's going for the *Nagini*.'

The ninja was with me by the time I reached the downward spiral pipe, Deprez a couple of steps behind. Both men hefted Sunjets, stocks folded back for easy handling. At the bottom of the pipe I thought I heard the clatter of someone falling, and a shriek of pain. I felt a brief snarl of wolf go through me.

Prey!

We ran, slithering and stumbling on the steep downward incline until we hit bottom and the empty, cherry-flashed expanse of the first chamber. There was blood smeared on the floor where Schneider had fallen. I knelt beside it and felt my lips draw back from my teeth. I got up and looked at my two companions.

'He won't be moving that fast. Don't kill him if you can avoid it. We still need to know about Carrera.'

'Kovacs!!'

It was Hand's voice from up the pipe, bawling with repressed fury. Deprez dropped me a taut grin. I shook my head and sprinted for the exit to the next chamber.

Hunt!

It isn't easy running when every cell in your body is trying to shut down and die, but the wolf gene splice and whatever else the Wedge biotechs had thrown into the cocktail rose through the midst of the nausea and snarled down the weariness. The Envoy conditioning rode it upward.

Check functionality.

Thanks, Virginia.

Around us the ship quivered and shook to wakefulness. We ran through corridors that pulsed with sequenced rings of the purple light I'd seen splash off the edge of the gate when it opened. In one chamber, one of the spine-backed machines moved to intercept us, facings awake with technoglyph display and chittering softly. I fetched up short, interface guns leaping to my hands, Deprez and Jiang flanking me. The impasse held for a long moment and then the machine slouched aside, muttering.

We exchanged glances. Beyond the tortured panting in my chest and the thudding in my temples, I found my mouth had bent itself into a smile.

'Come on.'

A dozen chambers and corridors further on, Schneider proved smarter than I'd expected. As Jiang and I burst into the open of a bubble, Sunjet fire spat and crackled from the far exit. I felt the sting of a near miss across my cheek and then the ninja at my elbow had floored me with a sideways flung arm. The next blast lashed where I had been. Jiang hit, rolled and joined me on the floor, face up, looking at a smouldering cuff with mild distaste.

Deprez slammed to a halt in the shadow of the entrance we'd come through, eye bent to the sighting system of his weapon. The barrage of covering fire he laid down boiled up and down the edges of Schneider's ambush point and – I narrowed my eyes – did absolutely no damage to the material of the exitway. Jiang rolled under the strafing beam and got a narrower angle on the corridor beyond. He fired once, squinted into the glare and shook his head.

'Gone,' he said, climbing to his feet and offering me his hand.

'I, uh, I, thanks.' I got upright. 'Thanks for the push.'

He nodded curtly, and loped off across the chamber. Deprez clapped me on the shoulder and followed. I shook my head clear and went after them. At the exitway I pressed my hand against the edge where Deprez had fired. It wasn't even warm.

The induction rig speaker fizzled against my throat. Hand's voice came through in static-chewed incoherence. Jiang froze ahead of us, head cocked.

'. . . vacs, an . . . me— . . . ow. —peat, re . . . ow . . .'

'Say. Again?' Jiang, spacing his words.

'—saiiii . . . —port no . . .—'

Jiang looked back at me. I made a chopping gesture and knocked my own rig loose. Finger stab forward. The ninja unlocked his posture and moved on, fluid as a Total Body dancer. Somewhat less graceful, we went after him.

What lead Schneider had on us had lengthened. We were moving more slowly now, edging up to entrances and exits in approved covert assault fashion. Twice we picked up movement ahead of us and had to creep forward, only to find another wakened machine ambling about the empty chambers chuntering to itself. One of them followed us for a while like a stray dog in search of a master.

Two chambers out from the docking bay, we heard the *Nagini*'s drives powering up. The covert assault caution shattered. I broke into a staggering sprint. Jiang passed me, then Deprez. Trying to keep up, I doubled over, cramping and retching, halfway across the last chamber. Deprez and the ninja were twenty metres ahead of me when they ducked around the entrance to the bay. I wiped a thin string of bile away from my mouth and straightened up.

A shrilling, ramming, detonating scream, like brakes applied fleetingly to the whole expanding universe.

The *Nagini*'s ultravibe battery firing in a confined space.

I dropped the Sunjet, had both hands halfway to my ears and the pulse stopped as abruptly as it had started. Deprez staggered back into view, painted bloody from head to foot, Sunjet gone. Behind him, the whine of the *Nagini*'s drives deepened to a roar as Schneider powered her up and out. A bang of disrupted air at the atmosphere baffles, barrelling back down the funnel of the docking bay and buffeting my face like a warm wind. Then nothing. Aching silence, tautened with the high-pitched hum of abused hearing trying to deal with the sudden absence of noise.

In the whining quiet, I groped after my Sunjet and made it to where Deprez was slumped on the floor, back to the curving wall. He was staring numbly at his hands and the gore that coated them. His face was streaked red and black with the same stuff. Under the blood, his chameleochrome battledress was already turning to match.

I made a sound and he looked up.

'Jiang?'

'This.' He lifted his hands towards me, and his features twisted momentarily, like the face of a baby not sure if it's going to cry. The words came one at a time, as if he was having to stop and glue them together. '*Is*. Jiang. This is.' His fists knotted up. '*Fuck*.'

At my throat, the induction rig fizzled impotently. Across the chamber, a machine moved and sniggered at us.

CHAPTER THIRTY-FOUR

A *Man Down is not a Man Dead. Leave No Stack Behind.*

Most tight spec ops units like to sing that particular song; the Envoy Corps certainly did. But in the face of modern weaponry it's getting harder and harder to sing it with a straight face. The ultravibe cannon had splashed Jiang Jianping evenly across ten square metres of docking bay deck and containing wall. None of the shredded and shattered tissue was any more solid than the stuff dripping off Luc Deprez. We walked back and forth through it for a while, scraping streaks in it with our boots, crouching to check tiny black clots of gore, but we found nothing.

After ten minutes, Deprez said it for us both.

'We are wasting our time, I think.'

'Yeah.' I lifted my head as something belled through the hull beneath our feet. 'I think Vongsavath was right. We're taking fire.'

'We go back?'

I remembered the induction rig and hooked it back on. Whoever had been yelling at us previously had given up; there was nothing on the channel but interference and a weird sobbing that might have been a carrier wave.

'This is Kovacs. Repeat, this is Kovacs. Status please.'

There was a long pause, then Sutjiadi's voice crashed in the mike.

'—pened? —e . . . —aw . . . launch. Schnei— . . . —ay?'

'You're breaking up, Markus. Status please. Are we under attack?'

There was a burst of distortion and what sounded like two or three voices trying to break in over Sutjiadi. I waited.

Finally, it was Tanya Wardani that came through, almost clear.

'. . . —ack here, . . . —acs . . . —afe. We . . . —ny, . . . —ger. —

peat, no . . . da . . . —ger.'

The hull sang out again, like a struck temple gong. I looked dubiously down at the deck beneath my feet.

'*Safe*, did you say?'

'—essss . . . —o dang— . . . —ack immedi— . . . —afe. —peat, safe.'

I looked at Deprez and shrugged.

'Must be a new definition of the word.'

'Then we go back?'

I looked around, up at the stacked snake-body tiers of the docking bay, then back at his gore-painted face. Decided.

'Looks that way.' I shrugged again. 'It's Wardani's turf. She hasn't been wrong yet.'

Back on the platform, the Martian datasystems had settled to a brilliant constellation of purpose, while the humans stood beneath it all and gaped like worshippers getting an unexpected miracle.

It wasn't hard to see why.

An array of screens and displays was stitched across the space around the central structure. Some were obvious analogues of any dreadnought's battle systems, some defied comparison with anything I'd ever seen. Modern combat gives you a familiarity with compound datadisplay, an ability to glean the detail you need from a dozen different screens and readouts at speed and without conscious thought. Envoy Corps conditioning refines the skill even further, but in the massive radiant geometries of the Martian datasystem, I could feel myself floundering. Here and there, I spotted comprehensible input, images that I could relate back to what I knew was happening in the space around us, but even amongst these elements there were chunks missing where the screens gave out frequencies for unhuman eyes. Elsewhere, I couldn't have told if the displays were complete, defective or totally fried.

Of the identifiable dataware, I spotted real-time visual telemetry, multi-coloured spectrograph sketches, trajectory mappers and battle dynamic analytical models, blast yield monitors and graphic maga-zine inventory, something that might have been grav gradient notation . . .

Centre screen in every second display, the attacker came on.

Skating down the curve of solar gravity at a rakish side-on angle, she was a slim, surgical-looking fusion of rods and elliptical curves that screamed *warship*. Hard on the heels of the thought, the proof dumped itself in my lap. On a screen that did not show real space, weaponry winked at us across the emptiness. Outside the dome, the shields our host had thrown up shimmered and fluoresced. The ship's hull shuddered underfoot.

Meaning . . .

I felt my mind dilate as I got it.

'Don't know what those are,' said Sun conversationally, as I arrived at her side. She seemed entranced by what she was watching. 'Faster-than-light weaponry at any rate; she's got to be nearly an astronomical unit out and we're getting hit instantaneously every time. They don't seem to do much damage, though.'

Vongsavath nodded. 'Prelim systems scramblers, I'd guess. To fuck up the defence net. Maybe it's some kind of grav disruptor, I've heard Mitoma are doing research into—' She broke off. 'Look, here comes the next torpedo spread. Man, that's a *lot* of hardware for a single launch.'

She was right. The space ahead of the attacking vessel had filled up with tiny golden traces so dense they could have been interference across the surface of the screen. Secondary displays yanked in detail and I saw how the swarm wove intricate mutual distract-and-protect evasion across millions of kilometres of space.

'These are FTL too, I think.' Sun shook her head. 'The screens deal with it somehow, gives a representation. I think this has all already happened.'

The vessel I was standing on thrummed distantly, separate vibrations coming in from a dozen different angles. Outside, the shields shimmered again, and I got the vague sense of a shoal of something dark slipping out in the microsecond pulses of lowered energy.

'Counterlaunch,' said Vongsavath with something like satisfaction in her voice. 'Same thing again.'

It was too fast to watch. Like trying to keep track of laser fire. On the screens, the new swarm flashed violet, threading through the approaching sleet of gold and detonating in blots of light that inked out as soon as they erupted. Every flash took specks of gold with it until the sky between the two vessels emptied out.

'Beautiful,' breathed Vongsavath. 'Fucking beautiful.'

I woke up.

'Tanya, I heard the word "safe."' I gestured up at the battle raging in rainbow representation over our heads. 'You call this *safe*?'

The archaeologue said nothing. She was staring at Luc Deprez's bloodied face and clothing.

'Relax, Kovacs.' Vongsavath pointed out one of the trajectory mappers. 'It's a cometary, see. Wardani read the same thing off the glyphs. Just going to swing past and trade damage, then on and out again.'

'A *cometary*?'

The pilot spread her hands. 'Post-engagement graveyard orbit, automated battle systems. It's a closed loop. Been going on for thousands of years, looks like.'

'What happened to Jan?' Wardani's voice was stretched taut.

'He left without us.' A thought struck me. 'He made the gate, right? You saw that?'

'Yeah, like a prick up a cunt,' said Vongsavath with unexpected venom. 'Man could fly when he needed to. That was my fucking ship.'

'He was afraid,' said the archaeologue numbly.

Luc Deprez stared at her out of his blood-masked face. 'We were all afraid, Mistress Wardani. It is not an excuse.'

'You fool.' She looked around at us. 'All of you, you fucking. Fools. He wasn't afraid of this. This fucking. *Light show*. He was afraid of *him*.'

The jerked nod was for me. Her eyes nailed mine.

'Where's Jiang?' asked Sun suddenly. In the storm of alien technology around us, it had taken that long to notice the quiet ninja's absence.

'Luc's wearing most of him,' I said brutally. 'The rest is lying back on the docking bay floor, courtesy of the *Nagini*'s ultravibe. I guess Jan must have been afraid of him as well, huh Tanya?'

Wardani's gaze flinched aside.

'And his stack?' Nothing showed on Sutjiadi's face, but I didn't have to see it. The wolf splice custom was trying to give me the same sinus-aching ride back behind the bridge of my nose.

Pack member down.

I locked it down with Envoy displacement trickery. Shook my head.

'Ultravibe, Markus. He got the full blast.'

'Schneider—' Vongsavath broke off and had to start again. 'I will—'

'Forget about Schneider,' I told her. 'He's dead.'

'Get in the queue.'

'No, he's dead, Ameli. Really dead.' And as their eyes fixed on me, as Tanya Wardani looked back disbelieving. 'I mined the *Nagini*'s fuel cells. Set to blow on acceleration under planetary gravity. He vaporised the minute he crashed the gate. Be lucky if there's tinsel left.'

Over our heads, another wave of gold and violet missiles found each other in the machine dance and, flickering, wiped each other out.

'*You blew up the Nagini?*' It was hard to tell what Vongsavath was feeling, her voice was so choked. '*You blew up my ship?*'

'If the wreckage is so dispersed,' said Deprez thoughtfully, 'Carrera may assume we were all killed in the explosion.'

'If Carrera is actually out there, that is.' Hand was looking at me the way he'd looked at the songspires. 'If this isn't all an Envoy ploy.'

'Oh, what's the matter, Hand? Did Schneider try to cut some kind of deal with you when you went walkabout?'

'I have no idea what you're talking about, Kovacs.'

Maybe he didn't. I was abruptly too weary to care one way or the other.

'Carrera will come out here whatever happens,' I told them. 'He's thorough that way, and he'll want to see the ship. He'll have some way of standing down the nanobe system. But he won't come yet. Not with little pieces of the *Nagini* littering the landscape, and emissions pick-up from the other side of the gate that reads like a full-scale naval engagement. That's going to back him up a little. It gives us some time.'

'Time to do what?' asked Sutjiadi.

The moment hung, and the Envoy crept out to play in it. Across splayed peripheral vision, I watched their faces and their stance, measured the possible allegiances, the possible betrayals. Locked down the emotions, peeled away the useful nuances they could give me, and dumped the remainder. Tied the wolf pack loyalty off, smothered whatever feeling still swam murkily in the space between Tanya Wardani and myself. Descended into the structured cold of Envoy mission time. Decided, and played my last card.

'Before I mined the *Nagini*, I stripped the spacesuits off the corpses we recovered, and stashed them in a recess in the first chamber outside the docking bay. Leaving aside the one with the blasted helmet, that's four viable suits. They're standard issue pull-ons. The airpacks will replenish from unpressured atmosphere environments like this one. Set the valves, they just suck it up. We leave in two waves. Someone from the first wave comes back with spare suits.'

'All this,' jeered Wardani, 'with Carrera waiting on the other side of the gate to snap us up. I don't think so.'

'I'm not suggesting we do it now,' I said quietly. 'I'm just suggesting we go back and recover the suits while there's time.'

'And when Carrera comes aboard? What do you suggest we do then?' The hatred welling up in Wardani's face was one of the uglier things I'd seen recently. '*Hide* from him?'

'Yes.' I watched for reactions. 'Exactly that. I suggest we hide. We move deeper into the ship and we wait. Whatever team Carrera deploys will have enough hardware to find traces of us in the docking bay and other places. But they won't find anything that can't be explained by our presence here before we all boarded the *Nagini* and blew ourselves to tinsel. The logical thing to do is assume that we all died. He'll do a sweep, he'll deploy a claim buoy, just the way we planned to, and then he'll leave. He doesn't have the personnel or the time to occupy a hulk over fifty klicks long.'

'No,' said Sutjiadi, 'But he'll leave a caretaker squad.'

I made an impatient gesture. 'Then we'll kill them.'

'And I have no doubt there'll be a second detachment waiting on the other side of the gate,' Deprez said sombrely.

'So what? Jesus, Luc. You used to do this for a living, didn't you?'

The assassin gave me an apologetic smile. 'Yes, Takeshi. But we are all of us sick. And this is the Wedge you are talking about. As many as twenty men here, perhaps the same again on the other side of the gate.'

'I don't think we really—' A sudden tremor jagged across the deck, enough to make Hand and Tanya Wardani stumble slightly. The rest of us rode it out with combat-conditioned ease, but still . . .

A moan in the fibres of the hull. The songspires across the platform seemed to gust sympathy at a level on the edge of hearing.

A vague unease coiled through me. Something was wrong.

I looked up at the screens and watched the attacking systems wiped out once again by the defence net. It all seemed to be taking place that little bit closer in this time.

'You *did* all decide, while I was gone, that we were safe here, right?'

'We did the maths, Kovacs.' Vongsavath nodded inclusively at Sun and Wardani. The systems officer inclined her head. Wardani just stared holes in me. 'Looks like our friend out there hooks up with us about once every twelve hundred years. And given the dating on most of the ruins on Sanction IV, that means this engagement has been fought about a hundred times already with no result.'

But still the feeling. Envoy senses, cranked up to snapping, and feeling something *not* right, something so far wrong, in fact, I could almost smell the scorching.

. . . sobbing carrier wave . . .

. . . songspires . . .

. . . time slowing down . . .

I stared at the screens.

We need to get out of here.

'Kovacs?'

'We need to—'

I felt the words moth their way out between dry lips, as if someone else was using the sleeve against my will, and then they stopped.

From the attacker, came the real attack at last.

It burst from the leading surfaces of the vessel like something alive. An amorphous, turbulent dark-body blob of something spat out at us like congealed hatred. On secondary screens you could see how it tore up the fabric of space around it and left a wake of outraged reality behind. It didn't take much to guess what we were looking at.

Hyperspace weaponry.

Experia fantasy stuff. And the sick wet dream of every naval commander in the Protectorate.

The ship, the Martian ship – and only now I grasped with instinctive Envoy-intuited knowledge that the other was *not* Martian, looked nothing like – pulsed in a way that sent nausea rolling through my guts and set every tooth in my head instantly on edge. I staggered and went down on one knee.

Something vomited into the space ahead of the attack. Something boiled and flexed and split wide open with a vaguely sensed detonation. I felt a recoil tremor go throbbing through the hull around me, a disquiet that went deeper than simple real-space vibration.

On the screen, the dark-body projectile shattered apart, flinging out oddly sticky-looking particles of itself. I saw the outside shield fluoresce, shudder and go out like a blown candle flame.

The ship screamed.

There was no other way to describe it. It was a rolling, modulating cry that seemed to emanate from the air around us. It was a sound so massive, it made the shriek of the *Nagini*'s ultravibe battery seem almost tolerable. But where the ultravibe blast had rammed and battered at my hearing, this sound sliced and passed through as effortlessly as a laser scalpel. I knew, even as I made the movement, that clapping hands over my ears would have no effect.

I did it anyway.

The scream rose, held and finally rolled away across the platform, replaced by a less agonising pastiche of fluting alert sounds from the datasystems and a splinter-thin fading echo from—

I whipped around.

—from the songspires.

This time there could be no doubt. Softly, like wind sawing over a worn stone edge, the songspires had collected the ship's scream and were playing it back to each other in skewed cadences that could almost have been music.

It was the carrier wave.

Overhead, something seemed to whisper response. Looking up, I thought I saw a shadow flicker across the dome.

Outside, the shields came back on.

'Fuck,' said Hand, getting to his feet. 'What was th—'

'Shut up.' I stared across at the place I thought I'd seen the shadow but the loss of the starscape background had drowned it in pearlish light. A little to the left, one of the Martian corpses gazed down at me from amidst the radiance of the datasystem. The sobbing of the songspires murmured on, tugging at something in the pit of my stomach.

And then, again, the gut-deep, sickening pulse and the thrum through the deck underfoot.

'We're returning fire,' said Sun.

On screen, another dark-body mass, hawked out of some battery deep in the belly of the Martian vessel, spat at the closing attacker. This time the recoil went on longer.

'This is incredible,' said Hand. 'Unbelievable.'

'Believe it,' I told him tonelessly. The sense of impending disaster had not gone with the decaying echo of the last attack. If anything, it was stronger. I tried to summon the Envoy intuition through layers of weariness and dizzying nausea.

'Incoming,' called Vongsavath. 'Block your ears.'

This time, the alien ship's missile got a lot closer before the Martian defence net caught and shredded it. The shockwaves from the blast drove us all to the ground. It felt as if the whole ship had been twisted around us like a wrung-out cloth. Sun threw up. The outside shield went down and stayed down.

Braced for the ship to scream again, I heard instead a long, low keening that scraped talons along the tendons of my arms and around my ribcage. The songspires trapped it and fed it back, higher now, no longer a fading echo but a field emanation in its own right.

I heard someone hiss behind me, and turned to see Wardani,

staring up in disbelief. I followed her gaze and saw the same shadow flitting clearly across the upper regions of the data display.

'What ...' It was Hand, voice fading out as another patch of darkness flapped across from the left and seemed to dance briefly with the first.

By then I knew, and oddly my first thought was that Hand, of all people, ought not to have been surprised, that he ought to have got it first.

The first shadow dipped and swooped around the corpse of the Martian.

I looked for Wardani, found her eyes and the numb disbelief there.

'No,' she whispered, little more than mouthing the word. 'It can't be.'

But it was.

They came from all sides of the dome, at first in ones and twos, sliding up the crystalline curve and peeling off into sudden full three-dimensional existence, shaken loose with each convulsive distortion that their ship suffered as the battle raged outside. They peeled off and swooped down to floor level, then soared up again and settled to circling the central structure. They didn't seem to be aware of us in any way that mattered, but none of them touched us. Overhead, their passage had no effect on the datadisplay system other than a slight rippling as they banked, and some of them seemed even to pass occasionally through the substance of the dome and out into hard space. More came funnelling up through the tube that had first led us to the platform, packing into a flying space that was already becoming crowded.

The sound they made was the same keening the ship had begun earlier, the same dirge that the songspires now gave out from the floor, the same carrier wave I'd picked up on the comset. Traces of the cherry-and-mustard odour wafted through the air, but tinged now with something else, something scorched and old.

Hyperspatial distortion broke and burst in the space outside, the shields came back on, tinged a new, violet colour and the ship's hull was awash with recoil as its batteries launched repeatedly at the other vessel. I was beyond caring. All feeling of physical discomfort was gone, frozen away to a single tightness in my chest and a growing pressure behind my eyes. The platform seemed to have expanded massively around me and the rest of the company were now too far out across the vast flattened space to be relevant.

I was abruptly aware that I was weeping myself, a dry sobbing in the small spaces of my sinuses.

'Kovacs!'

I turned, feeling as if I was thigh-deep in a torrent of icy water, and saw Hand, jacket pocket flapped back, raising his stunner.

The distance, I later reckoned, was less than five metres but it seemed to take forever to cross it. I waded forward, blocked the weapon arm at a pressure point and smashed an elbow strike into his face. He howled and went down, stunner skittering away across the platform. I dropped after him, looking through blurred vision for his throat. One weak arm fended me off. He was screaming something.

My right hand stiffened into the killing blade. Neurachem worked to focus my eyes through blurring.

'—all die, you fucking—'

I drew back for the blow. He was sobbing now.

Blurring.

Water in my eyes.

I wiped a hand across them, blinked and saw his face. There were tears streaming down his cheeks. The sobbing barely made words.

'What?' My hand loosened and I belted him hard across the face. 'What did you say?'

He gulped. Drew breath.

'Shoot me. Shoot us all. Use the stunner. *Kovacs. This is what killed the others.*'

And I realised my own face was soaked in tears, my eyes filled with them. I could feel the weeping in my swollen throat, the same ache that the songspires had reflected back, not from the ship, I knew suddenly, but from her millennia-departed crew. The knife running through me was the grief of the Martians, an alien pain stored here in ways that made no sense outside of folktales around a campfire out on Mitcham's Point, a frozen, unhuman hurt in my chest and the pit of my stomach that would not be dismissed, and a not-quite-tuned note in my ears that I knew when it got here would crack me open like a raw egg.

Vaguely, I felt the rip and warp of another dark-body near-miss. The flocking shadows above my head swirled and shrieked, beating upwards against the dome.

'*Do it, Kovacs!*'

I staggered upright. Found my own stunner, and fired it into Hand. Looked for the others.

Deprez, with his hands at his temples, swaying like a tree in a gale. Sun, apparently sinking to her knees. Sutjiadi between the two of them, unclear in the shimmering perspectives of my own tears. Wardani, Vongsavath . . .

Too far, too far off in the density of light and keening pain.

The Envoy conditioning scrabbled after perspective, shut down the flood of emotion that the weeping around me had unlocked. Distance closed. My senses reeled back in.

The wailing of the gathered shadows intensified as I overrode my own psychic defences and dimmer switches. I was breathing it in like Guerlain Twenty, corroding some containment system inside that lay beyond analytical physiology. I felt the damage come on, swelling to bursting point.

I threw up the stunner and started firing.

Deprez. Down.

Sutjiadi, spinning as the assassin fell at his side, disbelief on his face.

Down.

Beyond him, Sun Liping kneeling, eyes clamped tightly shut, sidearm lifting to her own face. Systems analysis. Last resort. She'd worked it out, just didn't have a stunner. Didn't know anyone else did either.

I staggered forward, yelling at her. Inaudible in the storm of grief. The blaster snugged under her chin. I snapped off a shot with the stunner, missed. Got closer.

The blaster detonated. It ripped up through her chin on narrow beam and flashed a sword of pale flame out the top of her head before the blowback circuit cut in and killed the beam. She toppled sideways, steam curling from her mouth and eyes.

Something clicked in my throat. A tiny increment of loss welling up and dripping into the ocean of grief the songspires were singing me. My mouth opened, maybe to scream some of the pain out, but there was too much to pass. It locked soundless in my throat.

Vongsavath stumbled into me from the side. I spun and grabbed her. Her face was wide-eyed with shock, drenched in tears. I tried to push her away, to give her some distance on the stunblast, but she clung to me, moaning deep in her throat.

The bolt convulsed her and she dropped on top of Sun's corpse.

Wardani stood on the other side of both of them, staring at me.

Another dark-body blast. The winged shadows above us screamed and wept and I felt something tearing inside me

'No,' said Wardani.

'Cometary,' I shouted at her across the shrieking. 'It has to pass, we just—'

Then something really did tear, somewhere, and I dropped to the deck, curled around the pain, gaping like a gaffed bottleback with the immensity of it.

Sun – dead by her own hand for the *second fucking time*.

Jiang – smeared pulp on the docking bay floor. Stack gone.

Cruickshank, ripped apart, stack gone. Hansen ditto. The count unreeled, speed review across time, thrashing like a snake in its death throes.

The stink of the camp I'd pulled Wardani out of, children starving under robot guns and the governance of a burnt-out wirehead excuse for a human being.

The hospital ship, limping interim space between killing fields.

The platoon, pack members torn apart around me by smart shrapnel.

Two years of slaughter on Sanction IV.

Before that, the Corps.

Innenin, Jimmy de Soto and the others, minds gnawed hollow by the Rawling virus.

Before that, other worlds. Other pain, most of it not mine. Death and Envoy deceit.

Before that, Harlan's World and the gradual emotional maiming of childhood in the Newpest slums. The life-saving leap into the cheerful brutality of the Protectorate Marines. Days of enforcement.

Strung-out lives, lived in the sludge of human misery. Pain suppressed, packed down, *stored* for an inventory that never came.

Overhead the Martians circled and screamed their grief. I could feel my own scream building, welling up inside, and knew it was going to rip me apart coming out.

And then discharge.

And then the dark.

I tumbled into it, thankful, hoping that the ghosts of the unavenged dead might pass me in the darkness unseeing.

CHAPTER THIRTY-FIVE

I t's cold down by the shoreline, and there's a storm coming in. Black flecks of fallout mingle with flurries of dirty snow, and the wind lifts splatters of spray off the rumpled sea. Reluctant waves dump themselves on sand turned muddy green beneath the glowering sky. I hunch my shoulders inside my jacket, hands jammed into pockets, face closed like a fist against the weather.

Further up the curve of the beach, a fire casts orange-red light at the sky. A solitary figure sits on the landward side of the flames, huddled in a blanket. Though I don't want to, I start in that direction. Whatever else, the fire looks warm, and there's nowhere else to go.

The gate is closed.

That sounds wrong, something I know, for some reason, isn't true. Still. . . .

As I get closer, my disquiet grows. The huddled figure doesn't move or acknowledge my approach. Before I was worried that it might be someone hostile, but now that misgiving shrivels up to make space for the fear that this is someone I know, and that they're dead—

Like everyone else I know.

Behind the figure at the fire, I see there's a structure rising from the sand, a huge skeletal cross with something bound loosely to it. The driving wind and the needle-thin sleet it carries won't let me look up far enough to see clearly what the object is.

The wind is keening now, like something I once heard and was afraid of.

I reach the fire and feel the blast of warmth across my face. I take my hands from my pockets and hold them out.

The figure stirs. I try not to notice. I don't want this.

'Ah – the penitent.'

Semetaire. The sardonic tone has gone; maybe he thinks he doesn't need it any more. Instead there's something approaching compassion. The magnanimous warmth of someone who's won a game whose outcome they never had that much doubt about.

'I'm sorry?'

He laughs. 'Very droll. Why don't you kneel at the fire, it's warmer that way.'

'I'm not that cold,' I say, shivering, and risk a look at his face. His eyes glitter in the firelight. He knows.

'It's taken you a long time to get here, Wedge Wolf,' he says kindly. 'We can wait a little longer.'

I stare through my splayed fingers at the flames. 'What do you want from me, Semetaire?'

'Oh, come now. What do I want? You know what I want.' He shrugs off the blanket and rises gracefully to his feet. He is taller than I remember, elegantly menacing in his ragged black coat. He fits the top hat on his head at a rakish angle. 'I want the same as all the others.'

'And what's that?' I nod up at the thing crucified behind him.

'That?' For the first time, he seems off balance. A little embarrassed, maybe. 'That's, well. Let's say that's an alternative. An alternative for you, that is, but I really don't think you want to—'

I look up at the looming structure, and suddenly it's easier to see through the wind and sleet and fallout.

It's me.

Pinned in place with swathes of netting, dead grey flesh pressing into the spaces between the cord, body sagging away from the rigid structure of the scaffold, head sunk forward on the neck. The gulls have been at my face. The eyesockets are empty and the cheeks tattered. Bone shows through in patches across my forehead.

It must, I think distantly, be cold up there.

'I did warn you.' A trace of the old mockery is creeping back into his voice. He's getting impatient. 'It's an alternative, but I think you'll agree it's a lot more comfortable down here by the fire. And there is this.'

He opens one gnarled hand and shows me the cortical stack, fresh blood and tissue still clinging to it in specks. I slap a hand to the back of my neck and find a ragged hole there, a gaping space at the base of my skull into *which my fingers slip with horrifying ease. Through on the other side of the damage, I can feel the slick, spongy weight of my own cerebral tissue.*

'See,' he says, almost regretfully.

I pull my fingers loose again. 'Where did you get that, Semetaire?'

'Oh, these are not hard to come by. Especially on Sanction IV.'

'You got Cruickshank's?' I ask him, with a sudden surge of hope.

He hesitates fractionally. 'But of course. They all come to me, sooner or later.' He nods to himself. 'Sooner or later.'

The repetition sounds forced. Like he's trying to convince. I feel the hope die down again, guttering out.

'Later then,' I tell him, holding my hands out to the fire one more time. The wind buffets at my back.

'What are you talking about?' The laugh tagged on the end of it is forced as well. I smile fractionally. Edged with old pain, but there's a strange comfort to the way it hurts.

'I'm going now. There's nothing for me here.'

'Go?' His voice turns abruptly ugly. He holds up the stack between thumb and forefinger, red glinting in the firelight. 'You're not going anywhere, my wolf-pack puppy. You're staying here with me. We've got some accounts to process.'

This time, I'm the one that laughs.

'Get the fuck out of my head, Semetaire.'

'You. Will.' One hand reaching crooked across the fire for me. 'Stay.'

And the Kalashnikov is in my hand, the gun heavy with a full clip of antipersonnel rounds. Well, wouldn't you know it.

'Got to go,' I say. 'I'll tell Hand you said hello.'

He looms, grasping, eyes gleaming.

I level the gun.

'You were warned, Semetaire.'

I shoot into the space below the hatbrim. Three shots, tight-spaced.

It kicks him back, dropping him in the sand a full three metres beyond the fire. I wait for a moment to see if he'll get up, but he's gone. The flames dampen down visibly with his departure.

I look up and see that the cruciform structure is empty, whatever that means. I remember the dead face it held up before and squat by the fire, warming myself until it gutters down to embers.

In the glowing ash, I spot the cortical stack, burnt clean and metallic shiny amidst the last charred fragments of wood, I reach in amongst the ashes and lift it out between finger and thumb, holding it the way Semetaire did.

It scorches a little, but that's OK.

I stow it and the Kalashnikov, thrust my rapidly chilling hands back into the pockets of my jacket and straighten up, looking around.

It's cold, but somewhere there's got to be a way off this fucking beach.

PART FIVE
Divided Loyalties

Face the facts. Then act on them. It's the only mantra I know, the only doctrine I have to offer you, and it's harder than you'd think, because I swear humans seem hardwired to do anything but. Face the facts. Don't pray, don't wish, don't buy into centuries-old dogma and dead rhetoric. Don't give in to your conditioning or your visions or your fucked-up sense of ... whatever. FACE THE FACTS. THEN act.

Quellcrist Falconer *Speech before the Assault on Millsport*

CHAPTER THIRTY-SIX

Night sky starscape, piercingly clear.

I looked at it dully for a while, watching a peculiarly fragmented red glow creep up over it from the left edge of my vision, then retreat again.

This ought to mean something to you, Tak.

Like some kind of code, webbed into the way the glow shattered across the rim of my vision, something designed in the way it levered itself up and then sank down again by fractions.

Like glyphs. Like numerals.

And then it did mean something to me, and I felt a cold wave of sweat break across my entire body as I realised where I was.

The red glow was a head-up display, printing out across the bowl of the spacesuit faceplate I was lying trapped beneath.

This is no fucking night sky, Tak.

I was outside.

And then the weight of recall, of personality and past came crashing in on me, like a micrometeorite punching through the thin seal of transparency that was keeping my life in.

I flailed my arms and found I couldn't move from the wrists up. My fingers groped around a rigid framework under my back, the faint thrum of a motor system. I reached around, twisting my head.

'Hey, he's coming out of it.'

It was a familiar voice, even through the thin metallic straining of the suit's comsystem. Someone else chuckled tinnily.

'Are you fucking surprised, man?'

Proximity sense gave me movement at my right side. Above me, I saw another helmet lean in, faceplate darkened to an impenetrable black.

'Hey, lieutenant.' Another voice I knew. 'You just won me fifty bucks UN. I told these fucking suitfarts you'd pull through faster than anyone else.'

'Tony?' I managed faintly.

'Hey, no cerebral damage either. Key another one in for 391 platoon, guys. We are *fucking* immortal.'

They brought us back from the Martian dreadnought like a vacuum commando funeral procession. Seven bodies on powered stretchers, four assault bugs and a twenty-five strong honour guard in full hard space combat rig. Carrera had been taking no chances when he finally deployed to the other side of the gate.

Tony Loemanako took us back through in immaculate style, as if Martian gate-beachheads were something he'd been doing all his professional life. He sent two bugs through first, followed with the stretchers and infantry, commandos peeling off in matched pairs on left and right, and closed it out with the last two bugs retreating through backwards. Suit, stretcher and bug drives all powered up to full grav-lift hover the second they hit Sanction IV's gravity field and when they grounded a couple of seconds after that, it was unified, on a single raise-and-clench command from Loemanako's suited fist.

Carrera's Wedge.

Propped up on the stretcher to the extent that the webbing allowed, I watched the whole thing and tried to damp down the sense of pride and belonging the wolf gene splice wanted me to feel.

'Welcome to base camp, lieutenant,' said Loemanako, dropping his fist to knock gently on my suit's breastplate. 'You're going to be fine now. Everything's going to be fine.'

His voice lifted in the comsystem. 'Alright, people, let's move. Mitchell and Kwok, stay suited and keep two of the bugs at standby. The rest of you, hit the shower – we're done swimming for now. Tan, Sabyrov and Munharto, I want you back here in fifteen, wear what you like but tooled up to keep Kwok and Mitchell company.

Everyone else, stand down. Chandra control, could we get some medical attention down here *today*, please.'

Laughter, rattling through the comset. There was a general loosening of stance around me, visible even through the bulk of vacuum combat gear and the non-reflective black polalloy suits beneath. Weapons went away, folded down, disconnected or simply sheathed. The bug riders climbed off their mounts with the precision of mechanical dolls and followed the general flow of suited bodies away down the beach. Waiting for them at water's edge, the Wedge battlewagon *Angin Chandra's Virtue* bulked on assault landing claws like some prehistoric cross between crocodile and turtle. Her heavily armoured chameleochrome hull shone turquoise to match the beach in the pale afternoon sunlight.

It was good to see her again.

The beach, now I came to look at it, was a mess. In every direction as far as my limited vision could make out, the sand was torn up and furrowed around the shallow crater of fused glass the *Nagini* had made when she blew. The blast had taken the bubblefabs with it, leaving nothing but scorchmarks and a sparse few fragments of metal that professional pride told me could not possibly be part of the assault ship itself. The *Nagini* had airburst, and the explosion would have consumed every molecule of her structure instantaneously. If the ground was for dead people, Schneider had certainly won clear of the crowd. Most of him was probably still up in the stratosphere, dissipating.

What you're good at, Tak.

The blast seemed to have sunk the trawler too. Twisting my head, I could just make out the stern and heat-mangled superstructure jutting above the water. Memory flickered brightly through my head – Luc Deprez and a bottle of cheap whisky, junk politics and government-banned cigars, Cruickshank leaning over me in—

Don't do this, Tak.

The Wedge had put up a few items of their own to replace the vaporised camp. Six large oval bubblefabs stood a few metres off the crater on the left, and down by the snout of the battlewagon, I picked out the sealed square cabin and the bulk pressure tanks of the polalloy shower unit. The returning vacuum commandos shucked their heavier items of weaponry on adjacent tent-canopied racks and filed in through the rinse hatch.

From the 'Chandra came a file of Wedge uniforms with the white shoulder flash of the medical unit. They gathered around the stretchers, powered them up and shunted us off towards one of the bubblefabs. Loemanako touched me on the arm as my stretcher lifted.

'See you later, lieutenant. I'll drop by once they got you shelled. Got to go and rinse now.'

'Yeah, thanks Tony.'

'Good to see you again, sir.'

In the bubblefab, the medics got us unstrapped and then unsuited, working with brisk, clinical efficiency. By virtue of being conscious, I was a little easier to unpack than the others, but there wasn't much in it. I'd been without the anti-rad dosing for too long and just bending or lifting each limb took major efforts of will. When they finally got me out of the suit and onto a bed, it was as much as I could do to answer the questions the medic put to me as he ran a series of standard post-combat checks on my sleeve. I managed to keep my eyes jacked half open while he did it, and watched past his shoulder as they ran the same tests on the others. Sun, who was pretty obviously beyond immediate repair, they dumped unceremoniously in a corner.

'So will I live, doc?' I mumbled at one point.

'Not in this sleeve.' Prepping an anti-rad cocktail hypospray as he talked. 'But I can keep you going for a while longer, I think. Save you having to talk to the old man in virtual.'

'What does he want, a debriefing?'

'I guess.'

'Well you'd better jack me up with something so I don't fall asleep on him. Got any 'meth?'

'I'm not convinced that's a good idea right now, lieutenant.'

That merited a laugh, dredged up dry from somewhere. 'Yeah, you're right. That stuff 'll ruin my health.'

In the end I had to pull rank on him to get the tetrameth, but he jacked me. I was more or less functional when Carrera walked in.

'Lieutenant Kovacs.'

'Isaac.'

The grin broke across his scarred face like sunrise on crags. He shook his head. 'You motherfucker, Kovacs. Do you know how many men I've had deployed across this hemisphere looking for you?'

'Probably no more than you can spare.' I propped myself up a little more on the bed. 'Were you getting worried?'

'I think you stretched the terms of your commission worse than a squad bitch's asshole, lieutenant. AWOL two months on a datastack posting. *Gone after something that might be worth this whole fucking war. Back later.* That's a little vague.'

'Accurate, though.'

'Is it?' He seated himself on the edge of the bed, chameleochrome coveralls shifting to match the quilt pattern. The recent scar tissue across forehead and cheek tugged as he frowned. 'Is it a warship?'

'Yes, it is.'

'Deployable?'

I considered. 'Dependent on the archaeologue support you've got to hand, I'd say yes, probably.'

'And how's your current archaeologue support?'

I glanced across the open space of the bubblefab to where Tanya Wardani lay curled up under a sheet-thin insulating quilt. Like the rest of the *Nagini* gang survivors, she'd been lightly sedated. The medic who did it had said she was stable, but not likely to live much longer than me.

'Wasted.' I started coughing, couldn't easily stop. Carrera waited it out. Handed me a wipe when I finished. I gestured weakly as I cleaned my mouth. 'Just like the rest of us. How's yours?'

'We have no archaeologue aboard currently, unless you count Sandor Mitchell.'

'I don't. That's a man with a hobby, not an archaeologue. How come you didn't come Scratcher-equipped, Isaac?' *Schneider must have told you what you were buying into*. I weighed it up, split-second, and decided not to give up that particular piece of information yet. I didn't know what value it held, if any, but when you're down to your last harpoon clip, you don't go firing at fins. 'You must have had some idea what you were buying into here.'

He shook his head.

'Corporate backers, Takeshi. Tower-dweller scum. You get no more air from people like that than you absolutely need to get aboard. All I knew until today was that Hand was into something big, and if the Wedge brought back a piece of it, it'd be made worth our while.'

'Yeah, but they gave you the codes to the nanobe system. Something more valuable than that? On Sanction IV? Come on Isaac, you must have guessed what it was.'

He shrugged. 'They named figures, that's all. That's how the Wedge works, you know that. Which reminds me. That's Hand over by the door, right? The slim one.'

I nodded. Carrera wandered over and looked intently at the sleeping exec.

'Yeah. Missing some weight off the pix I've got on stack.' He paced the makeshift ward, glancing left and right at the other beds and the corpse in the corner. Through the 'meth rush and the weariness, I felt an old caution go itching along my nerves. ''Course, that's not surprising, the rad count around here. I'm surprised any of you are still up and walking around.'

'We're not,' I pointed out.

'Right.' His smile was pained. 'Jesus, Takeshi. Why didn't you hold back a couple of days? Could have halved your dosage. I've got everybody on standard anti-rad, we'll all walk out of here with no worse than headaches.'

'Not my call.'

'No, I don't suppose it was. Who's the inactive?'

'Sun Liping.' It hurt more to look at her than I'd expected. Wolf pack allegiances are a slippery thing, it seems. 'Systems officer.'

He grunted. 'The others?'

'Ameli Vongsavath, pilot officer.' I pointed them out with a cocked finger and thumb. 'Tanya Wardani, archaeologue, Jiang Jianping, Luc Deprez, both stealth ops.'

'I see.' Carrera frowned again and nodded in Vongsavath's direction. 'So if that's your pilot, who was flying the assault launch when she blew?'

'Guy called Schneider. He's the one put me onto this whole gig in the first place. Fucking civilian pilot. He got rattled when the fireworks started out there. Took the ship, trashed Hansen, the guy we left on picket, with the ultravibe and then just blew hatches, left us to—'

'He went alone?'

'Yeah, unless you want to count the riders in the corpse locker. We lost two bodies to the nanobes before we went through. And we found another six on the other side. Oh, yeah and two more drowned in the trawler nets. Archaeologue team from back before the war, looks like.'

He wasn't listening, just waiting until I stopped.

'Yvette Cruickshank, Markus Sutjiadi. Those were the members of your team the nanobe system took out?'

'Yeah.' I tried for mild surprise. 'You got a crew list? Jesus, these tower-dwellers of yours cut some mean corporate security.'

He shook his head. 'Not really. These tower-dwellers are from the same tower as your friend over there. Rivals for promotion, in fact. Like I said, scum.' There was a curious lack of venom in his voice as he said it, an absent tone that seemed to my Envoy antennae to carry with it a tinge of relief. 'I don't suppose you recovered stacks for any of the nanobe victims?'

'No, why?'

'Doesn't matter. I didn't really think you would. My clients tell me the system goes after any built components. Cannibalises them.'

'Yeah, that's what we guessed too.' I spread my hands. 'Isaac, even if we had recovered stacks, they'd have been vaporised with just about everything else aboard the *Nagini*.'

'Yes, it was a remarkably complete explosion. Know anything about that, Takeshi?'

I summoned a grin. 'What do you think?'

'I think Lock Mit fast assault launches don't vaporise in mid-air for no reason. And I think you seem less than outraged about this guy Schneider running out on you.'

'Well, he is dead.' Carrera folded his arms and looked at me. I sighed. 'Yeah, OK. I mined the drives. I never trusted Schneider further than a clingfilm condom anyway.'

'With cause, it appears. And lucky for you we came along, given

373

the results.' He got up, brushed his hands together. Something unpleasant definitely seemed to have slid off his screen. 'You'd better get some rest, Takeshi. I'll want a full debriefing tomorrow morning.'

'Sure.' I shrugged. 'Not much more to tell, anyway.'

He raised an eyebrow. 'Really? That's not what my scanners say. We registered more energy discharged on the other side of that gate in the last seven hours than the sum generating cost of every hypercast to and from Sanction IV since it was settled. Myself, I'd say there's a reasonable chunk of story left to tell.'

'Oh, that.' I gestured dismissively. 'Well, you know, galactic ancients' automated naval engagement. No big deal.'

'Right.'

He was on his way out when something seemed to strike him. 'Takeshi.'

I felt my senses tilt like mission time.

'Yeah?' Striving to stay casual.

'Just out of curiosity. How did you plan to get back? After you blew the assault launch? You know, with the nanobes operative, the background rad count. No transport, except maybe that piece-of-shit trawler. What were you going to do, walk out? You're barely two steps ahead of inactive, all of you. What the hell kind of strategy was blowing your only available ride out?'

I tried to think back. The whole situation, the upward-sucking vertigo of the Martian ship's empty corridors and chambers, the mummified gaze of the corpses and the battle with weapons of unimaginable power raging outside – all of it seemed to have receded an immense distance into the past. I suppose I could have yanked it all back in with Envoy focus, but there was something dark and cold in the way, advising against it. I shook my head.

'I don't know, Isaac. I had suits stashed. Maybe swim out and hang around at the edge of the gate broadcasting a mayday squawk across to you guys.'

'And if the gate wasn't radio-transparent?'

'It's starlight-transparent. And scanner-transparent, apparently.'

'That doesn't mean a coherent—'

'Then I'd have tossed through a fucking remote beacon and

hoped it survived the nanobes long enough for you to get a fix. Jesus, Isaac. I'm an Envoy. We make this stuff up on the fly. Worse-case scenario, we had a close-to-working claim buoy. Sun could have fixed it, set it to transmit and then we could all have blasted our brains out and waited until someone came out to take a look. Wouldn't have mattered much – none of us have got more than a week left in these sleeves anyway. And whoever came out to check the claim signal would have had to re-sleeve us – we'd be the resident experts, even if we were dead.'

He smiled at that. We both did.

'Still not what I'd call leaktight strategic planning, Takeshi.'

'Isaac, you just don't get it.' A little seriousness dripped back into my voice, erasing my smile. 'I'm an Envoy. The strategic plan was to kill anyone who tried to backstab me. Surviving afterwards, well that's a bonus if you can do it, but if you can't.' I shrugged. 'I'm an Envoy.'

His own smile slipped slightly.

'Get some rest, Takeshi,' he said gently.

I watched him walk out, then settled to watching Sutjiadi's motionless form. Hoping the tetrameth would keep me up until he came round and found out what he had to do to avoid formal execution at the hands of a Wedge punishment squad.

CHAPTER THIRTY-SEVEN

Tetrameth is one of my favourite drugs. It doesn't ride as savagely as some military stimulants, meaning you won't lose track of useful environmental facts like *no, you can't fly without a grav harness* or *punching this will smash every bone in your hand*. At the same time, it does allow you access to cellular-level reserves that no unconditioned human will ever know they possess. The high burns clean and long, with no worse side-effects than a slight gleam on surfaces that shouldn't reflect light quite that well and a vague trembling around the edges of items you've assigned some personal significance to. You can hallucinate mildly, if you really want to, but it takes concentration. Or an overdose, of course.

The comedown is no worse than most poisons.

I was starting to feel slightly manic by the time the others woke up, chemical warning lights flashing at the tail-end of the ride, and perhaps I shook Sutjiadi over-vigorously when he didn't respond as fast as I'd have liked.

'Jiang, hey *Jiang*. Open your *fucking eyes*. Guess where we are.'

He blinked up at me, face curiously child-like.

'Whuhh—'

'Back on the beach, man. Wedge came and pulled us off the ship. Carrera's Wedge, my old outfit.' The enthusiasm was peeling a little wide of my known persona among my former comrades-in-arms, but not so wide that it couldn't be put down to tetrameth, radiation sickness and exposure to alien strangeness. And anyway, I didn't know for sure that the bubblefab was being monitored. 'Fucking *rescued* us, Jiang. The *Wedge*.'

'The Wedge? That's.' Behind the Maori sleeve's eyes, I saw him scrambling to pick up the situational splinters. 'Nice. Carrera's Wedge. Didn't think they did rescue-drops.'

I sat back again, on the edge of the bed and put together a grin.

'They came looking for me.' For all the pretence, there was a shivery warmth underlying that statement. From the point of view of Loemanako and the rest of 391 platoon at least, it was probably closing on true. 'You believe that?'

'If you say so.' Sutjiadi propped himself up. 'Who else made it out?'

'All of us except Sun.' I gestured. 'And she's retrievable.'

His face twitched. Memory, working its way across his brain like a buried shrapnel fragment. 'Back there. Did you. See?'

'Yeah, I saw.'

'They were ghosts,' he said, biting down on the words.

'Jiang, for a *combat ninja* you spook way too easy. Who knows what we saw. For all we know, it was some kind of playback.'

'That sounds like a pretty good working definition of the word *ghost* to me.' Ameli Vongsavath was sitting up opposite Sutjiadi's bed. 'Kovacs, did I hear you say the Wedge came out for us?'

I nodded, drilling a look across the space between us. 'What I was telling Jiang here. Seems I still have full membership privileges.'

She got it. Barely a flicker as she scooped up the hint and ran with it.

'Good for you.' Looking around at the stirring figures in the other beds. 'So who do I get the pleasure of telling we're not dead?'

'Take your pick.'

After that, it was easy. Wardani took Sutjiadi's new identity on board with camp-ingrained, expressionless dexterity – a paper twist of contraband, silently palmed. Hand, whose exec conditioning had probably been a little less traumatic but also more expensively tailored, matched her impassivity without blinking. And Luc Deprez, well, he was a deep-cover military assassin, he used to breathe this stuff for a living.

Layered across it all, like signal interference, was the recollection of our last conscious moments aboard the Martian warship. There was a quiet, shared damage between us that no one was ready to examine closely yet. Instead, we settled for final memories half and hesitantly spoken, jumpy, bravado-spiced talk poured out into a depth of unease to echo the darkness on the other side of the gate. And, I hoped, enough emotional tinsel to shroud Sutjiadi's transformation into Jiang from any scanning eyes and ears.

'At least,' I said at one point, 'we know why they left the fucking thing drifting out there now. I mean, it beats radiation and biohazard contamination out into the street. Those at least you can clean up. Can you imagine trying to run a dreadnought at battle stations when every time there's a near-miss the old crew pop up and start clanking their chains.'

'I,' said Deprez emphatically, 'Do not. Believe. In ghosts.'

'That didn't seem to bother them.'

'Do you think,' Vongsavath, picking her way through the thought as if it were snag coral at low tide, 'all Martians leave. Left. Something behind when they die. Something like that?'

Wardani shook her head. 'If they do, we haven't seen it before. And we've dug up a lot of Martian ruins in the last five hundred years.'

'I felt,' Sutjiadi swallowed. 'They were. Screaming, all of them. It was a mass trauma. The death of the whole crew, maybe. Maybe you've just never come across that before. That much death. When we were back in Landfall, you said the Martians were a civilisation far in advance of ours. Maybe they just didn't die violently, in large numbers, any more. Maybe they evolved past that.'

I grunted. 'Neat trick, if you can manage it.'

'And we apparently can't,' said Wardani.

'Maybe we would have, if that kind of thing was left floating around every time we committed mass murder.'

'Kovacs, that's absurd.' Hand was getting out of bed, possessed suddenly of a peculiar, bad-tempered energy. 'All of you. You've been listening to too much of this woman's effete, antihuman intellectualism. The Martians were no better evolved than us. You know what I saw out there? I saw two warships that must have cost billions to build, locked into a futile cycle of repetitions, of a battle that solved nothing a hundred thousand years ago, and still solves nothing today. What improvement is that on what we have here on Sanction IV? They were just as good at killing each other as we are.'

'Bravo, Hand.' Vongsavath clapped a handful of slow, sardonic applause. 'You should have been a political officer. Just one problem with your muscular humanism there – that second ship wasn't Martian. Right Mistress Wardani? Totally different config.'

All eyes fixed on the archaeologue, who sat with her head bowed. Finally, she looked up, met my gaze and nodded reluctantly.

'It did not look like any Martian technology I have ever seen or heard of.' She drew a deep breath. 'On the evidence I saw. It would appear the Martians were at war with someone else.'

The unease rose from the floor again, winding among us like cold smoke, chilling the conversation to a halt. A tiny premonition of the wake-up call humanity was about to get.

We do not belong out here.

A few centuries we've been let out to play on these three dozen worlds the Martians left us but the playground has been empty of adults all that time, and with no supervision there's just no telling who's going to come creeping over the fence or what they'll do to us. Light is fading from the afternoon sky, retreating across distant rooftops, and in the empty streets below it's suddenly a cold and shadowy neighbourhood.

'This is nonsense,' said Hand. 'The Martian domain went down in a colonial revolt, everyone agrees on that. Mistress Wardani, the Guild *teaches* that.'

'Yeah, Hand.' The scorn in Wardani's voice was withering. 'And why do you think they teach that? Who allocates Guild funding, you blinkered fuckwit? Who decides what our children will grow up believing?'

'There is evidence—'

'Don't *fucking* talk to me about evidence.' The archaeologue's wasted face lit with fury. For a moment I thought she was going to physically assault the executive. 'You ignorant mother*fucker*. What do you know about the Guild? I do this for a living, Hand. Do you want me to tell you how much evidence has been suppressed because it didn't suit the Protectorate worldview? How many researchers were branded antihuman and ruined, how many projects butchered, all because they wouldn't ratify the official line? How much *shit* the appointed Guild Chancellors spurt every time the Protectorate sees fit to give them a funding handjob?'

Hand seemed taken aback by the sudden eruption of rage from this haggard, dying woman. He fumbled. 'Statistically, the chances of two starfaring civilisations evolving so close to—'

But it was like walking into the teeth of a gale. Wardani had her own emotional 'meth shot now. Her voice was a lash.

'Are you *mentally defective?* Or weren't you paying attention when we opened the gate? That's instant matter transmission across interplanetary distance, technology that they *left lying around*. You think a civilisation like that is going to be limited to a few hundred cubic light years of space? The weaponry we saw in action out there was *faster than light*. Those ships could both have come from the other side of the fucking galaxy. *How would we know?*'

The quality of light shifted as someone opened the bubblefab flap. Glancing away from Wardani's face for a moment, I saw Tony Loemanako stood in the entrance to the bubblefab, wearing noncom-flashed chameleochrome and trying not to grin.

I raised a hand. 'Hello, Tony. Welcome to the hallowed chambers of academic debate. Feel free to ask if you don't follow any of the technical terms.'

Loemanako gave up trying to hide the grin. 'I got a kid back on Latimer wants to be an archaeologue. Says he doesn't want a profession of violence like his old man.'

'That's just a stage, Tony. He'll get over it.'

'Hope so.' Loemanako shifted stiffly, and I saw that under the chameleochrome coveralls, he wore a mobility suit. 'Commander wants to see you right away.'

'Just me?'

'No, he said bring anyone who's awake. I think it's important.'

Outside the bubblefab, evening had closed the sky down to a luminous grey in the west and thickening darkness in the east. Under it all, Carrera's camp was a model of ordered activity in the glow of tripod-mounted Angier lamps.

Envoy habit mapped it for me, cold detail floating over and above a tingling warm sense of hearthfire and company against the encroaching night.

Up by the gate, the sentries sat astride their bugs, leaning back and forth and gesturing. The wind carried down shreds of laughter I recognised as Kwok's, but distance rendered the rest inaudible. Their faceplates were hinged up, but otherwise they were swim-prepped and still armed to the teeth. The other soldiers Loemanako had detailed to back them up stood around a mobile ultravibe cannon in similar casual alertness. Further down the beach, another knot of Wedge uniforms busied themselves with what looked like the components for a blast shield generator. Others moved back and forth from the *Angin Chandra's Virtue* to the polalloy cabin and the other bubblefabs, carrying crates that could have been anything. Behind and above the scene, lights gleamed from the bridge of the *'Chandra* and at the loading level, where onboard cranes swung more equipment out of the battlewagon's belly and down onto the lamplit sand.

'So how come the mob suit?' I asked Loemanako, as he led us down towards the unloading area.

He shrugged. 'Cable batteries at Rayong. Our tinsel systems went down at a bad time. Got my left leg, hipbone, ribs. Some of the left arm.'

'Shit. You have all the luck, Tony.'

'Ah, it's not so bad. Just taking a fuck of a long time to heal right. Doc says the cables were coated with some kind of carcinogenic, and it's fucking up the rapid regrowth.' He grimaced. 'Been like this for three weeks now. Real drag.'

'Well, thanks for coming out to us. Especially in that state.'

'No worries. Easier getting about in vac than here anyway. Once you're wearing the mob suit, polalloy's just another layer.'

'I guess.'

Carrera was waiting below the *'Chandra*'s loading hatch, dressed in the same field coveralls he'd worn earlier and talking to a small, similarly-attired group of ranking officers. A couple of noncoms were busy with mounted equipment up on the edge of the hatch. About halfway between the *'Chandra* and the blast shield detail, a ragged-looking individual in a stained uniform perched on a powered-down loadlifter, staring at us out of bleary eyes. When I stared back, he laughed and shook his head convulsively. One hand lifted to rub viciously at the back of his neck and his mouth gaped open as if someone had just drenched him with a bucket of cold water. His face twitched in tiny spasms that I recognised. Wirehead tremors.

Maybe he saw the grimace pass across my face.

'Oh, yeah, *look* that way,' he snarled. 'You're not so smart, not so *fucking* smart. Got you for antihumanism, got you all filed away, *heard* you all and your counter-Cartel sentiments, how do you like—'

'Shut up, Lamont.' There wasn't much volume in Loemanako's voice, but the wirehead jerked as if he'd just been jacked in. His eyes slipped around in their sockets alarmingly, and he cowered. At my side, Loemanako sneered.

'Political officer,' he said, and toed some sand in the shivering wreck of a human's direction. 'All the fucking same. All mouth.'

'You seem to have this one leashed.'

'Yeah, well.' Loemanako grinned. 'You'd be amazed how quickly these political guys lose interest in their job once they've been socketed up and plugged in a few times. We haven't had a Correct Thought lecture all month, and the personal files, well, I've read 'em and our own mothers couldn't have written nicer things about us. Amazing how all that political dogma just sort of fades away. Isn't that right, Lamont?'

The political officer cringed away from Loemanako. Tears leaked into his eyes.

'Works better than the beatings used to,' said the noncom, looking at Lamont dispassionately. 'You know, with Phibun and, what was that other shit-mouthed little turd called?'

'Portillo,' I said absently.

'Yeah, him. See you could never be sure if he was really beaten or if he'd come back at you when he'd licked his wounds a bit. We don't have that problem any more. Think it's the shame that does it. Once you've cut the socket and shown them how to hook up, they do it to themselves. And then, when you take it away . . . Works like

382

magic. I've seen old Lamont here break his nails trying to get the interface cables out of a locked kitpack.'

'Why don't you leave him alone?' said Tanya Wardani unevenly. 'Can't you see he's already broken?'

Loemanako shot her a curious glance.

'Civilian?' he asked me.

I nodded. 'Pretty much. She's, uh, on secondment.'

'Well, that can work sometimes.'

Carrera seemed to have finished his briefing as we approached and the surrounding officers were beginning to disperse. He nodded acknowledgement at Loemanako.

'Thank you, sergeant. Did I see Lamont giving you some grief up there?'

The noncom grinned wolfishly. 'Nothing he didn't regret, sir. Think maybe it's time he was deprived again, though.'

'I'll give that some thought, sergeant.'

'Yes sir.'

'Meanwhile.' Carrera shifted his focus. 'Lieutenant Kovacs, there are a few—'

'Just a moment, commander.' It was Hand's voice, remarkably poised and polished, given the state he must be in.

Carrera paused.

'Yes?'

'I'm sure you're aware of who I am, commander. As I am aware of the intrigues in Landfall that have led to your being here. You may not, however, be aware of the extent to which you have been deceived by those who sent you.'

Carrera met my gaze and raised an eyebrow. I shrugged.

'No, you're mistaken,' said the Wedge commander politely. 'I am quite well informed of the extent to which your Mandrake colleagues have been economical with the truth. To be honest, I expected no less.'

I heard the silence as Hand's exec training stumbled. It was almost worth a grin.

'In any case,' Carrera went on, 'the issue of objective truth doesn't much concern me here. I have been paid.'

'Less than you could have been.' Hand rallied with admirable speed. 'My business here is authorised at Cartel level.'

'Not any more. Your grubby little friends have sold you out, Hand.'

'Then that was their error, commander. There seems no reason for you to share in it. Believe me, I have no desire for retribution to fall where it is not deserved.'

Carrera smiled faintly. 'Are you threatening me?'

'There is no need to view things in such—'

'I asked if you were threatening me,' The Wedge commander's tone was mild. 'I'd appreciate a straight yes or no.'

Hand sighed. 'Let us just say that there are forces I may invoke which my colleagues have not considered, or at least not assessed correctly.'

'Oh, yes. I forgot, you are a believer.' Carrera seemed fascinated by the man in front of him. 'A hougan. You believe that. Spiritual powers? Can be hired in much the same way as soldiers.'

Beside me, Loemanako sniggered.

Hand sighed again. 'Commander, what I *believe* is that we are both civilised men and—'

The blaster tore through him.

Carrera must have set it for diffuse beam – you don't usually get as much damage as that from the little ones and the thing in the Wedge commander's hand was an ultra compact. A hint of bulk inside the closed fist, a fish-tailed snap-out projector between his second and third knuckle, spare heat, the Envoy in me noticed, still dissipating from the discharge end in visible waves.

No recoil, no visible flash, and no punch backwards where it hit. The crackle snarled past my ears and Hand stood there blinking with a smoking hole in his guts. Then he must have caught the stench of his own seared intestines and, looking down, he made a high-pitched hooting noise that was as much panic as pain.

The ultra compacts take a while to recharge, but I didn't need peripheral vision to tell me jumping Carrera would be a mistake. Noncoms on the loading deck above, Loemanako beside me and the little knot of Wedge officers hadn't dispersed at all – they'd just fanned out and given us room to walk into the set-up.

Neat. Very neat.

Hand staggered, still wailing, and sat down hard on his backside in the sand. Some brutal part of me wanted to laugh at him. His hands pawed the air close to the gaping wound.

I know that feeling, some other part of me recalled, surprised into brief compassion. *It hurts, but you don't know if you dare touch it.*

'Mistaken again,' said Carrera to the ripped open exec at his feet. His tone hadn't shifted since the shooting. 'I am not a civilised man, Hand, I'm a soldier. A professional savage, and I'm on hire to men just like you. I wouldn't like to say what that makes you. Except out of fashion back at the Mandrake Tower, that is.'

The noise Hand was making shaped towards a conventional scream. Carrera turned to look at me.

'Oh, you can relax, Kovacs. Don't tell me you haven't wanted to do that before now.'

I manufactured a shrug. 'Once or twice. I probably would have got around to it.'

'Well, now you don't have to.'

On the ground, Hand twisted and propped himself. Something that might have been words emerged from his agony. At the edge of my vision, a couple of figures moved towards him: peripheral scan, still squeezed to aching point by the adrenalin surge, identified Sutjiadi and – *well, well* – Tanya Wardani.

Carrera waved them back.

'No, there's no need for that.'

Hand was definitely speaking now, a ruptured hissing of syllables that weren't any language I knew or, except once, had heard. His left hand was raised towards Carrera, fingers splayed. I crouched to his level, oddly moved by the contorted strength on his face.

'What's this?' The Wedge commmander leaned closer. 'What's he saying?'

I sat back on my heels. 'I think you're being cursed.'

'Oh. Well, I suppose that's not unreasonable under the circumstances. Still.' Carrera swung a long, heavy kick into the exec's side. Hand's incantation shredded apart in a scream and he rolled into a foetal ball. 'No reason why we have to listen to it either. Sergeant.'

Loemanako stepped forward. 'Sir.'

'Your knife please.'

'Yes, sir.'

Give Carrera credit – I'd never seen him ask any man in his command to carry out work he wouldn't do himself. He took the vibroknife from Loemanako, activated it and kicked Hand again, stamping him onto his belly in the sand. The exec's screams blurred into coughing and whooping sucked breath. Carrera knelt across his back and started cutting.

Hand's muffled shrieking scaled abruptly up as he felt the blade enter his flesh, and then stopped dead as Carrera sliced his spinal column through.

'Better,' muttered the Wedge commander.

He made the second incision at the base of the skull, a lot more elegantly than I had back in the Landfall promoter's office, and dug out the section of severed spine. Then he powered off the knife, wiped it carefully on Hand's clothing and got up. He handed knife and spinal segment to Loemanako with a nod.

'Thank you, sergeant. Get that to Hammad, tell him not to lose it. We just earnt ourselves a bonus.'

'Yes, sir.' Loemanako looked at the faces around us. 'And, uh . . . ?'

'Oh, yes.' Carrera raised one hand. His face seemed suddenly tired. 'That.'

His hand fell like something discarded.

From the loading deck above I heard the discharge, a muffled crump followed by a chitinous rustling. I looked up and saw what looked like a swarm of crippled nanocopters tumbling down through the air.

I made the intuitive leap to what was going to happen with a curious detachment, a lack of combat reflex that must have had its roots in the mingled radiation sickness and tetrameth comedown. I just had time to look at Sutjiadi. He caught my eye and his mouth twitched. He knew as well as I did. As well as if there'd been a scarlet decal pulsing across the screen of our vision.

Game—

Then it was raining spiders.

Not really, but it looked that way. They'd fired the crowd control mortar almost straight up, a low-power crimped load for limited dispersal. The grey fist-sized inhibitors fell in a circle not much wider than twenty metres. The ones at the nearest edge glanced off the curving side of the battlewagon's hull before they hit the sand, skidding and flailing for purchase with a minute intensity that I later recalled almost with amusement. The others bedded directly in puffs of turquoise sand and scuttled up out of the tiny craters they'd made like the tiny jewelled crabs in Tanya Wardani's tropical paradise virtuality.

They fell in thousands.

Game—

They dropped on our heads and shoulders, soft as children's cradle toys, and clung.

They scuttled towards us across the sand and scrambled up our legs.

They endured batting and shaking and clambered on undeterred.

The ones Sutjiadi and the others tore loose and flung away landed in a whirl of limbs and scuttled back unharmed.

They crouched knowledgeably above nerve points and plunged filament-thin tendril fangs through clothing and skin.

Game—

They bit in.

—Over.

CHAPTER THIRTY-EIGHT

There was no less reason for adrenalin to be pumping through my system than anyone else's, but the slow seep of radioactive damage had shrivelled my sleeve's capacity to deliver combat chemicals. The inhibitors reacted accordingly. I felt the nerve snap go through me, but it was a mild numbness, a fizzing that only dropped me to one knee.

The Maori sleeves were readier for a fight and so they took it harder. Deprez and Sutjiadi staggered and crashed into the sand as if shot with stunners. Vongsavath managed to control her fall, and rolled to the ground on her side, eyes wide.

Tanya Wardani just stood there looking dazed.

'Thank you gentlemen.' It was Carrera, calling up to the noncoms manning the mortar. 'Exemplary grouping.'

Neural inhib remotes. State-of-the-art public order tech. Only cleared colonial embargo a couple of years ago. In my capacity as a local military adviser, I'd had the shiny new system demonstrated to me on crowds in Indigo City. I'd just never been on the receiving end before now.

Chill, an enthusiastic young public order corporal had told me with a grin. *That's all you need to do. 'Course, that's extra funny in a riot situation. This shit lands on you, you're just going to get more 'dreened up, means they just go on biting you, maybe even stop your heart in the end. Have to be fucking Zen-rigged to break the spiral, and you know what, we're short on Zen riot activists this season.*

I held the Envoy calm like a crystal, wiped my mind of consequence and got up. The spiders clung and flexed a little as I moved, but they didn't bite again.

'Shit, lieutenant, you're *coated*. They must like you.'

Loemanako stood grinning at me from within a circle of clear sand, while surplus inhibitor units crawled around on the outer edge of the field his clean tag must be throwing down. A little to his right, Carrera moved in a similar pool of immunity. I glanced around and saw the other Wedge officers, untouched and watching.

Neat. Very fucking neat.

Behind them, political officer Lamont capered and pointed at us, jabbering.

Oh well. Who could blame him?

'Yes, I think we'd better get you brushed off,' said Carrera. 'I'm sorry for the shock, Lieutenant Kovacs, but there was no other comfortable way to detain this criminal.'

He was pointing at Sutjiadi.

Actually, Carrera, you could have just sedated everybody in the ward 'fab. But that wouldn't have been dramatic enough, and where transgressors against the Wedge are concerned, the men do like their stylised drama, don't they?

I felt a brief chill run along my spine, chasing the thought.

And tamped it down quick, before it could become the fear or anger that would wake up the coat of spiders I wore.

I went for weary-laconic.

'What the fuck are you talking about, Isaac?'

'This man,' Carrera's voice was pitched to carry. 'May have misrepresented himself to you as Jiang Jianping. His real name is Markus Sutjiadi, and he is wanted for crimes against Wedge personnel.'

'Yeah.' Loemanako lost his grin. 'Fucker wasted Lieutenant Veutin, and his platoon sergeant.'

'Veutin?' I looked back at Carrera. 'Thought he was down around Bootkinaree.'

'Yes, he was.' The Wedge commander was staring down at Sutjiadi's crumpled form. For a moment I thought he was going to shoot him there and then with the blaster. 'Until this piece of shit cut insubordinate and finished up feeding Veutin his own Sunjet. Killed Veutin really dead. Stack gone. Sergeant Bradwell went the same way when she tried to stop it. And two more of my men got their sleeves carved apart before someone locked this mother*fucker* down.'

'No one gets away with that,' said Loemanako sombrely. 'Right, lieutenant? No local yokel takes down Wedge personnel and walks away from it. Shithead's for the anatomiser.'

'Is this true?' I asked Carrera, for appearances' sake.

He met my gaze and nodded. 'Eye-witnesses. It's open and shut.'

Sutjiadi stirred at his feet like something stamped on.

They cleaned the spiders off me with a deactivator broom, and then dumped them into a storage canister. Carrera handed me a tag and the approaching tide of unoccupied inhibitors fell back as I snapped it on.

'About that debriefing,' he said, and gestured me aboard the *'Chandra*.

Behind me, my colleagues were led back to the bubblefab, stumbling as feeble adrenalin jags of resistance set off new ripples of bites from their new neural jailers. In the post-performance space we'd all left, the noncoms who'd fired the mortar went around with untamped canisters, gathering up the still crawling units that hadn't managed to find a home.

Sutjiadi caught my eye again as he was leaving. Imperceptibly, he shook his head.

He needn't have worried. I was barely up to climbing the entry ramp into the battlewagon's belly, let alone taking on Carrera in empty-handed combat. I clung to the remaining fragments of the tetrameth lift and followed the Wedge commander along tight, equipment-racked corridors, up a hand-rung-lined gravchute and into the confines of what appeared to be his personal quarters.

'Sit down, lieutenant. If you can find the space.'

The cabin was cramped but meticulously tidy. A powered-down grav bed rested on the floor in one corner, under a desk that hinged out from the bulkhead. The work surface held a compact datacoil, a neat stack of bookchips and a pot-bellied statue that looked like Hun Home art. A second table occupied the other end of the narrow space, studded with projector gear. Two holos floated near the ceiling at angles that allowed viewing from the bed. One showed a spectacular image of Adoracion from high orbit, sunrise just breaking across the green and orange rim. The other was a family group, Carrera and a handsome olive-skinned woman, arms possessively encompassing the shoulders of three variously aged children. The Wedge commander looked happy, but the sleeve in the holo was older than the one he was wearing now.

I found a spartan metal desk chair beside the projector table. Carrera watched me sit down and then leaned against the desk, arms folded.

'Been home recently?' I asked, nodding at the orbital holo.

His gaze stayed on my face. 'It's been a while. Kovacs, you knew damn well that Sutjiadi was wanted by the Wedge, didn't you?'

'I still don't know he *is* Sutjiadi. Hand sold him to me as Jiang. What makes you so sure?'

He almost smiled. 'Nice try. My tower-dweller friends gave me gene codes for the combat sleeves. That plus the sleeving data from the Mandrake stack. They were quite keen for me to know that Hand had a war criminal working for him. Added incentive, I imagine they saw it as. Grist to the deal.'

'War criminal.' I looked elaborately around the cabin. 'That's an interesting choice of terminology. For someone who oversaw the Decatur Pacification, I mean.'

'Sutjiadi murdered one of my officers. An officer he was supposed to be taking orders from. Under any combat convention I know of, that's a crime.'

'An officer? Veutin?' I couldn't quite work out why I was arguing, unless it was out of a general sense of inertia. 'Come on, would *you* take orders from Dog Veutin?'

'Happily, I don't have to. But his platoon did, and they were fanatically loyal, all of them. Veutin was a good soldier.'

'They called him Dog for a reason, Isaac.'

'We are not engaged in a pop—'

'—ularity contest.' I sketched a smile of my own. 'That line's getting a little old. Veutin was a fucking asshole, and you know it. If this Sutjiadi torched him, he probably had a good reason.'

'Reasons do not make you right, Lieutenant Kovacs.' There was a sudden softness in Carrera's tone that said I'd overstepped the line.

'Every graft-wrapped pimp on Plaza de los Caidos has a reason for every whore's face they carve up, but that doesn't make it right. Joshua Kemp has reasons for what he does and from his point of view they might even be good ones. That doesn't make him right.'

'You want to watch what you're saying, Isaac. That sort of relativism could get you arrested.'

'I doubt it. You've seen Lamont.'

'Yeah.'

Silence ebbed and flowed around us.

'So,' I said finally. 'You're going to put Sutjiadi under the anatomiser.'

'Do I have a choice?'

I just looked at him.

'We are the Wedge, lieutenant. You know what that means.' There was the slightest tug of urgency in his tone now. I don't know who he was trying to convince. 'You were sworn in, just like everyone else. You know the codes. We stand for unity in the face of chaos, and everyone has to know that. Those we deal with have to know that we are not to be fucked with. We need that fear, if we're going to operate effectively. And my soldiers have to know that that fear is an absolute. That it will be enforced. Without that, we fall apart.'

I closed my eyes. 'Whatever.'

'I'm not requiring you to watch it.'

'I doubt there'll be enough seats.'

Behind my closed eyelids, I heard him move. When I looked, he was leaning over me, hands braced on the edges of the projector table, face harsh with anger.

'You're going to shut up now, Kovacs. You're going to stand down that attitude.' If he was looking for resistance, he couldn't have seen any in my face. He backed off a half metre, straightened up. 'I won't let you piss away your commission like this. You're a capable officer, lieutenant. You inspire loyalty in the men you lead, and you understand combat.'

'Thanks.'

'You can laugh, but I know you. It's a fact.'

'It's the *biotech*, Isaac. Wolf gene pack dynamics, serotonin shutout and Envoy psychosis to pilot the whole fucking shambles. A *dog* could do what I've done for the Wedge. Dog fucking Veutin, for example.'

'Yes.' A shrug as he settled himself on the edge of the desk again. 'You and Veutin are, were, very similar in profile. I have the psychosurgeon assessments on file here, if you don't believe me. Same Kemmerich gradient, same IQ, same lack of generalisable empathy range. To the untutored eye, you could be the same man.'

'Yeah, except he's dead. Even to the untutored eye, that's got to stand out.'

'Well, maybe not quite the same lack of empathy, then. The Envoys gave you enough diplomatic training not to underestimate men like Sutjiadi. You would have handled him better.'

'So Sutjiadi's crime was he got underestimated? Seems as good a reason as any to torture a man to death, I suppose.'

He stopped and stared at me. 'Lieutenant Kovacs, I don't think I'm making myself clear. Sutjiadi's execution is not under discussion here. He murdered my soldiers, and at dawn tomorrow I will exact the penalty for that crime. I may not like it—'

'How gratifyingly humane of you.'

He ignored me. '—but it needs to be done, and I *will do it*. And you, if you know what's good for you, will ratify it.'

'Or else?' It wasn't as defiant as I'd have liked, and I spoilt it at the end with a coughing fit that racked me over in the narrow chair and brought up blood-streaked phlegm. Carrera handed me a wipe.

'You were saying?'

'I said, if I won't ratify the ghoul show, what happens to me?'

'Then I'll inform the men that you knowingly attempted to protect Sutjiadi from Wedge justice.'

I looked around for somewhere to toss the soiled wipe. 'Is that an accusation?'

'Under the table. No, there. Next to your leg. Kovacs, it doesn't matter whether you did it or not. I think you probably did, but I don't really care one way or the other. I have to have order, and justice must be seen to be done. Fit in with that, and you can have your rank back, plus a new command. If you step out of line, you'll be next on the slab.'

'Loemanako and Kwok won't like that.'

'No, they won't. But they are Wedge soldiers, and they will do as they are told for the good of the Wedge.'

'So much for inspiring loyalty.'

'Loyalty is a currency like any other. What you have earned, you can spend. And shielding a known murderer of Wedge personnel is more than you can afford. More than any of us can afford.' He leaned off the desk edge. Beneath the coveralls, Envoy scan read his stance at endgame. It was the way he always stood in the final round of sparring sessions that had gone down to the wire. The way I'd seen him stand when the government troops broke around us at Shalai Gap and Kemp's airborne infantry swept down out of the storm-front sky like hail. There was no fallback from here. 'I do not want to lose you, Kovacs, and I do not want to distress the soldiers who have followed you. But in the end, the Wedge is more than any one man within it. We cannot afford internal dissent.'

Outnumbered and outgunned and left for dead at Shalai, Carrera held position in the bombed-out streets and buildings for two hours, until the storm swept in and covered everything. Then he led a stalk-and-slaughter counteroffensive through the howling wind and street-level shreds of cloud until the airwaves crackled stiff with panicked airborne commanders ordering withdrawal. When the storm lifted, Shalai Gap was littered with the Kempist dead and the Wedge had taken less than two dozen casualties.

He leaned close again, no longer angry. His eyes searched my face.

'Am I – finally – making myself clear, lieutenant? A sacrifice is required. We may not like it, you and I, but that is the price of Wedge membership.'

I nodded.

'Then you are ready to move past this?'

'I'm dying, Isaac. About all I'm ready for right now is some sleep.'

'I understand. I won't keep you much longer. Now.' He gestured through the datacoil and it awoke in swirls. I sighed and groped after fresh focus. 'The penetration squad took an extrapolated line back from the *Nagini*'s angle of re-entry and fetched up pretty damn close to the same docking bay you breached. Loemanako says there were no apparent shut-out controls. So how did you get in?'

'Was already open.' I couldn't be bothered to construct lies, guessed in any case that he'd interrogate the others soon enough. 'For all we know, there are no shut-out controls.'

'On a warship?' His eyes narrowed. 'I find that hard to believe.'

'Isaac, the whole ship mounts a spatial shield that stands at least two kilometres out from the hull. What the fuck would they need with individual docking station shut out?'

'You saw that?'

'Yeah. Very much in action.'

'Hmm.' He made a couple of minor adjustments in the coil. 'The sniffer units found human traces a good three or four kilometres into the interior. But they found you in an observation bubble not much more than a kilometre and a half from your entry point.'

'Well, that couldn't have been hard. We painted the way with big fucking illuminum arrows.'

He gave me a hard look. 'Did you go walkabout in there?'

'Not me, no.' I shook my head, then regretted it as the little cabin pulsed unpleasantly in and out of focus around me. I waited it out. 'Some of them did. I never found out how far they went.'

'Doesn't sound very organised.'

'It wasn't,' I said irritably. 'I don't know, Isaac. Try and incubate a sense of wonder, huh? Might help when you get over there.'

'So it, ah, appears.' He hesitated, and it took me a moment to realise he was embarrassed. 'You, ah, you saw. Ghosts. Over there?'

I shrugged, suppressing an urge to cackle uncontrollably. 'We saw something. I'm still not sure what it was. Been listening in to your guests, Isaac?'

He smiled and made an apologetic gesture. 'Lamont's habits, rubbing off on me. And since he's lost the taste for snooping, seems a shame to let the equipment go to waste.' He prodded again at the datacoil. 'The medical report says you all showed symptoms of a heavy stunblast, except you and Sun, obviously.'

'Yeah, Sun shot herself. We . . .' Abruptly, it seemed impossible to explain. Like trying to shoulder a massive weight unaided. The last moments in the Martian starship, wrapped in the brilliant pain and radiance of whatever her crew had left behind them. The certainty that this alien grief was going to crack us open. How did you convey that to the man who had led you behind raging gunfire to victory at Shalai Gap and a dozen other engagements? How did you get across the ice-aching diamond-bright reality of those moments?

Reality? The doubt jolted rudely.

Was it? Come to that, come to the gun barrel-and-grime reality that Isaac Carrera lived, *was* it real any more? Had it ever been? How much of what I remembered was hard fact?

No, look. I've got Envoy recall—

But had it been that bad? I looked into the datacoil, trying wearily to muster rational thought. Hand had called it, and I bought in with something not much short of panic. Hand, the hougan. Hand, the religious maniac. When else had I ever trusted him as far as I could throw him?

Why had I trusted him then?

Sun. I grabbed at the fact. *Sun knew. She saw it coming and she blew her own brains out rather than face it.*

Carrera was looking at me strangely.

'Yes?'

You and Sun . . .

'Wait a minute.' It dawned on me. 'You said except Sun and *me*?'

'Yes. The others all show the standard electroneural trauma. Heavy blast, as I said.'

'But not me.'

'Well, no.' He looked puzzled. 'You weren't touched. Why, do you *remember* someone shooting you?'

When we were done, he flattened the datacoil display with one callused hand and walked me back through the empty corridors of the battlewagon and then across the night-time murmur of the camp. We didn't talk much. He'd backed up in the face of my confusion, and let the debriefing slide. Probably he couldn't believe he was seeing one of his pet Envoys in this state.

I was having a hard time believing it myself.

*She shot you. You dropped the stunner and she shot you, then herself.
She* must *have.*

Otherwise . . .

I shivered.

On a clear patch of sand to the rear of the *Angin Chandra's Virtue*,
they were erecting the scaffold for Sutjiadi's execution. The primary
support struts were already in place, sunk deep into the sand and
poised to receive the tilted, runnelled butcher's platform. Under the
illumination from three Angier lamps and the environ floods from
the battlewagon's rear drop hatch, the structure was a claw of
bleached bone rising from the beach. The disassembled segments of
the anatomiser lay close by, like sections of a wasp someone had
chopped to death.

'The war's shifting,' said Carrera conversationally. 'Kemp's a
spent force on this continent. We haven't had an air strike in weeks.
He's using the iceberg fleet to evacuate his forces across the
Wacharin straits.'

'Can't he hold the coast there?' I asked the question on
automatic, the ghost of attention from a hundred deployment
briefings past.

Carrera shook his head. 'Not a chance. That's a flood plain a
hundred klicks back south and east. Nowhere to dig in, and he
doesn't have the hardware to build wet bunkers. That means no
long-term jamming, no net-supported weapon systems. Give me six
more months and I'll have amphibious armour harrying him off the
whole coastal strip. Another year and we'll be parking the *'Chandra*
over Indigo City.'

'And then what?'

'Sorry?'

'And then what? When you've taken Indigo City, when Kemp's
bombed and mined and particle-blasted every worthwhile asset there
is and escaped into the mountains with the real diehards, *then what?*'

'Well.' Carrera puffed out his cheeks. He seemed genuinely
surprised by the question. 'The usual. Holding strategy across both
continents, limited police actions and scapegoating until everyone
calms down. But by that time . . .'

'By that time we'll be gone, right?' I shoved my hands into my pockets. 'Off this fucking mudball and somewhere where they know a losing game when they see one. Give me that much good news at least.'

He looked across at me and winked. 'Hun Home's looking good. Internal power struggle, lots of palace intrigue. Just your speed.'

'Thanks.'

At the bubblefab flap, low voices filtered out into the night air. Carrera cocked his head and listened.

'Come in and join the party,' I said morosely, pushing through ahead of him. 'Save you going back to Lamont's toys.'

The three remaining members of the Mandrake expedition were gathered in seats around a low table at the end of the ward. Carrera's security had broomed off the bulk of the inhib units and left each prisoner at detention-standard, a single inhibitor squatting like a tumour at the nape of the neck. It made everyone look peculiarly hunched, as if caught in mid-conspiracy.

They looked round as we entered the ward, reacting across a spectrum. Deprez was the least expressive; barely a muscle moved in his face. Vongsavath caught my eye and raised her brows. Wardani looked past me to where Carrera stood and spat on the quick-wipe floor.

'That's for me, I assume,' said the Wedge commander easily.

'Share it,' suggested the archaeologue. 'You seem close enough.'

Carrera smiled. 'I'd advise against cranking up your hate too far, Mistress Wardani. Your little friend back there is apt to bite.'

She shook her head, wordless. One hand rose in reflex, halfway to the inhib unit, then dropped away. Maybe she'd already tried removing it. It's not a mistake you make twice.

Carrera walked to the splatter of saliva, bent and scooped it up with one finger. He examined it closely, brought it to his nose and grimaced.

'You don't have long, Mistress Wardani. In your place I think I'd be a little more civil to the person who's going to advise on whether you're re-sleeved or not.'

'I doubt that'll be your decision.'

'Well.' The Wedge commander wiped his finger on the nearest bedsheet. 'I did say "advise". But then, this presupposes that you

398

make it back to Landfall in some re-sleevable capacity. Which you might not.'

Wardani turned to me, blocking Carrera off in the process. A subtle snub that made the diplomatic strand in my conditioning want to applaud.

'Is your catamite here threatening me?'

I shook my head. 'Making a point, I think.'

'Too subtle for me.' She cast a disdainful glance back at the Wedge commander. 'Perhaps you'd better just shoot me in the stomach. That seems to work well. Your preferred method of civilian pacification, presumably.'

'Ah, yes. Hand.' Carrera hooked a chair from the collection around the table. He turned it back forward and straddled it. 'Was he a friend of yours?'

Wardani looked at him.

'I didn't think so. Not your sort at all.'

'That has nothing to—'

'Did you know he was responsible for the bombing of Sauberville?'

Another wordless pause. This time the archaeologue's face sagged with shock, and suddenly I saw how very far the radiation had eaten into her.

Carrera saw it too.

'Yes, Mistress Wardani. Someone had to clear a path for your little quest, and Matthias Hand arranged for it to be our mutual friend Joshua Kemp. Oh, nothing direct of course. Military misinformation, carefully modelled and then equally carefully leaked along the right data channels. But enough to convince our resident revolutionary hero in Indigo City that Sauberville would look better as a grease stain. And that thirty-seven of my men didn't need their eyes any more.' He flipped a glance at me. 'You must have guessed, right?'

I shrugged. 'Seemed likely. A little too convenient otherwise.'

Wardani's eyes snapped sideways to mine, disbelieving.

'You see, Mistress Wardani.' Carrera got up as if his whole body ached. 'I'm sure you'd like to believe I'm a monster, but I'm not. I'm just a man doing a job. Men like Matthias Hand *create* the wars I make my living fighting. Keep that in mind next time you feel the need to insult me.'

The archaeologue said nothing, but I could feel her gaze burning into the side of my face. Carrera turned to go, then stopped.

'Oh, and Mistress Wardani, one more thing. Catamite.' He looked at the floor, as if pondering the word. 'I have what many would consider a rather limited range of sexual preferences, and anal penetration doesn't feature among them. But I see from your camp records that the same cannot be said for you.'

She made a noise. Behind it, I almost heard the creak and shift of the recovery scaffolding Envoy artifice had built inside her. The sound of damage done. I found myself, inexplicably, on my feet.

'Isaac, you—'

'You?' He was grinning like a skull as he faced me. '*You*, you *pup*. Had better sit down.'

It was nearly a command, nearly froze me in my tracks. Envoy bile rose sneering and beat it aside.

'Kovacs—' Wardani's voice, like a cable snapping.

I met Carrera halfway, one crooked hand rising for his throat, a muddled kick emerging from the rest of my sickness-tangled stance. The big Wedge body swayed in to meet me and he blocked both attacks with brutal ease. The kick slipped away left, taking me off balance and he locked out my striking arm at the elbow, then smashed it.

It made a crunching noise in the back of my head, an empty whisky tumbler crushed underfoot in some dimly lit bar. The agony swarmed my brain, wrenched out a single short scream and then subsided under neurachem pain management. Wedge combat custom – seemed the sleeve was still good for that much. Carrera had not released his hold, and I dangled from the grip he had on my forearm like a powered-down child's doll. I flexed my undamaged arm experimentally, and he laughed. Then he twisted hard on the shattered elbow joint, so pain rose back up like a black cloud behind my eyes, and dropped me. A casual kick to the stomach left me foetal, and not interested in anything much above ankle height.

'I'll send the medics,' I heard him say somewhere above me. 'And Mistress Wardani, I suggest you shut your mouth, or I will have some of my less sensitive men come and fill it for you. That and maybe give you a forcible reminder of what the word catamite means. Don't test me, woman.'

There was a rustle of clothing, and then he crouched at my side. One hand gripped my jaw and turned my face upward.

'You're going to have to get that sentimental shit out of your system if you want to work for me, Kovacs. Oh, and just in case you don't.' He held up a curled-up inhib spider in his hand. 'Temporary measure, purely. Just until we're done with Sutjiadi. We'll all feel a lot safer this way.'

He tipped his opened palm sideways, and the inhib unit rolled off into space. To my endorphin-dulled senses, it seemed to take a long time. I got to watch with something approaching fascination as the spider unrolled its legs in mid-air and fell flailing to the floor less than a metre from my head. There it gathered itself, spun about once or twice and then scuttled towards me. It clambered up over my face, then down around to my spine. A tiny spike of ice reached down into the bone, and I felt the cable-like limbs tighten around the back of my neck.

Oh well.

'Be seeing you, Kovacs. Have a think about it.' Carrera got up and apparently left. For a while, I lay there checking the seals on the cosy blanket of numbness my sleeve's systems had wrapped me in. Then there were hands on my body, helping me into a sitting position I had no real interest in attaining.

'Kovacs.' It was Deprez, peering into my face. 'You OK, man?'

I coughed weakly. 'Yeah, great.'

He propped me against the edge of the table. Wardani moved into view above and behind him. 'Kovacs?'

'Uhhhhhh, sorry about that, Tanya.' I risked a searching glance at the level of control on her face. 'Should have warned you not to push him. He's not like Hand. He won't take that shit.'

'Kovacs.' There were muscles twitching her face that might have been the first crumbling of the jerry-built recovery edifice. Or not. 'What are they going to do to Sutjiadi?'

A little pool of quiet welled up in the wake of the question.

'Ritual execution,' said Vongsavath. 'Right?'

401

I nodded.

'What does that mean?' There was an unnerving calm in Wardani's voice. I thought I might rewrite my assumptions about her state of recovery. 'Ritual execution. What are they going to do?'

I closed my eyes, summoned images from the last two years. The recollection seemed to bring a dull seeping ache up from my shattered elbow joint. When I'd had enough, I looked at her face again.

'It's like an autosurgeon,' I said slowly. 'Reprogrammed. It scans the body, maps the nervous system. Measures resilience. Then, they run a rendering programme.'

Wardani's eyes widened a little. 'Rendering?'

'It takes him apart. Flays the skin, flenses the flesh, cracks the bones.' I drew on memory. 'Disembowels him, cooks his eyes in their sockets, shatters his teeth and probes the nerves.'

She made a half-formed gesture against the words she was hearing.

'It keeps him alive while it does it. If he looks like going into shock, it stops. Gives him stimulants if necessary. Gives him whatever's necessary, apart from painkillers, obviously.'

Now it felt as if there was a fifth presence among us, crouched at my side, grinning and squeezing the shards of broken bone in my arm. I sat in my own biotech-damped pain, remembering what had happened to Sutjiadi's predecessors while the Wedge gathered to watch like the faithful at some arcane altar to the war.

'How long does this last?' asked Deprez.

'It depends. Most of the day.' The words dragged out of me. 'It has to be over by nightfall. Part of the ritual. If no one stops it earlier, the machine sections and removes the skull at last light. That usually does it.' I wanted to stop talking, but it seemed no one else wanted to stop me. 'Officers and noncoms have the option to call a *coup de grâce* vote from the ranks, but you won't get that until late afternoon, even from the ones that want it over. They can't afford to come across softer than the rank and file. And even late, even then, I've seen the vote go against them.'

'Sutjiadi killed a Wedge platoon commander,' said Vongsavath. 'I think there will be no mercy vote.'

'He's weak,' Wardani said hopefully. 'With the radiation poisoning—'

'No.' I flexed my right arm and a spike of pain ran up to my shoulder, even under the neurachem. 'The Maori sleeves are contam combat-designed. Very high endurance.'

'But the neurache—'

I shook my head. 'Forget it. The machine will adjust for that, kill the pain management systems first, rip them out.'

'Then he'll die.'

'No, he *won't*,' I shouted. 'It doesn't work that way.'

No one said much after that.

A pair of medics arrived, one the man who had treated me earlier, the second a hard-faced woman I didn't know. They checked my arm with elaborately non-committal competence. The presence of the inhib unit crouched on my nape and what it said about my status both went carefully unremarked. They used an ultravibe microset to break up the bone fragments around the shattered elbow joint, then set regrowth bios in deep, long monofilament feed lines topped off at skin level with the green marker tags and the chip that told my bone cells what to do and, more to the point, how fucking rapidly to get it done. *No slacking here. Never mind what you did back in the natural world, you're part of a military custom operation now, soldier.*

'Couple of days,' said the one I knew, peeling a rapid-dump endorphin dermal off the crook of my arm. 'We've cleared up the ragged edges, so flexing it shouldn't do any serious damage to the surrounding tissue. But it will hurt like fuck, and it slows down the healing process so try to avoid it. I'll grip-pad you so you remember.'

A couple of days. In a couple of days, I'd be lucky if this sleeve was still breathing. Recollection of the doctor aboard the orbital hospital flashed through my head. *Oh, for fuck's sake.* The absurdity of it bubbled through me and escaped as a sudden, unlooked-for grin.

'Hey, thanks. Don't want to slow down the healing process, do we?'

He smiled back weakly, then hurriedly turned his gaze to what he was doing. The grip-pad went on tight from bicep to lower forearm, warm and comforting, and constricting.

'You part of the anatomiser crew?' I asked him.

He gave me a haunted look. 'No. That's scan-related, I don't do it.'

'We're done here, Martin,' said the woman abruptly. 'Time to go.'

'Yeah.' But he moved slowly, unwillingly as he folded up the battlefield kitpack. I watched the contents disappearing, taped-over surgical tools and the strips of brightly coloured dermals in their tug-down sleeves

'Hey, Martin.' I nodded at the pack. 'You going to leave me a few of those pinks. I was planning to sleep late, you know.'

'Uh—'

The female medic cleared her throat. 'Martin, we aren't—'

'Oh, shut the *fuck* up, will you.' He turned on her with fury boiling up out of nowhere. Envoy instinct kicked me in the head. Behind his back, I reached for the pack. 'You don't rank me, Zeyneb. I'll dispense what I fucking like and you—'

''s OK,' I said quietly. 'I got them anyway.'

Both medics fixed on me. I held up the trailing strip of endorphin dermals I'd grabbed free in my left hand. I smiled thinly.

'Don't worry, I won't take them all at once.'

'Maybe you should,' said the female medic. 'Sir.'

'Zeyneb, I told you to shut up.' Martin gathered up the kitpack in a hurry, tightening it in his arms, cradling it. 'You, uh, they're fast-acting. No more than three at any one time. That will keep you under, whatever you h—' He swallowed. 'Whatever is going on around you.'

'Thanks.'

They gathered the rest of their equipment and left. Zeyneb looked back at me from the bubblefab flap and her mouth twisted. Her voice was too low for me to catch what she said. Martin raised his arm in a cuffing gesture, and they both ducked out. I watched them go, then looked down at the strip of dermals in my clenched fist.

'That's your solution?' asked Wardani in a small, cold voice. 'Take drugs and watch it all slide out of view?'

'Do you have a better idea?'

She turned away.

'Then get down off that fucking prayer tower and keep your self-righteousness to yourself.'

'We could—'

'We could *what*? We're inhibited, we're most of us a couple of days off death from catastrophic cell damage, and I don't know about you, but my arm hurts. Oh, yeah, and this whole place is wired for sight and sound to the political officer's cabin, which, I imagine, Carrera has ready access to when he wants it.' I felt a slight twinge from the thing on the nape of my neck, and realised my own anger was getting the better of my weariness. I locked it down. 'I've done all the fighting I'm going to do, Tanya. Tomorrow we get to spend the day listening to Sutjiadi die. You deal with that any way you want. Me, I'm going to sleep through it.'

There was a searing satisfaction in throwing the words out at her, like twisting shrapnel out of a wound in your own flesh. But somewhere underneath it, I kept seeing the camp commandant, shut down in his chair, current running, the pupil of his remaining human eye bumping idly against the upper lid.

If I lay down, I'd probably never get up again. I heard the words again, whispering out of him like dying breath. *So I stay in this. Chair. The discomfort wakes me. Periodically.*

I wondered what kind of discomfort I'd need at this stage of the game. What kind of chair I'd need to be strapped into.

Somewhere there's got to be a way off this fucking beach.

And I wondered why the hand at the end of my injured arm was not empty.

CHAPTER THIRTY-NINE

Sutjiadi started screaming shortly after it got light.

Outraged fury for the first few seconds, almost reassuring in its humanity, but it didn't last. In less than a minute, every human element boiled away to the white bone of animal agony. In that form it came searing up the beach from the butcher's slab, shriek after peeling shriek filling the air like something solid, hunting listeners. We had been waiting for it since before the dawn but it still hit like a shockwave, a visible flinch through each of us where we sat hunched on beds no one had even tried to sleep in. It came for us all, and touched us with a sickening intimacy. It laid clammy hands over my face and a clamped grip on my ribcage, stopping breath, spiked the hairs on my neck and sent a single twitch through one eye. At my nape, the inhib unit tasted my nervous system and stirred interestedly.

Lock it down.

Behind the shrieking ran another sound I knew. The low growl of an aroused audience. The Wedge, seeing justice done.

Cross-legged on the bed, I opened my fists. The dermal strips fell to the quilt.

Something flickered.

I saw the dead visage of the Martian, printed across my vision so clear it might have been a retinal display.

this chair—

—wakes me.

—spinning motes of shadow and light—

—dirge of alien grief—

. I could feel—

—a Martian visage, in amongst the swirl of brilliant pain, not dead—

—great unhuman eyes that met mine with something that—

I shuddered away from it.

The human scream ran on, ripping along nerves, digging into marrow. Wardani buried her face in her hands.

I shouldn't be feeling this bad, a detached part of me argued. *This isn't the first time I've—*

Unhuman eyes. Unhuman screams.

Vongsavath began to weep.

I felt it rising in me, gathering in spirals the way the Martians had done. The inhib unit tensed.

No, not yet.

Envoy control, cold and methodical unpicking of human response just when I needed it. I welcomed it like a lover on Wardani's sunset beach – I think I was grinning as it came on.

Outside on the slab, Sutjiadi screamed pleading denial, the words wrenched out of him like something drawn with pliers.

I reached down to the grip-pad on my arm and tugged it slowly towards my wrist. Twinges ran through the bone beneath as the movement snagged the regrowth biotags.

Sutjiadi screamed, ragged glass over tendon and gristle in my head. The inhibitor—

Cold. Cold.

The grip-pad reached my wrist and dangled loose. I reached for the first of the biotags.

Someone might be watching this from Lamont's cabin, but I doubted it. Too much else on the menu right now. And besides, who watches detainees with inhibitor systems crouched on their spines? What's the point? Trust the machine and get on with something more rewarding.

Sutjiadi screamed.

I gripped the tag and applied evenly mounting pressure.

You're not doing this, I reminded myself. *You're just sitting here listening to a man die, and you've done enough of that in the past couple of years for it not to bother you. No big deal.* The Envoy systems, fooling every adrenal gland in my body and plastering me with a layer of cool detachment. I believed what I told myself at a level deeper than thought. On my neck, the inhibitor twitched and snugged itself down again.

A tiny tearing and the regrowth bio filament came out.

Too short.

Fu—

Cold.

Sutjiadi screamed.

I selected another tag and tugged it gently side to side. Beneath the surface of the skin, I felt the monofilament slice tissue down to the bone in a direct line and knew it was also too short.

I looked up and caught Deprez looking at me. His lips framed a question. I gave him a distracted little smile and tried another tag.

Sutjiadi screamed.

The fourth tag was the one – I felt it slicing flesh in a long curve through and around my elbow. The single endorphin dermal I'd shot earlier kept the pain to a minor inconvenience, but the tension still ran through me like wires. I took a fresh grip on the Envoy lie that *absolutely nothing was happening here*, and pulled hard.

The filament came up like a kelp cable out of damp beach sand, ripping a furrow through the flesh of my forearm. Blood spritzed my face.

Sutjiadi screamed. Searing, sawing up and down a scale of despair and disbelief at what the machine was doing to him, at what he could feel happening to the sinewed fibres of his body.

'Kovacs what the fuck are you—' Wardani shut up as I cut her a look and jabbed a finger at my neck. I wrapped the filament carefully around my left palm, knotted it behind the tag. Then, not giving myself time to think about it, I splayed my hand and drew the noose smoothly and rapidly tight.

Nothing is happening here.

The monofilament sliced into my palm, went down through the pad of tissue as if through water and came up against the interface bioplate. Vague pain. Blood welled from the invisible cut in a thin line, then blotched across the whole palm. I heard Wardani's breath draw short, and then she yelped as her inhibitor bit.

Not here my nerves told the inhib unit on my own neck. *Nothing happening here.*

Sutjiadi *screamed*.

I unknotted the filament and drew it clear, then flexed my damaged palm. The lips of the wound across the palm split and gaped. I stuffed thumb into the split and—

NOTHING is happening here. Nothing at all.

—twisted until the flesh tore.

It hurt, endorphin or no fucking endorphin, but I had what I wanted. Below the mangled mass of meat and fatty tissue, the interface plate showed a clear white surface, beaded with blood and finely scarred with biotech circuitry. I worked the lips of the wound further apart until there was a clear patch of plate exposed. Then I reached back with no more conscious intent than you'd get from a back-cracking yawn, and jammed the gashed hand onto the inhibitor.

And closed my fist.

For just a moment, I thought my luck had run out. Luck that had seen me through removing the monofilament without major vascular damage, that had let me get to the interface plate without severing any useful tendons. Luck that had no one watching Lamont's screens. Luck like that had to run dry at some point and as the inhib unit shifted under my blood-slippery grip I felt the whole teetering structure of Envoy control start to come down.

Fuck

The interface plate – *user locked, hostile to any uncoded circuitry in direct contact* – bucked in my ripped palm and something shorted out behind my head.

The inhibitor died with a short electronic squeal.

I grunted, then let the pain come up through gritted teeth as I reached back with my damaged arm and began to unflex the thing's grip on my neck. Reaction was setting in now, a muted trembling racing up my limbs and a spreading numbness in my wounds.

'Vongsavath,' I said as I worked the inhibitor loose. 'I want you to go out there, find Tony Loemanako.'

'Who?'

'The noncom who came to collect us last night.' There was no longer any need to suppress emotion, but I found the Envoy systems were doing it anyway. Even while Sutjiadi's colossal agony scraped and raked along my nerve endings, I seemed to have discovered an inhuman depth of patience to balance against it. 'His name is Loemanako. You'll probably find him down by the execution slab. Tell him I need to talk to him. No, wait. Better just tell him I said I need him. Those words exactly. No reasons, just that. I need him right now. That should bring him.'

Vongsavath looked to the closed flap of the bubblefab. It barely muffled Sutjiadi's uncontrolled shrieking.

'Out there,' she said.

'Yes. I'm sorry.' I finally got the inhib unit off. 'I'd go myself, but it'd be harder to sell, that way. And you're still wearing one of these.'

I examined the carapace of the inhibitor. There was no outward sign of the damage the interface plate's counterintrusion systems had done, but the unit was inert, tentacles spasmed stiff and clawed.

The pilot officer got up unsteadily. 'Alright. I'm going.'

'And Vongsavath.'

'Yeah?'

'Take it easy out there.' I held up the murdered inhibitor. 'Try not to get excited about anything.'

It appeared I was smiling again. Vongsavath stared at me for a moment, then fled. Sutjiadi's screams blistered through in her wake for a moment, and then the flap fell back again.

I turned my attention to the drugs in front of me.

Loemanako came at speed. He ducked through the flap ahead of Vongsavath – another momentary lift in Sutjiadi's agony – and strode down the the centre aisle of the bubblefab to where I lay curled up on the end bed, shivering.

'Sorry about the noise,' he said, leaning over me. One hand touched my shoulder gently. 'Lieutenant, are you—'

I struck upward, into the exposed throat.

Five rapid-dump dermals of tetrameth from the strip my right hand had stolen the previous night, laid directly across major blood vessels. If I'd been wearing an unconditioned sleeve, I'd be cramped up and dying now. If I'd had less conditioning of my own, I'd be cramped up and dying now.

I hadn't dared dose myself with less.

The blow ripped open Loemanako's windpipe, and tore it across. Blood gushed, warm over the back of my hand. He staggered backwards, face working, eyes child-like with disbelieving hurt. I came off the bed after him—

—something in the wolf splice weeps in me at the betrayal—

—and finished it.

He toppled and lay still.

I stood over the corpse, thrumming inside with the pulse of the tetrameth. My feet shifted unsteadily under me. Muscle tremors skipped down one side of my face.

Outside, Sutjiadi's screams modulated upward into something new and worse.

'Get the mobility suit off him,' I said harshly.

No response. I glanced around and realised I was talking to myself. Deprez and Wardani were both slumped against their beds, stunned. Vongsavath was struggling to rise, but could not coordinate her limbs. Too much excitement – the inhibitors had tasted it in their blood and bitten accordingly.

'Fuck.'

I moved between them, clenching my mutilated hand around the spider units and tearing them loose as they spasmed. Against the shift and slide of the tetrameth, it was almost impossible to be more gentle. Deprez and Wardani both grunted with shock as their inhibitors died. Vongsavath's went harder, sparking sharply and scorching my opened palm. The pilot vomited bile, and thrashed. I knelt beside her and got fingers into her throat, pinning her tongue until the spasm passed.

'You O—'

Sutjiadi shrieked across it.

'—K?'

She nodded weakly.

'Then help me get this mob suit off. We don't have a lot of time 'til he's missed.'

Loemanako was armed with an interface pistol of his own, a

standard blaster and the vibroknife he'd loaned to Carrera the night before. I cut his clothes off and went to work on the mob suit beneath. It was combat spec – it powered down and peeled at battlefield speed. Fifteen seconds and Vongsavath's shaky assistance were enough to shut off the dorsal and limb drives and unzip the frame. Loemanako's corpse lay throat open, limbs spread, outlined in an array of upward-jutting flex-alloy fibre spines that reminded me fleetingly of bottleback corpses butchered and half-filleted for barbecue meat on Hirata beach.

'Help me roll him out of—'

Behind me, someone retched. I glanced back and saw Deprez propping himself upright. He blinked a couple of times and managed to focus on me.

'Kovacs. Did you—' His gaze fell on Loemanako. 'That's good. Now, do you want to share your plans for a change?'

I gave Loemanako's corpse a final shove and rolled it clear of the unwrapped mob suit. 'Plan's simple, Luc. I'm going to kill Sutjiadi and everyone else out there. While that's going on, I need you to get inside the 'Chandra and check for crew or conscientous objectors to the entertainment. Probably be a few of each. Here, take this.' I kicked the blaster across to him. 'Think you'll need anything else?'

He shook his head muzzily. 'You spare the knife? And drugs. Where are those fucking tetrameth.'

'My bed. Under the quilt.' I lay on the suit without bothering to undress and began to pull the support struts closed across my chest and stomach. Not ideal, but I didn't have the time. Ought to be OK – Loemanako was bigger framed than my sleeve, and the servoamp uptake pads are supposed to work through clothing at a push. 'We'll go together – I figure it's worth the risk of a run to the polalloy shed before we start.'

'I'm coming,' said Vongsavath grimly.

'No, you're fucking not.' I closed the last of the body struts and started on the arms. 'I need you in one piece; you're the only person can fly the battlewagon. Don't argue, it's the only way any of us get out of here. Your job is to stay here and stay alive. Get the legs.'

Sutjiadi's screams had damped down to semi-conscious moans. I felt a scribble of alarm run up my spine. If the machine saw fit to back off and leave its victim to recover for any length of time, those in the back rows of the audience might start to drift away for an interval cigarette. I hit the drives while Vongsavath was still fastening the last of the ankle joint struts and felt more than heard the servos murmur to life. I flexed my arms – jag of unwatched pain in the broken elbow, twinges in the ruined hand – and felt the power.

Hospital mob suits are designed and programmed to approximate normal human strength and motion while cushioning areas of trauma and ensuring that no part of the body is strained beyond its convalescent limits. In most cases the parameters are hardwired in to stop stupid little fucks from overriding what's good for them.

Military custom doesn't work like that.

I tensed my body and the suit got me to my feet. I thought a kick to groin height and the suit lashed out with speed and strength to dent steel. A left-handed back fist long strike. The suit put it there like neurachem. I crouched and flexed, and knew the servos would put me five metres into the air on demand. I reached out with machined precision and picked up Loemanako's interface gun right handed. Digits scrambled along the display as it recognised the Wedge codes in my undamaged palm. Red gleam of the load light, and I knew through the prickling in my palm what the magazine carried. The vacuum commando's standby. Jacketed slugs, short-fused plasma core. Demolition load.

Outside, the machine somehow licked Sutjiadi back up into screaming. Hoarse now, his voice was shredding. A deeper ground-swell rose behind the shrieks. Audience cheers.

'Get the knife,' I told Deprez.

CHAPTER FORTY

Outside, it was a beautiful day.

The sun was warm on my skin and glinting off the hull of the battlewagon. There was a slight breeze coming in off the sea, scuffing whitecaps. Sutjiadi screamed his agony at a careless blue sky.

Glancing down to the shoreline, I saw they'd erected metal-framed banks of seats around the anatomiser. Only the top of the machine showed above the heads of the spectators. Neurachem reeled in a tighter view – a sense of heads and shoulders tensed in fascination at what was happening on the slab, and then suddenly a glimpse of something flapping, membrane-thin and blood-streaked, torn loose from Sutjiadi's body by pincers and caught by the breeze. A fresh shriek floated up in its wake. I turned away.

You patched and evacuated Jimmy de Soto while he screamed and tried to claw out his own eyes. You can do this.

Functionality!

'Polalloy shed,' I muttered to Deprez and we moved down the beach to the far end of the *Angin Chandra's Virtue*, as rapidly as seemed safe without tripping some Wedge veteran's combat-amped peripheral vision. There's an art to it they teach you in covert ops – breath shallow, move smoothly. Minimise anything that might trigger the enemy's proximity senses. Half a minute of itching exposure was all it took, and then we were shielded from the seat banks by the swell of the *'Chandra*'s hull.

On the far side of the shed, we came across a young Wedge uniform, braced on the structure and vomiting his guts up in the sand. He looked up out of a sweat-beaded face as we rounded the corner, features twisted in misery.

Deprez killed him with the knife.

I kicked open the door with mob suit strength and swung inside, eyes flexed out to total scan in the sudden gloom.

Lockers stood tidily against one wall. A corner table held an assortment of helmet frames. Wall racks offered boot bases and breathing apparatus. The hatch to the showers was open. A Wedge noncom looked round from a datacoil at another desk, face haggard and angry.

'I've already fucking told Artola I'm not—' She spotted the mob suit and peered, getting up. 'Loemanako? What are you—'

The knife skipped through the air like a dark bird off my shoulder. It buried itself in the noncom's neck, just above the collar bone and she jerked in shock, came a wavering step towards me, still peering, and then collapsed.

Deprez stepped past me, knelt to check his handiwork and then withdrew the knife. There was a clean economy of motion in his movements that belied the state of his radiation-blasted cells.

He stood up and caught me looking at him.

'Something?'

I nodded at the corpse he'd just made. 'Not bad for a dying man, Luc.'

He shrugged. 'Tetrameth. Maori sleeve. I have been worse equipped.'

I dumped the interface gun on the table, picked up a pair of helmet frames and tossed one to him. 'You done this before?'

'No. I'm not a spaceman.'

'OK. Put this on. Hold the struts, don't smudge the faceplate.' I gathered boot bases and breathing sets at tetrameth speed. 'The air intake fits through here, like this. The pack straps over your chest.'

'We don't nee—'

'I know, but it's quicker this way. And it means you can keep the faceplate down. Might save your life. Now stamp down on the boot bases, they'll stick in place. I've got to power this thing up.'

The shower systems were set into the wall next to the hatch. I got one unit running, then nodded at Deprez to follow me, and went through into the shower section. The hatch cycled closed behind us, and I caught the thick solvent odour of the polalloy pouring in the confined space. The operational unit's lamps flashed orange in the low light surroundings, glinting off the dozens of twisting threads of polalloy where they ran down from the shower heads and spread like oil on the angled floor of the cubicle.

I stepped in.

It's an eerie feeling the first time you do it, like being buried alive in mud. The polalloy lands on you in a thin coating that quickly builds to a sliding sludge. It masses on the dome of cross-netting at the top of the helmet frame, then topples and pours down around your head, stinging your throat and nostrils even through your locked breathing. Molecular repulsion keeps it off the surface of the faceplate, but the rest of the helmet is sheathed in twenty seconds. The rest of your body, right down to the boot bases, takes about half as long again. You try to keep it away from open wounds or raw flesh; it stings before it dries.

fffffffuuuuck

It's airtight, watertight, utterly sealed, and it'll stop a high-velocity slug like battlewagon armour. At a distance, it even reflects Sunjet fire.

I stepped down and felt through the polalloy for the breathing set controls. Thumbed the vent control. Air hissed under my jaw, filling the suit and popping it loose around my body. I killed the air and chinned the faceplate control. The plate hinged silently up.

'Now you. Don't forget to hold your breath.'

Somewhere outside, Sutjiadi was still screaming. The tetrameth scratched at me. I almost yanked Deprez out of the shower, punched the air supply and watched as his suit popped.

'OK, that's it.' I dialled down to intake standard. 'Keep the plate down. Anyone challenges you, give them this signal. No, thumb crooked like this. It means the suit's malfunctioning. Might buy you the time you need to get close. Give me three minutes, then go. And stay away from the stern.'

The helmeted head nodded ponderously. I could not see his face through the darkened faceplate. I hesitated a moment, then clapped him on the shoulder.

'Try to stay alive, Luc.'

I chinned the faceplate closed again. Then I gave the tetrameth its head, collected the interface gun left-handed on my way through the locker room and let the momentum carry me back outside into the screaming.

It took me one of my three minutes to circle wide around the back of the polalloy shed and then the hospital bubblefab. The position gave me line of sight on the gate and the minimal security Carrera had left there. The same as last night – five strong guard, two suited and one powered-up bug. Looked like Kwok's hunched, cross-legged stance in one suit. Well, she'd never been a big fan of the anatomiser sessions. The other, I couldn't identify.

Machine support. The mobile ultravibe cannon and a couple of other chunks of automated firepower, but all turned the wrong way now, watching the darkness beyond the gate. I breathed out once and started up the beach.

They spotted me at twenty metres – I wasn't hiding. I waved the interface gun cheerily over my head, and gave the malfunction gesture with my other hand. The ragged hole in my left palm ached.

At fifteen metres, they knew something was wrong. I saw Kwok tense and used the only card I had left to play. I chinned the faceplate and waited twelve metres off for it to hinge up. Her face registered shock as she saw me, mingled pleasure, confusion and concern. She unfolded and got to her feet.

'Lieutenant?'

I shot her first. A single shot, in through the opened faceplate. The detonating plasma core blew the helmet apart as I ran forward.

—aching throatful of wolf loyalty, rubbed raw—

The second suit was moving when I got to him, a single leap in the mob suit and a mid-air kick that slammed him back against the carapace of the bug. He bounced off, one hand reaching to slap his faceplate closed. I grabbed the arm, crushed it at the wrist and fired down into his yelling mouth.

Something hammered me in the chest, threw me on my back in the sand. I saw an unsuited figure stalking towards me, hand gun flung out. The interface gun dragged my arm up a handsbreadth and I shot his legs out from under him. Finally, a scream to compete with Sutjiadi, and time running out. I chinned my faceplate closed and flexed my legs. The mob suit threw me to my feet again. A Sunjet blast lashed the sand where I had been. I tracked round and snapped off a shot. The Sunjet wielder spun about with the impact and red glinting fragments of spine exploded out of his back as the shell detonated.

The last one tried to close with me, blocking my gun arm upward and stamping down at my knee. Against an unarmoured man, it was a good move, but he hadn't been paying attention. The edge of his foot bounced off the mob suit and he staggered. I twisted and snapped out a roundhouse kick with all the balanced force the suit would give me.

It broke his back.

Something banged off the front of the bug. I looked down the beach and saw figures spilling from the makeshift amphitheatre, weapons levelling. I snapped a shot off in reflex, then got a grip on my 'meth-scrambled thought processes and straddled the bug.

The systems awoke at a slap to the ignition pad – lights and dataflow in the hooded and heavily armoured instrument panels. I powered up, lifted a quarter-turn about to face the advancing Wedge, selected weaponry and—

—*howl, howl, HOWL*—

some kind of snarling grin made it to my face as the launchers cut loose.

Explosives aren't good for much in vacuum combat. No shockwave to speak of, and any blast energy you generate dissipates fast. Against suited personnel, conventional explosives are next to useless, and nuclear yield, well, that really defeats the purpose of close-quarters combat. You really need a smarter kind of weapon.

The smart shrapnel motherframes cut twinned swerving trails among the soldiers on the beach, locators tilting the flight path with microsecond precision to dump their cub shells into the air just where they would wreak the most organic damage. Behind a barely visible haze of thrust that my faceplate enhancer painted pale pink, each blast unleashed a hail of monomolecular shards sewn with hundreds of larger tooth-sized razor-edged chunks that would bury themselves in organic matter and then fragment.

It was the weapon that ripped 391 platoon apart around me two months ago. Took Kwok's eyes, Eddie Munharto's limbs, and my shoulder.

Two months? Why does it feel like another lifetime?

The Wedge soldiers closest to each blast literally dissolved in the storm of metal fragments. Neurachem-aided vision showed it to me, let me watch them turned from men and women into shredded carcasses fountaining blood from a thousand entry and exit wounds and then into bursting clouds of shattered tissue. Those further off just died in sudden pieces.

The motherframes skipped joyously through them all, impacted on the banks of seats surrounding Sutjiadi, and blew. The whole structure lifted briefly into the air, and was gone in flame. The light from the explosion splashed itself orange on the hull of the *Angin Chandra's Virtue* and debris rained down into the sand and water. The blast rolled out across the beach, and rocked the bug on its grav field.

There were, I discovered, tears starting in my eyes.

I nudged the bug forward over the gore-splattered sand, kneeling upright and looking for survivors. In the quiet after the explosions, the grav drive made a ludicrously soft noise that felt like being stroked with feathers. The tetrameth glimmered at the edges of my vision and trembled in my tendons.

Halfway down to the blast zone, I spotted a pair of injured Wedgemen hidden between two of the bubblefabs. I drifted in their direction. One was too far gone to do anything other than cough up blood, but her companion heaved himself to a sitting position as the bug drew nearer. The shrapnel had, I saw, stripped off his face and left him blind. The arm nearest me was down to a shoulder stump and protruding bone fragments.

'What—' he pleaded.

The jacketed slug punched him flat. Beside him, the other soldier cursed me to some hell I hadn't heard of before, and then died strangling on her own blood. I hovered over her for a few moments, gun half levelled, then tipped the bug about as something banged flatly, down by the battlewagon. I scanned the shoreline beside Sutjiadi's impromptu funeral pyre, and picked out motion at the water's edge. Another soldier, almost uninjured – he must have crawled under the structure of the battlewagon and escaped the worst of the blast. The gun in my hand was below the level of the bug's screen. He saw only the polalloy suit and the Wedge vehicle. He got up, shaking his head numbly. There was blood running out of his ears.

'Who?' he kept saying. 'Who?'

He wandered distractedly into the shallows, looking around him at the devastation, then back at me. I chinned up my faceplate.

'Lieutenant Kovacs?' His voice boomed, overloud with his sudden deafness. 'Who did this?'

'We did,' I told him, knowing he couldn't hear me. He watched my lips, uncomprehending.

I raised the interface gun. The shot pinned him up against the hull for a moment, then blew him clear again as it exploded. He collapsed into the water and floated there, leaking thick clouds of blood.

Movement from the 'Chandra.

I whipped about on the bug and saw a polalloy-suited figure stumble down the entry rank and collapse. A mob suit leap over the bug's screen and I landed in the water, kept upright by the suit's gyros. A dozen strides took me to the crumpled form, and I saw the Sunjet blast that had charred through the stomach at one side. The wound was massive.

The faceplate hinged up, and Deprez lay gasping beneath it.

'Carrera,' he managed hoarsely. 'Forward hatch.'

I was already moving, already knowing bone-deep I was too late.

The forward hatch was blown on emergency evac. It lay half buried in a crater of sand with the force of the explosive bolts that had thrown it there. Footprints beside it where someone had jumped the three metres from hull to beach. The prints led off in a sprinted line to the polalloy shed.

Fuck you, Isaac, fuck you for a diehard motherfucker.

I burst through the door to the shed brandishing the Kalashnikov. Nothing. Not a fucking thing. The locker room was as I'd left it. The female noncom's corpse, the scattering of equipment in low light. Beyond the hatch, the shower was still running. The reek of the polalloy drifted out to me.

I ducked inside, checked corners. Nothing.

Fuck.

Well, it figures. I shut down the shower system absently. *What did you expect, that he'd be easy to kill?*

I went back outside to find the others, and tell them the good news.

Deprez died while I was gone.

When I got back to him, he'd given up breathing and was staring up at the blue sky as if slightly bored with it. There was no blood – at close range, a Sunjet cauterises totally, and from the wound it looked as if Carrera had got him point blank.

Vongsavath and Wardani had found him before me. They were knelt in the sand a short distance away on either side of him. Vongsavath clutched a captured blaster in one hand, but you could tell her heart wasn't in it. She barely looked up as my shadow fell across her. I dropped a hand on her shoulder in passing, and went to crouch in front of the archaeologue.

'Tanya.'

She heard it in my voice. 'What now?'

'It's a lot easier to shut the gate than to open it, right?'

'Right.' She stopped and looked up at me, searching my face. 'There's a shutdown procedure that doesn't require encoding, yes. How did you know?'

I shrugged, inwardly wondering myself. Envoy intuition doesn't usually work this way. 'Makes sense, I guess. Always harder to pick the locks than slam the door afterwards.'

Her voice lowered. 'Yes.'

'This shutdown. How long will it take?'

'I, *fuck*, Kovacs. I don't know. A couple of hours. Why?'

'Carrera isn't dead.'

She coughed up a fractured laugh. 'What?'

'You see that big fucking hole in Luc.' The tetrameth thrummed in me like current, feeding a rising anger. 'Carrera made it. Then he got out the forward escape hatch, painted himself in polalloy and is by now on the other side of the fucking gate. That clear enough for you?'

'Then why don't you leave him there?'

'Because if I do,' I forced my own voice down a couple of notches, tried to get a grip on the 'meth surge. 'If I do, he'll swim up while you're trying to close the gate and he'll kill you. And the rest of us. In fact, depending on what hardware Loemanako left aboard the ship, he may be right back with a tactical nuclear warhead. *Very* shortly.'

'Then why don't we just get the fuck out of here right now?' asked Vongsavath. She gestured at the *Angin Chandra's Virtue.* 'In this thing, I can put us on the other side of the globe in a couple of minutes. Fuck it, I could probably get us out of the whole system in a couple of months.'

I glanced across at Tanya Wardani and waited. It took a few moments, but finally she shook her head.

'No. We have to close the gate.'

Vongsavath threw up her hands. 'What the fuck for? Who care—'

'Stow it, Ameli.' I flexed the suit upright again. 'Tell the truth, I don't think you could get through the Wedge security blocks in much less than a day anyway. Even with my help. I'm afraid we're going to have to do this the hard way.'

And I will have a chance to kill the man who murdered Luc Deprez.

I wasn't sure if that was the 'meth talking, or just the memory of a shared bottle of whisky on the deck of a trawler now blasted and sunk. It didn't seem to matter that much.

Vongsavath sighed and heaved herself to her feet.

'You going on the bug?' she asked. 'Or do you want an impeller frame?'

'We'll need both.'

'Yeah?' she looked suddenly interested. 'How come? Do you want me—'

'The bugs mount a nuclear howitzer. Twenty kiloton yield. I'm going to fire that motherfucker across and see if we can't fry Carrera with it. Most likely, we won't. He'll be backed off somewhere, probably expecting it. But it will chase him away for long enough to send the bug through. While that draws any long-range fire he can manage, I'll tumble in with the impeller rig. After that,' I shrugged. 'It's a fair fight.'

'And I suppose I'm not—'

'Got it in one. How does it feel to be indispensable?'

'Around here?' She looked up and down the corpse-strewn beach. 'It feels out of place.'

CHAPTER FORTY-ONE

'**Y**ou can't do this,' said Wardani quietly.

I finished angling the nose of the bug upward towards the centre of the gate-space, and turned to face her. The grav field murmured to itself.

'Tanya, we've seen this thing withstand weapons that ...' I searched for adequate words. 'That I for one don't understand. You really think a little tickle with a tactical nuke is going to cause any damage?'

'I don't mean that. I mean you. Look at you.'

I looked down at controls on the firing board. 'I'm good for a couple more days.'

'Yeah – in a hospital bed. Do *you* really think you stand a chance going up against Carrera, the state you're in? The only thing holding you up right now is that suit.'

'Rubbish. You're forgetting the tetrameth.'

'Yeah, a lethal dose from what I saw. How long can you stay on top of that?'

'Long enough.' I skipped her look and stared past her down the beach. 'What the hell is keeping Vongsavath?'

'Kovacs.' She waited until I looked at her. 'Try the nuke. Leave it at that. I'll get the gate closed.'

'Tanya, why didn't you shoot me with the stunner?'

Silence.

'Tanya?'

'Alright,' she said violently. '*Piss* your fucking life away out there. See if I care.'

'That wasn't what I asked you.'

'I,' she dropped her gaze. 'I panicked.'

'That, Tanya, is bullshit. I've seen you do a lot of things in the last couple of months, but panic hasn't been any of them. I don't think you know the meaning of the word.'

'Oh, yeah? You think you know me that well?'

'Well enough.'

She snorted. 'Fucking soldiers. Show me a soldier, I'll show you a fucked-in-the-head romantic. You know nothing about me, Kovacs. You've fucked me, and that in a virtuality. You think that gives you insight? You think that gives you the right to *judge* people?'

'People like Schneider, you mean?' I shrugged. 'He would have sold us all out to Carrera, Tanya. You know that, don't you. He would have sat through Sutjiadi and let it happen.'

'Oh, you're feeling proud of yourself, is that it?' She gestured down at the crater where Sutjiadi had died and the brightly reddened spillage of corpses and spread gore stretching up towards us. 'Think you've achieved something here, do you?'

'You wanted me to die? Revenge for Schneider?'

'No!'

'It's not a problem, Tanya.' I shrugged again. 'The only thing I can't work out is why I *didn't* die. I don't suppose you've got any comment on that? As the resident Martian expert, I mean.'

'I don't know. I, I panicked. Like I said. I got the stunner as soon as you dropped it. I put myself out.'

'Yeah, I know. Carrera said you were in neuroshock. He just wanted to know why I wasn't. That, and why I woke up so fast.'

'Maybe,' she said, not looking at me, 'you don't have whatever is inside the rest of us.'

'Hoy, Kovacs.'

We both shifted to look down the beach again.

'Kovacs. Look what I found.'

It was Vongsavath, riding the other bug at crawling pace. In front of her stumbled a solitary figure. I narrowed my eyes and reeled in a closer look.

'I don't fucking believe it.'

'Who is it?'

I rustled up a dry chuckle. 'Survivor type. Look.'

Lamont looked grim, but not noticeably worse than the last time we'd met. His ragged-clad frame was splattered with blood, but none of it seemed to be his. His eyes were clenched into slits and his trembling seemed to have damped down. He recognised me and his face lit up. He capered forward, then stopped and looked back at the bug that was herding him up the beach. Vongsavath snapped something at him and he started forward again until he stood a couple of metres away from me, jigging peculiarly from one foot to another.

'Knew it!' He cackled out loud. 'Knew you'd do it. Got *files* on you, I knew you would. I *heard* you. *Heard* you, but I didn't say.'

'Found him in the armoury crawlspace,' said Vongsavath, bringing the bug to a halt and dismounting. 'Sorry. Took a while to scare him out.'

'*Heard* you, *saw* you,' said Lamont to himself, rubbing ferociously at the back of his neck. 'Got *files* on you. Ko-ko-ko-ko-kovacs. *Knew* you'd do it.'

'Did you,' I said sombrely.

'*Heard* you, *saw* you, but I didn't say.'

'Yeah, well that was your mistake. A good political officer always relays his suspicions to higher authority. It's in the directives.' I picked up the interface gun from the bug console and shot Lamont through the chest. It was an impatient shot and it sheared through him too high to kill immediately. The shell exploded in the sand five metres behind him. He flopped on the ground, blood gouting from the entry wound, then from somewhere he found the strength to get to his knees. He grinned up at me.

'*Knew* you'd do it,' he said hoarsely, and keeled slowly over on his side. Blood soaked out of him and into the sand.

'Did you get the impeller?' I asked Vongsavath.

I sent Wardani and Vongsavath to wait behind the nearest rock bluff while I fired the nuke. They weren't shielded and I didn't want to waste the time it would take to get them into polalloy. And even at a distance, even in the freezing vacuum on the other side of the gate, the nuclear shells the bug mounted would throw back enough hard radiation to cook an unshielded human very dead.

Of course, previous experience suggested the gate would handle the proximity of dangerous radiation in much the same way it had dealt with the proximity of nanobes – it wouldn't permit it. But you could be wrong about these things. And anyway, there was no telling what a Martian would consider a tolerable dose.

Then why are you sitting here, Tak?

Suit'll soak it up.

But it was a little more than that. Sat astride the bug, Sunjet flat across my thighs, interface pistol tucked into a belt pouch, face on to the bubble of starscape the gate had carved into the world before me, I could feel a long, dragging inertia of purpose setting in. It was a fatalism running deeper than the tetrameth, a conviction that there wasn't that much more to do and whatever result was waiting out there in the cold would just have to do.

Must be the dying, Tak. Bound to get to you in the end. Even with the 'meth, at a cellular level, any sleeve is going to—

Or maybe you're just scared of diving through there and finding yourself back on the Mivtsemdi *all over again.*

Shall we just get on with it?

The howitzer shell spat from the bug carapace slow enough to be visible, breached the gate-space with a faint sucking sound and trailed off into the starscape. Seconds later the view was drenched white with the blast. My faceplate darkened automatically. I waited, seated on the bug, until the light faded. If anything outside visual spectrum radiation made it back through, the contam alert on the suit helmet didn't think it worth mentioning.

Nice to be right, huh?

Not that it matters much now anyway.

I chinned up the faceplate and whistled. The second bug lifted from behind the rock bluff and ploughed a short furrow through the sand. Vongsavath set it down with casual perfection, aligned with mine. Wardani climbed off from behind her with aching slowness.

'Two hours, you said, Tanya.'

She ignored me. She hadn't spoken since I shot Lamont.

'Well.' I checked the security tether on the Sunjet one more time. 'Whatever you've got to do, start doing it now.'

'What if you're not back in time?' objected Vongsavath.

I grinned. 'Don't be stupid. If I can't waste Carrera and get back here in two hours, I'm not coming back. You know that.'

Then I knocked the faceplate shut and put the bug into drive. Through the gate. Look – easy as falling.

My stomach climbed into my throat as the weightlessness swarmed aboard. Vertigo kicked in behind it.

Here we fucking go again.

Carrera made his play.

Minute blotch of pink in the faceplate as a drive kicked in somewhere above me. Envoy reflex fielded it the moment it happened and my hands yanked the bug about to face the attack. Weapons systems flickered. A pair of interceptor drones spat out of the launch pods. They looped in to avoid any direct defences the approaching missile had, then darted across my field of vision from opposite sides and detonated. I thought one of them had begun to spin off course, tinselled out, when they blew. Silent white light flared and the faceplate blotted out my view.

By then, I was too busy to watch.

I kicked back from the body of the bug, nailing down a sudden surge of terror as I let go of its solidity and fell upward into the dark. My left hand clawed after the impeller control arm. I froze it.

Not yet.

The bug tumbled away below me, drive still lit. I shut out thoughts of the infinite emptiness I was adrift in, focused instead on the dimly sensed mass of the ship above me. In the sparse light from the stars, the polalloy combat suit and the impeller rack on my back would be next to invisible. No impeller thrust meant no trace on anything but the most sensitive of mass-sensing sets, and I was willing to bet that Carrera didn't have one of those to hand. As long as the impellers stayed dead, the only visible target out here was the bug's drive. I lay crouched upright in the weightless quiet, tugged the Sunjet to me on its tether line and cuddled the stock into my shoulder. Breathed. Tried not to wait too hard for Carrera's next move.

Come on you motherfucker.

Ah-ah. You're expecting, Tak.

428

We will teach you not to expect anything. That way, you will be ready for it.

Thanks, Virginia.

Properly equipped, a vacuum commando doesn't have to do most of this shit. A whole rack of detection systems load into the helmet frames of a combat suit, coordinated by a nasty little personal battlecomputer that doesn't suffer from any of the freezing awe humans are prone to in hard space. You have to roll with it, but as with most warfare these days, the machine does most of the work.

I hadn't had time to find and install the Wedge's battletech, but I was tolerably sure Carrera hadn't either. That left him with whatever Wedge-coded hardware Loemanako's team had left aboard the ship, and possibly a Sunjet of his own. And for a Wedge commando, it goes against the grain to leave hardware lying around unwatched – there wouldn't be much.

You hope.

The rest was down to one-on-one at levels of crudity that stretched all the way back to orbital champions like Armstrong and Gagarin. And that, the tetrameth rush was telling me, had to work in my favour. I let the Envoy senses slide out over my anxiety, over the pounding of the tetrameth, and I stopped waiting for anything to happen.

There.

Pink flare off the darkened edge of the looming hull.

I pivoted my weight as smoothly as the mob suit would allow, lined myself up on the launch point and kicked the impellers up into overdrive. Somewhere below me, white light unfolded and doused the lower half of my vision. Carrera's missile homing in on the bug.

I cut the impellers. Fell silently upward towards the ship. Under the faceplate, I felt a grimace of satisfaction creep across my face. The impeller trace would have been lost in the blast from the exploding bug, and now Carrera had nothing again. He might be expecting something like this, but he couldn't see me, and by the time he could . . .

Sunjet flame awoke on the hull. Scattered beam. I quailed for a moment inside my suit, then the grin stitched itself back as I saw. Carrera was firing wide, too far back along an angle between the death of the bug and where I really was now. My fingers tightened around the Sunjet.

Not yet. Not—

Another Sunjet blast, no closer. I watched the beam light up and die, light up and die, getting my own weapon lined up for the next one. The range had to be less than a kilometre now. A few more seconds and a beam on minimal dispersal should punch right through the polalloy Carrera was wearing and whatever organic matter was also in the way. A lucky shot would take off his head or melt through heart or lungs. Less lucky would do damage he'd have to deal with, and while he was doing that I'd get close.

I could feel my lips peeling back from my teeth as I thought it.

Space erupted in light around me.

For a moment so brief it only registered at Envoy speeds, I thought the crew of the ship had come back again, outraged at the nuclear blast so close to their funeral barge, and the irritating pinprick firefighting in its wake.

Flare. You stupid fuck, he's lit you up.

I snapped on the impellers and whirled away sideways. Sunjet fire chased me from a rampart on the hull over my head. On one spin, I managed to get off returning fire. Three sputtering seconds, but Carrera's beam shut off. I fled for the roof, got some piece of hull architecture between me and Carrera's position, then reversed the impeller drive and braked to slow drift. Blood hammered in my temples.

Did I get him?

Proximity to the hull forced recoding of my surroundings. The alien sculpted architecture of the vessel overhead was suddenly the surface of a planetoid and I was head down five metres over it. The flare burnt steadily a hundred metres out, casting twisted shadows past the chunk of hull architecture I was floating behind. Weird detail scarred the surfaces around me, curls and scrapings of structure like scrawlings in bas relief, glyphs on a monumental scale.

Did I—

'Nice evasion, Kovacs.' Carrera's voice spoke into my ear as if he was sitting in the helmet beside me. 'Not bad for a non-swimmer.'

I checked the head up displays. The suit radio was set for receive only. I nudged sideways in the helmet space and the transmit symbol glowed on. A cautious body flex put me parallel to the hull. Meanwhile . . .

Keep him talking.

'Who told you I was a non-swimmer?'

'Oh, yes, I was forgetting. That fiasco with Randall. But a couple of outings like that hardly make you a VacCom veteran.' He was playing for avuncular amusement, but there wasn't much hiding the raw ugliness of the rage underneath it. 'Which fact explains why it's going to be very easy for me to kill you. That is what I'm going to do, Kovacs. I'm going to smash in your faceplate and watch your face boil out.'

'Better get on with it, then.' I scanned the solidified bubbling of hull in front of me, looking for a sniper vantage point. 'Because I don't plan to be here much longer.'

'Only came back for the view, huh. Or did you leave some holoporn with sentimental value lying around the docking bay?'

'Just keeping you out of the way while Wardani closes the gate, that's all.'

A short pause, in which I could hear him breathing. I shortened the tether line on the Sunjet until it floated close beside my right arm, then touched the trim controls on the impeller arm and risked a half-second impulse. The straps tugged as the racked motors on my back lifted me delicately up and forward.

'What's the matter, Isaac? You sulking?'

He made a noise in his throat. 'You're a piece of shit, Kovacs. You've sold out your comrades like a tower dweller. Murdered them for credit.'

'I thought that's what we were about, Isaac. Murder for credit.'

'Don't give me your fucking Quellisms, Kovacs. Not with a hundred Wedge personnel dead and blown apart back there. Not with the blood of Tony Loemanako and Kwok Yuen Yee on your hands. *You* are the murderer. They were soldiers.'

A tiny stinging in my throat and eyes at the names.

Lock it down.

'They slaughtered sort of easily for soldiers.'

'*Fuck* you, Kovacs.'

'Whatever.' I reached out for the approaching curve of the hull architecture where a small bubble formed a rounded spur on one side of the main structure. Behind my outstretched arms, the rest of my body shifted into a dead stop posture. A momentary sense of panic sweated through me at the sudden thought that the hull might be contact-mined in some way—

Oh well. Can't think of everything.

—and then my gloved hands came to rest on the curving surface and I stopped moving. The Sunjet bumped gently off my shoulder. I risked a rapid glance through the gull-winged space where the two bubble forms intersected. Ducked back. Envoy recall built me a picture and mapped it against memory.

It was the docking bay, centred at the bottom of the same three-hundred-metre dimple and set about with bubbled hillocks that were themselves distorted by other smaller swellings rising haphazardly from their flanks. Loemanako's squad must have left a locater beacon, because there was no other way Carrera could have found the place this fast on a hull nearly thirty klicks across and sixty long. I looked at the suit receiver display again, but the only channel showing was the one Carrera's slightly hoarse breathing came through on. No big surprise; he would have killed the broadcast as soon as he got set up. No point in telegraphing his ambush point to anyone else.

So where the fuck are you, Isaac? I can hear your breathing, I just need to see you so I can stop it.

I eased myself painstakingly back to a viewing position and started scanning the globular landscape below me a degree at a time. All I needed was a single careless move. Just one.

From Isaac Carrera, decorated VacCom commander, survivor of half a thousand vacuum combat engagements and victor in most. A careless move. Sure, Tak. Coming right up.

'You know, I wonder, Kovacs.' His voice was calm again. He'd cranked his anger back under control. Under the circumstances, the last thing I needed. 'What kind of deal did Hand offer you?'

Scan, search. Keep him talking.

'More than you're paying me, Isaac.'

'I think you're forgetting our rather excellent healthcare cover.'

'Nope. Just trying to avoid needing it again.'

Scan, search.

'Was it so bad, fighting for the Wedge? You were guaranteed re-sleeving at all times, and it's not as if a man of your training was ever likely to suffer real death.'

'Three of my team would have to disagree with you, there, Isaac. If they weren't already really fucking dead, that is.'

A slight hesitation. '*Your* team?'

I grimaced. 'Jiang Jianping got turned into soup by an ultravibe blast, the nanobes took Hansen and Cruicksha—'

'*Your* tea—'

'I heard what you fucking said the first time, Isaac.'

'Oh. I'm sorry. I merely wonder—'

'Training's got fucking nothing to do with it, and you know it. You can go sell that fucking song to Lapinee. Machines and luck, that's what kills you or keeps you alive on Sanction IV.'

Scan, search, find that motherfucker.

And calm down.

'Sanction IV and any other conflict,' Carrera said quietly. 'You of all people should know that. It's the nature of the game. If you didn't want to play, you shouldn't have dealt yourself in. The Wedge isn't a conscript army.'

'Isaac, the whole fucking planet has been conscripted into this war. No one's got any choice any more. *You're going to be involved, you might as well have the big guns.* That's a Quellism for you, in case you wondered.'

He grunted. 'Sounds like common sense to me. Didn't that bitch ever say anything original?'

There. My 'methed-out nerves jumped with it. *Right there.*

The slim edge of something built by human technology, stark angular outline caught by flarelight among the curves at the base of a bubble outcrop. One side of an impeller set frame. I settled the Sunjet into place and lined up on the target. Drawled response.

'She wasn't a philosopher, Isaac. She was a soldier.'

'She was a terrorist.'

'We quibble over terms.'

I triggered the Sunjet. Fire lanced across the concave arena and splashed off the outline. Something exploded visibly off the hull, in fragments. I felt a smile tug at the corners of my mouth.

Breathing.

It was the only thing that warned me. The papery whisper of breath at the bottom of the suit receiver. The suppressed sound of effort.

Fu—

Something invisible shattered and shed light over my head. Something no more visible spanged off my faceplate, leaving a tiny glowing V of chipped glass. I felt other tiny impacts off my suit.

Grenade!

Instinct had me already spinning to the right. Later, I realised why. It was the quickest route between Carrera's position and mine, working round the rim of hull architecture that ringed the docking bay. A single third of the circle, and Carrera had crept round it while he talked to me. Shed of the impellers that had decoyed me and would in any case telltale his movement, he'd dragged and shoved himself from handhold to boot purchase point, all the way round. He'd used anger to disguise the stress in his voice as he worked, held down his breathing elsewhere, and at some point he judged close enough, he'd lain still and waited for me to give myself away with the Sunjet. And with the experience of decades in vacuum combat, he'd hit me with the one weapon that wouldn't show up.

Exemplary, really.

He came at me across fifty metres of space like a flying version of Semetaire on the beach, arms reaching. The Sunjet sprouted recognisably from his right fist, a Philips squeeze launcher from his left. Though there was no way to detect it, I knew the second electromag-accelerated grenade was already in flight between us.

I jammed the impellers to life and backflipped. The hull vanished from view, then hinged back in from the top as I spiralled away. The grenade, deflected by the wash from the impeller drives as I flipped, exploded and sewed space with shrapnel. I felt shards of the stuff bang through one leg and foot, sudden numbing impacts and then traceries of pain through the flesh like biofilaments slicing. My ears popped painfully as suit pressure dropped. The polalloy socked inward at a dozen other points, but it held.

434

I tumbled up and over the bubble outcrop, a sprawling target in the flarelight, hull and bearings spinning around me. The pain in my ears eased as the polalloy congealed across the damage. No time to look for Carrera. I trimmed the impeller thrust, then dived once more for the globular landscape stretching below me. Sunjet fire flashed around me.

I hit the hull a glancing blow, used the impact to change trajectories and saw another Sunjet blast scythe past on the left. I caught a glimpse of Carrera as he adhered briefly to a rounded surface back up the slope of the dimple. I already knew the next move. From there, he'd push off with a single well-controlled kick and ride the simple linear velocity down towards me, firing as he came. At some point he'd get close enough to punch molten holes through the suit that the polalloy could not congeal over.

I bounced off another bubble. More idiot tumbling. More near-miss Sunjet fire. I trimmed the impellers again, tried for a line that would take me into the shadow of the outcrop, and cut off the thrust. My hands groped after something to hold and caught on one of the bas relief scroll effects I'd spotted earlier. I killed my motion and twisted round to look for Carrera.

No sign. I was out of line of sight.

I turned back and crept gratefully further around the bubble outcrop. Another curl of bas relief offered itself and I reached down—

Oh, shit.

I was holding the wing of a Martian.

Shock held me unstirring for a second. Time enough for me to think this was some kind of carving in the hull surface, time enough to know at some deep level that it wasn't.

The Martian had died screaming. The wings were flung back, sunk into the hull surface for most of their width, protruding only at the curled extremities and where their muscled webbing rose up under the arched spine of the creature. The head was twisted in agony, beak gaping open, eyes glaring like comet-tailed orbs of washed jet. One clawed limb lifted talons above the hull surface. The whole corpse was sheathed in the material of the hull it had flailed against, drowning there.

435

I shifted my gaze and looked out across the surface ahead of me, the scattered scrawl of raised detail, and knew finally what I was looking at. The hull around the docking-bay dimple – all of it, the whole bubbling expanse – was a mass grave, a spider's web trap for thousands upon thousands of Martians who had all died entombed in whatever substances had run and foamed and burst here when –

When *what?*

The shape of the catastrophe was outside anything I could envisage. I could not imagine the weapons that would do this, the circumstances of this conflict between two civilisations as far ahead of humanity's scavenger-built little empire as we were from the gulls whose bodies had clogged the water around Sauberville. I could not see how it could happen. I could only see the results. I could only see the dead.

Nothing ever changes. A hundred and fifty light years from home and the same shit just keeps going down.

Got to be some kind of universal fucking constant.

The grenade bounced off another hull-drowned Martian ten metres away, careened up and exploded. I rolled away from the blast. A brief pummelling over my back and one searing penetration under my shoulder. Pressure drop like a knife through my eardrums. I screamed.

Fuck this.

I fired the impellers and burst out of the cover of the bubble outcrop, not knowing what I was going to do until I did it. Carrera's gliding figure showed up less than fifty metres off. I saw Sunjet fire, turned on my back and dived directly at the docking-bay mouth. Carrera's voice trailed me, almost amused.

'Where do you think you're going, Kovacs?'

Something exploded at my back and the impeller thrust cut out. Scorching heat across my back. Carrera and his fucking VacCom skills. But with the residual velocity, and well, maybe a little spirit realm luck cadged off the vengeful ghost of Hand – *he shot you after all, Matt, you did curse the fucker* – just to grease the palm of whatever fate . . .

I ploughed through the atmosphere baffles of the docking bay at a slewed angle, found gravity beneath me and battered into one of the stacked fat-snake containing walls, bounced off with the sudden shock of weight from the grav field and crashed to the deck, trailing wings of smoke and flame from the wrecked impeller frame.

For a long moment, I lay still in the cavernous quiet of the bay.

Then, from somewhere, I heard a curious bubbling sound in my helmet. It took me several seconds to realise I was laughing.

Get up, Takeshi.

Oh, come on ...

He can kill you just as dead in here, Tak. Get UP.

I reached out and tried to prop myself up. Wrong arm – the broken elbow joint bent soggily inside the mob suit. Pain ran up and down the abused muscles and tendons. I rolled away, gasping and tried with the other arm. Better. The mob suit wheezed a little, something definitely awry in the works here, but it got me up. Now get rid of the wreckage on my back. The emergency release still worked, sort of. I hauled myself clear, the Sunjet caught in the frame and would not tug loose on the tether line. I yanked at it for a senseless moment, then unseamed the tether instead and bent to free the weapon from the other side.

'Alri ... vacs.' Carrera's voice, trampled out by the interference from the interior structure. 'If ... tha ... ay ... ant it.'

He was coming in after me.

The Sunjet stuck.

Leave it!

And fight him with a pistol? *In* polalloy?

Weapons are an extension screamed an exasperated Virginia Vidaura, in my head – you *are the killer and destroyer. You are whole, with or without them. Leave it!*

'kay, *Virginia.* I sniggered a little. *Whatever you say.*

I lurched away towards the lintel-braced exit from the bay, drawing the interface pistol from its pouch. Wedge equipment was crated and stacked across the bay. The locater beacon, dumped unceremoniously, still powered at standby, the way Carrera had presumably left it. A nearby crate cracked open, sections of a disassembled Philips launcher protruding. Haste written into the details of the scene, but it was a soldierly haste. Controlled speed. Combat competence, a man at his trade. Carrera was in his element.

437

Get the fuck out of here, Tak.

Into the next chamber. Martian machines stirred, bristled and then sloped sullenly away from me, muttering to themselves. I limped past them, following the painted arrows, *no, don't fucking follow the arrows.* I ducked left at the next opportunity and plunged along a corridor the expedition had not taken before. A machine snuffled after me a few paces, then went back.

I thought I heard the sound of motion behind and above me. A jerked glance up into the shadowed space overhead. Ludicrous.

Get a grip, Tak. It's the 'meth. You did too much and now you're hallucinating.

More chambers, intersecting curves one into another and always the space above. I stopped myself rigidly from looking up. The pain from the grenade shards in my leg and shoulder was beginning to seep up through the chemical armour of the tetrameth, waking echoes in my ruined left hand and the shattered joint in my right elbow. The furious energy I'd felt earlier had decayed to a jumpy sense of speed and vibrating riffs of inexplicable amusement that threatened to emerge as giggling.

In that state, I backed through into a tight, closed chamber, turned about and came face to face with my last Martian.

This time, the mummified wing membranes were folded down around the skeletal frame, and the whole thing was crouched on a low roost bar. The long skull drooped forward over the chest, hiding the light gland. The eyes were closed.

It lifted its beak and looked up at me.

No. It fucking didn't.

I shook my head, crept closer to the corpse and stared at it. From somewhere, an impulse arose to caress the long bone ridge on the back of the skull.

'I'll just sit here for a while,' I promised, stifling another giggle. 'Quietly. Just a couple of hours, that's all I need.'

I lowered myself to the floor on my uninjured arm, leaned against the sloping wall behind us, clutching the interface gun like a charm. My body was a warm twisting together of limp ropes inside the cage of the mob suit, a faintly quivering assemblage of soft tissue with no more will to animate its exoskeleton. My gaze slipped up into the gloomy space at the top of the chamber and for a while I thought I saw pale wings beating there, trying to escape the imprisoning curve. At some point, though, I spotted the fact that they were in my head, because I could feel their paper-thin texture brushing around the inner surface of my skull, scraping minutely but painfully at the insides of my eyeballs and obscuring my vision by degrees, pale to dark, pale to dark, pale to dark, to dark, to dark—

And a thin, rising whine like grief.

'Wake up, Kovacs.'

The voice was gentle, and there was something nudging at my hand. My eyes seemed to be gummed shut. I lifted one arm and my hand bumped off the smooth curve of the faceplate.

'Wake up.' Less gentle now. A tiny jag of adrenalin went eeling along my nerves at the change in tone. I blinked hard and focused. The Martian was still there – *no shit, Tak* – but my view of the corpse was blocked by the figure in the polalloy suit that stood a safe three or four metres out of reach, Sunjet carried at a wary angle.

The nudging at my hand recommenced. I tipped the helmet and looked down. One of the Martian machines was stroking at my glove with an array of delicate-looking receptors. I shoved it away, and it backed up chittering a couple of places, then came sniffing back undeterred.

Carrera laughed. It rang too loud in the helmet receiver. I felt as if the fluttering wings had somehow hollowed out my head so that my whole skull wasn't much less delicate than the mummified remains I was sharing the chamber with.

'That's right. Fucking thing led me to you, can you believe that? Really helpful little beastie.'

At that point, I laughed too. It seemed the only thing appropriate to the moment. The Wedge commander joined in. He held up the interface gun in his left hand, and laughed louder.

'Were you going to kill me with this?'

'Doubt it.'

We both stopped laughing. His faceplate hinged up and he looked down at me out of a face gone slightly haggard around the eyes. I guessed even the short time he'd spent tracking me through the Martian architecture hadn't been a lot of fun.

I flexed my palm, once, on the off-chance that Loemanako's gun might not have been personally coded, that any Wedge palm plate might be able to call it. Carrera caught the move and shook his head. He tossed the weapon into my lap.

'Unloaded anyway. Hold on to it if you like – some men go better that way, holding a gun tight. Seems to help at the end. Substitute for something, I guess. Mother's hand. Your dick. You want to stand up to die?'

'No,' I said softly.

'Open your helmet?'

'What for?'

'Just giving you the option.'

'Isaac—' I cleared my throat of what felt like a web of rusted wire. Words scraped through. It seemed suddenly very important to say them. 'Isaac, I'm sorry.'

You will be

It flared through me like tears up behind my eyes. Like the wolf-weeping loss that Loemanako's and Kwok's deaths had brought up through my throat.

'Good,' he said simply. 'But a little late.'

'Have you seen what's behind you, Isaac?'

'Yeah. Impressive, but very dead. No ghosts that I've seen.' He waited. 'Do you have anything else to say?'

I shook my head. He raised the Sunjet.

'This is for my murdered men,' he said.

'*Look* at the fucking thing,' I screamed, every increment of Envoy intonation pushed into it and for just a fraction of a second his head shifted. I came up off the floor, flexing in the mob suit, hurling the interface gun into the space below his hinged-up faceplate and diving at him low.

Miserly shavings of luck, a tetrameth crash and my fading grip on Envoy combat poise. It was all I had left and I took it all across the space between us, teeth bared. When the Sunjet crackled, it hit where I'd been. Maybe it was the shouted distractor, shifting his focus, maybe the gun hurtling towards his face, maybe just this same tired general sense that it was all over.

He staggered backwards as I hit him, and I trapped the Sunjet between our bodies. He slid into a combat judo block that would have thrown an unarmoured man off his hip. I hung on with the stolen strength of Loemanako's suit. Another two stumbling backsteps and we both smashed into the mummified Martian corpse together. The frame tipped and collapsed. We tumbled over it like clowns, staggering to get up as we slipped. The corpse disintegrated. Powder burst of pale orange in the air around us.

I'm sorry.

You will be, if the skin crumbles.

Faceplate up, panting, Carrera must have sucked in a lungful of the stuff. More settled on his eyes and the exposed skin of his face.

The first yell as he felt it eating in.

Then the screams.

He staggered away from me, Sunjet clattering to the deck, hands up and scrubbing at his face. Probably it only ground the stuff harder into the tissue it was dissolving. A deep-throated shrieking poured out of him and a pale red froth began to foam through between his fingers and over his hands. Then, the powder must have eaten through some part of his vocal cords, because the screams collapsed into a sound like a faltering drainage system.

He hit the floor making that sound, gripping at his face as if he could somehow hold it in place and bubbling up thick gouts of blood and tissue from his corroded lungs. By the time I got to the Sunjet and came back to stand over him with it, he was drowning in his own blood. Beneath the polalloy, his body quivered as it went into shock.

I'm sorry.

I placed the barrel of the weapon on the hands that masked his melting face, and pulled the trigger.

CHAPTER FORTY-TWO

When I finished telling it, Roespinoedji clasped his hands together in a gesture that made him look almost like the child he wasn't.

'That's wonderful,' he breathed. 'The stuff of epics.'

'Stop that,' I told him.

'No, but really. We're such a young culture here. Barely a century of planetary history. We need this sort of thing.'

'Well,' I shrugged and reached for the bottle on the table. Shelved pain twinged in the broken elbow joint. 'You can have the rights. Go sell it to the Lapinee group. Maybe they'll make a construct opera out of the fucking thing.'

'You may laugh.' There was a bright entrepreneurial gleam kindling in Roespinoedji's eyes. 'But there's a market for this homegrown stuff. Practically everything we've got here is imported from Latimer, and how long can you live on someone else's dreams?'

I poured my glass half full of whisky again. 'Kemp manages.'

'Oh, that's *politics*, Takeshi. Not the same thing. Mishmashed neoQuellist sentiment and old time Commin, Commu—' he snapped his fingers. 'Come on, you're from Harlan's World. What's that stuff called?'

'Communitarianism.'

'Yes, that.' He shook his head sagely. 'That stuff isn't going to stand the test of time like a good heroic tale. Planned production, social equality like some sort of bloody grade school construct. Who'd bite into that, for Samedi's sake? Where's the savour? Where's the blood and adrenalin?'

I sipped the whisky and stared out across the warehouse roofs of Dig 27 to where the dighead's angular limbs stood steeped in the glow of sunset. Recent rumour, half-jammed and scrambled as it unreeled on illicitly-tuned screens said the war was heating up in the equatorial west. Some counterblow of Kemp's that the Cartel hadn't allowed for.

Pity they didn't have Carrera around any more, to do their thinking for them.

I shivered a little as the whisky went down. It bit well enough, but in a polite, smoothly educated way. This wasn't the Sauberville blend I'd killed with Luc Deprez, a subjective lifetime ago, last week. Somehow I couldn't imagine someone like Roespinoedji giving that one house room.

'Plenty of blood out there at the moment,' I observed.

'Yes, *now* there is. But that's the revolution. Think about afterwards. Suppose Kemp won this ridiculous war and implemented this voting thing. What do you think would happen next? I'll tell you.'

'Thought you would.'

'In less than a year he'd be signing the same contracts with the Cartel for the same wealth-making dynamic, and if he didn't, his own people would, uh, *vote* him out of Indigo City and then do it for him.'

'He doesn't strike me as the sort to go quietly.'

'Yes, that's the problem with voting,' said Roespinoedji judiciously. 'Apparently. Did you ever actually meet him?'

'Kemp? Yeah, a few times.'

'And what was he like?'

He was like Isaac. He was like Hand. He was like all of them. Same intensity, same goddamned fucking conviction that he was right. Just a different dream of what he was right about.

'Tall,' I said. 'He was tall.'

'Ah. Well, yes, he would be.'

I turned to look at the boy beside me. 'Doesn't it worry you, Djoko? What's going to happen if the Kempists fight their way through this far?'

He grinned. 'I doubt their political assessors are any different to

443

the Cartel's. Everyone has appetites. And besides. With what you've given me, I think I have bargain capital enough to go up against old Top Hat himself and buy back my much-mortgaged soul.' His look sharpened. 'Allowing that we have dismantled *all* your dead hand datalaunch security, that is.'

'Relax. I told you, I only ever set up the five. Just enough so that Mandrake could find a few if it sniffed around, so it'd know they were really out there. It was all we had time for.'

'Hmm.' Roespinoedji rolled whisky around in the base of his glass. The judicious tone in the young voice was incongruous. 'Personally, I think you were crazy to take the risk with so few. What if Mandrake had flushed them all out?'

I shrugged. 'What if? Hand could never risk assuming he'd found all of them, too much at stake. It was safer to let the money go. Essence of any good bluff.'

'Yes. Well, you're the Envoy.' He prodded at the slim hand-sized slab of Wedge technology where it lay on the table between us. 'And you're quite sure Mandrake has no way to recognise this broadcast?'

'Trust me.' Just the words brought a grin to my lips. 'State-of-the-art military cloaking system. Without that little box there, transmission's indistinguishable from star static. For Mandrake, for anyone. You are the proud and undisputed owner of one Martian starship. Strictly limited edition.'

Roespinoedji stowed the remote and held up his hands. 'Alright. Enough. We've got an agreement. Don't beat me over the head with it. A good salesman knows when to stop selling.'

'You'd just better not be fucking with me,' I said amiably.

'I'm a man of my word, Takeshi. Day after tomorrow at the latest. The best that money can buy,' he sniffed. 'In Landfall, at any rate.'

'And a technician to fit it properly. A real technician, not some cut-rate virtually qualified geek.'

'That's a strange attitude for someone planning to spend the next decade in a virtuality. I have a virtual degree myself, you know. Business administration. Three dozen virtually experienced case histories. Much better than trying to do it in the real world.'

'Figure of speech. A good technician. Don't go cutting corners on me.'

'Well, if you don't trust me,' he said huffily, 'why don't you ask your young pilot friend to do it for you?'

'She'll be watching. And she knows enough to spot a fuck-up.'

'I'm sure she does. She seems very competent.'

I felt my mouth curve at the understatement. Unfamiliar controls, a Wedge-coded lockout that kept trying to come back online with every manoeuvre and terminal radiation poisoning. Ameli Vongsa-vath rode it all out without much more than the odd gritted curse, and took the battlewagon from Dangrek to Dig 27 in a little over fifteen minutes.

'Yes. She is.'

'You know,' Roespinoedji chuckled. 'Last night, I thought my time was finally up when I saw the Wedge flashes on that monster. Never occurred to me a Wedge transport could be hijacked.'

I shivered again. 'Yeah. Wasn't easy.'

We sat at the little table for a while, watching the sunlight slide down the support struts of the dighead. In the street running alongside Roespinoedji's warehouse, there were children playing some kind of game that involved a lot of running and shouting. Their laughter drifted up to the roof patio like woodsmoke from someone else's beach barbecue.

'Did you give it a name?' Roespinoedji wondered finally. 'This starship.'

'No, there wasn't really that kind of time.'

'So it seems. Well, now that there is. Any ideas?'

I shrugged.

'The *Wardani*?'

'Ah.' He looked at me shrewdly. 'And would she like that?'

I picked up my glass and drained it.

'How the fuck would I know?'

She'd barely spoken to me since I crawled back through the gate. Killing Lamont seemed to have put me over some kind of final line for her. Either that or watching me stalk mechanically up and down in the mob suit, inflicting real death on the hundred-odd Wedge corpses that still littered the beach. She shut the gate down with a face that held less expression than a Syntheta sleeve knock-off, followed Vongsavath and myself into the belly of the *Angin Chandra's Virtue* like a mandroid, and when we got to Roespinoedji's place, she locked herself in her room and didn't come out.

I didn't feel much like pushing the point. Too tired for the conversation we needed to have, not wholly convinced we even needed to have it any more and in any case, I told myself, until Roespinoedji was sold, I had other things to worry about.

Roespinoedji was sold.

The next morning, I was woken late by the sound of the tech-crew contractors arriving from Landfall in a badly landed aircruiser. Mildly hungover with the whisky and Roespinoedji's powerful black market anti-rad/painkiller cocktails, I got up and went down to meet them. Young, slick and probably very good at what they did, they both irritated me on sight. We went through some introductory skirmishing under Roespinoedji's indulgent eye, but I was clearly losing my ability to instil fear. Their demeanour never made it out of *what's with the sick dude in the suit*. In the end I gave up and led them out to the battlewagon where Vongsavath was already waiting, arms folded, at the entry hatch and looking grimly possessive. The techs dropped their swagger as soon as they saw her.

'It's cool,' she said to me when I tried to follow them inside. 'Why don't you go talk to Tanya? I think she's got some stuff she needs to say.'

'To me?'

The pilot shrugged impatiently. 'To someone, and it looks like you're elected. She won't talk to me.'

'Is she still in her room?'

'She went out.' Vongsavath waved an arm vaguely at the clutter of buildings that constituted Dig 27's town centre. 'Go. I'll watch these guys.'

I found her half an hour later, standing in a street on the upper levels of the town and staring at the facade in front of her. There was a small piece of Martian architecture trapped there, perfectly preserved blued facets now cemented in on either side to form part of a containing wall and an arch. Someone had painted over the glyph-brushed surface in thick illuminum paint: FILTRATION RECLAIM. Beyond the arch, the unpaved ground was littered with dismembered machinery gathered approximately into lines across the arid earth like some unlikely sprouting crop. A couple of coveralled figures were rooting around aimlessly, up and down the rows.

She looked round as I approached. Gaunt-faced, gnawed at with some anger she couldn't let go of.

'You following me?'

'Not intentionally,' I lied. 'Sleep well?'

She shook her head. 'I can still hear Sutjiadi.'

'Yeah.'

When the silence had stretched too much, I nodded at the arch. 'You going in here?'

'Are you fucking—? No. I only stopped to . . .' and she gestured helplessly at the paint-daubed Martian alloy.

I peered at the glyphs. 'Instructions for a faster-than-light drive, right?'

She almost smiled.

'No.' She reached out to run her fingers along the form of one of the glyphs. 'It's a schooling screed. Sort of cross between a poem and a set of safety instructions for fledglings. Parts of it are equations, probably for lift and drag. It's sort of a grafitti as well. It says.' She stopped, shook her head again. 'There's no way to say what it says. But it, ah, it promises. Well, enlightenment, a sense of eternity, from dreaming the use of your wings before you can actually fly. And take a good shit before you go up in a populated area.'

'You're winding me up. It doesn't say that.'

'It does. All tied to the same equation sequence too.' She turned away. 'They were good at integrating things. Not much compartmentalisation in the Martian psyche, from what we can tell.'

The demonstration of knowledge seemed to have exhausted her. Her head drooped.

'I was going to the dighead,' she said. 'That café Roespinoedji showed us last time. I don't think my stomach will hold anything down, but—'

'Sure. I'll walk with you.'

She looked at the mob suit, now rather obvious under the clothes the Dig 27 entrepreneur had lent me.

'Maybe I should get one of those.'

'Barely worth it for the time we've got left.'

We plodded up the slope.

'You sure this is going to come off?' she asked.

'What? Selling the biggest archaeological coup of the past five hundred years to Roespinoedji for the price of a virtuality box and a black market launch slot? What do you think?'

'I think he's a fucking merchant, and you can't trust him any further than Hand.'

'Tanya,' I said gently. 'It wasn't Hand that sold us out to the Wedge. Roespinoedji's getting the deal of the millennium, and he knows it. He's solid on this one, believe me.'

'Well. You're the Envoy.'

The café was pretty much as I remembered it, a forlorn-looking herd of moulded chairs and tables gathered in the shade cast by the massive stanchions and struts of the dighead frame. A holomenu fluoresced weakly overhead, and a muted Lapinee playlist seeped into the air from speakers hung on the structure. Martian artefacts stood about the place in no particular pattern that I could discern. We were the only customers.

A terminally bored waiter sloped out of hiding somewhere and stood at our table, looking resentful. I glanced up at the menu then back at Wardani. She shook her head.

'Just water,' she said. 'And cigarettes, if you've got them.'

'Site Sevens or Will to Victory?'

She grimaced. 'Site Sevens.'

The waiter looked at me, obviously hoping I wasn't going to spoil his day and order some food.

'Got coffee?'

He nodded.

'Bring me some. Black, with whisky in it.'

He trudged away. I raised an eyebrow at Wardani behind his back.

'Leave him alone. Can't be much fun working here.'

'Could be worse. He could be a conscript. Besides,' I gestured around me at the artefacts, 'look at the decor. What more could you want?'

A wan smile.

'Takeshi.' She hunched forward over the table. 'When you get the virtual gear installed. I, uh, I'm not going with you.'

I nodded. *Been expecting this.*

'I'm sorry.'

'What are you apologising to me for?'

'You, uh. You've done a lot for me in the last couple of months. You got me out of the camp—'

'We pulled you out of the camp because we needed you. Remember.'

'I was angry when I said that. Not with you, but—'

'Yeah, with me. Me, Schneider, the whole fucking world in a uniform.' I shrugged. 'I don't blame you. And you were right. We got you out because we needed you. You don't owe me anything.'

She studied her hands where they lay in her lap.

'You helped put me back together again, Takeshi. I didn't want to admit it to myself at the time, but that Envoy recovery shit works. I'm getting better. Slowly, but it's off that base.'

'That's good.' I hesitated, then made myself say it. 'Fact remains, I did it because I needed you. Part of the rescue package; there was no point in getting you out of the camp if we left half your soul behind.'

Her mouth twitched. 'Soul?'

'Sorry, figure of speech. Too much time hanging around Hand. Look, I've got no problem with you bailing out. I'm kind of curious to know why, is all.'

The waiter toiled back into view at that point, and we quietened. He laid out the drinks and the cigarettes. Tanya Wardani slit the pack and offered me one across the table. I shook my head.

'I'm quitting. Those things'll kill you.'

She laughed almost silently and fed herself one from the pack. Smoke curled up as she touched the ignition patch. The waiter left. I sipped at my whisky coffee and was pleasantly surprised. Wardani plumed smoke up into the dighead frame space.

'Why am I staying?'

'Why are you staying?'

She looked at the table top. 'I can't leave now, Takeshi. Sooner or later, what we found out there is going to get into the public domain. They'll open the gate again. Or take an IP cruiser out there. Or both.'

'Yeah, sooner or later. But right now there's a war in the way.'

'I can wait.'

'Why not wait on Latimer? It's a lot safer there.'

'I can't. You said yourself, transit time in the *Chandra* has got to be eleven years, minimum. That's full acceleration, without any course correction Ameli might have to do. Who knows what's going to have happened back here in the next eleven years?'

'The war might have ended, for one thing.'

'The war might be over next year, Takeshi. Then Roespinoedji's going to move on his investment, and when that happens, I want to be here.'

'Ten minutes ago you couldn't trust him any more than Hand. Now you want to work for him?'

'We, uh,' she looked at her hands again. 'We talked about it this morning. He's willing to hide me until things have calmed down. Get me a new sleeve.' She smiled a little sheepishly. 'Guild Masters are thin on the ground since the war kicked in. I guess I'm part of his investment.'

'Guess so.' Even while the words were coming out of my mouth, I couldn't work out why I was trying so hard to talk her out of this. 'You know that won't help much if the Wedge come looking for you, don't you.'

'Is that likely?'

'It could ha—' I sighed. 'No, not really. Carrera's probably backed up somewhere in a sneak station, but it'll be a while before they realise that he's dead. While longer before they sort the authorisation to sleeve the back-up copy. And even if he does get out to Dangrek, there's nobody left to tell him what happened there.'

She shivered and looked away.

'It had to be done, Tanya. We had to cover our traces. You of all people should know that.'

'What?' Her eyes flicked back in my direction.

'I said. You of all people should know that.' I kept her gaze. 'It's what you did last time around. Isn't it.'

She looked away again, convulsively. Smoke curled up off her cigarette and was snatched away by the breeze. I leaned into the silence between us.

'It doesn't much matter now. You don't have the skills to sink us between here and Latimer, and once we're there you'll never see me again. Would. Never have seen me again. And now you're not coming with us. But like I said, I'm curious.'

She moved her arm as if it wasn't connected to her, drew on the cigarette, exhaled mechanically. Her eyes were fixed on something I couldn't see from where I was sitting.

'How long have you known?'

'Known?' I thought about it. 'Honestly, I think I've known from the day we pulled you out of the camp. Nothing I could lock down, but I knew there was a problem. Someone tried to bust you out before we came. The camp commandant let that slip, in between fits of drooling.'

'Sounds unusually animated, for him.' She drew more smoke, hissed it out between her teeth.

'Yeah, well. Then of course there were your friends down on the rec deck at Mandrake. Now that one I *really* should have spotted on the launch pad. I mean, it's only the oldest whore's trick in the book. Lead the mark up a darkened alley by his dick, and hand him over to your pimp.'

She flinched. I forced a grin.

'Sorry. Figure of speech. I just feel kind of stupid. Tell me, was that gun-to-your-head stuff just tinsel, or were they serious?'

'I don't know.' She shook her head. 'They were revolutionary guard cadres. Kemp's hard men. They took out Deng when he came sniffing around after them. Really dead, stack torched and body sold off for spares. They told me that while we were waiting for you. Maybe to scare me, I don't know. They probably would have shot me sooner than let me go again.'

'Yeah, they convinced the fuck out of me as well. But you still called them in, didn't you?'

'Yes,' she said it to herself, as if discovering the truth for the first time. 'I did.'

'Care to tell me why?'

She made a tiny motion, something that might have been her head shaking, or just a shiver.

'OK. Want to tell me *how*?'

She got herself back together, looked at me. 'Coded signal. I set it up while you and Jan were out casing Mandrake. Told them to wait on my signal, then placed a call from my room in the tower when I was sure we were definitely going to Dangrek.' A smile crossed her face, but her voice could have been a machine's. 'I ordered underwear. From a catalogue. Locational code in the numbers. Basic stuff.'

I nodded. 'Were you always a Kempist?'

She shifted impatiently. 'I'm not from here, Kovacs. I don't have any political, I don't have any *right* to a political stance here.' She shot me an angry look. 'But for Christ's sake, Kovacs. It's their fucking planet, isn't it?'

'That sounds pretty much like a political stance to me.'

'Yeah, must be really nice not to have any beliefs.' She smoked some more, and I saw that her hand was trembling slightly. 'I envy you your smug sanctimonious fucking detachment.'

'Well, it's not hard to come by, Tanya.' I tried to curb the defensiveness in my voice. 'Try working local military adviser to Joshua Kemp while Indigo City comes apart in civil riots around you. Remember those cuddly little inhib systems Carrera unloaded on us? First time I saw those in use on Sanction IV? Kemp's guardsmen were using them on protesting artefact merchants in Indigo City, a year before the war kicked in. Maxed up, continuous discharge. No mercy for the exploitative classes. You get pretty detached after the first few street cleanups.'

'So you changed sides.' It was the same scorn I'd heard in her voice that night in the bar, the night she drove Schneider away.

'Well, not immediately. I thought about assassinating Kemp for a while, but it didn't seem worth it. Some family member would have stepped in, some fucking cadre. And by then, the war was looking pretty inevitable anyway. And like Quell says, these things need to run their hormonal course.'

'Is that how you survive it?' she whispered.

'Tanya. I have been trying to leave ever since.'

'I,' she shuddered. 'I've watched you, Kovacs. I watched you in Landfall, in that firefight at the promoter's offices, in the Mandrake Tower, the beach at Dangrek with your own men. I, I envied you what you have. How you live with yourself.'

I took brief refuge in my whisky coffee. She didn't seem to notice.

'I can't.' A helpless, fending gesture. 'I can't get them out of my head. Dhasanapongsakul, Aribowo, the rest of them. Most of them, I didn't even see die, but they. Keep.' She swallowed hard. 'How did you know?'

'You want to give me a cigarette now?'

She handed over the pack, wordlessly. I busied myself with lighting and inhaling, to no noticeable benefit. My system was so bombed on damage and Roespinoedji's drugs, I would have been amazed if there had been. It was the thin comfort of habit, not much more.

'Envoy intuition doesn't work like that,' I said slowly. 'Like I said, I knew something was wrong. I just didn't want to take it on board. You uh, you make a good impression, Tanya Wardani. At some level, I didn't want to believe it was you. Even when you sabotaged the hold—'

She started. 'Vongsavath said—'

'Yeah, I know. She still thinks it was Schneider. I haven't told her any different. I was pretty much convinced it was Schneider myself after he ran out on us. Like I said, I didn't *want* to think it might be you. When the Schneider angle showed up, I went after it like a heatseeker. There was a moment in the docking bay when I worked him out. You know what I felt? I was relieved. I had my solution and I didn't have to think about who else might be involved any more. So much for detachment, huh.'

She said nothing.

'But there were a whole stack of reasons why Schneider couldn't be the whole story. And the Envoy conditioning just went on racking them up 'til there was too much to ignore any more.'

'Such as?'

'Such as this.' I reached into a pocket and shook out a portable datastack. The membrane settled on the table and motes of light evolved in the projected datacoil. 'Clean that space off for me.'

She looked at me curiously, then leaned forward and lobbed the display motes up to the top left-hand corner of the coil. The gesture echoed back in my head, the hours of watching her work in the screens of her own monitors. I nodded and smiled.

'Interesting habit. Most of us flatten down to the surface. More final, more satisfying I guess. But you're different. You tidy upward.'

'Wycinski. It's his.'

'That where you picked it up?'

'I don't know.' She shrugged. 'Probably.'

'You're not Wycinski, are you?'

It startled a short laugh out of her. 'No, I'm not. I worked with him at Bradbury, and on Nkrumah's Land, but I'm half his age. Why would you think something like that?'

'Nothing. Just crossed my mind. You know, that cybersex virtuality. There was a lot of male tendency in what you did to yourself. Just wondered, you know. Who'd know better how to live up to male fantasy than a man?'

She smiled at me. 'Wrong, Takeshi. Wrong way round. Who'd know better how to live up to male fantasy than a woman.'

For just a moment, something warm sparked between us, already fading as it came into being. Her smile washed away.

'So you were saying?'

I pointed at the datacoil. 'That's the pattern you leave after shutdown. That's the pattern you left in the cabin datacoil on board the trawler. Presumably after you slammed the gate on Dhasana-pongsakul and his colleagues, after you took out the two on the trawler and dumped them in the nets. I saw it the morning after the party. Didn't notice at the time, but like I said that's Envoys for you. Just go on acquiring little scraps of data until it means something.'

She was staring intently at the datacoil, but I still spotted the tremor go through her when I said Dhasanapongsakul's name.

'There were other scraps, once I started to look. The corrosion grenades in the hold. Sure, it took Schneider to shut down the

454

onboard monitors on the *Nagini*, but you were fucking him. Old flame, in fact. I don't suppose you had any harder time talking him into it than you did in getting me down to the rec deck at Mandrake. It didn't fit at first, because you were pushing so hard to get the claim buoy aboard. Why go to the trouble of trying to put the buoys out of commission in the first place, then work so hard to get the remaining one placed.'

She nodded jerkily. Most of her was still dealing with Dhasanapongsakul. I was talking into a vacuum.

'Didn't make sense, that is, until I thought about what else had been put out of commission. Not the buoys. The ID&A sets. You trashed them all. Because that way no one was going to be able to put Dhasanapongsakul and the rest into virtual and find out what had happened to them. Of course, eventually we'd get them back to Landfall and find out. But then. You didn't plan for us to make it back, did you?'

That got her back to me. A haggard stare across wreathed smoke.

'You know when I worked most of this out?' I sucked in my own smoke hard. 'On the swim back to the gate. See, I was pretty much convinced it'd be closed by the time I got there. Wasn't quite sure why I thought that at first, but it sort of fell into place. They'd gone through the gate, and the gate had closed on them. Why would that happen, and how did poor old Dhasanapongsakul end up on the wrong side wearing a T-shirt. Then I remembered the waterfall.'

She blinked.

'The waterfall?'

'Yeah, any normal human being, post-coital, would have shoved me in the back into that pool and then laughed. We both would have. Instead, you started crying.' I examined the end of my cigarette as if it interested me. 'You stood at the gate with Dhasanapongsakul, and you pushed him through. And then you slammed it shut. It doesn't take two hours to shut that gate, does it, Tanya?'

'No,' she whispered.

'Were you already thinking you might have to do the same thing to me? Then, at the waterfall?'

'I.' She shook her head. 'Don't know.'

'How did you kill the two on the trawler?'

'Stunner. Then the nets. They drowned before they woke up. I.' She cleared her throat. 'I pulled them up again later, I was going to, I don't know, bury them somewhere. Maybe even wait a few days and drag them to the gate, try to open it so I could dump them through as well. I panicked. I couldn't stand to be there, wondering if Aribowo and Weng might find some way to open the gate again before their air ran out.'

She looked at me defiantly.

'I didn't really believe that. I'm an archaeologue, I know how . . .' She was silent for a few moments. 'I couldn't even have opened it again myself in time to save them. It was just. The gate. What it meant. Sitting there on the trawler, knowing they were just the other side of that. Thing, suffocating. Millions of kilometres away in the sky above my head and still right there in the cavern. So close. Like something huge, waiting for me.'

I nodded. Back on the beach at Dangrek, I'd told Wardani and Vongsavath about the corpses I'd found sealed in the substance of the Martian vessel while Carrera and I hunted each other across the hull. But I never told either of them about my last half hour inside the ship, the things I'd seen and heard as I stumbled back out to the echoing desolation of the docking bay with Carrera's impeller frame on my shoulders, the things I'd felt swimming beside me all the way back to the gate. After a while, my vision had narrowed down to that faint blur of light orbiting out in the blackness, and I didn't want to look round for fear of what I might see, what might be hunched there, offering me its taloned hand. I just dived for the light, scarcely able to believe it was still there, terrified that at any moment it would slam shut and leave me locked out in the dark.

Tetrameth hallucination, I told myself later, and that was just going to have to do.

'So why didn't you take the trawler?'

She shook her head again and stubbed out her cigarette.

'I panicked. I was cutting the stacks out of the two in the nets, and I just.' She shivered. 'It was like something was staring at me. I dumped them back in the water, threw the stacks out to sea as far as I could. Then I just ran away. Didn't even try to blow the cavern or cover my tracks. Walked all the way into Sauberville.' Her voice changed in some way I couldn't define. 'I got a ride with this guy in a ground car the last couple of klicks. Young guy with a couple of kids he was bringing back from a grav-gliding trip. I guess they're all dead now.'

'Yes.'

'I. Sauberville wasn't far enough. I ran south. I was in the Bootkinaree hinterlands when the Protectorate signed the accords. Cartel forces picked me up from a refugee column. Dumped me in the camp with the rest of them. At the time, it seemed almost like justice.'

She fumbled out a fresh cigarette and fitted it in her mouth. Her gaze slanted my way.

'That make you laugh?'

'No.' I drained my coffee. 'Point of interest, though. What were you doing around Bootkinaree? Why not head back for Indigo City? You being a Kempist sympathiser and all.'

She grimaced. 'I don't think the Kempists would have been pleased to see me, Takeshi. I'd just killed their entire expedition. Would have been a little hard to explain.'

'Kempists?'

'Yeah.' There was a gritted amusement in her tone now. 'Who'd you think bankrolled that trip? Vacuum gear, drilling and construction equipment, the analogue units and the dataprocessing system for the gate. Come on, Takeshi. We were on the edge of a war. Where do you think all that stuff came from? Who'd you think went in and wiped the gate from the Landfall archive?'

'Like I said,' I muttered. 'I didn't want to think about it. So it was a Kempist gig. So why'd you waste them?'

'I don't know,' she gestured. 'It seemed like. I don't know, Kovacs.'

'Fair enough.' I crushed out my cigarette, resisted the temptation to take another, then took it anyway. I watched her and waited.

'It.' She stopped. Shook her head. Started again, enunciating with exasperated care. 'I thought I was on their side. It made sense. We all agreed. In Kemp's hands the ship would be a bargaining chip the Cartel couldn't ignore. It could win the war for us. Bloodlessly.'

457

'Uh-uh.'

'Then we found out it was a warship. Aribowo found a weapons battery up near the prow. Pretty unmistakeable. Then another one. I, uh.' She stopped and sipped some water. Cleared her throat again. 'They changed. Almost overnight, they all changed. Even Aribowo. She used to be so . . . It was like possession. Like they'd been taken over by one of those sentiences you see in experia horror flicks. Like something had come through the gate and . . .'

Another grimace.

'I guess I never knew them all that well after all. The two on the trawler, they were cadres. I didn't know them at all. But they all went the same way. All talking about what could be done. The *necessity* of it, the revolutionary *need*. Vaporise Landfall from orbit. Power up whatever drives the ship had, they were speculating FTL now, talking about taking the war to Latimer. Doing the same thing there. Planetary bombardment. Latimer City, Portausaint, Soufriere. All gone, like Sauberville, until the Protectorate capitulated.'

'Could they have done that?'

'Maybe. The systems on Nkrumah's Land are pretty simple, once you get to grips with the basics. If the ship was anything like.' She shrugged. 'Which it wasn't. But we didn't know that then. They thought they could. That was what mattered. They didn't want a bargaining chip. They wanted a war machine. And I'd given it to them. They were cheering the death of millions as if it was a good joke. Getting drunk at night talking it up. Singing fucking revolutionary songs. Justifying it with rhetoric. All the shit you hear dripping off the government channels, twisted a hundred and eighty degrees. Cant, political theory, all to shore up the use of a planetary massacre machine. And I'd given it to them. Without me, I don't think they could have got the gate open again. They were just Scratchers. They needed me. They couldn't get anyone else, the Guild Masters were all already on their way back to Latimer in cryocap liners, way ahead of the game, or holed up in Landfall waiting for their Guild-paid hypercasts to come through. Weng and Aribowo came looking for me in Indigo City. They begged me to help them. And I did.' There was something like a plea in her face as she turned to look at me. 'I gave it to them.'

'But you took it away again,' I said gently.

Her hand groped across the table. I took it in mine, and held it for a while.

'Were you planning to do the same to us?' I asked, when she seemed to have calmed. She tried to withdraw her hand, but I held onto it.

'It doesn't matter now,' I said urgently. 'These things are done, all you have to do now is live with them. That's how you do it, Tanya. Just admit it if it's true. To yourself, if not to me.'

A tear leaked out of the corner of one eye in the rigid face opposite me.

'I don't know,' she whispered. 'I was just surviving.'

'Good enough,' I told her.

We sat and held hands in silence until the waiter, on some aberrational whim, came to see if we wanted anything else.

Later, on our way back down through the streets of Dig 27, we passed the same junk salvage yard, and the same Martian artefact trapped in cement in the wall. An image erupted in my mind, the frozen agony of the Martians, sunk and sealed in the bubblestuff of their ship's hull. Thousands of them, extending to the dark horizon of the vessel's asteroidal bulk, a drowned nation of angels, beating their wings in a last insane attempt to escape whatever catastrophe had overwhelmed the ship in the throes of the engagement.

I looked sideways at Tanya Wardani, and knew with a flash like an empathin rush that she was tuned in to the same image.

'I hope he doesn't come here,' she muttered.

'Sorry?'

'Wycinski. When the news breaks, he'll. He'll want to be here to see what we've found. I think it might destroy him.'

'Will they let him come?'

She shrugged. 'Hard to really keep him out if he wants it badly enough. He's been pensioned off into sinecure research at Bradbury for the last century, but he still has a few silent friends in the Guild. There's enough residual awe for that. Enough guilt as well, the way he was treated. Someone'll turn the favour for him, blag him a hypercast at least as far as Latimer. After that, well he's still independently wealthy enough to make the rest of the running himself.' She shook her head. 'But it'll kill him. His precious Martians, fighting and dying in cohorts just like humans. Mass graves and planetary wealth condensed into war machines. It tears down everything he wanted to believe about them.'

'Well, predator stock . . .'

'I *know*. Predators have to be smarter, predators come to dominate, predators evolve civilisation and move out into the stars. That same old fucking song.'

'Same old fucking universe,' I pointed out gently.

'It's just . . .'

'At least they weren't fighting amongst themselves any more. You said yourself, the other ship wasn't Martian.'

'Yeah, I don't know. It certainly didn't look it. But is that any better? Unify your race so you can go beat the shit out of someone else's. Couldn't they get *past* that?'

'Doesn't look like it.'

She wasn't listening. She stared blindly away at the cemented artefact. 'They must have known they were going to die. It would have been instinctive, trying to fly away. Like running from a bomb blast. Like putting your hands out to stop a bullet.'

'And then the hull what, melted?'

She shook her head again, slowly. 'I don't know, I don't think so. I've been thinking about this. The weapons we saw, they seemed to be doing something more basic than that. Changing the,' she gestured, 'I don't know, the *wavelength* of matter? Something hyperdimensional? Something outside 3-D space. That's what it felt like. I think the hull disappeared, I think they were standing in space, still alive because the ship was still *there* in some sense, but knowing it was about to flip out of existence. I think that's when they tried to fly.'

I shivered a little, remembering.

'It must have been a heavier attack than the one we saw,' she went on. 'What we saw didn't come close.'

I grunted. 'Yeah, well, the automated systems have had a hundred thousand years to work on it. Stands to reason they'd have it down to a fine art by now. Did you hear what Hand said, just before it got bad?'

'No.'

'He said *this is what killed the others*. The one we found in the corridors, but he meant the others too. Weng, Aribowo, the rest of the team. That's why they stayed out there until their air burned out. It happened to them too, didn't it.'

She stopped in the street to look at me.

'Look, if it did . . .'

I nodded. 'Yeah. That's what I thought.'

'We calculated that cometary. The glyph counters and our own instruments, just to be sure. Every twelve hundred standard years, give or take. If this happened to Aribowo's crew as well, it means.'

'It means another near-miss intersection, with another warship. A year to eighteen months back, and who knows what kind of orbit that might be locked into.'

'Statistically,' she breathed.

'Yeah. You thought of that too. Because statistically, the chances of two expeditions, eighteen months apart both having the bad luck to stumble on deep-space cometary intersections like that?'

'Astronomical.'

'And that's being conservative. It's the next best thing to impossible.'

'Unless.'

I nodded again, and smiled because I could see the strength pouring back into her like current as she thought it through.

'That's right. Unless there's so much junk flying around out there that this is a very common occurrence. Unless, in other words, you're looking at the locked-in remains of an entire naval engagement on a system-wide scale.'

'We would have seen it,' she said uncertainly. 'By now, we would have spotted some of them.'

'Doubtful. There's a lot of space out there, and even a fifty-klick hulk is pretty small by asteroidal standards. And anyway, we haven't been looking. Ever since we got here, we've had our noses buried in the dirt, grubbing up quick dig/quick sale archaeological trash.

Return on investment. That's the name of the game in Landfall. We've forgotten how to look any other way.'

She laughed, or something very like it.

'*You're* not Wycinski, are you, Kovacs? Because you talk just like him sometimes.'

I built another smile. 'No. I'm not Wycinski, either.'

The phone Roespinoedji had lent me thrummed in my pocket. I dug it out, wincing at the way my elbow joint grated on itself.

'Yeah?'

'Vongsavath. These guys are all done. We can be out of here by tonight, you want it that way.'

I looked at Wardani and sighed. 'Yeah. I want it that way. Be down there with you in a couple of minutes.'

I pocketed the phone and started down the street again. Wardani followed.

'Hey,' she said.

'Yeah?'

'That stuff about looking out? Not grubbing in the dirt? Where did that come from all of a sudden, Mr I'm-Not-Wycinski?'

'I don't know.' I shrugged. 'Maybe it's the Harlan's World thing. It's the one place in the Protectorate where you tend to look outward when you think about the Martians. Oh, we've got our own dig sites and remains. But the one thing about the Martians you don't forget is the orbitals. They're up there every day of your life, round and round, like angels with swords and twitchy fingers. Part of the night sky. This stuff, everything we've found here, it doesn't really surprise me. It's about time.'

'Yes.'

The energy I'd seen coming back to her was there in her tone, and I knew then that she'd be alright. There'd been a point when I thought that she wasn't staying for this, that anchoring herself here and waiting out the war was some obscure form of ongoing punishment she was visiting upon herself. But the bright edge of enthusiasm in her voice was enough.

She'd be alright.

It felt like the end of a long journey. A trip together that had started with the close contact of the Envoy techniques for psychic repair in a stolen shuttle on the other side of the world.

It felt like a scab coming off.

'One thing,' I said as we reached the street that wound down in dusty hairpins to the Dig 27's shabby little landing field. Below us lay the dust coloured swirling of the Wedge battlewagon's camouflage cloaking field. We stopped again to look down at it.

'Yeah?'

'What do you want me to do with your share of the money?'

She snorted a laugh, a real one this time.

'Needlecast it to me. Eleven years, right? Give me something to look forward to.'

'Right.'

Below on the landing field, Ameli Vongsavath emerged abruptly from the cloaking field and stood looking up at us with one hand shading her eyes. I lifted an arm and waved, then started down towards the battlewagon and the long ride out.

EPILOGUE

The Angin Chandra's Virtue *blasts her way up off the plane of the ecliptic and out into deep space. She's already moving faster than most humans can clearly visualise, but even that's pretty slow by interstellar standards. At full acceleration, she'll still only ever get up to a fraction of the near-light speeds the colony barges managed coming the other way a century ago. She's not a deep space vessel, she's not built for it. But her guidance systems are Nuhanovic, and she'll get where she's going in her own time.*

Here in the virtuality, you tend to lose track of external context. Roespinoedji's contractors have done us proud. There's a shoreline in wind- and wave-gnawed limestone, slumped down to the water's edge like the layers of melted wax at the base of a candle. The terraces are sunblasted a white so intense it hurts to look at without lenses, and the sea is dappled to brilliance. You can step off the limestone, straight into five metres of crystal-clear water and a cool that strips the sweat off your skin like old clothes. There are multicoloured fish down there, in amongst the coral formations that rise off the bed of pale sand like baroque fortification.

The house is roomy and ancient, set back in the hills and built like a castle someone has sliced the top off. The resulting flat roof space is railed in on three sides and set with mosaic patios. At the back, you can walk straight off it into the hills. Inside, there's enough space for all of us to be alone if we want to be, and furnishings that encourage gatherings in the kitchen and dining area. The house systems pipe in music a lot of the time, unobtrusive Spanish guitar from Adoracion and Latimer City pop. There are books on most of the walls.

During the day, the temperatures crank up to something that makes you want to get in the water by a couple of hours after breakfast. In the evenings, it cools off enough that you pull on thin jerseys or jackets if you're going to sit out on the roof and watch the stars, which we all do. It isn't any night sky you'd see from the pilot deck of the Angin Chandra's Virtue *right now – one of the contractors told me they've drawn the format from some archived Earth original. No one really cares.*

As afterlives go, it's not a bad one. Maybe not up to the standards someone like Hand would expect – not nearly restricted enough entry for one thing – but then this one was designed by mere mortals. And it beats whatever the dead crew of the Tanya Wardani *are locked into. If the* 'Chandra's *deserted decks and corridors give it the feel of a ghost ship, the way Ameli Vongsavath says they do, then it's an infinitely more comfortable form of haunting than the Martians left us on the other side of the gate. If I am a ghost, stored and creeping electron-swift in the tiny circuitry in the walls of the battlewagon, then I have no complaints.*

But there are still times when I look around the big wooden table in the evenings, past the emptied bottles and pipes, and I wish the others had made it. Cruickshank, I miss especially. Deprez and Sun and Vongsavath are good company, but none of them has quite the same abrasive cheeriness the Limon Highlander used to swing about her like a conversational mace. And of course none of them are interested in having sex with me the way she would have been.

Sutjiadi didn't make it either. His stack was the only one I didn't turn into slag on the beach at Dangrek. We tried downloading it before we left Dig 27, and he came out shrieking insane. We stood around him in a cool marbled courtyard format, and he didn't know us. He screamed and gibbered and drooled, and shrank away from anyone who tried to reach out to him. In the end, we turned him off, and then wiped the format as well, because in all of our minds the courtyard was contaminated for good.

Sun has muttered something about psychosurgery. I remember the Wedge demolitions sergeant they re-sleeved once too often, and I wonder. But whatever psychosurgery there is on Latimer, Sutjiadi will get. I'm buying.

Sutjiadi.

Cruickshank.

Hansen.

Jiang.

Some would say we got off lightly.

Sometimes, when I'm sitting out under the night sky with Luc Deprez and a shared bottle of whisky, I almost agree.

Periodically, Vongsavath disappears. A primly-dressed construct modelled after a Hun Home Settlement Years bureaucrat comes to collect her in an antique, soft top airjeep. He fusses with her collision safety harness, to the amusement of everyone watching, and then they wheel about and drone off into the hills behind the house. She's rarely gone more than half an hour.

Of course in real time, that's a couple of days. Roespinoedji's contractors slowed the onboard virtuality down for us, about as far as it would go. It must have been some kind of a first for them – most clients want virtual time running at tens or hundreds of times reality standard. But then most people don't have a decade and more with nothing better to do than sit around. We're living out the eleven year transit in here at about a hundred times the speed it's really passing. Weeks on the 'Chandra's shadow-crewed bridge pass in hours for us. We'll be back in the Latimer system by the end of the month.

It really would have been easier to just sleep through it, but Carrera was no worse a judge of human nature than any of the other carrion birds gathered about the paralysed body of Sanction IV. Like all vessels with potential to escape the war, the battlewagon is grudgingly equipped with a single emergency cryocap for the pilot. It isn't even a very good one – most of Vongsavath's time away is taken up with the de- and refrosting time required by the overcomplex cryosystems. That Hun Home bureaucrat is an elaborate joke on Sun Liping's part, suggested and then written into the format when Vongsavath returned one evening spitting curses at the inefficiency of the cryocap's processor.

Vongsavath exaggerates, of course, the way you do about minor annoyances when life is so close to perfect in its major aspects. Most of the time she's not gone long enough for her coffee to get cold, and the systems checks she performs on the pilot deck have so far proved one hundred per cent superfluous. Nuhanovic guidance systems. Like Sun once said, in the hull of the Martian ship, they don't build the stuff any better than this.

I mentioned that comment to her a couple of days ago as we lay floating on our backs in the long aquamarine swells out beyond the headland, eyes slitted against the sun overhead. She could barely remember saying it. Everything that happened on Sanction IV is already starting to seem like a

466

lifetime ago. In the afterlife, you lose track of time, it seems, or maybe you just no longer have the need or desire to keep track. Any one of us could find out from the virtuality datahead how long we've been gone, when exactly we'll arrive, but it seems none of us want to. We prefer to keep it vague. Back on Sanction IV, we know, years have already passed, but exactly how many seems – and probably is – irrelevant. The war may already be over, the peace already being fought over. Or it may not. It's hard to make it matter more than that. The living do not touch us here.

For the most part, anyway.

Occasionally, though, I wonder what Tanya Wardani might be doing by now. I wonder if she is already out on the edges of the Sanction system somewhere, turning the face of some new sleeve tired and intent as she pores over the glyph locks on a Martian dreadnought. I wonder how many other deadwired hulks there are spinning around out there, whirling up to trade fire with their ancient enemies and then falling away injured into the night again, machines creeping out to soothe and repair and make ready for the next time. I wonder what else we're going to come across in those unexpectedly crowded skies, once we start looking. And then, occasionally, I wonder what they were all doing there in the first place. I wonder what they were fighting for in the space around that nondescript little star and I wonder if in the end they thought it was worth it.

Even more occasionally, I turn my mind to what I have to do when we do get to Latimer, but the detail seems unreal. The Quellists will want a report. They'll want to know why I couldn't twist Kemp closer to their designs for the whole Latimer sector, why I changed sides at the critical moment, and worst of all, why I left things no better aligned than they were when they needlecast me in. It's probably not what they had in mind when they hired me.

I'll make something up.

I don't have a sleeve right now, but that's a minor inconvenience. I've got a half-share in twenty million UN dollars banked in Latimer City, a small gang of hardened spec ops friends, one of whom boasts blood connection to one of the more illustrious military families on Latimer. A psychosurgeon to find for Sutjiadi. A bad-tempered determination to visit the Limon Highlands and give Yvette Cruickshank's family the news of her death. Beyond that, a vague idea that I might go back to the silver-grassed ruins of Innenin and listen intently for some echo of what I found on the Tanya Wardani.

These are my priorities when I get back from the dead. Anyone who has a problem with them can line right up.

In some ways, I'm looking forward to the end of the month.

This afterlife shit is overrated.

ACKNOWLEDGEMENTS

Once again, thanks to my family and friends for putting up with me during the making of *Broken Angels*. It can't have been easy. Thanks once again also to my agent Carolyn Whitaker for her patience, and to Simon Spanton and his crew, notably the very passionate Nicola Sinclair, for making *Altered Carbon* fly like a golden eagle on sulphate.

This is a work of science fiction, but many of the books that influenced it are not. In particular, I'd like to express my deepest respect for two writers from my non-fiction inspiration bank; my thanks go to Robin Morgan for *The Demon Lover*, which is probably the most coherent, complete and constructive critique of political violence I have ever read, and to John Pilger for *Heroes*, *Distant Voices* and *Hidden Agendas*, which together provide an untiring and brutally honest indictment of the inhumanities perpetrated around the globe by those who claim to be our leaders. These writers did not invent their subject matter as I did, because they did not need to. They have seen and experienced it for themselves at first hand, and we should be listening to them.

ABOUT GOLLANCZ

Gollancz is the oldest SF publishing imprint in the world. Since being founded in 1927 Gollancz has continued to publish a focused selection of bestselling and award-winning authors. The front-list includes **Ben Aaronovitch**, **Joe Abercrombie**, **Charlaine Harris**, **Joanne Harris**, **Joe Hill**, **Alastair Reynolds**, **Patrick Rothfuss**, **Nalini Singh** and **Brandon Sanderson**.

As one of the largest Science Fiction and Fantasy imprints in the UK it is no surprise we have one of the most extensive backlists in the world. Find high-quality SF on Gateway written by such authors as **Philip K. Dick**, **Ursula Le Guin**, **Connie Willis**, **Sir Arthur C. Clarke**, **Pat Cadigan**, **Michael Moorcock** and **George R.R. Martin**.

We also have a strand of publishing in translation, which includes French, Polish and Russian authors. Gollancz is home to more award-winning authors than any other imprint, with names including **Aliette de Bodard**, **M. John Harrison**, **Paul McAuley**, **Sarah Pinborough**, **Pierre Pevel**, **Justina Robson** and many more.

The SF Gateway
More than 3,000 classic, rare and previously out-of-print SF novels at your fingertips.
www.sfgateway.com

The Gollancz Blog
Bringing you news from our worlds to yours. Stories, interviews, articles and exclusive extracts just for you!
www.gollancz.co.uk

GOLLANCZ
LONDON